MIDDLE

THE JAGUAR STONES
Book One

WORLD

J&P VOELKEL

SCHOLASTIC INC.
New York Toronto London Auckland
Sydney Mexico City New Delhi Hong Kong

AUTHORS' NOTE

The Jaguar Stones are fictional, as are all the characters in this book except for Friar Diego de Landa, the true-life Spanish priest who made one big bonfire of ancient Maya books and artworks. San Xavier is a fictional country based on present-day Belize.

ISBN 978-0-545-39715-5

12 11 10 9 8 7 6 5 4 3 2 1   11 12 13 14 15 16/0

Printed in the U.S.A.   75

First Scholastic printing, September 2011

Book design by Becky Terhune

To Harry, Charly, and Loulou
k yahkume'ex

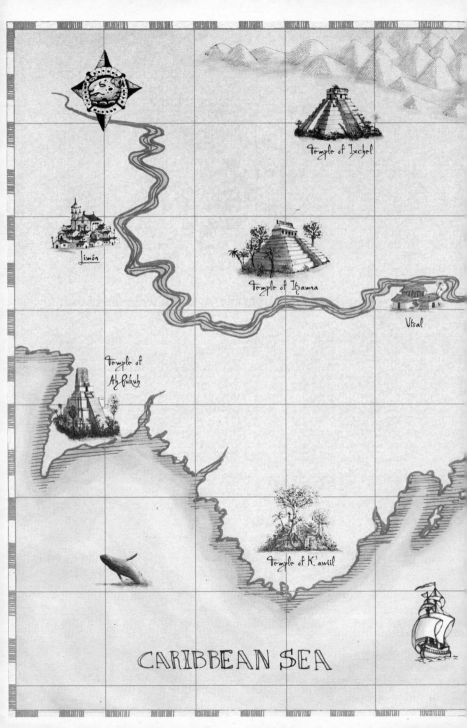

Temple of Ixchel

Limón

Temple of Itzamna

Utsal

Temple of
Ah Pukuh

Temple of K'awiil

CARIBBEAN SEA

CONTENTS

CHARACTERS

In order of appearance

In Boston

MAX (Massimo Francis Sylvanus) MURPHY: fourteen years old, only child, videogamer, drummer, pizza connoisseur

ZIA: the Murphys' mysterious housekeeper

FRANK AND CARLA MURPHY: Max's parents, famous archaeologists

In San Xavier

OSCAR POOT: head of the Maya Foundation

LUCKY JIM: Uncle Ted's foreman and bodyguard

TED MURPHY: Max's uncle, a banana exporter

VICTOR: waiter at hotel

ANTONIO DE LANDA: Spanish aristocrat

RAUL: Uncle Ted's butler

CHULO and SERI: Lola's tame howler monkeys

LOLA (Ix Sak Lol—*each sock loll*): Maya girl about Max's age

CHAN KAN: Maya wise man

OCH and little OCH: village boys, brothers

EUSEBIO: chili farmer and boatman

HERMANJILIO (*herman kee leo*): Maya archaeologist, university professor

LORD 6-DOG (Ahaw Wak Ok—*uh how walk oak*): ancient Maya king

LADY COCO (Ix Kan Kakaw—*each con caw cow*): Lord 6-Dog's mother

In Xibalba

LORDS of DEATH: twelve lords of the underworld, minions of Ah Pukuh

TZELEK: evil priest and Lord 6-Dog's twin brother

Maya Gods

IXCHEL (*each shell*): moon goddess

CHAHK (*chalk*): god of storms and warfare

ITZAMNA (*eats um gnaw*): ruler of heaven, lord of day and night

K'AWIIL (*caw wheel*): god of kingship and lineage

AH PUKUH (*awe pooh coo*): god of violent and unnatural death

It's not easy
being fourteen.
Especially when your parents
have accidentally unleashed
the forces of chaos and
destruction into the world—
and left you to sort out the mess.

This is the story of a city boy,
a jungle girl, and, quite possibly,
the end of the world as we know it.

It's set in the present day,
but it all begins on a moonlit
night, twelve hundred
years ago, in the ancient
Maya city of Itzamna. . . .

Preface
THE DREAM

Lord 6-Dog was awakened by the sound of his own screaming.

For a few moments he lay still on his sleeping mat, trying to shake off the memory of the dream. He told himself to calm down, but still his body trembled and the sweat ran down his forehead (no small journey, as his mother had strapped his head between two boards after he was born to lengthen his skull like a corn cob).

A howler monkey . . . ?

Suddenly the door curtain was ripped aside and the royal guards burst in to investigate the noise. They filled the tiny room. Lord 6-Dog quickly composed himself and signaled to them that all was well.

Then it occurred to him that perhaps all was *not* well.

14

As soon as the guards had gone, he examined himself all over, looking for monkey fur. Only when he was sure that his muscular body was still as smooth as a turtle shell did he start to relax.

But a howler monkey . . . ?

It was unthinkable.

He was the famous Lord 6-Dog—most powerful king, most fearless warrior, most handsome hero of the mighty Maya. Yet in his dream, he'd been an ugly, stinking, flea-infested monkey. How could it be?

What did it mean?

Like all his people, Lord 6-Dog took dreams very seriously. But this one was unthinkable. How could a king become a lowly monkey? If dreams were messages from the gods, surely this one had gone astray in the cosmic sorting office. . . .

Then again, perhaps it was *not* the gods who'd sent this dream.

Only yesterday, Lord 6-Dog's advisers had warned him about the growing powers of his twin brother, Tzelek. It was no secret that Tzelek coveted the throne—and, as a high priest, he was an accomplished sorcerer. Could he have sent this dream?

Lord 6-Dog sighed. It seemed that his advisers were always warning him about something. If it wasn't the machinations of Tzelek, it was a challenge from another city-state or some impending natural disaster. One court astrologer had even foreseen the fall of the whole Maya civilization.

No wonder everyone was jumpy.

Vowing never to tell another soul about his dream, Lord

6-Dog rubbed his heavy-lidded eyes, blew his huge hooked nose, and went outside for some air.

The royal sleeping quarters were at the top of the palace, and he could see for miles from the terrace outside his rooms. All around him, the silhouettes of other pyramids rose out of the jungle. Facing him, across the plaza, loomed the massive temple where his father, Lord Punak Ha, was buried. And below him, still and quiet, lay the beautiful city of Itzamna, jewel of the Monkey River. Its citizens slept peacefully tonight, trusting the young king they worshipped as a living god to protect them from all misfortune.

Lord 6-Dog shivered, even though the night was warm.

Stars were twinkling in the jungle sky, and a big round moon was shining down. It reminded him of another night, long ago, when he'd stood on this very spot with his mother, Lady Kan Kakaw. She'd been pointing out the image of a leaping rabbit on the surface of the moon, but little 6-Dog couldn't see it. He'd said it looked like the face of a man to him. How his mother had laughed and kissed him.

He smiled at the memory. It was a long time since he'd seen his mother happy. Since the death of his father, she'd turned into a bad-tempered old woman who never had a kind word for anyone.

As if on cue, her angry voice interrupted his reverie. "Where's that idiot son of mine?"

Lady Kan Kakaw came running out onto the terrace, flaming torch in hand, four long gray braids flying behind her. She slapped her son hard on the head. "That's for waking me with your screaming."

"I am sorry if I disturbed thee, Mother," said Lord 6-Dog.

"'I am sorry if I disturbed thee, Mother,'" she mimicked in a singsong voice. "Why must you talk in that old-fashioned way?"

"I believe it is fitting for a king to use the language of his ancestors."

"You sound ridiculous."

"So thou art always telling me."

"You young people don't know how lucky you are. In my day, children were seen and not heard."

"I am not a child, Mother. I am nineteen years old."

She peered at him. "Nineteen already? Is it really five years since your father was taken from us?"

He braced himself for her usual speech about how he wasn't fit to lick his father's jaguar-skin sandals. But tonight she seemed distracted. She was just staring out across the moonlit valley, as if mesmerized by the rustling of the treetops and the screeching of the monkeys in the jungle.

"Is something out there, Mother?" he asked.

"Of course not!" she said, a little too quickly.

He tried to follow her gaze, but her crossed eyes made it impossible. (Crossed eyes were a sign of beauty, and his mother's eyes had been trained to focus inward by hanging a bead between them when she was a baby.) "Thou art lying, Mother. What dost thou look at? I command thee to tell me!"

"There's nothing to tell."

"Speak—or I will bid Tzelek to rip out thine old heart in one of his rituals."

"You wouldn't dare," she said.

Lord 6-Dog suppressed a smile. He drew himself up to his full height and tried to look frightening. "Art thou sure, Mother? The day of 12-Blade approaches, and the people expect a human sacrifice. They would be most impressed if the chosen one were of royal blood. Thine image would be painted on souvenir plates, the poets would write odes in thy memory . . . unless, of course, thou hast something to tell me, old woman?"

She gaped in disbelief. "How dare you speak to your mother that way?"

"I am the mighty Lord 6-Dog. I will speak to thee any way I wish."

"Even you are not mightier than the gods, 6-Dog, and tonight I have found favor with them. Treat me with respect, or you may feel their wrath."

Lord 6-Dog inspected his mother more closely. There was something different about her tonight. She seemed younger, happier, almost girlish.

"What nonsense has filled thy deluded old head?"

"Oh, I am not deluded. For tonight, the gods blessed me with the most wonderful dream. In fact, before you so rudely awakened me, I was happy for the first time since your father died."

To her son's amazement, the old woman began to whirl around like a temple dancer, her crossed little eyes as bright as two shiny cocoa beans.

"I dreamed I was a howler monkey," she intoned, as if in a trance. "I was swinging through the trees as free as a bird. . . . I was sucking on wild plums and spitting out the stones. . . . I was picking lice off my head and eating them." She paused theatrically. "And I loved every moment of it!"

She registered the horror on her son's face, and her performance ended abruptly. "It's not something a cold fish like you would understand," she said.

If she had not hung her head at that moment—whether in shame or to hide her happiness—she would have noticed her son's expression change from disgust to fascination.

Now he was the one who was mesmerized.

He could hear his mother talking in the background. But whatever she was rambling on about could not distract him from the small insect that had landed on her head and was now crawling over her hair.

Very slowly, almost tenderly, he leaned over and picked it off.

Then, before he knew what he was doing, the mighty Lord 6-Dog opened his mouth and popped it in.

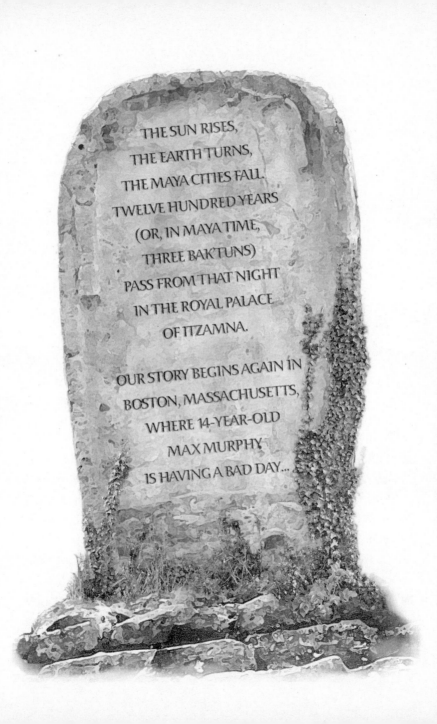

THE SUN RISES,
THE EARTH TURNS,
THE MAYA CITIES FALL,
TWELVE HUNDRED YEARS
(OR, IN MAYA TIME,
THREE BAK'TUNS)
PASS FROM THAT NIGHT
IN THE ROYAL PALACE
OF ITZAMNA.

OUR STORY BEGINS AGAIN IN
BOSTON, MASSACHUSETTS,
WHERE 14-YEAR-OLD
MAX MURPHY
IS HAVING A BAD DAY...

Chapter One
BAD NEWS

All was quiet.

Suddenly a flock of parrots exploded from the trees, shrieking and squawking, and three men burst out of the rainforest. One of them pushed a hostage, a young girl, in front of him. The other two shot at anything and everything as they ran across the clearing toward the steps of the pyramid.

The noise was terrifying—guns shooting, men shouting, birds screeching—but Max tried to stay calm, waiting for the right moment. He knew he would only get one chance. And, armed with only a blowgun, he also knew the odds were against him.

In the end, it happened so quickly that he hardly had time to think.

Just as the men reached the bottom step, something caught their attention high above Max's head, and they stopped to blitz the treetops with bullets. He crouched behind a log, not daring to breathe, as leaves and twigs exploded and rained down onto the forest floor. An animal shrieked and fell through the branches, landing with a thud somewhere behind him.

It was now or never.

Adrenaline pumped through his veins as he fired his three darts in quick succession.

Yes! Yes! No!

He'd hit the hostage—again.

GAME OVER.

Max threw down the controller in disgust.

What was he doing wrong? He'd jumped over the massive tree roots, sidestepped the boa constrictor sleeping in the leaf pile, bypassed the battalion of army ants, and outswum the hungry crocodiles that lurked under the surface of the river. He'd got everything right, but he still couldn't get past this level.

And what was that cross-eyed monkey trying to tell him?

He grabbed the case and scrutinized the small print. Nope, definitely nothing about cross-eyed monkeys. In fact, no rules at all.

Stupid game.

Where had it come from anyway? It was just lying on his bed when he came home. The case looked new, but it smelled musty, like the gym lockers at school.

As Max's hand reached for the controller again, a vacuum cleaner roared into life outside his door. No one could shoot a blowgun with that racket going on. He decided to go downstairs for a snack.

On the landing, he stepped around Zia, the housekeeper and wielder of the vacuum. As usual, she didn't look at him. Or maybe she did. It was hard to tell. Max had never seen her eyes because she wore heavy black sunglasses, even on the grayest of days. In her fist, she carried a crumpled handkerchief to wipe away the tears that often rolled down her cheeks. Max's mother said it was dust allergies and not to mention it. (A *housekeeper with dust allergies–just what you need*, thought Max.)

Zia had lived with Max's family for as long as he could remember. She rarely spoke, except to discuss household matters with his mother or to whisper in some strange language on the phone. She was just someone who cooked and cleaned and slept in the room over the garage. She never sat with the family or ate with them, and Max was so used to her snuffling around the house that he hardly registered her existence.

At the bottom of the stairs, he paused by the hallway mirror to check out his hair. (He was trying to grow it, and he'd got into the habit of reviewing its progress in every reflective surface he passed.) He combed his bangs with his fingers and struck a moody pose. His hair was over his ears now, he noted with satisfaction, straight and shiny, the color of roasted chestnuts.

Max called it brown.

The kids at school called it red.

It came from his father and all the Irish Murphys before him, with their pale blue eyes and invisible eyelashes. Max had inherited his Italian mother's dark eyes and, one of these days, he intended to dye his hair black and disown the Irish gene altogether.

He slunk into the kitchen and opened the fridge in search of food.

Nothing.

Just a huge dish of Zia's homemade tamales, and he'd rather starve than eat one of them. He'd tried one once, just

24

once, and the memory still made him feel nauseous. They'd looked so tempting, wrapped in their corn husks and tied up with twine like a row of little surprise presents.

Yeah, the worst surprise of your life, thought Max. He'd sunk his teeth into the greasy dough, and the sticky filling had expanded in his mouth like insulation foam. He'd only just reached the sink in time. The worst thing was that Zia had witnessed the whole thing.

Come to think of it, that was possibly why she didn't speak to him.

Max's mother said he was a picky eater. But she was from Venice, Italy, where the local specialty was boiled tripe. Tripe! The stomach lining of a cow! Why would anyone eat tripe in the country that invented pizza?

Tripe aside, Max's Italian grandmother—Nonna—was a fantastic cook. And as soon as school finished for the summer, Max and his parents were flying to Italy to see her for a long vacation. In a couple of weeks' time, he'd be eating Nonna's pizza, the dough thin and crisp and chewy all at the same time, homemade tomato sauce, bubbling mozzarella . . .

Max was still daydreaming about pizza when the back door flew open and his parents, Frank and Carla Murphy, burst in.

"Mom . . . Dad . . . what are you doing here?"

It was only fiveish, and they never came home before seven. They were archaeology professors at Harvard—specialist subject, the ancient Maya. It seemed ironic to Max that his parents spent all their waking hours with people who'd been dead as dodos for a thousand years, and neglected him, their own living, breathing son.

But this was a big year for Maya studies.

Max usually zoned out when his parents talked about work, but even he knew that the Maya calendar, which had counted the days since the world began, was supposed to be coming to an end. The Internet was buzzing with theories about comets and volcanoes and spacemen and tidal waves and polar shifts caused by planetary alignments predicted by the Maya centuries ago.

His father said it was all hogwash.

But then, his father could talk for hours about how people should do their own research rather than believing everything they read on the Internet.

Max thought this attitude was shortsighted.

Archaeologists should be pleased to have so many people blogging and spreading crazy rumors about the Maya. At least they were the center of attention for once. The rest of the time, they bored everyone stiff.

After all, what had the Maya ever given the world?

No mummies, no gladiators, no Olympic Games.

Just some tumbledown pyramids and a few old pots.

Yet Max's parents couldn't get enough of them.

His father seemed to prefer the ancient world, full stop.

Even his clothes were ancient. He'd worn the same hideous beige safari jacket for as long as Max could remember. It was covered in pockets, more pockets than any normal person could ever need, and every pocket bulged with notebooks and leaking pens. Add to this a thinning ponytail and a frizzy red beard, and Max wondered if his father ever glanced in the mirror at all. He seemed to have no interest in how he looked. He was always lost in the past, too preoccupied—Max assumed—with the ancient Maya to spare a thought for his appearance.

His mother went too far the other way. She wouldn't leave the house without lipstick and she ironed creases down the front of her jeans. Max supposed it was an Italian thing.

"*Ciao, bambino,*" she said now, attempting to plant a kiss on his cheek. "How was your day? Did you like your new video game?"

"*Pyramid of Peril?* It's a piece of junk."

The smile faded on his mother's face.

"It smells bad," Max explained. "And the rules are missing. Where did it come from?"

"Zia found it," said his mother. "In a yard sale, I think."

Max wrinkled his nose. "That explains the musty smell."

"There's gratitude for you," said his father.

"It's just that my friends get the new limited edition *Hellhounds 3-D*, and I get garbage from a yard sale," protested Max.

"I'm not interested in what your friends get or don't get," said his father. "You all spend far too much time playing silly games and sending cretinous messages to each other on Face Space—"

"It's not called—"

"I don't care what it's called. It's a waste of time."

Max's mother rubbed her temples as if she had a headache. "You know, Frank, perhaps we should order this"—she paused, wincing in distaste at the title—"Hellhounds game"—she pronounced it in the Italian way, *'Ell 'Oundz*, which made it sound a bit more sophisticated—"to keep him busy while we're away."

"Shopping is not the answer, Carla," said his father. "He needs to learn to make his own entertainment."

"I just thought, with this trip and everything . . . ," said his mother defensively.

"What trip?" said Max. "Do you mean Italy?"

"No, *bambino*," his mother said with a sigh. "We need to talk to you. Something's come up . . . a dig. . . . It's very important. . . . The permits just came through today. . . ."

"A dig?" echoed Max dully. "When do you go?"

"We leave in a few hours' time," said his father, trying to hide his excitement.

"Tonight?" wailed Max. "For how long?"

"We're . . . um . . . we're not sure," said his father.

"But what about the end-of-year concert? My drum solo?"

His mother put an arm around him. "I'm sorry, *bambino*. We'll ask one of the other parents to record it, and we'll watch it when we get back. . . ."

Max shook off her arm.

"You're the worst parents in the world!" he said. "You've missed every single performance of the school band! You promised you'd come to the end-of-year concert. I've been rehearsing for weeks. . . ."

"Calm down, Max," said his father. "It's out of our control. We didn't plan for this to happen. We said we're sorry."

He didn't sound sorry.

"Can't you wait a couple of weeks?" Max pleaded. "Then you could come to my concert and I could come on your dig."

"Not possible," said his father. "These permits are like gold dust. They could be revoked at any moment, and we won't get another chance."

"So where is this dig?" asked Max sulkily.

"San Xavier," said his father.

"San Xavier?" Max sounded outraged. "But that's where you grew up! You said you'd take me there one day."

"Not this time," said his father firmly. "This trip is work. Hard work."

"But . . ."

"The answer's no, Max."

"Well, just hurry back," said Max sadly, "so we can go to Italy."

Neither parent replied.

His father looked at his watch.

His mother adjusted the gold hoops in her ears.

Why wouldn't they look at him?

"We *are* still going to Italy, aren't we?" he asked anxiously.

There was another moment's silence, and then his father said, "It looks like we'll have to take a rain check, Max." He seemed oblivious to his son's disappointment. "Let's face it," he continued in a cheery tone, "you're getting a bit old for family vacations. You teenagers want to be with friends your own age, not boring old folks like us. Am I right?"

Max said nothing.

His mother read his thoughts. "I was looking forward to Italy, too, *bambino*," she said. "I promise we wouldn't do this if it wasn't very important."

Some people think their kids are important, thought Max.

He tried to look as if he didn't care. He opened the fridge, took out the milk, and gulped it down straight from the carton.

"Massimo!" roared his mother. "Use a glass!"

Massimo was the name on Max's birth certificate.

And there were more.

Massimo Francis Sylvanus Murphy.

Luckily, he'd always been called Max for short, and no

one, except his family in Italy and his mother when she was angry, ever called him Massimo.

He wiped his mouth with the back of his hand—"Massimo! Use a napkin!"—and replaced the milk. Then he slammed the fridge door hard enough to make the cans and bottles rattle inside, and gave it a little kick.

His father raised an eyebrow. "Very mature," he said.

"What do you expect?" asked Max.

"I expect you to think about someone besides yourself for once," replied his father. "We've already explained that we didn't plan on this, but there's no alternative. I've drawn up a full list of activities to make sure you spend your time productively when school ends."

He took a piece of paper out of one of his many pockets, unfolded it, and handed it to Max.

"'Weeding the yard, painting the fence, washing the windows . . . ,'" read Max, with mounting outrage. "When do I get to have any fun?"

"I've also included sports activities," said his father, "like running five miles a day, and tennis lessons twice a week."

"What about the things *I* like to do?" protested Max.

"I don't want you frittering away the summer playing video games. It's not healthy, Max. When I was your age, I was outdoors all the time, climbing trees, exploring ruins, swimming in water holes. . . ."

"But we live in the middle of Boston," Max protested. "You grew up in the jungle."

"That's right. No shopping malls, no movie theaters, but my brother and I had a fine old time, let me tell you."

"If you had such a fine old time, how come you and Uncle Ted don't speak to each other anymore?"

"Massimo! Don't be cheeky!"

"As a matter of a fact," said his father, "we'll be staying with my brother for a couple of nights when we get to San Xavier."

"Really? So you're friends again?"

His father ignored the question. "I've made a chart for you to keep track of your progress, so you can monitor your achievements."

"I can't believe this! It's going to be the worst summer ever."

"Nonsense, Max! It can do a fourteen-year-old boy a world of good to be thrown back on his inner resources once in a while—"

"But Dad, it takes a lot of inner resources to play *Hellhounds 3-D*—"

"Enough!" said his father. "Haven't you got homework to do?"

Max stomped up to his room and slammed the door. Then he grabbed his iPod, turned his current favorites—the Plague Rats—up to full volume, and threw himself on the bed, fuming with rage.

After a while, his mother came in with pizza. She tried to talk to him, but her voice could not compete with the throbbing bass in his ears. Max lay there, nodding along to his music and staring at her blankly.

There were tears in her eyes as she left the room.

Serves her right, he thought. *She wanted to go to Italy as much as I did. She should stand up to Dad and tell him that his own family's more important than the stupid Maya.*

Max opened the pizza box. Pepperoni Supreme with extra cheese—his favorite. As he gobbled it down, he thought about Italy. Dinners under the orange trees with everyone crammed around one long table . . . playing pickup soccer games in the piazza . . . wandering around Venice with his cousins . . . eating gelato at night in Saint Mark's Square . . . feeling part of one big happy family.

He sighed.

Boston was dead in the summer. All his friends would be at camp or away on vacation. To be stuck here with Zia was the pits.

The next minute, his father was pulling off Max's headphones.

"I said the taxi's here," he yelled. "Time to go!"

Max's mother ran in, looking frazzled. "I'll call or e-mail as soon as I can," she said, "but it's like the Stone Age in San Xavier, so don't worry if you don't hear from us right away." She felt his forehead. "Are you all right, *bambino*? You look pale."

"Of course he looks pale," snapped his father. "He spends his whole life in his room! There's nothing wrong with him that a bit of healthy exercise won't cure. I'm sorry you're not happy, Max, but we can't always get what we want."

You always get what you want, thought Max.

"Remember to wear a hat in the sun—with your fair skin, you have to be careful," said his mother, bending to kiss him.

For once, he didn't duck away.

"You be careful, too, Mom," he said.

A tear rolled down her face.

"Oh, for Pete's sake," said his father. "Don't do this, Max."

"What am *I* doing? You're the one who's walking out on his only child."

"You're fourteen," said his father, "hardly a child. There

were ancient Maya kings younger than you."

Outside, the taxi was revving its motor.

"Remember to floss twice a day, *bambino*. . . ."

"Come *on*, Carla," said his father. "Zia will look after him. We need to go."

As her husband chivvied her out the door, Max's mother turned back. "Look up at the moon rabbit, Max, and I'll be looking at it, too. I love you. . . ."

And then they were gone.

The moon rabbit?

It sounded familiar, but he couldn't place it. . . .

And then it came to him.

It was an evening long ago. He was sitting on the window seat over there, and his mother was pointing up at the night sky. "We see the man in the moon," she was saying, "but ancient Maya children saw a leaping rabbit, the pet of the moon goddess."

After that, little Max had waved to the moon rabbit every night.

Big Max cringed at the memory and went back to thinking

about the injustice of the day's events. He was still slightly in shock. This was definitely the worst thing his parents had ever done. And he couldn't believe he'd let them leave without buying him *Hellhounds 3-D*. If only he hadn't wasted so much time being angry. Kicking the fridge was definitely not cool.

His mother said he got his temper from the hotheaded Irish Murphys. His father said it was her Italian blood that made Max so temperamental.

Either way, he reflected, everything was his parents' fault. Everything.

He fixed himself a big bowl of ice cream with fudge sauce and took it into the sitting room to find something unsuitable to watch on TV.

There was still no sign of Zia. Yet, as he rooted under the sofa cushions for the remote, he felt he was being watched.

He looked around the room. His mother's prized collection of ancient Maya sculptures looked back at him. Usually these little pottery figures blended into the wallpaper, but tonight they seemed to be perched on the edges of their shelves, following his every move with their hollow clay eyes.

He slumped down so they couldn't see him anymore. He was still slumped on the sofa watching rock videos when Zia marched in at midnight and switched off the TV.

When he didn't move right away, she reached behind him, pulled out the cushion he'd been leaning on, and started beating it furiously. Max got the impression she'd like to beat him as well, so he meekly went upstairs.

He could still hear her beating up cushions when he got into bed and switched out the light. *It's going to be a long summer*, he thought.

Next morning, Friday, Max awoke to the smell of bacon

frying. Instead of the usual cold cereal, he found a cooked breakfast waiting for him in the kitchen. When he came home from school, a cheeseburger and a piece of home-made blueberry pie were set out on a tray. He was about to take it upstairs, when he heard a familiar snuffle from the sitting room.

"Zia!" he called. "Zia! I'm home!"

She didn't hear him. She was kneeling down with her back to him. She'd arranged some of his mother's Maya figurines like an audience in front of her. On the floor between Zia and the figurines, there was something on the carpet. Pebbles, maybe, and bits of yellow corn. She looked like a little girl playing with dolls. Was she trying to feed the statues? Had she lost her mind?

"Zia!" he shouted. "What are you doing?"

She jumped at the sound of his voice, but she didn't turn around. With trembling hands, she gathered up the bits on the carpet and stuffed them into her apron pocket. Then she pulled out a duster from her other pocket and started wiping the figurines. "I clean!" she said, nodding at him. "You eat!"

She was the weirdest housekeeper in Boston, all right.

For the rest of the weekend, Max lay around playing video games, chatting with his friends online, practicing for his upcoming drum solo, and gelling his hair into spikes.

A vague sense of unease was growing at the back of his mind.

He knew his mother had said not to worry if he didn't hear from them, but he couldn't shake off the feeling that something was wrong.

The days went by.

On the Friday morning a week and a day since his parents

had left, he came down to a breakfast of cold cereal and an e-ticket to San Xavier with his name on it. The flight was departing in a few hours' time.

"Zia!" he yelled.

She walked calmly into the kitchen with an armful of laundry.

He waved the piece of paper at her.

"What's this, Zia? Where did it come from?"

"They tell me to buy it," she said. "They say you must go there."

"They? Who's they? My parents? They want me to go to San Xavier? But why? What else did they say?"

"They say you are special," said Zia with a shrug, as if this was the most baffling statement she had ever heard.

She'd even packed a backpack for him.

"But what about the last week of school? The concert? My drum solo?"

"Go!" she said. "You must not keep them waiting."

Chapter Two
THE CURSE OF THE MAYA

Torrential rain beat against the windows of the small plane as it rolled to a stop. Max wiped away the condensation and peered out. Water was streaming in waves over the runway. It wasn't exactly dry land, but he was glad to be on it. It had been a bumpy ride.

"Welcome to San Xavier City," said the pilot glumly. "The local temperature is ninety-five degrees and the forecast is for rain."

At least English was the official language here, thanks to some British pirates who'd settled this coast three hundred years ago and eventually laid claim to the whole country. Before them, the Spanish had ruled San Xavier. And before them, it had been home to the ancient Maya, whose kingdoms had stretched across Central America from the Caribbean to the Pacific.

Max had learned all this—plus more than he wanted to know about the ancient Maya enthusiasm for human sacrifice—from the in-flight magazine.

He'd only picked it up because his iPod had run out of

juice. But what an eye-opening read it had been.

He'd leafed through the magazine eagerly, looking for photos of luxury hotels on palm-fringed beaches. But all he'd found were blurry old snapshots of ruined temples and gloomy caves, plus the occasional artist's gory impression of a sacrifice or a bloodletting in progress.

Even the article on flora and fauna was unnerving.

It seemed that all the biggest, nastiest, ugliest insects in the world had chosen to live in San Xavier. Max was particularly daunted by the picture of a hairy brown spider as big as a dinner plate. And how could such a small country be home to so many species of poisonous snakes?

The San Xavier tourist board certainly had its work cut out.

But here he was.

And even San Xavier had to be better than a summer in Boston, washing windows.

Max's only luggage was the backpack Zia had packed for him. He pulled it down from the overhead bin and shuffled along the narrow aisle toward the door. Most of the other passengers stayed in their seats, glumly watching as the ground crew pushed a set of rusty steps across the tarmac through the blowing rain.

No one else seemed keen to disembark, and Max was first in line when the steward swung open the door. It was like standing behind a waterfall. The roar of the rain was deafening, and the wet wind blew in a thick, musty smell of earth and decaying plants.

Max hesitated, savoring his final moment of being dry before ducking into the torrent. By the time he reached the little terminal building, he was literally soaked to the skin. He couldn't have been wetter if he'd been sitting in a bathtub.

As the official at the immigration desk studied his passport, a puddle formed around Max's feet. Eventually, the official put down the passport, leaned back in his chair, and stared at Max.

As Max looked back at him, he realized that the man seemed familiar. Where had he seen that high forehead, those heavy-lidded eyes, that huge nose before? Then it hit him. This guy was the embodiment of one of his mother's Maya figurines. Max glanced around the terminal. And there they all were. Behind desks, in lines, slumped in chairs, leaning against walls. Wherever he looked, faces from ancient history stared back.

And they didn't look entirely friendly.

The official's voice, when it finally came, made Max jump.

"Massimo Francis Sylvanus Murphy?"

"Yes?" said Max, cringing to hear his full name spoken out loud.

"What brings you to San Xavier?"

"I'm here to meet my parents."

"Ah, the famous Frank and Carla Murphy."

"You know them?"

"I know of them."

"What does that mean?"

"It means that your parents make life difficult for government officials like myself. They ignore our warnings. They think they are above such things."

This was news to Max. He'd always thought his parents were the most boringly upright and law-abiding citizens on the planet.

"Have they done something wrong?"

"Tell them from me," said the official, as he cracked his knuckles menacingly, "that they are not welcome here. They may have procured the necessary permits"—he rubbed his thumb and forefinger together to suggest a bribe—"but some things are better left alone."

A chill ran down Max's spine. The official's eyes were as cold and hard as flint. It wouldn't be difficult to imagine him conducting a human sacrifice.

At last, Max's passport was stamped.

"Take care," said the official as he handed it back. It sounded more like a threat than a friendly farewell.

Max walked into the arrivals hall. It was a sea of people, noise, and color. He scanned the faces of the waiting throng expectantly. Somewhere in there, his mother would be waving and calling to him—"Over here, *bambino*, over here!"

Why couldn't he see her? Both his parents were taller than most of the locals who crushed around the barriers. He looked again more slowly.

His confident smile faded.

It was unbelievable. Here he was, ready to make a fresh start by a hotel swimming pool—but where were they?

They were late.

Late for the big reunion scene.

It was the last straw.

All Max's feelings of forgiveness evaporated. First his parents abandoned him, then they made him fly two thousand miles on a rickety plane to some snake-infested dump in the rainy season, and then they couldn't even be bothered to pick him up on time.

Through a gap in the crowd, he noticed a wiry, nervous-looking little man, no bigger than a child, trying to make eye contact with him. Max looked away, but out of the corner of his eye, he was horrified to see the little man darting over.

"Mister Max?"

"Yes?"

"I am Oscar Poot, head of the Maya Foundation here in San Xavier City, and I have the privilege to work with the great Frank and Carla Murphy."

"Where are they?" asked Max, returning Oscar's handshake distractedly.

"I am sorry, but they could not come."

"Why not? Too busy with work, I suppose?"

Oscar nodded. "You must feel very proud of them."

What Max actually felt was like he'd been kicked in the stomach. His parents were off somewhere with their beloved ancient Maya and, once again, he was on his own.

"Where are they?"

"I last spoke to them four days ago, on the satellite phone. They were at the Temple of Ixchel." Oscar said the name slowly, and the way he pronounced it, *each-shell*, reminded Max of the wind that whistled every time the terminal doors were opened and of the angry rain that lashed the windows. "It's in the north, a remote site, Late Classic. . . ."

"So when will they be back?"

"I do not know," said Oscar. "There was a big storm and we have lost contact. Communications often fail in the jungle, especially in bad weather."

"But they're all right?"

"Why wouldn't they be?"

"The immigration guy said—"

"Let me guess. He told you that Frank and Carla are mixed up in something dangerous?"

"No, but—"

"People in San Xavier have overactive imaginations. It comes from living with so much history." He picked up Max's backpack. "Let's go."

"Where to?"

"You are to stay with your uncle, Mister Theodore Murphy."

"Uncle Ted?"

"Exactly."

"Is it far?"

"To the bus station? Five minutes."

"To my uncle's house?"

"It is over the mountains, but only a day by bus." Oscar turned up the collar of his jacket. "Are you ready to run?"

His car was parked just a short sprint from the terminal doors, but the rain was so fierce that once again Max got soaked.

"How do you like this weather?" Oscar gestured at the dark gray sky as he tried to start up the engine of his battered little car. "It is most unusual for the time of year. Even the old people say they have never seen anything like it."

It was not much drier inside the car. Max's window refused to roll all the way up, and his face was stung by the rain that pelted in through the gap. His feet were sitting in a pool of water at least three inches deep.

He was still groping for a nonexistent seat belt as they roared off into the rain, narrowly missing a collision with an airport fuel tanker. The stubby wipers struggled to cope with the volume of water, and Max wondered how Oscar could see anything at all as he wove crazily through the traffic.

"Are you hungry?" asked Oscar, as he swerved into

oncoming traffic to avoid a large pothole.

Max considered the question. His primary emotion right now was terror at Oscar's driving. Next to that, he was wet, tired, and confused. But underneath it all, he was amazed to detect the ever-present flicker of hunger.

A short time later, they were seated at a rickety table in the bus station café.

Max looked around in distaste. It was the least appetizing eating place he'd ever seen. There was no counter or bar, just a small, low-ceilinged room containing a few ill-matched tables and chairs. The walls were yellowed with cigarette smoke and sticky with grease. A naked lightbulb hung from the ceiling, illuminating the cockroaches that scuttled across the dirty floor. Max tried not to think about the class on food hygiene he'd taken last term.

An ancient waitress in bright red lipstick, a miniskirt, and carpet slippers made her way over. Max looked at the silvery gray roots of her stringy blond hair as she flicked the crumbs off the table and onto the floor. *She looks like Madonna's great-great-grandmother*, he thought.

While Oscar ordered the daily special for both of them, Max tried to dry himself off with some paper napkins. He noticed that he'd already acquired several nasty insect bites on his arms.

When the waitress had shuffled back with their drinks (a glass of evil-smelling fizzy brown liquid masquerading as Coke for Max, a glass of rum for Oscar), Oscar proposed a toast.

"To your parents," he said.

Max didn't even bother to raise his glass.

"Where does Uncle Ted live?" he asked.

Oscar looked surprised that Max hadn't joined in the

toast. It was evident from his expression that he liked the parents a lot more than the son. "Your uncle runs a banana business near Puerto Muerto," he said, a little coolly.

"Puerto Muerto? 'Dead Port'?" Spanish was one of Max's least favorite subjects at school, but a few words had seeped into his brain. "What kind of name is that?"

"It is called Puerto because it is an old Spanish port at the mouth of the Monkey River. And it is called Muerto for many reasons. . . ."

Max wished he'd never asked. "I'm starving," he said. "I hope the food comes soon."

But Oscar was warming to his theme. "The port was built for the logwood trade. Do they teach you about logwood?"

"No," said Max, "but it doesn't matter. I'm not really—"

Oscar launched into his story anyway.

"Logwood contained a red dye that was highly prized in seventeenth-century Europe. The trees were felled upriver and floated down to the port, so the water flowed as red as blood. It carried with it the bodies of Maya slaves who died in the logging camps."

"So it's called Puerto Muerto for the dead slaves," Max guessed, hoping to put an end to the story.

But Oscar had not finished. "It was not just logwood the Spanish stole from us. Every day, they loaded plunder onto their galleons. . . ."

Max became aware that other diners were straining to overhear.

"Could you talk a little quieter?" he whispered. "People are looking."

"One day," proclaimed Oscar, louder than ever, "a sea chest waiting on the dock bore the crest of Friar Diego de Landa."

He pronounced the name with great force and infused hatred into every syllable.

Max looked blank.

"You have not heard of him?" asked Oscar, in disbelief.

"Shh," begged Max, conscious that all eyes were on them.

But Oscar was in full flow. "Diego de Landa was the curse of the Maya. He tortured us, he burned our books, he told the world we were savages."

There was a murmur of assent from the diners.

"The food's taking a long time," said Max, looking pointedly at the old waitress, who'd pulled up a chair nearby.

Oscar made a dismissive gesture, as if food was the last thing on his mind. "Among the ill-gotten gains in Landa's sea chest were two of our five sacred Jaguar Stones."

An ominous whisper went around the restaurant. It reminded Max of a zombie movie he'd seen on late-night TV, where the zombies chanted in unison like, well, zombies, as they moved in, blank-faced, for the kill. The diners' whispering sounded like *"bah lawm toon oh ob, bah lawm toon oh ob, bah lawm toon oh ob,"* and whatever it meant, it sent shivers down Max's spine.

"What are they saying?" he asked.

"Bahlamtuuno'ob," said Oscar. "It means 'Jaguar Stones.'"

"What are Jaguar Stones?"

"They are your father's life's work. The five sacred stones and the five sacred pyramids. He is probably the world expert on the subject."

Max tried to suppress a yawn.

"He has not mentioned that to you? That is so typical of your father. He is a genius and yet so modest. Do you know how lucky you are to have such brilliant parents? They are

45

such a wonderful couple, and both so talented—"

Max was not in the mood to sing his parents' praises. "So what happened when this Landa guy got the stones back to Spain?" he asked, to change the subject.

Oscar launched back into his tale. "The ship was lost at sea. The *Espada*, as it was called, set sail for Cadiz on a perfect day and was never seen again. Some think it was dragged down to the underworld by the weight of the sacred stones. Others think it hit a reef and sank. Who knows? No trace of the galleon or the sea chest has ever been found."

"So the Jaguar Stones were lost forever?"

"And with them, my people's future." Oscar reached for his rum. "It was hope that died at Puerto Muerto."

"Things can't be that bad," said Max, unmoved. "Didn't you say there were five Jaguar Stones? What about the other three?"

"Lost, all lost." Oscar sighed, draining his glass.

His face brightened as the waitress set down two steaming plates. "Mmm," he murmured, "who doesn't like tamales?"

The revenge of Zia, thought Max.

Tamales, it turned out, were quite a favorite in San Xavier. There were at least three tamale stands in the bus station, adding their distinctive moldy aroma to the already toxic mixture of exhaust fumes, cigarette smoke, and sweat.

But it was the noise that made Max's eyes water.

Horns blared, doors slammed, adults shouted, children wailed, babies screamed, and underneath it all, tinny piped music screeched out from loudspeakers on poles.

A convoy of gaudily painted buses streamed into the flooded parking lot.

"That one's yours," said Oscar, pointing to a rusty pink-and-green-striped bus that was just pulling in. The name Estelly was painted on its side.

Max watched as Estelly disgorged twice as many people as could possibly have fit inside. The conductor, a boy of about twelve, climbed up onto the roof and threw down the wet bags and threadbare cases, letting each land with a muddy splat. At the same time, a barrage of identical pieces was thrown up at him from all sides, as if he were a goalie in some manic soccer practice. Meanwhile, at ground level, a heaving mass of humanity fought to get on board.

"They sell more tickets than seats, so you will need to push." Oscar handed him his ticket and shoved him into the crowd. Before Max could protest or even say good-bye, he was carried along in the throng toward Estelly.

He fought his way onto the bus and was instantly enveloped in the reek of too many unwashed bodies packed into too small a space. He found a seat at the back and slid in. Moments later, a fat man in a cowboy hat eased in next to him. Max was now pinned against the window, his feet on his backpack and his knees under his chin.

He became aware of a tapping on the window. He swiveled his gaze and saw Oscar on tiptoes, way down below, gesturing at him to open the window. "Something for the journey," yelled Oscar, trying to make himself heard above the din of the bus station. He passed up a greasy bag of tamales. "Good-bye, Mister Max. Your uncle will meet you at Puerto Muerto."

As the driver revved the engine, a question sprang into

Max's head. "Oscar," he called, "if you haven't spoken to my parents in four days, who told you to meet me at the airport?"

Oscar strained to hear him, and he repeated the question.

The little conductor jumped aboard and banged on the side of the bus with his fist. With a blast on the air horn, the driver crashed the gears and splashed out of the parking lot.

Max was sitting stunned in the backseat.

It had been hard to hear Oscar's reply, but it had definitely sounded like, "Zia."

Chapter Three
PUERTO MUERTO

Oscar was right. Hope had died in Puerto Muerto.

The streets were lined with wooden shacks. Their tin roofs were rusty. Their walls, once gaily painted, were cracked and stained. On nearly every corner was a dimly lit bar where men hunched over empty glasses. Old women in black sat in doorways, but none bothered to look up as the bus went past. Even the scrawny little dogs lay still, their heads on their paws, while flies buzzed halfheartedly around them.

The bus entered a rubbish-strewn square and, with a final squeal of brakes, skidded to a stop in front of a crumbling cathedral and a statue of some long-forgotten Spanish general on his horse.

How the mighty had fallen.

Once the general and his compatriots, their hands stained red with logwood, had built lavish palaces on this square. Once their wives had paraded around it in the latest European fashions.

But now the looters themselves had been looted.

Their palaces were scrawled with graffiti and festooned

with washing lines. Their cathedral was an empty shell. And their general was just a droppings-encrusted roost for the pigeons that scratched a living in the square.

Max jumped off the bus, took a deep breath—and almost choked. The salty sea air was overpowered by a stench of rotting fish and diesel oil. Still, it felt good to stretch his legs. Actually, given those blind corners on the mountain roads, it felt good to be alive.

"*Adiós, americano,*" called the little conductor, as the bus lurched off in a grinding of gears. When the cloud of exhaust smoke cleared, Max was left standing alone. There was no one around except two shifty-looking men on the cathedral steps, who were smoking and watching him like cats watching a mouse.

Uncle Ted, where are you?

If only he'd asked Oscar for his uncle's address or phone number. All Max knew about him was that *Ted* was short for *Theodore*, he was Frank Murphy's older brother, and he'd inherited the family banana business. Max didn't even know what Uncle Ted looked like, although he assumed he had Murphy hair.

Mindful of the two men watching him, Max tried to look

inconspicuous. This worked for approximately five seconds before he was dive-bombed by a swarm of yellow butterflies who had, apparently, never seen a tourist before. They flapped excitedly around him, trying to land on his head, his face, his hands, any piece of exposed skin they could find.

He was still swatting butterflies when he saw the two men walking toward him. A knife glinted in the sunlight.

Max started to run. A big car rolled into the square and stopped right in front of him. It was a shiny new Mercedes with blackened windows. In that squalid little town, it looked as out of place as an alien spaceship.

The butterflies took off in a yellow cloud.

The two men melted into the shadows.

The door of the Mercedes opened, and the driver slowly got out.

He looked like the Maya mafia, a block of solid muscle in a black suit, dark sunglasses, and black leather driving gloves. He wasn't that old, but his twenty or so years had obviously been hard-lived. A long scar ran down his face from his high, sloping forehead to the bottom of one ear. His nose looked as if it had been on the losing end of a fight with an iron bar. From his big bull neck to his barrel chest to his tree-trunk legs, every inch of this guy exuded menace. "Give me your backpack," he said.

"T-t-take it," stammered Max. "Please don't hurt me. My uncle will be here any minute. . . ."

The rear door of the Mercedes opened.

"He's here," said a voice that sounded uncannily like Max's father.

"Uncle Ted?"

A handsome but slightly haggard man emerged from

51

the backseat. He wore a cream linen suit and a panama hat. A wisp of reddish hair was visible beneath the brim.

His pale blue eyes regarded Max sadly.

"You are Massimo, I presume?"

"My friends call me Max."

"Massimo, this is Lucky Jim," said Uncle Ted, introducing the driver. "You don't want to get on the wrong side of Lucky. He comes from a long line of fierce Maya warriors."

Max swallowed hard. They weren't exactly making him feel welcome. "Have you heard from Mom and Dad?" he asked.

"No," said Uncle Ted. "I was going to ask you the same question." He looked at his watch. "Please get in the car, I'm late for a meeting."

Max slid into the Mercedes. He was stiff and bruised from the bus ride, and his bones sank gratefully into the soft leather cushions. Enveloped in luxury, with the electric windows tightly closed and the air-conditioning gently fanning him, he allowed himself to relax slightly. He sat back and, without thinking, put his feet up against the seat in front of him.

"Feet down!" barked his uncle, getting in next to him.

Lucky carefully wiped the imprint of Max's dusty shoes off the leather seat back before slamming the car door. Max got the impression that, if he could, he would have wiped away every trace of him.

The Mercedes headed out of town, rolling smoothly over rocks and potholes, until they came to a driveway marked GRAN HOTEL DE LAS AMERICAS.

"Do you live in a hotel?" Max asked his uncle hopefully.

"Of course not," snapped Uncle Ted. "I'm meeting a new client here."

Inwardly, Max groaned. All he wanted to do was collapse into a soft bed.

As they rounded a curve in the drive, an imposing colonial-style building came into view. It hadn't seen a coat of paint for a hundred years but, unlike the rest of Puerto Muerto, it managed to be charming rather than depressing.

They drew up at the colonnaded entrance, and a liveried doorman came running over to open the car door for Uncle Ted.

"Can I wait in the car?" asked Max.

"No."

"But—"

"You'll do as I say. There are some dangerous people around."

Uncle Ted pressed a tip into the doorman's hand and strode past him into the hotel. Max followed him through the run-down lobby and out onto a stone terrace overlooking the Caribbean Sea. It was a beautiful spot, with steps leading from the terrace through formal gardens down to a small pebble beach. Uncle Ted and Max sat at a table in the far corner, while Lucky Jim assumed a lookout position in the garden.

They certainly took security seriously in the banana business.

A waiter in a starched white jacket glided out of a side door and set down little dishes of olives, cashew nuts, and tiny cocktail tamales.

"Good afternoon, Mr. Murphy. May I bring your usual?"

"Thank you, Victor."

"And for you, sir?" the waiter asked Max.

"What is there?" asked Max without enthusiasm,

expecting to be offered the vile brown concoction from the bus station café.

The waiter rattled off a list of brand-name sodas.

"I'll have a Coke, please. And vanilla ice cream."

The waiter bowed and was gone.

The clouds were clearing now, and the estuary below sparkled like emeralds in the sun.

"Is that the Monkey River?" Max asked.

Uncle Ted was sitting bolt upright, his eyes darting nervously around the garden as if he was expecting a ninja attack.

"What?" he said irritably.

"I was just asking if that's the Monkey River down there."

"I hope you're not going to plague me with questions while you're here, Massimo; I'm not running a tourist information center. It was bad enough getting a phone call from that madwoman, telling me you were coming to stay."

"What madwoman?"

"You call her Zia, don't you? I told her not to send you, but she wouldn't listen to me."

Max watched the boats bobbing on the green water. He didn't know what Zia had been thinking, but she'd made a big mistake. "I'm sure Mom and Dad will be back soon," he said.

"Let us hope so," said Uncle Ted.

They sat in silence until Victor the waiter came back with their order.

Max poured half the Coke into his glass and carefully dropped a large spoonful of ice cream into it. Then he closed his eyes and sucked it all down until his straw made loud gurgling noises on the bottom of his empty glass.

When he opened his eyes, Uncle Ted and the waiter were both staring at him, appalled.

"I'm sorry, Victor," said Uncle Ted. "I can only apologize for my nephew's table manners."

Victor smiled indulgently at Max, then, on the pretext of scraping crumbs off the table, he leaned down by Uncle Ted and murmured, "Heard anything from the police yet, sir?"

Uncle Ted froze. He looked at Max out of the corner of his eye to see if he'd overheard. He had.

"The police?" spluttered Max. "Is this about Mom and Dad?"

Victor shot an apologetic glance at Uncle Ted and fled inside.

"Calm down, Massimo," said Uncle Ted. "The chief of police is a friend of mine. I just asked him to send a chopper up to Ixchel to check things out."

"What things?"

"Nothing in particular. Just to have a look round. See if your parents are still there and bring them back if they are. I am concerned that the trails will be blocked after the storm."

There was a shout from the garden.

A flash of steel.

A gardener held up the headless, writhing body of a snake. It was about three feet long, bright red with yellow and black bands.

Uncle Ted gave a low whistle. "It's a coral snake," he said. "You don't want to get bitten by one of those."

"It's the second one he's found today," said Victor, who'd come to see what all the shouting was about. "The rain seems to bring them out." He called something to the gardener in Spanish and went back inside, shaking his head.

Uncle Ted looked at his watch. "My client will be here in a moment. Until he's gone, Massimo, I must ask you to stay inside with Victor. Off you go, now. . . ."

Victor was polishing glasses behind the bar. He regarded Max with a mixture of sympathy and suspicion. "Are you having a pleasant vacation?" he inquired stiffly.

"Yes, thank you," said Max, sitting at the bar and picking at a bowl of cashew nuts.

Victor's eyes kept darting nervously toward the door onto the terrace, and Max turned to see what he was looking at.

"We have postcards," said Victor quickly, as if to distract him. He indicated a small basket next to the register.

Max flicked idly through the cards. They were dog-eared and too faded to be recognizable. "Do you know anything about a place called Ixchel?" he asked.

Victor narrowed his eyes. "What did you want to know?"

Max shrugged. "Just tourist stuff."

Victor looked relieved. "Ixchel is one of the five sacred pyramids of the Monkey River. Ixchel herself was the moon goddess. Her name means 'Lady Rainbow.' The ancient Maya thought rainbows were bad omens. Lady Rainbow was greatly feared."

"Why?"

"When mortals angered her, which was often, she would empty her water jar over us, causing terrible floods and rainstorms."

Above them, the sky was clouding over again.

"It does seem to rain a lot here," said Max.

"Lady Rainbow has been very angry lately," agreed Victor. "The farmers are worried for their crops." He winked at Max. "Maybe they should make some offerings to her."

"What kind of offerings?"

"I am joking. These days, the farmers get their weather reports from TV."

"What kind of offerings did they *used* to make?"

"Jade, incense, sacrifices, that sort of thing."

"Human sacrifices?" asked Max.

"Sometimes."

Upstairs in the bathroom, Max looked at himself in the tarnished mirror. His face was white as death. Human sacrifices, snakes, tamales . . . he didn't want to stay in San Xavier a day longer than he had to. Maybe when his parents got back from wherever they were, they could all fly to Italy for a proper vacation. They owed him, big-time.

He turned on the tap. After a lot of banging in the pipes, a trickle of brown water dripped out. He splashed his face. The water smelled of drains. He stumbled into the corridor, intending to stick his head out the nearest window for some fresh air. But what he saw made him jump back.

There were men with guns all over the garden. They were all dressed in black. Half of them were pointing their weapons at Lucky Jim. The other half were focused on something that was happening directly under the window.

Max flattened himself against the wall and peered down.

There were two men on the path. One was his uncle. The other was a dark-haired man with a neatly trimmed beard and a mustache that curled up at the ends. Like his bodyguards, he was dressed in black, with a short cape around his shoulders and black leather gloves.

This must be Uncle Ted's client.

The banana business was evidently more cutthroat than Max had realized.

Voices drifted up to the window.

"I understand you have certain objects for sale," the dark-haired man was saying in a strong Spanish accent.

"Objects?" repeated Uncle Ted cagily.

"Let us not play games, Señor Murphy. It has come to my attention that you recently sold a sword, a fine blade of Toledo. I must know where you found this piece."

"I cannot divulge that information."

The Spaniard clicked his tongue impatiently. "*Bueno.* But you will confirm that it was the sword of Friar Diego de Landa?"

"It was sold as such," conceded Uncle Ted.

"If that sword is authentic, Señor Murphy, it was last seen in the hold of the ship *Espada* that sailed from this very port in 1553 and was lost en route to Cadiz." He pronounced it *cah-deeth.*

"I am aware of the history of the piece."

"Then you will know that the same ship was said to be carrying two important stone carvings?"

"If you say so."

"Señor Murphy, let us get to the point. . . ."

The Spaniard clicked his fingers and one of his bodyguards came forward, carrying a metal briefcase. The guard tripped slightly on the terrace steps and before he could regain his balance, the Spaniard grabbed the briefcase from him, pulled out a gun, and pistol-whipped him across the face. As the guard fell to the ground in pain, the Spaniard kicked him savagely in the stomach.

"Clumsy pig," he screamed.

This guy's a complete psycho! thought Max.

The Spaniard resumed negotiations as if nothing had happened. "The stone carving that I seek," he began, before noticing a drop of the bodyguard's blood on his shiny black boots. "*Momentito*," he said, clicking his fingers again. Another guard materialized to wipe away the offending stain.

"*Bueno*," said the Spaniard. "As I was saying, the stones that I seek are the brothers of this one. It is my wish to collect the full set."

With that, he placed the briefcase on the garden wall and unlocked it. The breeze died down and the birds stopped singing as he threw back the lid.

A faint glow emanated from the case. It was was lined with foam, and nestled inside was a glassy black stone about the size of a football. It looked very old and it was crudely carved into the shape of a cat's head with the mouth open, ready to bite. An unpleasant smell, like rotting meat, wafted up to the window.

Uncle Ted's face looked even more deeply wrinkled in the glow of the stone. He spoke in an admiring whisper. "The Black Jaguar of Ah Pukuh . . . lost for centuries . . . But where did you get it?"

The Spaniard snapped the briefcase closed.

"I, too, have my secrets, *señor*. But I see that you recognize the stone. Tell me, do you have its brothers?"

"If I did," said Uncle Ted, "I'd be a fool to sell."

"Everything has its price, Señor Murphy."

A songbird trilled noisily in a nearby tree. The Spaniard wheeled around and shot it dead. "I will give you time to think."

He replaced his gun in its holster and strolled casually

over to admire a rosebush in a painted pot.

He picked one perfect red bloom and sniffed it delicately. "Aaah," he sighed. "*Una rosa muy rara*, a rare hybrid grandiflora, if I am not mistaken." He let the flower drop to the ground and crushed it with the toe of his boot.

It lay on the path like a smear of blood.

"It touched me in the heart to hear that your brother and his wife are missing, Señor Murphy. How unfortunate. And your nephew is with you now, is he not? It is to be hoped that he does not also . . . disappear."

Uncle Ted looked like he might punch the guy in the nose, and Max clenched his own fists in sympathy, mentally egging him on.

Then the moment for retaliation was lost as—*bang, bang, bang!*—the Spaniard pumped one bullet after another into the painted flowerpot, his face contorted with rage, until the pot was broken into tiny pieces and the uprooted rosebush fell to the ground. A lizard darted out to hunt for beetles in the spilled dirt, and he would have shot that as well, but he'd run out of bullets. He threw the gun at it and missed.

"Sell me the Jaguar Stone or you will be sorry," he hissed in a fury.

Shocked by the force of the Spaniard's temper, Uncle Ted put up his hands to signal defeat. "May I at least inquire with whom I am to do business?"

In a moment of pure cartoon villainy, the Spaniard threw back his cape, stuck out his chest, and looked down his aquiline nose. It was a wonder he didn't twirl his mustache. "Count Antonio de Landa," he announced, making an elaborate bow, "at your service."

"Landa?" repeated Uncle Ted in surprise.

"Yes, Señor Murphy, your ears do not play tricks. My ancestor was the famous Friar Diego de Landa. So you see, I am merely seeking the return of my family's rightful property."

Uncle Ted's eyebrows shot up as if to dispute that claim, but he quickly masked his skepticism. "Of course, this changes everything," he said. "It will take me a little time to retrieve the object in question, but I will contact you tomorrow to arrange the details of the sale."

"*Hasta luego,*" said Landa. He turned on his heel and was gone.

Max took a few deep breaths, then headed for the stairs. As he went down, he saw Uncle Ted come in from the terrace and say something to Victor. Victor pointed up at the staircase.

"Ah, there you are, Massimo," called his uncle. "We can go now; my business here is done."

"Uncle Ted, what exactly is your business?"

"Bananas, of course," he answered.

Out on the terrace, Max could see workmen sweeping up the damage wrought by Landa.

Lucky came in and nodded at Uncle Ted. "All clear, boss," he said.

"Let's go," said Uncle Ted.

It was a beautiful drive along the coast, with banana groves on one side and rolling surf on the other. But Max saw none of it. As soon as his head touched the cool leather of the backseat, he fell fast asleep in the Mercedes.

As they drove along the rutted highway, a rainbow arched in the sky above them.

Chapter Four
VILLA ISABELLA

All that night and late into the morning, Max dreamed about snarling jaguars prowling the streets of Boston. He was finally awakened by the tropical sun streaming in through the French windows.

For a moment he thought he was in a hotel on vacation. But as he took in the bare white walls and plain wooden furniture of Uncle Ted's guest room, he remembered that his parents were missing in action and his uncle was doing shady deals with trigger-happy Spaniards.

He got out of bed and stepped onto the balcony. The heat hit him like a blast from a blowtorch. A toucan with a beak like an upturned canoe gave a croak of protest and flapped away. A bright green insect the size of a toy helicopter loomed menacingly at him before landing on a purple flower as big as a Frisbee. And everywhere Max looked, yellow butterflies were dancing in the sunshine. Everything was so big and bright and colorful, it seemed unreal.

Even Uncle Ted's house looked like a film set. Villa Isabella sat on a ridge at one end of a sheltered bay. It was an old colonial mansion, built of honey-colored stones that glowed in the sun. But despite its blue-painted shutters and flower-decked balconies, it also had the aspect of a fortress.

From the depth of the windows, Max estimated that the walls were two feet thick. He could see a tall, battlemented tower on one corner and, by leaning out as far as he dared, he noted that the lowest floor had arrow slits like a medieval castle.

An old stone wall, topped by a walkway and fortified with crumbling guard posts, encircled the villa's grounds. Was that to keep predators out or to keep guests in? Max wondered.

From his second-floor vantage point, he could see over the wall from the bay on one side to the rainforest on the other. Faint animal sounds—whoops and cackles—floated over from the forest. Max scanned it for signs of wildlife, but the tops of the trees were packed tightly together like evil mutant broccoli and he could see nothing move in their impenetrable green depths.

A blast from a ship's horn made him look toward the sea. The bay was wide and horseshoe-shaped, a natural harbor; a big white yacht—surely Uncle Ted's?—floated at anchor in the turquoise water.

Only the beach spoiled the picture-postcard view. Instead of fine white sand, this was black and gritty, strewn with palm fronds, old tires, strips of plastic, and other garbage that had washed up in the storm.

But this was a work zone, not a tourist resort. Along the curve of the bay, about half a mile from the house, there was a large warehouse connected to a pier. A crane was loading crates into the hold of a rusty freighter. This must be the banana business in action. But given the conversation Max had overheard at the hotel, he couldn't help wondering if those

crates contained something more valuable than bananas.

His musings were interrupted by a growl from his stomach. Time to go and find some breakfast.

He got dressed and peered out of the bedroom doorway. His room opened onto a long corridor lined with suits of armor and oil paintings of stern-looking men with pointed beards, all richly dressed in ruffs and capes. They reminded him of that crazy cape-twirling Spaniard in the garden.

Max followed the corridor to the main staircase. His footsteps echoed loudly as he ran down the huge stone steps leading into the great hall.

Wow. He must have passed through this room the night before, but he'd been so tired he hadn't seen it properly. Now its size and scale amazed him.

The great hall was arranged as a reception room with clusters of antique sofas, dark wood tables, and stiff-backed chairs. Against the far wall was an enormous stone fireplace that could have burned a small forest in one go. A coat of arms with crossed swords was carved into the over-mantel.

It would have looked like a castle in medieval Europe,

were it not for the Maya sculptures occupying every ledge, every side table, every niche. In pride of place in the center of the floor were two gigantic stone heads.

It was only when he stood in front of these heads that Max realized how big the great hall was. The heads were taller than a school bus and yet not out of proportion for the room. As he looked from one hook-nosed face to the other, they seemed to stare right back at him—one with sadness, one with anger.

Max began to feel uncomfortable. There was a sense of tension between the statues that gave him goose bumps. He reached out to feel the stone.

"Please do not touch," came a voice behind him.

Max turned to see an immaculately groomed old man in a black tailcoat.

"Welcome to the Villa Isabella, sir. I am Raul, head butler and household administrator. You slept well, I trust?"

"Yes, thank you," said Max. He turned back to the heads. "Who are these guys?"

"The one on the left is Lord 6-Dog."

"Lord 6-Dog? What kind of name is that?"

"It is the name of a great ancient Maya king who united the cities of the Monkey River and brought a golden age of prosperity to the people of this region."

"And who's Mr. Angry next to him?"

"That's Lord 6-Dog's twin brother, Tzelek the Black Priest."

"What's his problem?"

"In a nutshell, sir, he's a bad loser."

"What happened?" asked Max, looking quickly from one head to the other, as if to catch them blinking.

"A classic case of sibling rivalry."

"It's a classic case of sibling rivalry, sir. When 6-Dog inherits the Jaguar Throne, Tzelek is consumed with jealousy. Determined to wrest the throne from his twin brother, he turns to the dark arts. In their final showdown, Tzelek conjures up a demon army and attacks Lord 6-Dog, who counterattacks with his veteran Jaguar Warriors. It is the greatest battle between good and evil in Maya history."

Max liked the way Raul told the story in the present tense, as if he were a sports commentator and it was all happening right there and then.

"Who won?" he asked.

"It is not over," said Raul cryptically. He rubbed his hands briskly together. "And now, sir, brunch will be served out on the terrace." He pointed to some glass doors farther down the hallway.

Max was heading toward them when, through a half-open door, he noticed a circular room. Thinking it must be the base of the battlemented tower he'd seen from his balcony, he looked inside.

What he saw astounded him.

If the rest of the house was channeling medieval Spain, this room was like something out of a James Bond movie.

With varnished wood paneling from floor to ceiling, it had the sleek, tight feel of a luxury yacht. Plasma screens hanging from the ceiling transmitted security shots of the house, grounds, and warehouse. On the desk were several laptop computers, some night-vision goggles, and an array of high-tech equipment whose purpose Max couldn't even guess.

His eye was drawn to a poster-size aerial photograph showing the locations of various Maya ruins. Max tried to find the Temple of Ixchel, but there were too many sites and the captions were too small.

On another wall was a diploma from the Royal College of Art in London and some old photographs. There were of Ted and Frank as teenagers, striking cool poses in the jungle, and there was Ted holding a red-haired baby. Uncle Ted had no children, had never been married as far as Max knew, so that baby had to be him—little Max. The thought that Uncle Ted kept his picture on the wall made him feel more at home, and he looked around for any other family mementos.

In front of a window was a brass telescope. It was focused on the luxury yacht he'd seen from the balcony, and Max could just about make out the lettering on the stern: LA ESPADA, CADIZ. *That's a coincidence*, he thought, *same name as that old galleon in Oscar's story*. But this yacht couldn't have been more twenty-first century. It was bristling with electronic masts and radar dishes.

Max was trying to find the zoom for a closer look, when a hand tapped him on the shoulder.

He turned to see Raul standing behind him.

What was this guy's problem? That was the second time today he'd sneaked up behind Max and scared him half to death.

"This is Mr. Murphy's private office, sir," said Raul.

"I was just looking at the yacht," said Max. "Is it Uncle Ted's?"

"No, sir. It belongs to a Spaniard by the name of Count Antonio de Landa—a most unsavory character, by all accounts. They say he killed his own brother to inherit the family estate. And now, sir, if you don't mind . . ."

Raul ushered Max out of the room, pulled the door tightly

shut, and stalked imperiously back to the kitchen.

Max went out onto the terrace. It was more like an outdoor room, enclosed as it was on three sides by frescoed walls and fronted by a stone balustrade. It was cooled by wooden ceiling fans and shaded by a yellow awning that gave the light an unreal quality, as if everything was inside a tent.

A table, covered by a starched white tablecloth, had been set for two with china plates, sparkling glass, and heavy silver flatware. A newspaper was placed to one side. Even the newspaper looked ironed.

Max took a seat and Raul appeared behind him.

"Tea, coffee, or hot chocolate, sir?"

"Hot chocolate," said Max decisively.

Raul nodded and went inside.

Instantly, Max wished he'd asked for a cold soda instead. He jumped up to follow Raul and change his order but only got as far as the doorway before freezing in his tracks. In front of his astonished eyes, the closed door to the office flew open and Uncle Ted emerged, brushing dust off his shoulders.

How was it possible?

There was only one door to that room, and it had been barely a minute since Max himself had vacated it. Had Uncle Ted climbed in through a window?

Unseen by his uncle, Max crept back to his seat to ponder the problem.

A few minutes later, Uncle Ted strode out onto the terrace.

"Good morning, Massimo," he said, a little frostily. "Raul tells me you've been exploring."

"I was just—"

"I must ask you not to poke around. Raul runs a tight

ship, and I don't want you making work for him. Do you understand?"

"Yes," said Max, "but I was only—"

"The matter is closed," said Uncle Ted, as he scanned the newspaper headlines.

Raul brought out a platter of scrambled eggs and smoked salmon, a bowl of freshly sliced pineapple, and a big basket of toast, rolls, and pastries. Max watched him as he set the food down. What a tattletale. Was he going to report back to Uncle Ted on every little thing? It was like being five years old.

"Help yourself," said Uncle Ted to Max as Raul gave a small bow and withdrew.

Max took a large spoonful of eggs and picked out the salmon. Next, he cut the crusts off a piece of toast and removed all the raisins from a Danish. Then he settled down to enjoy what was left, surrounded by little piles of rejected food.

Uncle Ted set down the newspaper. "I have good news," he said. "I spoke to the chief of police this morning. Your parents have left the camp, so they must be on their way back. Many of the trails are impassable after the storm, but it turns out they have an excellent guide. He's a local archaeologist who was working with them at Ixchel, Herman something-or-other, and, apparently, he knows the jungle like the back of his hand."

"That's great," said Max. "Did the chopper find anything?"

"No, the camp was deserted."

"Was it all neatly packed up?"

"Let's leave the detective work to the police, shall we? We'll get a full report later."

"But was it packed up or not?"

"Since you ask, clothes and papers were strewn every-where—due to the storm, no doubt."

"Aha!" Max pounced on this clue. "So we know they left in a hurry. Otherwise, Mom would have tidied up. She hates mess."

"I know how she feels," said Uncle Ted, pointedly eyeing the piles of discarded food around Max's plate and the drips of hot chocolate on the white tablecloth.

"If they're on their way back," mused Max, "I wonder why the chopper didn't see them from the air?"

"The tree canopy's too thick," replied Uncle Ted.

"The evil mutant broccoli," muttered Max.

"Excuse me?" said Uncle Ted.

"That's what it looks like from my balcony."

"Ah," said Uncle Ted. "But the broccoli—I mean the canopy—is a good thing for our purposes. It blocks out the sunlight, so not much grows on the ground. Makes it easier to walk through the rainforest."

"You said the trails were impassable," Max reminded him

"The storm has done a lot of damage, but I'm sure they'll find a way through. More toast?"

While Max dissected another Danish, Uncle Ted read the newspaper. They'd been sitting like this in silence for a while when Raul came rushing out. "Sorry to interrupt your breakfast, sir, but you have an urgent phone call." From the way Raul avoided his eyes, Max guessed the call was about his parents. As he sat and waited, he threw crumbs of pastry to the little birds that hopped about under the table.

"The chopper pilot has filed his report," announced Uncle Ted when he came back. "The chief of police told me to stress that it's probably not significant, but they found a gold hoop earring near the cenote and they wanted me to ask you if Carla—"

"Yes! Mom wears earrings like that!"

"And so do most of the women in San Xavier. It means nothing."

"Where did you say they found it?"

"By the cenote."

"*Say-note-eh?* What's that?"

"It's the local name for a sinkhole. The jungle's full of underground lakes and rivers. When the roof collapses, you get a cenote. It's like a deep well. The Maya used to think they were entrances to the underworld."

A bell rang in Max's brain. "Didn't the Maya use them for human sacrifice?"

"How did you know that?" said Uncle Ted in surprise.

"I read it in the magazine on the plane."

"That figures. They like to lay the human sacrifice story on thick for the tourists—but I'd advise you to take it with a pinch of salt."

"Do the police think Mom and Dad are on their way back?"

"Absolutely."

"Are they doing anything to find them?"

"There's not much they *can* do. It's the old needle-in-a-haystack scenario. Forensics are going to run a few tests on your father's jacket, but . . ."

Max's blood ran cold. "They found Dad's jacket?"

"Yes, that disgusting old thing with all the pockets."

"But he never takes it off."

"Maybe not in Boston, but it's hotter here—in case you hadn't noticed."

"I've seen him wear it at noon in a heat wave." A note of panic crept into Max's voice. "Was there anything in the pockets?"

"I don't think so. Why?"

"That's where he keeps his research notes."

This was bad. His father would never willingly be parted from his jacket. Max tried to calm himself by taking a sip of hot chocolate, but his hands were shaking too much to hold the cup.

"Did you know," said Uncle Ted, "that the ancient Maya were the first to make a drink out of chocolate? They served it on special occasions like we serve champagne."

Max pushed his cup away.

"Why are they running tests on Dad's jacket?"

Uncle Ted tried to sound casual. "It had a mark on it. But I told them, that old jacket was so dirty, it was always covered in stains."

"What mark? What was it?"

"It looked like blood, but—"

"*Blood?*"

"Don't panic, Massimo, it's not Frank's blood. In fact, they don't think it's human blood at all."

"Not human? I don't understand."

"No one understands yet. Things are never what they seem around here. We must wait for forensics to finish their tests."

"When will that be?"

Uncle Ted shrugged. "Who knows? Things don't move

as quickly in San Xavier as they do in Boston."

"Can't you bribe someone?" suggested Max.

Uncle Ted raised an eyebrow. "Certainly not."

The ceiling fans whirred lazily in the rafters. A honeybee hovered over a flower. A lizard perched motionless on the balustrade. It was as if time had stood still. Max felt jet-lagged and tired and confused. He was angry at his parents, angry at Uncle Ted, angry at the yellow butterfly that was fluttering in front of his face.

He tried to wave away the butterfly and his hand caught the lid of the chocolate pot, sending the whole thing flying. The pot smashed on the tiled floor. Chocolate dregs spattered Uncle Ted's white shirt, and shards of bone china flew everywhere.

Raul ran out with a dustpan and brush.

Uncle Ted poured some water onto a napkin and dabbed at his shirt. "I must ask you to be more careful while you're staying here, Massimo," he said. "I like an orderly house."

But Max didn't care about a few hot-chocolate stains.

It was the blood on his father's jacket that preoccupied him.

As they sat there, the sky darkened to a purple bruise and raindrops began drumming on the canvas awning. When Uncle Ted finally spoke again, he had to shout to make himself heard above the rainstorm. "There's no sense in sitting around moping, Massimo. You need to keep busy. As of tomorrow, I'm starting you in the banana warehouse."

Max looked at him warily. "How much will you pay me?"

"Hard work is its own reward," replied Uncle Ted. "You're living here at my expense. You should be glad to earn your keep."

"That's slave labor!" protested Max.

But Uncle Ted didn't seem to hear him. "Breakfast at five tomorrow, and report straight to Lucky Jim in the warehouse."

"Breakfast at five? But it's my summer vacation."

"You have to rise early in the tropics to beat the heat. If you get an early start, you can look forward to a productive day's work."

Hard work is its own reward? Breakfast at five? A productive day's work?

Max stared at his uncle openmouthed.

"Something wrong?" asked Uncle Ted.

"You sound like my father," said Max in surprise.

Uncle Ted said nothing. But his face reminded Max of his mother's expression the day she stepped in dog poop on Boston Common.

Chapter Five

MAX GOES BANANAS

"There's only one way to learn the banana business," said Lucky Jim. "And that's from the bottom up."

"Does that mean I get to drive one of those?" asked Max, eyeing the forklift trucks that zoomed around the warehouse moving pallets of green bananas.

"No," said Lucky, "it means you can clean up the beach. See all the old tires and palm fronds and dead fish washed up by the storm?"

"But that's a huge job," spluttered Max as Lucky passed him the rake.

As he glumly set to work, he consoled himself that it was better to be outside in the fresh air than sweltering inside the warehouse, even if all the insects in San Xavier had decided to keep him company.

No matter how much bug spray he used, they attacked him relentlessly. He had so many bites, he looked like a human dot-to-dot puzzle. He was only grateful there were no girls around to witness this deeply uncool turn of events.

As he worked—or more accurately, slacked off—Max

brooded on events at Ixchel. The more he went over things—the bloodstained jacket, the earring—the weirder it all seemed.

And then there was the mystery of Uncle Ted. What was he hiding? Every time Max asked to make a phone call or send an e-mail, he was told there was no connection. It was obviously untrue.

The old Max Murphy, the one who had kicked the fridge in Boston, would have made a scene about it, for sure. But some survival instinct made him hold his tongue. After all, Uncle Ted moved in dangerous circles, and Max didn't want to provoke his anger.

But why was he trying to cut his nephew off from the outside world?

Sometimes, as Max halfheartedly raked the sand, he had a distinct sensation of being watched. He never caught anyone in the act, but he guessed that Lucky Jim had his binoculars trained on him at all times. It made him feel like a performing monkey.

One morning when the rains came and he was running to the warehouse for shelter, he noticed a space under the loading pier. The tide was out and the rocks were dry. It was the perfect hideout. He could sit on the rocks without being seen by anyone. Plus, he'd be able to hear everything that happened on the dock above, which would help him keep tabs on Lucky Jim.

Surrounded by a curtain of rain, Max sat under the pier and thought things through for the billionth time. It was obvious that Uncle Ted was up to no good. But the question was, did he have anything to do with the disappearance of Max's parents?

His thoughts were interrupted by noises above him.

He realized that the downpour had stopped and work had resumed on the dock.

He heard his uncle's voice.

"It's all hands on deck tonight, Lucky. We load at two a.m."

"No worries, boss, the shipment is ready."

"Splendid! And how's that nephew of mine shaping up?"

"I'm sorry to say this about your own flesh and blood, boss, but he's as lazy as a three-toed sloth."

Both men laughed heartily.

"Bit of a spoiled brat, eh?"

"He's not used to hard work, boss, that's for sure."

"He's an only child—I think he usually gets his own way."

"Should I go easier on him, boss?"

"Absolutely not. It could ruin everything, him showing up like this. We have to keep him out of the house, at all costs. Raul caught him snooping around the office the other day—and you know what that could lead to. Work him till he drops, Lucky—make sure he's too tired to cause trouble."

"Whatever you say, boss."

Max was shaking with rage. So his uncle thought he was a spoiled brat, did he? And cleaning this stinking beach was just a ruse to keep him out of the house? Well, Uncle Ted's game was up.

Max would expose him for the crook he was.

There was obviously something incriminating hidden in the office. Max thought back to the day he'd looked around. Had he noticed anything strange? Not really. The only strange thing had been the way Uncle Ted had come out of the office without Max seeing him go in.

And, just like that, Max knew what he was looking for.

A secret door.

Maybe it led to the battlemented tower.

Maybe there was a money-laundering company up there. Or a passport-forging operation. Or—the idea struck him like a knock on the head—maybe, just maybe, his parents were being held prisoner up there.

Now Max was tingling with anticipation.

If they were loading a shipment at two a.m., he'd make his first search tonight. Everyone would be out of the house long enough for him to have a good look around. A spoiled brat indeed! For once, Max was proud of the anger that burned in his veins and spurred him on to vengeance. Uncle Ted was going to regret the day he'd ignited the wrath of Max Murphy!

That afternoon, Max worked with a new energy and enthusiasm. Even Lucky Jim noticed his efforts and signaled his approval from the pier. Max waved to him cheerily. And as he raked, he laid his plans.

Straight after dinner, Uncle Ted excused himself, saying he needed an early night.

Big fat liar, thought Max.

"Sounds good," he said. "Me, too."

Once in his room, he got ready for action. He found a flashlight in the side pocket of his backpack (*Thanks, Zia!*) and changed into a dark T-shirt and jeans. Then he set his alarm clock for quarter to two and lay down on the bed to get as much rest as possible before zero hour.

When the alarm went off, he felt as if he'd just gone to sleep. He forced himself out of bed and staggered to the window.

No movement at the pier.

He looked up and down the coast.

Still nothing.

Maybe the rendezvous had been cancelled.

Maybe Uncle Ted really did make it an early night.

The minutes ticked by.

Max was just about to get back into bed, when he realized that a shadow on the water was actually a boat slowly and silently making its way to the pier. This was it. His big chance. He guessed he had at least twenty minutes before they finished loading and came back to the house.

He stuck his head out of the bedroom doorway. All was still. The only sound was the beating of his own heart and the tick of an antique clock. He crept into the corridor, past the suits of armor, past the disapproving frowns of the long-dead Spaniards, and down the big stone staircase to the great hall.

Uncle Ted's huge collection of Maya sculptures shimmered in the moonlight. With the furniture receding into the darkness, they seemed to hover in the air like ghosts. A faint chatter of insects outside the window fell quiet as Max entered. He felt as if he'd walked in on a secret meeting, presided over by the two great stone heads.

Max hesitated. The heads looked even more alive tonight. Luminous in the moonlight, they seemed to glow from within. He told himself that their animated expressions were just the flickering shadows of the palm fronds at the window.

But they were looking straight at him.

And they did not look pleased to see him.

"Excuse me, guys," he said under his breath, and steeled himself to walk past them.

On shaking legs, he reached the door to his uncle's office. It was closed.

Worse than that, it was locked.

No, wait, it was just stuck.

He gently eased the old door open with a creak that seemed to reverberate through the house. He froze, listening for any sound or movement. Nothing. He breathed again. But time was passing. He had to hurry.

Quickly. Get inside and close the door.

Where to look?

He didn't dare switch on his flashlight in case they saw him from the dock. So with only the moon for light, he started searching the room. He tapped walls, looked behind shelves, lifted rugs for a trapdoor, but found nothing.

What had he missed? How can you hide a whole door?

He sat down on a bookcase that ran under the window and took one last look. He yawned and shivered at the same time. It was cold in this room.

Time to abort the mission and go to bed.

He put a hand on the edge of the bookcase to push himself up and, as he did so, the rush of cold air took his breath away. It was coming from directly behind him.

Wide awake now, he got down on his hands and knees to inspect the woodwork. There was a crack where the bookcase joined the wall. He pulled at the bookcase and felt a slight movement, just enough to tell him that he'd found his secret door. Now he had to find the lock.

Heart thumping, he took the books off the shelves and felt around inside the bookcase. His fingers closed on a small lever. He pushed it down and, with a click, the shelf unit swung away from the wall. He'd done it!

Still on his hands and knees, he was looking straight down

into a narrow steel staircase that spiraled into the bowels of the earth.

Down?

This was not what he'd been expecting at all. He'd been looking for an entrance to the tower, not the dungeons.

But a secret door was a secret door.

Spurred on by the spirit of revenge, he took a few steps down and pulled the bookcase back into position behind him. When it clicked shut, dim green lights came on to illuminate the stairwell. There was no sound but a faint dripping. Down and down he went, trying not to slip on the wet steel treads. With every step, the temperature dropped another few degrees.

At the bottom of the staircase it was as cold and clammy as a tomb.

He stepped under a small archway and into a tunnel hewn out of the rock. All he could hear was the soft hum of machinery and the dripping of water. The tunnel seemed deserted, but he could see arched openings at regular intervals all the way along. Anyone—or anything—could be inside them.

He crept down the tunnel and looked through the first archway. It opened into a large room, dimly lit by rows of computer screens. The walls were papered with charts and maps. Long metal tables supported stacks of computer hardware and electronic boxes covered with dials and switches. Cables and wires snaked across the ground and lay heaped in coils. Was he dreaming? There must have been a million dollars' worth of equipment in there.

The next archway revealed a locker room, packed with

camouflage gear and wet suits, and after that came a smaller tunnel that sloped steeply downward.

Max followed it for about twenty paces before he tripped on something. The beam of his flashlight revealed several rusty iron rings embedded in the cobbles. As he circled them, trying to work out what they were, he saw water lapping at his feet. Ah, they were boat moorings. The rest of the tunnel was flooded, and Max guessed it led to the open sea.

He retraced his steps back up to the main tunnel.

What was next? he wondered. A weapons cache? An underground firing range? A submarine dock?

But it was none of those. In fact, the next room was more extraordinary than anything Max could ever have imagined.

He was standing in the entrance to an Aladdin's cave.

The long vaulted space was lined with shelves. On them, nestled in foam rubber and laid out as carefully as a museum display, was a magnificent array of Maya artifacts as well as pieces of antique armor and weaponry.

Max stepped in to have a closer look. Nearer the doorway, the pottery was chipped and the swords were broken and rusty. But the farther back he went, the more perfect—and, presumably, more valuable—the artifacts became. At the far end, displayed on double thicknesses of foam, were pieces of jade jewelry, inlaid masks, ornately painted bowls, and beautifully carved stone figurines.

Max had seen it all before.

How many times had his parents dragged him around museums, oohing and aahing over this kind of stuff?

He hated it.

He was just turning to leave and go back to the techno room, when he saw a small metal suitcase on a high shelf. It seemed to be calling to him. Without thinking, he reached up for it.

It was heavier than he expected, and he nearly fell backward as he pulled it down. Then he flipped open the latches and lifted the lid.

A warm breeze blew out of the case and filled the air with the earthy smell of jungle. Inside the case, nestled in foam, was a head, a cat's head, carved in blood-red stone. The style was primitive, but the head was so full of life and energy, it almost seemed to snarl.

At that moment, Max felt metal on the back of his neck.

"Freeze."

He knew that voice. It was Lucky Jim. And he didn't sound like he was joking.

"Lucky, it's me, Max Murphy, I—"

"No tourists allowed down here."

"But I'm not a tourist, I'm—"

"Stop talking." There was the sound of a gun being cocked. "Now walk. Or I'll blow your head off."

Lucky Jim pushed and prodded him back to the flooded tunnel, all the while mumbling into a walkie-talkie.

"Sit," he said, pushing Max down onto the wet cobbles. "Put your hands behind your back." Max felt cold steel around his wrists as Lucky handcuffed him to a boat mooring. A vein as thick as a jungle vine throbbed in Lucky's forehead. "You're in big trouble, boy," he said.

Max was thinking fast. He looked up at Lucky Jim. "Are you really descended from a long line of Maya warriors?" he asked.

"What if I am?"

"So why do you allow Uncle Ted to loot your treasures? This stuff should be in a museum. Don't you want your children to see the amazing things the Maya were doing when Europe was still in the Dark Ages?"

Max thought it was a brilliant speech for the spur of the moment, and he waited expectantly for Lucky to realize the error of his ways. But Lucky showed no trace of shame. Instead, he drew himself up to his full man-mountain height, folded his arms, and sneered down at Max.

"If I ever have kids," he said, "I'd want to keep them as far away from this stuff as possible. I want them to break free of the past."

"B-b-but what about their heritage?"

Lucky Jim was beyond anger. He was so angry he was almost calm.

"Heritage? If you want heritage, go to one of those Maya theme parks in Mexico. You can watch a Maya show, eat Maya food, have your picture taken with a Maya warrior—

the complete Maya experience. It won't be the real thing, of course, because you tourists don't want the real thing."

"What's the real thing?" whimpered Max.

"You really want to know?"

Max nodded.

"Time for a history lesson," said Lucky Jim, bending down until the pulsing vein on his forehead was inches from Max's face. "Those old Maya may have been good at pottery and math, but they were ruled by violence and superstition. Problem is, they're still alive. And they're still trying to run things around here. You can call that heritage, but I call it a dangerous reality."

"You're crazy!" blurted Max.

Lucky Jim laughed like a crazy person. "You tourists don't get it, do you? Maya time is different from your time. Our world is different from your world."

He sat down and leaned back against the tunnel wall.

"Take those pyramids in the jungle, like the one your parents were working on. You tourists wouldn't be so quick to climb all over them if you knew how many doors to the underworld they conceal. And those doors are still open. Your parents knew that. . . ."

"What else did my parents know?" whispered Max.

Lucky Jim grabbed Max by the neck of his T-shirt and pulled him close.

"*Bahlamtuuno'ob*," he growled.

"The Jaguar Stones?" asked Max. But before he got his answer, there was a sound of approaching footsteps.

Lucky Jim let him go and stood up. "I've seen some bad things in the jungle," he said as he backed away, "but I wouldn't like to be in your shoes now."

As Lucky Jim's footsteps faded away, the other footsteps got louder until Uncle Ted stood over his terrified nephew.

"Got a little lost on our way for milk and cookies, did we?" he said. "I'm disappointed in you, Massimo. I distinctly remember asking you not to poke around. The only question now is what to do with you. . . ."

Max said nothing. There was nothing he could say. He'd been caught red-handed.

"Lucky thinks we should dump you in the ocean . . . tell the police you went looking for your parents in the jungle and never returned. It's an interesting idea, don't you think? The undertow would carry your body halfway to Cuba before the sun comes up."

Max stared at him in disbelief. How could his own uncle, a man who had held him in his arms as a baby, talk to him this way? "Now I understand why my father has always hated you," he spat.

"To hell with your father," said Uncle Ted. "It's your own skin you need to worry about."

Chapter Six
FAMILY SECRETS

o hell with your father."

That's what he'd said.

The words were still ringing in Max's ears as Uncle Ted unlocked the handcuffs and pulled him to his feet. He suddenly knew, with a horrible certainty, that Uncle Ted had killed his parents.

"Walk," said Uncle Ted. "And don't try anything. The villa is crawling with security guards tonight. And their orders are to shoot to kill."

"You'll go to jail for this," said Max.

"Silence!" said Uncle Ted.

Keeping Max in front of him, Uncle Ted prodded him back through the tunnels and up the spiral staircase. By the time they emerged into the office, the sun was rising over the sea. Max shivered in the dawn light. He was wet and cold and weary to his bones.

"Sit!" said Uncle Ted, pushing him into a chair. "I can see I need to teach you a lesson you won't forget." He opened the desk drawer and took out a vicious-looking hunting knife.

Max swallowed. Was this the knife that Uncle Ted had used to kill his parents? He couldn't take his eyes off its glinting blade. He thought about running, but he was too weak to move. In any case, where would he go?

This was it.

His parents were dead. And now it was his turn to die.

There was just one thing he had to know.

"Why did you kill them?" he asked dully.

"What?"

"Why did you kill my parents?"

Uncle Ted looked at him blankly. "What are you talking about?"

Max looked at the knife.

Uncle Ted followed his eyes. Then he started to laugh.

"Don't be ridiculous," he said. "This rusty old thing couldn't cut butter." He crouched in front of an old storage chest and starting working the blade under the lid. "I keep the knife handy for this," he explained. "Darn thing always sticks. The sea air warps everything."

Eventually the lid came free, and Uncle Ted pulled a blanket out of the chest. He wrapped it around Max's shoulders. "How could you think I killed your parents?" he asked, shaking his head in disbelief.

Max shrugged. "You were acting suspiciously."

"I'll admit there's no love lost between your father and me, but surely I don't strike you as a murderer?"

"Down there"—Max indicated the secret door—"you threatened to kill me."

"Did I? Well, I *was* very angry with you, Massimo. You could have got hurt with your silly games tonight. I'm just trying to keep you safe until your parents reappear."

"So having Lucky Jim stick a gun in my neck was keeping me safe?"

"He was trying to scare some sense into you. It's one thing when you slack off at the banana warehouse, but tonight's little escapade was unforgivable. What were you thinking, getting up in the middle of the night and . . . and"—he searched for the correct criminal term—"*trespassing* like that?"

Max was unrepentant. "It's a good thing I did, or I wouldn't have known about that treasure trove down there. It's stolen, isn't it?"

Uncle Ted had the grace to look sheepish. "That's no concern of yours."

"It is if I'm living here."

"Let us hope you will not be living here much longer."

"So what are you going to do with me? Throw me in the dungeons?"

"It's tempting."

They glared at each other for a while, until Uncle Ted broke the silence.

"Here's what I suggest," he said eventually. "Since I am stuck with you for the foreseeable future, we will have to find a way to live together. From now on, you must obey my rules to the letter. You will stay in your room at night, and you are forbidden to set foot in my office. Agreed?"

Uncle Ted held out his hand to shake on it.

Max thought for a moment. "I'll shake on one condition."

"Which is?"

"You tell me the truth about what's going on around here."

"Why on earth would I do that?"

Max had seen enough gangster movies to know the answer.

"Because I know too much already," he said. "And because blood is thicker than water."

To Max's surprise, Uncle Ted started to laugh. "Spoken like a true Murphy!" he said.

"What does that mean?"

"Frank hasn't told you our family history? Then it will be my pleasure to tell you everything he doesn't want you to know."

Which was how, ten minutes later, Max found himself tucked up on a sofa in the great hall, as Raul brought in a tray of hot chocolate and buttery, freshly baked croissants.

Uncle Ted selected a silver photo frame from a collection on a side table. "Do you know who this is?" he asked.

Max studied the faded picture of a handsome young farmer in a flat cap and plaid shirt, riding a white horse bareback.

"Grandpa Murphy?" he guessed.

Uncle Ted nodded. "Life on the farm was too quiet for him. Soon after that photo was taken, he headed to America to seek his fortune, working his passage on a freighter from Dublin to New York. From there, he hustled and brawled his way south until he pitched up in San Xavier. It was still a young country then, like the Wild West, full of adventurers and opportunists. He tried big-game fishing and logging before winning the banana business in a poker game."

"Grandpa was a gambler?" Max was half shocked and half delighted to be descended from a poker-playing renegade.

"From that day forward, he never gambled again. He devoted himself to building up the business until he had enough money to buy this house. He turned it into the finest mansion on the coast."

"Why did he want such a big house?"

"He was trying to impress someone."

"A girl?"

"Her father."

Uncle Ted jumped up to get another photograph. This one showed a family posing stiffly in their Sunday best. The women wore flowery dresses, pearl necklaces, and shawls. The men wore dark suits, slicked-back hair, and pencil mustaches. To Max, they looked like a family of tango dancers.

Uncle Ted pointed to a stern-looking man. "Don José Pizarro, descendant of the original conquistadores, wealthy landowner, and, most importantly, father of the beautiful Isabella." His finger moved to a young girl with long black hair and dancing eyes. "Naturally Don José opposed the marriage of his daughter to the son of dirt-poor Irish farmers. But eventually, won over by the Villa Isabella, he gave his blessing."

"Grandma Isabel was a Spanish aristocrat? Why did Dad never tell me?"

"Think about it, Massimo. 'Leading Maya scholar is direct descendant of the very people who tried to wipe out Maya culture.' It doesn't look good on his résumé."

"But he could have told me," said Max indignantly. "It's my history, too."

"I bet I know something else he hasn't told you," said Uncle Ted. "Your father has a guilty secret. Something that happened when we were teenagers. In fact, it's the reason he was at Ixchel last week."

"Go on," said Max, wide-eyed.

"So Patrick and Isabella were married, and Frank and I came along. We were so close, people thought we were twins.

It's hard to imagine now, but we used to be best friends."

"Why did you fall out?"

Uncle Ted's face clouded over. "After Mother died, we pretty much ran wild. Frank's always been obsessed with the Maya and he'd drag me out for days at a time, looking for Maya ruins in the jungle. In the summer that changed our lives, we were camping with a friend when we discovered a different kind of ruin. Not a Maya temple this time, but a Franciscan monastery from the days of the conquest. There wasn't much left of it and we wouldn't have stayed, but it started to rain. So we took shelter in the ruins and built a fire against one of the old walls. I don't know if it was the heat of the fire, but the wall suddenly collapsed and there, in the rubble, was a small cedar box. We forced it open, expecting to find gold coins and jewels. What a letdown! It was just some rosary beads and an old book wrapped in deerskin! I was disappointed, but Frank was dancing a jig like he'd scored the winning touchdown in the Super Bowl."

Max groaned. "I've seen him do that dance at weddings."

"Well, this time he had good reason—he'd realized that the old book was the private journal of Friar Diego de Landa! Have you heard of him?"

"Oscar Poot called him the curse of the Maya."

"He was bad news, that was for sure," said Uncle Ted. "He single-handedly attempted to wipe out Maya culture. Even the authorities in Spain were shocked, and had him imprisoned in the monastery."

"Did you find his skeleton in the ruins?"

"No, he was sent back to Spain to face charges."

"So what happened to the journal?"

"Well, that's what we argued about. It was one of the greatest archaeological finds of the century, but your father refused to report it."

"Where is it now?"

"Let's just say that its existence is known only to a select few."

Max could not believe his ears. His father had been hiding stolen goods all these years. He was an archaeological outlaw, a desperado in a safari jacket.

"The jacket!" spluttered Max.

"What jacket?" asked Uncle Ted.

"Dad's old safari jacket! I bet that's where he kept the journal! It must be missing with the rest of his notes."

"Surely he wouldn't have been stupid enough to bring it back to San Xavier?" Uncle Ted sighed. "If you're right, Massimo, this is a disaster."

"Why? Because it's priceless?"

"No, because it contains a secret that could destroy the world."

Max made a face. "You're supposed to be telling me the truth," he said.

"This is the truth, Massimo. I've seen the journal and I can tell you that Friar Landa had no interest in saving souls. He directed all his energies to finding a certain set of stone carvings with supposedly mystical powers."

"The Jaguar Stones!"

"You've heard of them?"

"Oscar mentioned them. But what's the harm in a few old stones?"

"Landa tortured thousands of men, women, and children to get his hands on them. He believed that if he could gather all five stones together, he would become a living god."

"But that's stupid, isn't it?"

"The point is, Max, that Landa believed it—and so will plenty of other power-crazy megalomaniacs. That journal contains full instructions for using the five sacred stones at the five sacred pyramids. If it falls into the wrong hands, every rogue nation on the planet will be racing to find the Jaguar Stones. Major wars have started for less."

"I can't believe Dad's kept this secret for so long. Isn't that against some kind of archaeological code of honor?"

"Honor doesn't come into it. Ever since Frank read the journal, he's been obsessed by the idea of putting Landa's instructions to the test."

"But what good are the instructions without a Jaguar Stone?"

Uncle Ted said nothing.

Max did a double take. "Don't tell me Dad had a Jaguar Stone?"

Uncle Ted slowly wiped his mouth with a napkin.

Then he carefully refolded the napkin and put it down next to his cup.

He straightened the spoon on his saucer.

He flicked a crumb off the table.

When he could no longer avoid answering Max's question, he spoke in a whisper.

One word.

One word that changed everything.

"Yes."

"What!" Max sat bolt upright.

"Frank had the White Jaguar of Ixchel."

"Where did he get it?"

"From me."

Max considered this information. "That carved head in the suitcase on the shelf down there—was that a Jaguar Stone?"

Uncle Ted nodded. "The Red Jaguar of Chahk."

"Where you *you* getting them from?"

"I think I've said enough."

"But what about your underground cache?"

"It's not a cache, Massimo, it's a storeroom. Those limestone caves are the perfect temperature for storing antiques."

Max narrowed his eyes. "Are you forging Jaguar Stones? You promised you'd tell me *everything*." He lay back on the sofa and pulled up the blanket, like a child waiting for a bedtime story.

"It could be dangerous for you to know more, Massimo."

"If you want me to stop poking around, you have to tell me."

Uncle Ted sighed. "I'm a smuggler."

Max's eyes widened in surprise.

"Are you shocked?" asked Uncle Ted.

"It's just that Dad always says . . . ," began Max. Then he stopped himself.

"I know what Frank says," said Uncle Ted. "He says smugglers and looters are the scum of the earth."

Max nodded glumly.

Uncle Ted laughed. "You must have realized by now, Massimo, that I don't give a fig for what Frank says. It was partly his fault that I had to start smuggling. Has he ever talked about what happened when your grandpa died?"

"He never talks about the past," said Max, "unless it's about the Maya."

"Patrick Murphy died about twenty years go. I was pursuing my studies at art school in London, and Frank was at Harvard. Neither of us wanted to take charge of family affairs, but Frank insisted it should be me. He said it was my duty as the eldest, but I got the sense he thought my studies were less important. I came back to find the business in tatters. There was a blight in the banana groves and production was at an all-time low. I wanted to close down, but people were depending on me. Lucky Jim's father was foreman at the time and supporting a huge family. I couldn't let them starve. I had to find the money to keep things going until the blight was over. So I decided to put my artistic training to good use and start dealing in Maya artifacts. Frank said I was no better than a thieving conquistador. I thought that was rich, given that he was sitting on Landa's journal, so I called him a few names, too. To cut a long story short, we've been like oil and water ever since. He got to live out his dream digging up old pots, while I stayed in San Xavier, packing bananas."

"Why didn't you go back to London when the blight was over?"

"The usual story . . . *cherchez la femme.*"

Max looked blank.

"I fell in love," explained Uncle Ted.

"Who—?" began Max.

"It ended badly. That's when I decided to forget about pointless concepts like art and love, and throw myself into making money. Maya artifacts are just another commodity to me—like bananas."

"Dad says—"

"Your father is a hypocrite! In public, he denounces the black market, but in private he's been blackmailing me to get him a Jaguar Stone."

Max's mouth fell open. "You're kidding!"

"I'm not. He made me swear that if I ever came across a Jaguar Stone, I would pass it straight to him, no questions asked. That was his price for not reporting my smuggling activities. Of course, I never dreamed for a moment that not one, but two Jaguar Stones would fall into my lap."

"Where did they come from?"

"It was pure chance." Uncle Ted leaned forward conspiratorially. "One day last year, we'd just set sail with a load of bananas and our 'special cargo,' when the local coast guard pulled alongside to board us for inspection. Luckily, we were using the old Chinese smugglers' trick of towing the loot in a crate underwater. We cut the rope, the crate sank to the bottom of the sea, and there was nothing for the coast guard to find."

"But didn't you lose it?" asked Max, fascinated by this master class in smuggling techniques.

"No, that's the clever bit. We fit our crates with small transmitters. If we have to cut one loose, we can track it with a GPS—a global positioning system. The waters around here aren't deep, so we just send down a diver to retrieve it."

"Why don't the coast guards see the signal?"

"They do. But there are so many environmentalists tracking whales and dolphins with the same system, no one pays any attention. Even so, we thought it would be wise to lay low for a while. So we left the crate and just monitored the signal for several months. That's when we noticed something strange."

Max sat up again. "What was it?"

"The crate was moving toward land. You expect things to drift with the current, but this was like a magnetic attraction.

Eventually the signal indicated that the crate was no longer underwater. Yet the depth gauge showed it was still way below sea level. It didn't make sense."

"Was it in an air pocket or something?"

"I went down with the divers to find out. Tracking the signal, we found ourselves in an underwater tunnel. We followed it for a hundred yards or so, until it opened into a huge cavern. And I mean huge. I'm talking about Madison Square Garden. When we surfaced and shone our flashlights around, we couldn't believe our eyes. Washed up on the rocks was the wreck of a Spanish galleon. It was the long-lost *Espada*."

"That's the ship that disappeared!"

"Exactly! And can you imagine the riches that were in its hold?"

A ray of sunshine lit up the room, and when Uncle Ted shielded his eyes, he looked like he was blinded by the glare from the *Espada*'s gold.

"It took us months to bring up the haul. But the best was yet to come. . . ."

Uncle Ted paused for dramatic effect.

"On our final dive before the tide changed, we found an old sea chest at the back of the hold. It was perfectly preserved in the cave and there, burned into the wood, was the crest of Friar Diego de Landa! Can you believe it?"

Uncle Ted's face was shining with excitement and Max knew that, this time, Landa's box had contained more than rosary beads and old books.

"We opened the lid, and a ghostly glow lit up the cavern. Inside the chest, along with a jeweled sword and some solid-gold candlesticks, were two—two!—of the legendary Jaguar

Stones. One in pure white alabaster and one in ruby-red Mexican fire opal. There in front of me were the White Jaguar of Ixchel and the Red Jaguar of Chahk. What a moment!"

Uncle Ted shook his head at the memory.

"Your father came for the White Jaguar last week and took it as if it was his birthright. But no matter. I've fulfilled my side of the bargain and I was not expecting to see him ever again—until his son turned up on my doorstep."

"I'm sorry," said Max.

Uncle Ted shook his head. "I'm the one who should be sorry. I've enjoyed our little chat. I haven't talked so much in years. Maybe blood *is* thicker than water, Massimo."

"Please call me Max."

"I will try and be a better host, Max." Uncle Ted smiled ruefully. "When it comes to houseguests, I've always agreed with Jean-Paul."

"Is he one of your servants?"

"Jean-Paul Sartre, the French philosopher. He said, 'Hell is other people.' Of course, he said it in French. But my point is, I don't like visitors at the best of times, and seeing your father always puts me in a bad mood."

"He has that effect on me sometimes," said Max.

Uncle Ted roared with laughter. "I'm looking forward to getting to know you, Max. I hope we can make a fresh start."

Max nodded eagerly.

"But no more nocturnal rambles, okay?" continued Uncle Ted. "I'm selling the Red Jaguar tomorrow night, and I need you to stay in your room. My buyer is a nasty piece of work, and anything could happen."

Max guessed he was talking about the gun-crazed Spaniard. "No problem," he said. He had no desire to bump into that cape-twirling weirdo. It was a shame to miss all the excitement, though. "Maybe I could help you?" he suggested.

"I'd rather you didn't," said Uncle Ted firmly.

"Let me do something safe, like keeping a lookout. There's a great view from my balcony, and I could use those night-vision goggles I saw in your office. Please, Uncle Ted; I'd keep out of sight."

His uncle thought for a moment. "Maybe it's not such a bad idea. At least I'd know where you were. But you have to promise to stay in your room, whatever happens. These thugs mean business."

"I give you my word."

When Raul came in to clear away the breakfast things, he saw them shaking hands and smiled to himself as he loaded the tray. It was a long time since he'd seen his boss look so happy.

"Ah, Raul," said Uncle Ted, "have you packed the boy's lunch?"

"What?" said Max indignantly. "You mean, after all this, I still have to go and rake the beach?"

"Absolutely." Uncle Ted tried to look stern. "Now get to work."

Chapter Seven
THIEVES IN THE NIGHT

That evening Max sat on his balcony, waiting for it to get dark enough to try out the night-vision goggles and thinking over everything Uncle Ted had told him. His head was throbbing from information overload. If he were a computer, he would have crashed for sure.

Back in Boston, life had been black and white. Parents led dull lives and went to bed early. Smugglers were low-life jerks. The Maya were dead as dodos.

Here in the jungle, none of that was true.

All bets were off.

How had Uncle Ted put it?

Things are never what they seem around here.

It was unsettling, but also exciting.

Max liked the sense of possibility, the idea that he could reinvent himself. He could be irresistible to girls . . . he could ace tests without studying . . . maybe he could—dare he even think it?—be an interesting enough person to make his parents want to spend more time with him.

As he took stock of his current situation, he realized he'd changed a lot already. He'd traveled all this way on his own. He'd survived Lucky Jim's gun on his neck. He'd even bonded with child-hating Uncle Ted. It wasn't a bad start. In fact, tonight, standing on the balcony of his rich uncle's beautiful house, he felt like a new person.

Older, wiser, more mature.

That's the spirit, he encouraged himself.

He smiled—a sardonic, James Bond kind of smile.

Out here, with the waves lapping the shore and the sounds of the rainforest beyond the garden wall, it was easy to feel like an international playboy.

Max Murphy, Man of Mystery.

It had a ring to it.

Finally the sun was setting, and Max inspected the night-vision goggles. They looked like heavy binoculars attached to a web of straps. It took him a while to get them on, but once he did . . .

Boy, did they work!

It was fantastic! Everything was cast in a green glow, but he could see almost as well as in daylight. In fact, thanks to thermal imaging and infrared detectors, he could see some things even better than usual.

Ha-hah! Those guards patrolling the beachfront thought they were keeping a low profile, but their body heat made them stand out like luminous green ghosts!

Excited, Max turned his goggles onto the rainforest. Surely tonight he'd be able to spot signs of life in the normally inscrutable mass of foliage.

Nothing.

Nothing.

Nothing.

Wait.

He saw a movement.

He focused in on it.

Gotcha!

Something was coming out of the jungle and heading this way. As Max watched, the faint green glow formed itself into two distinct heat spots. He increased the magnification on the goggles until he could make out two monkeys, one a little bigger than the other.

With their long tails curved in the air behind them, the monkeys loped quickly toward the perimeter wall. For a few minutes they disappeared from view, but soon appeared again on the edge of the wall. Max smiled to himself. They must sneak in all the time to steal bananas.

The monkeys certainly seemed to know where they were going, but it was not toward the banana warehouse. They were headed straight toward the house. Max was tingling with excitement. Seeing animals in the wild felt very different from seeing them in the zoo. He kept absolutely still so as not to frighten them away.

What were they up to? They seemed to be interested in a particular stone pillar in the garden. Was there some sort of tasty vine growing on it? What was the special attraction? Max's smile faded as he watched the monkeys remove a metal grate off the side of the pillar and climb inside. It must be a ventilation shaft for the underground rooms!

He kept his eyes fixed on the pillar, but the monkeys had vanished.

Just when he was wondering if he'd dreamed the whole thing (had he fallen asleep for a moment?), the monkeys reappeared.

But what was that? They were carrying something. Max's jaw dropped when he recognized the metal case containing the Red Jaguar.

This was not remotely funny anymore. It was deadly serious and Max seemed to be the only one who was aware of it. Where were the guards? Where was Lucky Jim? Where was Uncle Ted?

If only someone would come before it was too late. . . .

The monkeys moved awkwardly across the lawn toward the perimeter wall. The case was heavy and they were having difficulty lifting it. But even so, they would soon be over the wall and into the jungle.

Max was in turmoil. Should he shout for the guards and try to convince them that two monkeys had staged a commando raid? Or should he go after the monkeys himself and break his promise to Uncle Ted about staying in his room?

Max made his decision.

A promise was a promise.

He basked in a glow of self-righteousness. For once, he would act in a mature and responsible manner. He would do as he was told—even if the monkeys got clean away.

He ran to the door to raise the alarm.

It was locked.

Uncle Ted had locked him in!

So much for mutual trust and respect!

As of now, all promises were null and void.

In a hotheaded rage, Max grabbed his backpack and reviewed the jumbled contents: flashlight, towel, mosquito net, shades, and—what was that, at the bottom?—ugh, granola bars. (He would never, never be that hungry.) What else? He threw in his Red Sox cap for good luck.

Ready to go.

He slung his backpack over his shoulder and climbed over the balcony railing. It was a little high to jump down, but with the aid of a climbing vine he made it to the ground.

Uncle Ted was going to be mad.

Very mad.

But there was no going back.

Besides, if Uncle Ted had trusted him and not locked him in his room, he wouldn't have attempted this crazy escapade. Now he was master of his own destiny. And if he could just get those monkeys to drop the Jaguar Stone, Uncle Ted would have to kiss his feet and beg his forgiveness.

Through the night-vision goggles, Max spotted the monkeys disappearing over the perimeter wall. He raced across the garden toward them. Steps led up to a battlemented walkway that ran along the top of the wall. Max took the steps two at time and peered over. About forty more feet of lawn lay between the wall and the start of the jungle. He could see the monkeys slowly dragging the case toward the tree line. They seemed to be heading for a gap in the undergrowth, maybe some sort of trail.

Max swung over the wall and found footholds to climb down in the crumbling stone. Then he sprinted across the lawn and . . . after a moment's hesitation . . . he plunged down the trail and into the forest. His

pace slowed. It was like entering a tunnel. The noise was incredible. *Whook-whook. Whook-whook.* At first, he thought a chopper was circling above him, but then he realized that this deafening sound was coming from the tiny pop-eyed frogs that looked down at him from every tree.

Though no competition for the frogs in the decibel stakes, nocturnal birds were shrieking, insects were buzzing—and every so often something a whole lot bigger would let out a hungry growl that shook the air like a subway train passing through.

Max told himself that the creatures were more scared of him than he was of them, but he doubted it was true. He wanted to turn back. But which would he rather face—a wild beast or an angry Uncle Ted?

He decided to keep going.

With every step, the din of the jungle grew louder. The trees rustled and shook. Bats darted in front of his face. Lightning bugs and click beetles lit up his goggles with their fluorescent green trails. He seemed to be surrounded by creeping, crawling, jumping things.

Okay. Concentrate.

Max could clearly see the path and he picked his way carefully over the tangled mass of tree roots. His pace was slow and he was grateful the Red Jaguar was so heavy. If it had been lighter, the monkeys could have swung through the trees and he wouldn't have had a chance of following.

As it was, they continued their slow, shuffling progress until they came to an open space under a tall stand of bamboo. Then they inspected the ground fastidiously before choosing a place to set down the suitcase, like two old ladies getting ready for a picnic.

Max hid behind a tree, hardly daring to breathe. *Any minute now*, he thought, *I'll run into the clearing, frighten them away, and grab the suitcase.* But as he stood there, gathering his nerve, the bigger monkey opened its mouth and began to roar. Max couldn't believe the sheer volume of it. It was like something out of *Jurassic Park*. If he hadn't seen with his own eyes that it was coming from a monkey, he would have thought a T. rex was loose in the jungle. Make that a T. rex with a megaphone. But who or what was the monkey calling?

A human figure, dressed all in black, emerged from the forest. The monkeys jumped up and down excitedly. The figure patted them and gave them something to eat. The monkeys grabbed at the food and leapt into the trees, whooping and screeching at each other.

Then the figure opened the case and took out the Red Jaguar.

Its glow illuminated the whole clearing.

Suddenly, the air was silent. The insects, the birds, even the tree frogs ceased their calling. The whole jungle seemed to be waiting and watching.

Quickly, the figure wrapped the stone in a cloth and put it into a small backpack. Then he started digging in the ground, scooping out the dirt with both hands until he'd made a hole big enough to bury the metal case. Only when both stone and case were hidden from view did the jungle cacophony resume.

Who was this mysterious thief who trained monkeys to do his dirty work? Was it one of Landa's henchmen? Or a business rival of Uncle Ted's?

An unearthly noise made Max jump out of his skin.

It sounded close.

He peeped out from behind the tree.

The noise was coming from the thief! With his hands cupped around his mouth, he was making a series of throaty, inhuman growls. Loud monkey grunts rained down from the trees in reply. At one point Max's legs turned to jelly when it seemed the thief was looking directly at him, but it was a false alarm and the thief resumed his "conversation" before taking off again into the jungle.

Max followed, trying to be as quiet and light-footed as he could.

It was harder than before, because the pace was faster and the trail was much less distinct. Even with the night-vision goggles, he had to use all his wits and concentration to keep the figure in view. Roots tripped him, vines clung to him, branches pulled at him. But none of these obstacles seemed to bother his quarry, who made the trek look as effortless as a stroll in the park.

They came to a stagnant river with a layer of green scum floating on top. A large tree had fallen across it, creating a natural bridge. The thief ran nimbly over the tree trunk and continued up the path.

Max paused before crossing. A division of army ants was marching toward him across the tree trunk. Their column was as wide as the log, and there was no end in sight to their ranks.

They're only ants, he told himself, and stepped gingerly onto the log.

It was perilously slippery.

Max concentrated every fiber of his being on keeping his balance. Now he could see that many of the ants were dragging prey—dead beetles, wasps, and crickets—underneath their bodies. He stomped on them with his thick-soled sneakers as he inched his way across. He'd made it about halfway when he felt a searing pain in his legs. He looked down to see ants on his sneakers, crawling up inside his jeans. Instinctively, he leaned over to swat at them and fell headfirst into the murky river.

It tasted disgusting. Max spluttered to the surface and stood up on the oozy bottom. The water came up to his knees. He couldn't see much because his goggles were smeared with mud, but the pain in his legs seemed to be subsiding so he guessed the ants had been washed off. Now he just had to get to the bank without being attacked by bloodsucking leeches or razor-toothed piranhas. . . .

The glutinous mud of the riverbed made every step a struggle. At one point the suction pulled off a sneaker, and he had to stick a hand in and feel around for it. The thick, green water stank like rotten eggs, and his whole body shook with revulsion.

Something slimy touched his face.

A piece of weed? A water snake?

Splashing hysterically, he made it to the bank. He sat down on a rock. His heart was pounding. Where was he? What had he done? Dripping wet and trembling with fear, he rammed his sneaker back on. Then he ran his hands all over his body to wipe down every inch of himself. He didn't want any creepy jungle thing to touch any bit of him.

This was it, the end of the line.

He would sit here until he was found.

Or until he starved to death.

Or until something ate him.

It was at this low point that Max realized what an idiot

he'd been. He was lost in the treacherous forest, alone, wet, bitten, scared, and hungry. Now the police would have to break off their search for his parents to look for him instead (if Uncle Ted even bothered to report him missing).

He drew his feet up, put his head on his knees, and hugged himself. His clothes smelled sulfurous and moldy. Overwhelmed by self-pity, he unzipped his wet backpack and looked inside. It seemed to be pretty dry. He pulled out a towel and dried himself off as much as he could. Then he stuck his hand in again and groped around. Among the tangle of mosquito netting and odd socks, his fingers closed on something unnaturally hard and dense.

The granola bars.

It had come to this.

Miserably, he unwrapped a bar. He brought the compacted brown mass to his lips. With a heavy heart, he opened his mouth and prepared his tongue to receive the foul-tasting grunge.

Then, in the nick of time, he recovered his fighting spirit.

Things were bad, but not that bad.

He still wasn't desperate enough to eat a granola bar.

So he sat on the rock and pulled himself together and thought about what he should do. The most sensible thing would be to retrace his steps. But going back over that ant-covered log was not an option. Nor was wading across that slimy river. And they both paled in comparison with the terror he felt about facing Uncle Ted without bringing back the Jaguar Stone.

He wiped the last of the mud off his goggles and looked around.

Trees, trees, nothing but trees.

Big, thick trees with buttress roots taller than he was.

Tall, thin trees with sinister, twisted trunks and long, sinewy roots, gnarled and warty like a witch's fingers.

He looked harder. Now he was seeing things.

In the unreal green light of the goggles, he could see a mark hacked into one of the tree trunks.

It looked like an arrow. And it was freshly carved.

He thought again about that late-night zombie movie. *We've been expecting you, Max Murphy,* cackled the zombies in his head.

Stop it.

He told himself there was a natural explanation for the mark, that it was made by the beak of a giant woodpecker or the teeth of some demented rodent. Possibly something that was watching him right now.

Was something watching him?

He couldn't see any eyes in the darkness, but he had the same sensation that he'd had on the beach.

Something was watching him for sure.

How tasty he must look, sitting on this rock in the moonlight like the last jelly doughnut in the school cafeteria.

Any moment now, something big would come along and eat him.

Or maybe it wouldn't, and he'd be forced to eat the granola bars.

Either way, the future was looking grim.

Something fell out of the arrow-scarred tree with a thump.

With his heart in his mouth, Max turned to look. A ripe mango lay squashed on the ground. Squashed and rotten like his hopes for survival.

He put his head in his hands.

He was lost in the middle of a jungle. If only he'd marked the way he'd come so he could find his way back. This was Boy Scout 101, and he'd flunked it.

There was a rustling in the leaves. Two more mangoes fell to the ground and landed by the first one. As Max regarded them miserably, he noticed a faint trail at the base of the tree, eerily illuminated like a ghostly runway by phosphorescent mushrooms on either side.

A trail. Any trail was better than nothing.

He got to his feet and headed for the mushrooms.

His feet squelched in the mud as he tramped along, but he no longer cared if he made any noise. He was miserable and tired, and his quarry was long gone. The important thing now was to keep to the trail, watch out for snakes in the leaf litter, and try to find somewhere safe to wait for daybreak.

After an hour or so, he came to a part of the forest that was quieter and airier. By now, he was bone tired. His legs ached, his feet ached, his arms ached, his head ached.

He looked around and saw a massive tree trunk, easily twenty feet in diameter. The bottom of the trunk was bare, but its higher reaches had some kind of vine growing down them. The vine had big leathery leaves and exposed roots that dangled from the tree like bits of frayed rope. Where the trunk split into two, about ten feet off the ground, the crook was cushioned by a thick green mattress of leaves that seemed to have been flattened down, just for him. In Max's exhausted state, it looked as cozy and inviting as a featherbed.

Using a neighboring tree stump as a step and pulling on the dangling roots to haul himself the rest of the way up, Max reached the crook of the tree quite easily. Then he wedged himself between the branches, hung up his mosquito net as best he could, and lay back, using his backpack as a pillow.

Now all he had to do was watch out for predators and wait for the dawn. As long as he didn't fall asleep, he should be safe here. He scratched the insect bites on his arms and face, and allowed himself to relax a little. He'd been awake for two days and it felt good to finally rest. Stars twinkled in the little patch of sky that was visible through the leaves above his head. Stars meant a clear sky and no rain clouds. His clothes still stank from the river, but at least they were beginning to dry out. He'd survived this far and, with a whole day ahead of him, he was sure he could find his way back to the Villa Isabella. He remembered a time in the distant past when he'd walked through a rainforest like this one. Or was it a video game? Past and present, waking and sleeping, games and reality . . . it was all merging into one.

It was surprisingly comfortable in this tree.

As Max's thoughts settled like roosting doves, the hum of the jungle arranged itself into a soothing lullaby.

His eyelids felt heavy. He'd close them just for a moment.

Soon he curled up like a baby bird in its cozy nest and nodded off to sleep.

"Ow! Ow! Ow!"

The next thing he knew, he was screaming in pain and terror.

He'd been attacked as he slept.

He woke up to find great black hairy hands all over him, pinching him, squeezing him, pulling out his hair by the roots.

Chapter Eight

THE MONKEY GIRL

They weren't hands, they were paws. Great hairy paws with long fingers.

Max tried to bat them away, but he was tangled up in his mosquito net and he fell out of the tree. He landed in a heap on his backpack.

Seconds later, the night-vision goggles landed next to him with a dull crunch.

He peered up to see what had attacked him.

Two monkeys were sitting high in the branches. One was big and black. The other was smaller and reddish in color. The bigger one was wearing Max's baseball cap. They both had thick hair and wispy beards that would have made them look quite intellectual had they not been baring their teeth and screeching with monkey laughter.

They looked suspiciously like the monkeys who'd stolen the Red Jaguar. But before Max could study them in any detail, they were off, leaping from branch to branch, still screeching raucously.

Max looked around. The leaf canopy above him blocked

out most of the sun, but he could have guessed it was morning just from the energy in the air. Thousands of busy little life-forms scuttled around, intent on getting breakfast before it got too hot to move. Bugs buzzed and whirred and clicked. Birds shrieked and squawked and whooped. Flowers pumped out their heady scents, competing with each other to lure the passing insects like those salespeople who lurked in Macy's doorway with sprays of perfume.

Everything was shrouded in a humid mist. In the dim light, Max felt like he was underwater, but with butterflies instead of fish.

On the positive side, it was the most amazing morning of his life.

On the negative side, he was lost, sore, itchy, hungry, smelly, and caked in mud. Somehow he had to find his way back and face the wrath of Uncle Ted. He felt sick at the thought. If only he could have returned in triumph, bringing the Red Jaguar with him. But it was too late for that now.

Thud!

A wild avocado, hard as a rock, landed at his feet.

Deep in the foliage he saw a flash of Red Sox cap and heard the whooping of monkey laughter.

Max was sure now that these were the monkeys who'd stolen the Red Jaguar. After all, they seemed to like hanging around humans, they were intelligent in an annoying sort of way, and they were light-fingered enough to have pilfered his baseball cap.

A seed of hope began to grow.

Maybe the human thief and the Red Jaguar weren't far away, either. Maybe Max's triumphal-return scenario was still a possibility.

There was a crashing of branches as the monkeys moved off through the trees. They seemed to be headed in the direction of the trail. Every so often, they stopped and looked at Max as if waiting for him to catch up.

He decided to follow them.

Although it was just after dawn, the air felt wet and heavy. There was an insistent drumming sound that Max could not identify. As the noise grew louder and louder, water began to drip from the leaves above. Soon the drops became a downpour. Of course! The drumming sound—it was rain on the forest canopy!

Max ducked under a huge leaf for cover. He watched the rain running down the center of the leaf in front of him, and he caught as much as he could in his cupped hands. It was the sweetest water he'd ever tasted.

When the deluge was over, a hailstorm of nutshells told Max that the monkeys were waiting for him to resume his trek through the dripping jungle. With his wet clothes chafing, bugs biting him, and thorns tearing at his skin, his high spirits soon plummeted. He trudged along, trying to ignore the voices in his head that were telling him how lost he was, how stupid he was, how doomed he was to follow a pair of crazy monkeys. The voices were right, of course, but there wasn't much he could do about it now.

A shaft of sunlight burst through a gap in the tree canopy.

At the same moment, Max rounded a turn in the path.

In front of him was an ancient stone slab, about eight feet tall, standing in a spotlight of brilliant sunshine. Brushing aside the purple flowers that clung to it, he saw that the slab was covered in worn hieroglyphs. A swarm of yellow butterflies danced around his head, and the sun bathed the whole incredible scene in a golden glow.

Max paused for a moment to take it all in: the stone, the butterflies, the smoky scent of the flowers . . . Smoky? Wait—

He caught the unmistakable whiff of campfire.

The thief had made camp!

The monkeys had led him to his quarry!

The Red Jaguar was at hand!

But what now?

He'd been so intent on the chase, he hadn't considered what he'd do if he actually caught up with the thief. With no knowledge of any combat technique that wasn't computer-generated, how could he hope to overpower this criminal and steal back the Red Jaguar? It might be wiser to follow at a safe distance and wait for the police to show up. But first, he'd take a closer look at the enemy camp.

Grabbing a fallen branch as a weapon, his senses on high alert, Max tiptoed down the path. The trees were thinning out, and he was approaching an open space. For the last ten yards, he crept forward on his hands and knees. Then, using a large tree as cover, he peered into the clearing.

The remains of a campfire smoldered in the middle. Behind it, some leaning at crazy angles, others lying on the ground, were ranks of carved stone slabs like the one he'd just seen by the trail. And behind them, as if they were guarding it, was a small, square building, half buried by earth and vegetation.

After so many hours of traipsing through the tentacled, tangled jungle, it was extraordinary to come upon something so angular, so solid, so . . . man-made. It should have been a welcome sight, but this architecture was distinctly disturbing.

The rubble-filled doorway was unmistakably a mouth, edged top and bottom by rows of pointed stone teeth. Above the door, Max made out two square eyes and a flat, stubby nose. The rest of the face was carved into intricate geometric patterns, like a tattooed Maori warrior. The overall expression was of intense malevolence. Even the lack of greenery around the face was sinister, as if the nose and mouth were keeping the facade clear of weeds with their toxic exhalations.

Hiding behind the tree, Max scanned the area for signs of life.

No one.

He'd arrived too late.

Secretly, he was relieved.

But hey, he'd been hot on the trail, and he took pride in that. For his first time in the jungle—with no map and no compass—he'd done really well to get this far. He'd slept in a tree, he'd survived the night, and the worst was surely over. This clearing would be plainly visible to the rescue helicopter. If he revived the fire and sent out some smoke signals, he could be back at Villa Isabella in time for lunch.

He was so busy congratulating himself that he didn't hear the swish of a machete behind him, didn't hear the thief creeping up on him, until a voice whispered in his ear, "Looking for me?"

Max spun around.

There in front of him was the mysterious figure in black.

It was a girl.

A pretty girl.

She was taller than him and maybe a little older.

She had amber-colored eyes and coppery black hair.

She was wearing black cargo pants, a Ramones T-shirt, and hiking boots. A black sweatshirt was knotted around her waist. She held the machete loosely in one hand with the ease of one who knew how to use it.

Max had the strangest feeling he'd seen her somewhere before.

She spoke again. "What took you so long, Hoop?"

Max was speechless. So many questions were going through his mind. He stood there with his mouth open, until one question formed itself into words.

"Who are you?" he stammered.

"My name is Ix Sak Lol." (To Max, it sounded like *Eech Sock Loll.*) "It's Mayan for 'Lady White Flower.' But most people call me Lola."

"But who are you? Why did you steal the Red Jaguar?"

She ignored his questions. "Come and sit down, Hoop."

He couldn't move. He just stood there, staring at her.

"Oh, I'm sorry, do excuse my manners," she said, affecting a formal bow. "Please do me the honor of taking a seat in my humble campsite, Massimo Francis Sylvanus Murphy."

She led him into the clearing and indicated that he should sit on one of the fallen stone slabs. "Perhaps you would care for some jungle soda, otherwise known as water?"

"How do you know my name?" he asked, grabbing the canteen she offered him.

"*Massimo* is Italian, after your grandfather," she announced confidently. "*Francis* is after your father. And *Sylvanus* is after Sylvanus Griswold Morley, the famous archaeologist who excavated Chichén Itzá. He was also a spy, you know."

Max stopped drinking and gawked at her in amazement. "But how . . . ?"

She laughed. "I met your parents at Ixchel last week. They talk about you a lot. My friend Hermanjilio Bol"—she pronounced it *herman kee leo*—"was working with them. I went to help him set up camp before your parents arrived."

"Have you heard from this Herman guy?" asked Max eagerly. "Mom and Dad haven't come back yet, and Uncle Ted thinks the trails might be impassable after the storm. He thinks your friend is probably leading them to safety."

"I left Ixchel before the storm, and I haven't talked to Hermanjilio since. But I'm sure everyone's okay, Hoop."

Another question formed in Max's addled brain. "Why do you keep calling me Hoop?" He tried to copy her pronunciation, which was somewhere between *hoop* and *hope*.

"That's what I called you in my head, when I was tracking you. It's short for *chan hiri'ich hoop*, which means 'little matchstick' in Mayan. With your red hair and your thin little legs, that's what you look like!"

"My hair is brown," said Max. "But what do you mean, when you were tracking me? I was tracking you."

"Ha! You'd have been eaten by jaguars if I hadn't kept an

eye on you. And what about that crocodile's nest you nearly disturbed when you fell in the river? Or the vampire bat that was hovering around while you slept—in the strangler fig bed that I made for you?"

"Liar," said Max, but he swallowed uncomfortably.

"How about the arrow I cut into the tree? And the bioluminescent fungi?"

"What?"

"The glow-in-the-dark mushrooms I placed by the trail. You'd still be sitting on that rock, feeling sorry for yourself, if I hadn't shown you the way. Which reminds me"— she handed him a mud-caked towel—"this is yours."

It was his, all right. He must have left it by the stagnant river. He shook off the dried mud and pushed the towel into his backpack.

"I think the phrase you're looking for is *thank you*," said Lola.

"What should I thank you for? Luring me into the jungle in the middle of the night? Leading me across that bridge to be attacked by killer ants? Setting those monkeys on me?"

"Oh, poor Hoop," said Lola, ruffling his hair.

He pushed her away.

She pushed him back.

Next thing, they were scuffling on the ground and, a split second later, Lola had Max flat on his back and trussed up with a vine.

"So, Hoop, admit that I am the better fighter."

"No."

"Admit it."

Max looked her straight in the eyes. "I admit it, Monkey Girl," he said. "You are the better . . . thief!"

Lola tightened the vine around Max's body. "It's not stealing when you take back something that belongs to you," she said.

"Liar!" squeaked Max, his voice constricted by the vine. "If it belongs to anyone, the Red Jaguar belongs to the ancient Maya."

"That's what I said."

"Right," said Max. "So you're ancient Maya, are you? You're over a thousand years old, and you chop up tourists for human sacrifices?"

"Maybe I do," said Lola, raising her machete.

"I'm not stupid," said Max. "Even I know that the ancient Maya disappeared hundreds of years ago. It's a big mystery. Some experts think they were abducted by aliens."

"What experts?" Lola was laughing so hard, she relaxed the vine a little.

"I read it on the Internet. The Maya are living in another galaxy, and when their calendar ends this year, they might come back in spaceships to reclaim their land. That's if the world isn't destroyed by a tsunami, of course."

"Do you believe every crazy thing you read on the Internet, Hoop?"

"Well, I don't believe you're a Maya. They vanished. Everyone knows that."

"Is that so? Well, maybe I'll vanish and leave you tied up like a tamale."

She walked away and began stamping out the fire.

Max tried to break free of the vine, but he wasn't strong enough.

"Hey, Monkey Girl . . . ?"

"That's not my name."

"Lola . . . ? Lady White Flower . . . ? Untie me!"

"How can I? I don't exist, remember?"

A column of ants was making its way toward him.

"Stop messing around! Untie me!"

She came back and stood over him, hands on hips. "I'll untie you because I like your parents. But get it into your head that I'm just as Maya as the guys who built that temple behind me."

"Are you a ghost?" said Max dubiously.

"*No!*" Lola looked like she didn't know whether to laugh or be angry. "Don't you know that the Maya are still alive? There are millions of us! We didn't disappear. There's no mystery. We just left the old cities."

"In spaceships?"

She rolled her eyes. "On foot."

"Why?"

"All sorts of reasons. Drought, deforestation, over-population, conquest . . . but it didn't happen overnight. Different cities rose and fell over time. We've been around for three thousand years. I wear jeans and eat pizza, but I'm still Maya."

"Pizza?" echoed Max, all other thoughts disappearing at this mention of food. "Do you have any?"

Lola slashed through the vine with her machete. Then she reached into her backpack and pulled out a little parcel wrapped in a leaf.

"Here," she said. "No pizza on the menu today."

Max opened the leaf and found a rough-looking tortilla filled with a paste of brown beans. He inspected it with distaste. "Haven't you got anything else?"

"You're welcome," said Lola sarcastically.

"Some people say the old temples are still alive."

Max tried a bite—it didn't taste as bad as it looked. As he wolfed down the tortilla, he looked at the building. "Did you say that's a temple?"

"They think so. The archaeologists just call it Structure Thirteen. They started excavating it a few years ago but they ran out of money. Whenever you see a hill or a mound around here, it's usually a Maya structure waiting to be excavated."

"What a waste! If this place was in the States, they'd dig it out in no time. They'd have souvenir shops and snack bars and costumed interpreters. It'd make a fortune."

"And you think that's a good idea?"

Max shrugged defensively. "Why not?"

"Some people say the old temples are still alive," said Lola.

"I bet it's just a rumor to keep looters away." He looked sharply at Lola. "Are you a looter? Or a tomb raider?"

"No!" she said, shocked at the suggestion.

"But you stole the Red Jaguar. Are you working for Count de Landa?"

"No! I work with howler monkeys, not snakes!"

Max became aware of several large black and brownish monkeys sitting in the nearest tree, watching them. One of the lighter-colored monkeys dropped to the ground and sat in front of him, regarding him with an air of disappointment.

"What's the matter with him?" asked Max.

"Her," corrected Lola, stroking the monkey's head. "This is Seri. She and her brother Chulo woke you up this morning. Your snoring was disturbing the whole forest."

"Oh, ha-ha," said Max. "I'm amazed I got any sleep at all."

"What a lazy boy you are. I watched you on the beach. I've never seen anyone work so little and complain so much."

Max ignored the insult. "So it was you! I knew someone was spying on me."

"I wasn't the only one. Landa's men are everywhere," said Lola as she smoothed over the earth to remove all traces of the campfire. She put a finger to her lips and cocked her head to one side. Max had no idea which of the many forest sounds she was listening to. After a few seconds, she whispered, "The monkeys say men are coming." She shouldered her backpack. "Can you swim?"

"Why?"

"There's a place near here, the Blue Pool; we can give them the slip. . . ."

"But what if it's Uncle Ted? I'll tell him how you saved me in the jungle—"

"Ah, so you admit I saved you?"

"No, but I'll say it so he won't be mad at you. We'll give the Red Jaguar back to him and—"

"Forget it. Are you coming with me or not?"

"To swim in a pool?"

"It leads to an underground cave system. There are caves and tunnels under the whole jungle in this area. You're not claustrophobic, are you?"

Max shook his head, without conviction. He didn't like the sound of this at all. But meeting this girl felt like fate. And besides, she had the Red Jaguar.

"Let's go then," he said, trying to sound casual.

She fished some waterproof zipper bags out of her backpack. "Here, put your flashlight and anything else in one of these."

While Max fiddled with the bags, Lola called to the

monkeys. From the wistful tone of the growls, he guessed she was saying good-bye.

Then, with a nod at Max to follow her, she ran across the clearing and into the trees. After a while, the ground sloped down and they came to a large pool with a rocky cliff on the far side. The water was light blue in the shallows, darkening to a brilliant cobalt as the bottom fell away.

Lola waded purposefully in, with Max trailing cautiously behind. A few more steps and they had to swim. She seemed to be heading for the cliff face. As they got closer, Max saw a small opening in the shadow of an overhanging rock.

Lola swam straight into it.

Max swam to the mouth of the cave and held on to the side, afraid to go farther. All he could see was inky blackness. There was a strange sound like the hissing of gas.

"Come on, Hoop," said an impatient voice from out of the darkness. "The water's shallow inside the cave. Just swim toward my voice."

A few strokes later, his feet touched bottom. He stood for a moment as his eyes adjusted to the dim light coming from the entrance. He could just see Lola several yards ahead, pulling herself up onto a ledge. Max splashed his way over to her and tried to scramble up beside her.

To his embarrassment, she had to give him a hand.

"Where are we?" he asked.

"Take a look," said Lola.

When they switched on their flashlights, Max saw that the ledge was in a huge cavern. In some places, the stream below them was narrow; in others, it spilled out into wide expanses of dark, still water. Minerals had seeped through the cave walls, staining them in rich metallic colors of blue, gold, silver, and red. Against this vibrant backdrop, white calcite formations rose up like abstract marble statues.

"It looks like a cathedral," gasped Max. It was then he realized that the hissing sound was coming from the hundreds— maybe thousands—of brown furry creatures that were clinging to the roof of the cave.

"Bats!" he whispered to Lola, but she'd gone.

He could hear her splashing on ahead. He quickly climbed down into the stream and followed her into the darkness.

"How much farther?" he asked, but she didn't answer.

They waded deeper and deeper into the cavern, following the course of the stream. Bats swooped over Max's head, making him duck and stumble. Most of the time, the water came up only to his ankles, but it was cold and the stones on the streambed were sharp, so the going was difficult. It was also slightly surreal, due to the ever-increasing amount of pottery they passed.

Pots had been placed in small pools, on ledges, stuffed between stalagmites, tucked into small niches: anywhere there was a pot-sized hole, a pot was filling it. It reminded Max of his grandmother's house in Italy, where every available space was filled with china figurines. But the oddest thing about this display was that every single pot was cracked or broken.

"What's with all the pots?" asked Max.

"Caves were sacred places," said Lola. "People came to this one to pray for rain. They would bring a piece of pottery with them and break it to release the spirits inside. It's a way of saying thank you to the gods."

Max was enjoying the image of holding a Maya Thanks-giving at Nonna's house and smashing all her china, when he heard a noise behind them. One glance at Lola told him she'd heard it, too.

They upped their pace.

Presently, they entered an even bigger cavern, where the stream formed a wide, shallow pool. In this chamber, the tops of the stalagmites had been cut off and the insides hollowed out. Max slipped and bumped into one of them. It rang like a bell, with a low vibration that echoed through the cave. The other stalagmites in the chamber also began to resonate, creating a haunting melody.

"Idiot!" hissed Lola. "You'll lead them straight to us. Don't touch anything else. And stay on the edge of the pool."

"Wouldn't it be quicker to just wade straight across?" he asked.

In answer, Lola shone her flashlight onto the pool. Several skeletons were lying in the water, their centuries-old bones covered in a layer of calcite, which gave them a more fleshly appearance. Rising from the pool's center was a small island on which a stone altar had been built. On the front of the altar was carved a fearsome figure with bulbous eyes, a long nose, and two curving tusks. In one hand, the figure held what looked like a bolt of lightning. In the other, it held a bowl containing a sinister-looking lump.

"What's in his bowl?" asked Max.

"A human heart."

"Oh."

Max's own heart was pounding as they circled the rest of the pool.

On the far side was a narrow cleft in the rock. As they drew closer, he heard a low rumbling. They turned sideways to squeeze through the gap, and as they inched along, the rumbling got louder and louder until it became a deafening roar.

"Not much farther now," called Lola.

The passageway gave another turn and opened into a tall, narrow cavern. They were on a stone platform overlooking a rushing underground river. Facing outward from each corner of the platform was the stone head of a snarling jaguar. In the center of the platform, steps led down into the raging torrent.

"It's a dead end," screamed Max. "We're trapped!"

"It's the Sacred River of the Jaguar Kings—our escape route!"

Max looked down at the whirling, surging, foaming maelstrom beneath them. It wasn't possible that anyone could survive in those perilous waters.

"No way!" he yelled.

"It's the only way!" she yelled back.

Chapter Nine
SHOOTING THE RAPIDS

Y ou're crazy!" Max screamed over the noise of the water. "We can't swim in that—we'll drown!"

"The water *is* a little high," conceded Lola. "But we won't be swimming."

Max watched, puzzled, as she climbed up behind a cluster of stalagmites and pulled out a large bundle. When she shook it out, he saw it was a six-foot rubber raft. Rolled up inside were two collapsible paddles and a foot pump.

"I had a feeling I'd need a fast getaway." Lola looked pleased with herself.

"You planned this?"

She nodded.

"But look at the water. Nothing could survive that."

"Where's your sense of adventure, Hoop? You pump, I'll pack. Hurry!"

His brain paralyzed with fear, Max inflated the raft and assembled the paddles. Lola tied the backpacks onto the raft's handles and taped the flashlights to the front as headlamps, so their hands would be free for paddling.

She seemed to know what she was doing.

They dragged the raft down the steps, and Lola held it steady while Max scrambled in on shaking legs.

Before Lola could follow him, they were both caught in a powerful beam of light.

"Stop!" commanded a heavily accented voice. "There is no way out. Surrender now, or these will be the waters of your death."

Max recognized the lisping tones of Count Antonio de Landa.

He was ready to surrender there and then, but Lola jumped in and started paddling furiously. They were swept away from the steps and into the darkness.

Bang!

A shot echoed in the cave, and a red light high above them illuminated the raft as it careened and bucked in the churning water.

"What was that?" whimpered Max.

"Flare gun," said Lola as she dug her paddle into the water. "They're lighting up the cave to shoot at us."

Max started paddling like his life depended on it—which it did.

A burst of gunfire ricocheted off the cave wall. Max threw himself onto the floor of the raft, but Lola yelled at him to get back up. As he dipped his paddle shakily into the water, he braced himself for the bullet that never came. The swift current swept them out of Landa's view, and the last they heard of him was a volley of Spanish curses echoing through the cavern.

There was no time to relax. The tunnel narrowed and the current strengthened, shooting them into a twisting passageway. They bounced from one wall to another until, soaked in spray, they were swept sideways into a cavern filled with stalactites and stalagmites, like a forest of stone.

At times, they glided through vast chambers where the water was calm and their flashlights found blind catfish lurking in the depths, their eyes atrophied from centuries of darkness. At other times, the current was fierce and they had no time to look at anything as they struggled to keep the raft off the rocks.

All the time, Max was trying to keep his mind a blank, trying not to think about the blackness around them, the weird shapes of the rocks, what it would be like to fall into the water, the impossibility of ending this day alive.

They entered a place where the cave roof had collapsed, and they had to shade their eyes from the blinding sunlight that poured down on them. The water here was a sparkling green, and it flowed slowly as if reluctant to reenter the darkness. All around the chamber, strange forms like giant hairy turnips twisted out of the water and up through the roof of the cave.

"What are those?" asked Max.

"Tree roots from above," said Lola. "They've burrowed down through the limestone to get to this river."

"I can't believe roots could bore through solid rock," marveled Max.

Lola turned around to look at him. "Life is hard in the rainforest," she said. "Everything is fighting for survival."

"Including you?"

She didn't answer, and they paddled on in silence.

All too soon, they slipped back into darkness. The river was quiet now and the air was stale. It was getting harder to

135

breathe. The cave ceiling came down lower and lower, and they had to lean back to pass underneath. Sometimes they had to lie completely flat on their backs as they pushed themselves along with their fingertips in the pitch black.

Once there was the terrible sound of rock scraping on rubber as they got wedged under a particularly low overhang. Then they had to try not to scream and calmly maneuver themselves to the left or the right, to find a place where the raft could squeeze through. (By unspoken agreement, Max did the trying not to scream, while Lola did the calm maneuvering.)

"Are we nearly there?" gasped Max. It was so hot, he thought he might dissolve like a lump of butter in a frying pan. Claustrophobia didn't really cover it. There was no air, no space, no light. This raft was like a floating coffin. Except that he knew he wasn't dead because he could hear the blood roaring in his ears.

"I need you to concentrate, Hoop," said Lola. "Do you hear that roaring noise?"

"You can hear it, too?" asked Max in surprise.

Lola nodded. "It's the rapids."

"Rapids?"

"Calm down, Hoop, it's okay. The river splits in two: our branch meanders calmly to the outside, the other way gets a bit wild. We must stay close to this wall. If we drift into the middle and get caught in the current, we'll be swept over the rapids and we don't want that, do we?"

Max shook his head. He definitely didn't want that.

They inched along, hanging on to rocks and tree roots to keep them close to the wall. The water was placid on their side, and ahead of them was a silent tunnel filled with darkness.

Lola groaned.

She waved her paddle into the darkness. It made a dull thud. What had looked like a tunnel was a solid wall of black stone. The raft lurched to a stop. The river disappeared under the rock.

"Now what? We're trapped! You said you knew the way!" Max was panicking.

"It's not my fault," said Lola. "The water has risen after the storm."

"What are we going to do?"

"How do I know? Just don't freak out, you're tipping the raft."

She pulled one of the flashlights off the front of the raft and shone the light along the surface of the water where it met the wall of rock.

There was no way through.

"The rapids it is, then," said Lola.

"No way!"

"Let's just go back and check it out. We can't stay here."

Reluctantly, Max helped her turn the raft and maneuver it back to the splitting point. Bits of vegetation flew along in the fast-flowing water rushing to the rapids. The roaring noise was almost deafening now.

"I vote we get it over with," said Lola.

Before Max could argue, she pulled his hand off the rock and they were off, slowly at first and then gathering speed until they became one with the roaring river. The twisting tunnel curved sharply down and they shot through it, whirling and pitching. The jumping beam of the flashlight made it hard to see what was ahead. Boulders loomed at them out of the darkness.

Max screamed all the way.

You'd pay a fortune for this at Disneyland, he told himself.

They struggled frantically to keep the raft centered in the current. A jagged outcrop loomed on the right. Max used all his strength to push off of it with his paddle. The raft hung there for a moment before veering back into the current. Max's paddle, still wedged in the rocks, was ripped from his hand.

Caught off balance, he almost fell overboard.

He'd just scrabbled back inside when the raft was thrown into the air as they dropped over a small waterfall. He was pitched over the side of the raft and under the foaming water. The current swirled around him and raged in his ears. Everything was black. He couldn't breathe. He didn't know which way was up.

His lungs were gasping for air.

Suddenly, something pushed him from underneath and he shot up through the surface like a whale rider at SeaWorld.

He was in some sort of underground lake.

The water was still.

The rapids were behind him.

The raft was about ten feet away. He could see Lola outlined in a circle of light, surrounded by the menacing darkness on all sides. He splashed over through the icy-cold water, trying not to think about what might lurk in its depths.

"Give me a hand," he sputtered, pulling at the side of the raft.

A hand! A hand! A hand! his voice echoed back at him from all directions.

"Hold on," called Lola. "The raft's full of water."

"Hurry, the catfish are biting my legs."

This wasn't true, but in his imagination they were circling him like sharks. He was sure it was only a matter of time before they pounced.

"No, they're not! Don't be such a baby!"

Baby! Baby! sang the echoes, as if the cave walls themselves were taunting him.

Lola helped him aboard.

"Where's your paddle?" she said.

"I lost it."

"You lost it?"

"I nearly drowned."

"But you didn't drown, did you? I think the Jaguar Kings are helping us."

Max remembered how something had pushed him to the surface. He was shivering uncontrollably, out of cold and fear. "Y-yeah, sure," he said as cynically as he could through chattering teeth. "J-just get me out of here."

"Get a grip," said Lola sternly. "We're coming to the tricky bit."

"The tricky bit? Trickier than those rapids? You've got to be kidding me!"

"Calm down, Hoop. The Jaguar Kings will look after us."

"But—"

"Shh," she said, holding up a finger and listening intently. She paddled hesitantly onward, then stopped and listened again. She did this a few times, paddling and listening, paddling and listening, until she announced triumphantly, "Found it!"

"What?"

"The way out!"

"But we're in the middle of an underground lake."

"Can you hear that faint sucking noise? This lake drains from below."

"No way!" said Max. "Forget it!" Being sucked through an underwater drain sounded even more terrifying than bodysurfing through the rapids of an underground river.

"Do you have a better idea?" asked Lola.

Max looked at her with terror.

"No? Then we have no choice." When she unfixed the one flashlight they had left, darkness fell like dirt on a grave.

"I'm not getting back into that water," he said.

He heard Lola splash over the side, and then there was silence.

"Lola? Lola?"

Out of the darkness, her arm snaked around his waist, there was a quick scuffle, and he was flipped overboard. Spluttering and coughing, he grabbed hold of the side of the raft, too shocked even to protest.

"I'm sorry, Hoop, it was for your own good," she said. "Just hold on tight."

He didn't need telling twice. He was gripping so tightly, his hands were starting to cramp up.

There were strange sounds in the dark.

"What's that noise?"

"I'm slashing the raft."

"No!" he cried, but it was too late.

"It's done," said Lola. "Just let me put the machete away."

Weighted down by the backpacks, the deflated raft started sinking. It would have gone straight to the bottom if they hadn't been holding it.

"Take a deep breath," said Lola, "and let the current take you. The raft will pull us down. The Jaguar Kings will help us, I promise."

"I can't do it," said Max.

"We'll go on three," said Lola.

"*I can't do it!*"

"One . . ."

"*Stop!*"

"Two . . ."

"*No!*"

"Three!"

He heard Lola take a deep breath and then he felt the raft pulling him down as she disappeared under the water.

He could let go or he could follow her.

He followed her under the water and heard a roar coming up through the lake. In a panic, he let go of the raft and swam back up to the surface. He gulped great mouthfuls of air, treading water in the pitch black.

What now?

He called Lola's name, and it echoed back at him mockingly.

Lola! Lola! Lola!

Echoes surrounded him and closed in on him. The crazy count had been right. These would be the waters of Max's death. When he was too tired and too cold to tread water anymore, he would slide under and drown.

The current tugged at his ankles.

His only chance was to follow Lola.

He took a big breath and forced his face into that black water.

He swam down.

One, two, three strokes. The roar was deafening.

Four, five, six strokes. His ears hurt and he felt dizzy.

Seven, eight, nine. His hand exploded with pain as it smashed on a rock.

Ten, eleven, twelve. He tried to fight it, but it was too late. He closed his eyes and gave in to the force that was pulling him down and squeezing him and squirting him out like mustard on a hot dog. Pictures from his life flashed before his eyes, faces and places and long-forgotten moments.

Strangely, Max Murphy's last thought was of Zia's tamales.

Chapter Ten
STRANGE WEATHER

When Max opened his eyes, he was lying on his back in shallow water.

Somewhere in the distance he could hear a rushing torrent, but the pool around him was as warm and still as a bath. Light bounced off the water and cast an unworldly light throughout the chamber, reflecting the ripples of the waves on the rock walls above him.

He was just wondering if this was a special watery heaven for drowning victims, when a familiar voice called him back to the land of the living.

"Are you going to lie around all day?"

He turned his head to one side and saw Lola sitting on a sandbank, cutting the backpacks from the remnants of the raft.

"Did we make it?" he gasped.

"Yes," she said, "no thanks to you."

Max sat up. His hand hurt like crazy and he guessed the rest of him was covered with bruises. "Some escape route," he grumbled. "I feel like I've been through a washing machine."

"You're alive, aren't you?" said Lola. "Stop complaining."

"So how did we get here?" he asked.

Max followed Lola's eyes to the jet of water that crashed into the pool from a large hole in the cave wall.

"We didn't . . . ?"

She laughed. "We did."

"But how?"

As she explained, Lola drew a diagram in the sand. "The lake is like a bowl, with a hole way down in the side. All we had to do was swim low enough for the current to suck us through."

"How did you know about it?"

"My friend Hermanjilio told me. He said that Maya warriors used to prove their bravery by swimming through it, as some sort of initiation rite."

"Ha! So now I'm a full-fledged Maya warrior?"

"Never in a million years," said Lola. "Maya warriors were brave and fearless. And handsome."

Max made a face at her. "They had big noses."

Lola made a face back at him. "How's your hand?" she asked. "That's a nasty gash."

"How do you *think* it is? It hurts!"

Lola pursed her lips.

"Sorry," said Max, "I didn't mean to snap at you. It's just that some crazy girl made me shoot the rapids in an underground river and then she got me trapped like a hair ball in an underground sink. Oh yes, and some cape-twirling psycho is trying to kill me."

"Don't take it personally," said Lola. "He's trying to kill me, too."

"That's true," Max admitted grudgingly. He looked

144

around the cavern. "So how do we get out of here?"

"You see that skylight up there?" Max looked where she was pointing. High, high above them, he could see a pinprick of blue sky. "I came here once with Hermanjilio," she continued. "We rappelled down from the outside on a rope and pulled ourselves back up. We were planning to come back, so we left the rope in place for next time."

"I don't see any rope," said Max.

"I do," said Lola.

She waded through the water to some rocks on the far side and picked up a length of dirty rope. "It's fallen in," she said. She inspected the end. "Maybe an animal gnawed through it."

"Or Landa cut it," said Max.

They looked at each other. For the first time, Max saw something like fear on Lola's face.

"We're going to die, aren't we?" he said.

"Of course not," said Lola, coiling up the rope and bringing it back with her. "Hermanjilio will find us."

"What if he doesn't?"

"Studies show," said Lola, "that the people who survive emergency situations are usually the ones who maintain a positive attitude."

"We could sing," suggested Max.

Lola shook her head vehemently.

"I could tell you about Italy. That's where I'm supposed to be now, sitting down to dinner at my grandmother's house . . . . maybe thin-crust pizza, chewy on the inside and burned at the edges . . . or spaghetti with meatballs . . . or lasagna . . . or pumpkin ravioli—"

"Stop!" yelled Lola. "We have to think about something

"The sacred pool at the Temple of Chahk."

else. How about I show you a bit of the temple to pass the time?"

"What temple?"

"This is the sacred pool at the Temple of Chahk, the god of storms and warfare."

"A Maya temple? It must have doors to the outside. . . ."

Lola shook her head. "Sorry, Hoop. This place was swallowed up by the jungle hundreds of years ago. The whole pyramid is buried under earth and trees. It's really spooky in there, but there's an old map room at the entrance that's worth a look."

"I hate archaeology," said Max.

"It will take your mind off food," said Lola.

She led him to the back wall of the cavern and up some steps carved out of the rock to look like tree roots. The thick carved trunks of the limestone trees stood to attention on either side of a doorway.

"This is the Map Chamber," said Lola.

As Max's eyes adjusted to the gloom, he saw that he was in a circular room with a low ceiling. The walls were polished smooth and glowed faintly green with a natural phosphorescence. In the middle of the room was a long stone table with raised carvings on its surface.

"Isn't it wild?" said Lola, indicating the table. "It's a relief map of the Monkey River basin as it would have been a thousand years ago."

It reminded Max of the table he'd played with his train set on when he was little. But instead of stations and railway tracks, the surface of this table had been carved into clusters of little pyramids, palaces, and thatched huts. Five of the pyramids were inlaid with colored stones and connected by a network of stone causeways.

As Max peered at it, Lola crept up behind him.

"Gotcha!" she said, clamping a hand on his shoulder.

Max jumped out of his skin. "What did you do that for?" he yelled.

"Only kings and high priests were allowed in this chamber. If they caught a peasant like you in here, they'd flay you alive and rip out your heart."

Max looked around uneasily.

"So," said Lola, studying the map, "want to see where we are?"

"Isn't it a bit out of date?"

"The coastline and the river and the sites of the temples haven't changed." She pointed to the pyramid colored white. "Look, there's Ixchel." She traced the course of the Monkey River down to the sea. "There's Puerto Muerto and the bay near your uncle's house." She pointed to the red pyramid. "Here's Chahk, where we are now. And that little green pyramid is the old city of Itzamna, where Hermanjilio lives."

"Is Hermanjilio your boyfriend?"

Lola laughed. "He's the archaeologist in charge of excavating Itzamna. I told you, he's a colleague of your parents."

"Maybe Hermanjilio will take my parents to Itzamna," said Max, assessing the distance from the white pyramid to the green. He noticed that Itzamna was in the middle, with the other four colored pyramids around it. "What's the significance of the five colored pyramids?" he asked.

"Who knows?" said Lola, looking flustered. But she didn't meet his eyes.

And suddenly, he understood.

"Uncle Ted said there are five sacred pyramids and five Jaguar Stones! My parents had the White Jaguar, and the pyramid at Ixchel is colored white. This place is colored red—and we have the red stone! Yes, I remember—Uncle Ted called it the Red Jaguar of Chahk! It must belong in this temple somewhere! If only we knew how to use it. . . ."

"No, Hoop, leave it to your parents—"

"Aha! So I'm right, aren't I?"

"Yes . . . No . . . I don't know. . . . It's dangerous. . . ."

With Lola pulling at him to leave, Max circled the map table, studying it from different angles.

"Stand here," he said. "If you screw your eyes up, it kind of looks like a headless cat standing on four clawed feet."

"I don't see it," said Lola stubbornly.

"And look! At the end where the head should be, there's a space about the size of the Jaguar Stone. We have to see if the Red Jaguar fits in there!"

"That would be a very bad idea."

"But Oscar said the Jaguar Stones are my parents' life's work! I have to try this for them. . . ."

"No, you don't."

"Why did you steal the Red Jaguar, if you're scared to use it?"

"It's for Hermanjilio, not me."

"Then test it out for Hermanjilio. Come on, Monkey Girl. We're stuck here anyway. What have we got to lose?"

Lola sighed. "You win. Get the stone. But I don't like it."

Before she could change her mind, Max ran and got the backpacks. Eagerly, he unwrapped the Red Jaguar.

"It's a bit chipped," he said, looking at it closely for the first time.

"You're bleeding on it," she said crossly. She pulled a bandanna out of her back pocket. "Here, wrap your hand in this and give the stone to me. . . ."

She was holding the Red Jaguar over the niche, looking for a way to slot it in, when it seemed to jump out of her hand and click into the space on its own.

"Told you!" said Max.

They waited for something to happen.

"Nothing's happening," said Lola. "Take it out."

"It's glowing, I'm sure of it."

"You're imagining things."

"Wait—look at that!"

Lola gasped. "It's repairing itself."

Sure enough, where the stone had been chipped, it was growing back to its original shape. When the stone was restored, the map table began to glow and slowly come to life. The stone river flowed in shining blue plasma. Several temples disappeared under luminous green jungle. The map room lit up as a ball of yellow fire formed over the table and warmed their heads with its heat.

"That fireball," whispered Max, "I think it's the sun."

"And the map's updated itself," said Lola. "There's your uncle's house and the banana warehouse and that statue of the guy on the horse in Puerto Muerto. And look at this temple—you can't even see it anymore under all the foliage. The jungle's taken over everything. Just like in real life."

Dark clouds formed over parts of the map, the air flashed with sparks, and it began to rain. Max poked one of the clouds. It felt cold and moist and it moved.

"Lola, look! This is crazy! I can make it rain wherever I want!"

"Wow!" she gasped. "Let me try!"

They amused themselves by directing the rainstorms for a while, before the same thought occurred to them both at the same time. Their eyes met.

"You don't suppose—" began Lola.

"—that what we do in here—" continued Max.

"—has any effect on what happens out there?" finished Lola.

She studied the map, found the small hole in the cave ceiling, and blocked it with her finger. Max ran back to the steps. The cavern was dark. "Move your finger," he called. Right away, a beam of light lit up the cavern.

"It still works after all these years," said Lola, her eyes shining. "Can you imagine the control my ancestors had over their world? They could make it rain. They could divert rivers. They could destroy their enemies' crops. I've never understood how they could sustain so many people in such a small area. This is how they did it! They would never have had a bad harvest."

In the excitement of the moment, Max had a brilliant idea. He began to scratch at the glowing green foliage that covered the little red pyramid. Lola saw what he was doing and instantly understood. "This might just work," she said, as she helped him scrape away the centuries of vegetation until the pyramid was bare and the outline of a door could be seen on the top platform.

"A way out! We're saved!" whooped Max.

Lola was more subdued. "Have you ever been inside a Maya pyramid, Hoop?"

Max thought for a moment. Strange as it seemed, given that his parents spent half their lives at Maya sites, he was pretty sure that he never had. "I don't think so," he said.

"Well, brace yourself. It's creepy up there."

"It's creepy down here. Let's go!"

"Just don't say I didn't warn you."

She pulled out the Jaguar Stone, wrapped it, and put it back into her backpack. Then she took out a candle, lit it, and handed it to Max.

"Where's *my* flashlight?" he protested.

"You lost it in the river."

"Can't I use yours?"

With a sigh of irritation, Lola gave Max the flashlight and took the candle. She led him through a doorway into a passage that quickly became a narrow staircase, zigzagging steeply to and fro, up and up and up. Every so often an ice-cold drip from the ceiling would land on his neck in the darkness, making him jump every time.

"It's just water, don't make such a fuss," said Lola.

The steps were wet and slippery, but when Max put a hand on the wall to steady himself, his fingers sank into a spongy, putrid-smelling fungus. He slipped over in surprise and, as he got back to his feet, something cold and squelchy landed on his head.

"Ew! Ew! Ew!" he cried.

"It's just water, Hoop!"

Max ran a hand through his hair and heard something drop to the ground. A huge white centipede, maybe six inches long, like a slug on legs, glistened in the beam of his flashlight.

"Look at this!" he called to Lola. "It wasn't just . . ."

But the centipede had scurried into the shadows.

Max pulled his T-shirt over his head like a hood until the

staircase ended and they emerged into a large, roughly hewn room. The ceiling was so low they had to crouch, and the floor was cracked and uneven. On the far side of the room was a doorway, and carved above it was a ghoulish face contorted in agony.

"Is it this way?" asked Max, making for the doorway.

"Stop!" yelled Lola, pulling him back. "Don't go in there."

Now that Max looked more closely, he saw that the murky interior was scattered with skulls and bones. He sensed that something lurked in there, something dead yet alive, something that was trying to lure him in. Out of the corner of his eye he saw a movement and he leapt back in fear, but it was just a centipede wriggling out of an eye socket in the nearest skull.

"You're very jumpy, Hoop. Are you sure you want to do this?"

"Just show me the way out."

"Up here." Lola was standing under a dark square in one corner of the ceiling, pointing up at a narrow shaft that shot

up into blackness. "It's not difficult," she said. "There are footholds, but it's too tight to climb with the backpacks. I'll go up first with the flashlight and let down the rope. You tie on the backpacks, then use the rope to help you get up. Okay?"

Bossy, bossy, bossy, he thought. "Just hurry," he said.

Max pressed himself into the corner and watched the glow of the flashlight recede.

He shivered.

Was it fear making his blood run cold? Or was the temperature dropping?

He held the candle under his chin for heat.

It was so cold he could see his breath.

He exhaled slowly, watching how the crystals hung in the air and sparkled in the candlelight. He exhaled again, harder this time. To his horror, a cloud of white breath shot out like spray from a fire extinguisher and—*No, no, no!*—put out the flame.

He couldn't believe it.

He'd blown out the candle.

How could he have been so stupid?

The icy darkness crowded in on him.

The blackness was suffocating, like a blanket of evil.

What was that scratching noise?

Fingernails? Centipedes? The presence in the bone room?

His heart beat faster and faster. He stamped his feet to keep warm and to frighten away anything that might be thinking of scurrying around his feet.

"Hurry, Lola!" he called. "The candle's gone out!"

By the time the end of the rope dropped down, a light frost had formed on his head and shoulders. His damp clothes were freezing against his skin. Fumbling with cold, he tied on the backpacks.

He looked up at the distant circle of light that was Lola's face. Focusing only on her, refusing to think about the darkness that clutched at his feet like invisible fingers, he began to climb. It was hard going and his wounded hand throbbed, but his fear was greater than his pain. He was aware of nothing but the need to maintain upward motion.

Eventually, he reached the room above. He threw himself on the stone floor, breathing heavily, while Lola pulled up the backpacks.

"I told you it was creepy in here," she said.

She relit the candle, and Max looked around. This room was smaller than the one below and empty apart from something in one corner, something that reflected candlelight in its shiny, gelatinous skin, something gently pulsating with the pump of a million heartbeats. . . .

Max jumped to his feet. "It's a monster! It's alive!"

"Frog spawn," said Lola. "I should have warned you."

A dark chill was rising out of the shaft and spreading like dry ice. The room was starting to fill with a clammy, foul-smelling fog.

"Let's keep moving." Lola coughed.

"Me first," said Max, grabbing the rope and tying it around him.

The shaft was shorter this time, and he soon arrived at the top.

A wave of heat engulfed him. It was like entering an oven. His cold, wet clothes dried instantly in a haze of steam.

Nervously, he shone the flashlight around, wondering

what could follow giant centipedes and throbbing frog spawn, but his light found no life-forms of any kind. Apart from the heat, this level was almost pleasant. It had the smallest floor area, but a high ceiling made it less claustrophobic, and all four walls were painted with colorful murals.

While he waited for Lola to tie on the backpacks, Max looked closer at the paintings. Mostly they were life-size figures of Maya warriors, monsters, and bizarre animal people with crocodile heads and lobster claws. They were so freaky, it took Max a moment to register the most disturbing thing of all.

This room had no door.

They were at the top and there was no way out.

Chapter Eleven
RAT ON A STICK

Phew," said Lola, pulling herself up. "It's hot in here."

"Like a furnace," agreed Max, hauling up the backpacks.

He took out Lola's canteen of water and went to take a swig.

"Stop!" protested Lola, trying to take it back from him. "Give me that. We don't know how long it has to last."

Max fended her off and took a long, gulping drink. "I'm thirsty. What's the big deal?"

"This is the temple of Chahk, the god of storms and warfare. The king came here to offer his blood in return for rainstorms to water the corn. Water is life. You should treat every drop with respect, especially in here."

"Let's get out of here then. Where's the hidden door?"

"How should I know?"

"But I thought you'd been here before."

"Hermanjilio and I stuck our heads in once, but we knew

the pyramid was buried under jungle, so there was no point in looking for a door."

"Oh, great," said Max sarcastically. "We're trapped."

A lump of self-pity formed in his throat. He hoped the guys at school would know he'd died in the company of a girl. And she definitely wasn't ugly. He pictured their waxy bodies lying side by side in this stone tomb, like Romeo and Juliet. He smiled mistily at Lola.

"Don't just stand there like a moron," she said. "Help me find the door."

Max cast a lethargic look around. His head was pounding from the oppressive heat. It felt like summer in the city, just before a thunderstorm.

"We should feel for a current of air," he said. "That's what led me to the secret door at my uncle's house."

But there was no current of air.

It was getting hotter.

Max's throat was so dry he couldn't swallow.

"I need more water," he gasped.

"No," said Lola.

"Who made you guardian of the water?"

"Who made you such a baby?"

They searched the room from top to bottom again, but found nothing. The floor was burning their feet.

"There has to be a hidden switch," said Lola.

After their third fruitless search, it was getting hard to breathe. They stood on their backpacks to protect their feet and looked at each other in despair, the sweat running down their faces.

"It's no good," said Lola. "We'll have to go back the way we came."

"No!" said Max, terrified of what might be waiting in the foul fog below.

He forced himself to think.

Head hurts.

Think.

Throat hurts.

Think.

If this was a video game, how would it work?

Enter a new room. No exit. Look for the clues.

There were always clues.

He stared at the painted figures on the wall in front of him. "I bet they know the secret," he said. He was alarmed to realize that a particularly monstrous character with bulbous eyes, a long nose, and tusklike protuberances looked vaguely familiar. "Who's that ugly one on the end?"

"You've met him," said Lola. "That's the great Lord Chahk. We passed his statue in the Cave of Broken Pots, remember? He was holding a lightning-bolt ax and a bowl with a human heart in it."

Max did remember. And, as he stared at Lord Chahk,

he began to feel a connection. It was the same feeling he'd had when he saw the metal case on the shelf in Uncle Ted's vault.

He went over to the painting and examined every inch of it.

Nothing.

He looked into Lord Chahk's goggly eyes.

Nothing.

But the answer was here, he knew it. Call it a gamer's sixth sense.

"Pass me the water," he said.

"No," said Lola. "We have to save it."

"Not for me, for him. It's so hot and dry in here. Don't you think he'd like to feel the rain on his skin?"

"You're crazy," began Lola, but she didn't try to stop him as he took the canteen and poured the last of their precious water onto the wall above Lord Chahk's head. Max watched expectantly as it streamed down the storm god's face and chest.

Nothing happened.

He shook out the last drop of water.

Nothing.

The water evaporated instantly. The wall was still as dry as old bones.

Max looked at Lola miserably. His throat was so parched that his tongue felt swollen. "Sorry," he whispered. The word had never sounded so inadequate.

But Lola wasn't listening. She was totally focused on Lord Chahk.

"Blood!" she said. "He wants blood!"

Ignoring Max's howls of pain, she ripped the bandanna off

his gashed hand and pressed his wound against the painted bowl. Then she rubbed the bloodstained bandanna into it as well, for good measure. "Greetings, Lord Chahk," she intoned. "In return for this blood, we ask for our freedom."

As the blood soaked into the limestone, there was a noise like a frog croaking. Then another and another, until the room echoed with a frogs' chorus. The atmosphere in the room seemed to lift slightly, and the air felt a little cooler.

Lola, who was still pressing the bandanna against the bowl, yelped in surprise.

"What happened?" shouted Max above the din of frogs.

"Electric shock—"

A string of red sparks made their way up from Lord Chahk's bowl to his lightning-bolt ax. There was a flash, a crash of thunder, and the sound of stone rolling on stone.

One of the carved panels swung out.

Light flooded into the room, momentarily blinding them.

The croaking grew to a deafening buzz as hundreds of frogs materialized out of the temple walls and leapt across the floor to the open door. For a few seconds, Max and Lola couldn't move for the sea of frogs around their feet. Then, like a wave rolling in to shore, the amphibian tide swept out of the temple and into the torrential rain, with a farewell croak that even Max could identify as pure pleasure.

Max and Lola stepped outside.

Rain had never felt so good.

"We did it!" yelled Max, punching the air. "We did it!"

A flock of parrots screeched disapprovingly as they flew overhead.

"We make a good team!" whooped Lola, high-fiving him.

A team. He liked the sound of that.

He put his head back and tried to catch the rain in his parched mouth, whirling around, letting the downpour wash away the dust of the temple. He felt himself rehydrating like a packet of instant noodles.

His headache had gone.

His hand had stopped throbbing.

But his brain was still in shock.

The list of contenders for Most Terrifying Experience of This Trip So Far grew longer every day, but the Temple of Chahk won the category hands down.

"Hey, Monkey Girl," he said, trying to sound cool, "I thought ruins were just a bunch of old stones. That place was definitely alive."

"I warned you," said Lola.

They were about a hundred feet up, on the top platform of a giant pyramid. The tips of other pyramids could be seen rising through the jungle canopy like distant islands in a sea of green. As the rain stopped, a rainbow formed in the distance.

Max uttered a cry of horror. "Is that what I think it is?" he asked, pointing with his toe to a large reddish-brown stain.

"Blood?" said Lola, unfazed. "Probably. I'm sure they held bloodlettings and sacrifices up here."

Max shook his head in disgust. "Why were the Maya so bloodthirsty?"

"It wasn't like that. Blood was sacred. Blood was the breath of the soul. Blood had to flow to keep the gods happy and the sun shining and the crops growing. Even the king had to shed his blood. The people expected it."

"They must have gone through a lot of kings."

"No, the kings just gave a little blood, a token."

"It's still barbaric."

"Oh, I don't know." Lola looked thoughtful. "It's interesting, the idea of making a sacrifice for the common good. Like, if people stopped buying mahogany furniture, the loggers might stop chopping down the rainforest. . . ."

Max wasn't listening.

He was standing on the edge of the pyramid, staring down into the jungle.

So this was how it felt to be an ancient Maya king. Above you, the heavens and the gods who spoke through you. Below you, the awestruck faces of your adoring people.

Lola touched his arm. "Let's go."

As she skipped down the steep stone steps, Max picked his way slowly behind her. In the end, he found it easiest to sit down and lower himself step by step. Way below, he heard Lola calling to her monkeys and a distant roar floating back over the rainforest in reply.

When he reached the ground, he looked back to see how far he'd come, but the pyramid was already half covered in vegetation. Vines were writhing their way across the platform, earth was accumulating on the steps, and trees were literally growing in front of his eyes. Soon the Temple of Chahk would be hidden again beneath its blanket of jungle.

Lola was waiting for him, a length of thick vine over her shoulders, like the snake lady at the circus.

"Still thirsty?" she asked.

She slashed the end of the vine and held it over his mouth like a hose. Sweet water came gushing out.

"Remember this plant," she said. "Its Mayan name is *Ha Ix Ak. Ha* means 'water,' *Ix* means 'lady,' *Ak* means 'vine.' Lady

Water Vine has saved many lives in the rainforest."

"I don't suppose she has a friend called Lady Pizza Plant?" asked Max.

"Sure, do you want the one with extra cheese?"

"Don't even joke about it," said Max. "I'm starving."

"First, we must make camp. Darkness falls fast in the jungle. I'll find saplings to make a shelter. You get wood for the fire."

"Did anyone ever tell you you're bossy?" said Max.

"Did anyone ever tell you you're lazy?" said Lola.

"Yes," said Max proudly, "all the time."

"In the rainforest, lazy boys get eaten by jaguars. You must start the fire before dark to keep them away." She handed Max her machete. "Ever used one of these?"

"As a matter of a fact, I have," said Max.

"Where?"

"Oh, you know, son of archaeologists and all that . . ."

She didn't need to know that his previous experience with a machete consisted of swishing through a computer-animated jungle in *Pyramid of Peril*, that day his parents came home early.

Was that really just two weeks ago? It seemed like another lifetime.

Suddenly, Max remembered where he'd seen Lola before. Level two!

She looked like the girl who was taken hostage in the shoot-out. And now, here they were, having survived a real-life pyramid of peril! For one brief moment Max entertained the possibility that his entire life was just a video game.

"Hey, Monkey Girl, listen to this," he began, but she was gone.

He hacked his way clumsily into the jungle in search of kindling. Swinging a machete wasn't as easy as it had looked on-screen. But despite his lack of technique, he felt like a Hollywood action hero.

Max Murphy: Man of Mystery and Explorer Extraordinaire.

A movement caught his eye, and he looked down to see a long, brownish-gray snake sliding out of the leaf litter toward him.

Max froze, not even breathing, and tried to remember what he'd read about snakes in the in-flight magazine. He seemed to recall that the more garish they were, the more likely they were to be poisonous. That deadly coral snake in Puerto Muerto had been brightly colored. This snake was drab, apart from a yellow flash under its head. Reassured, he stayed absolutely still as the snake passed six inches to the side of his foot and slithered away into the bush. After that, he was more careful, probing the ground with his machete and checking overhanging branches for reptilian residents.

By the time he returned to the campsite with an armful of wood, the monkeys had arrived. Seri was sitting grooming herself while her brother, Chulo, still wearing Max's baseball cap, was swinging languidly from a tree branch by his tail. Max's backpack lay open on the ground, and both monkeys were chewing on the dreaded granola bars.

"Good snack?" he asked in a friendly tone.

Chulo growled in a most unfriendly tone.

"No, I don't like those bars, either," said Max. "Ever had pizza, Chulo?"

Chulo took off the baseball cap and covered his face with it.

"So you're a Red Sox fan, too?" asked Max, reaching for the cap.

Chulo snapped at Max's hand and Max quickly withdrew it.

He decided to get on with making the fire.

As he chose a patch of flat ground, he could feel Chulo watching his every move. The monkey's critical gaze made him feel self-conscious, and it took him a while to assemble his teepee of twigs, as taught in Cub Scouts.

He paused to admire his creation before striking the match. Quick as a flash, Chulo jumped on Max's head and scattered the wood with his tail. Then he hopped about, screeching with monkey laughter.

After this had happened several times, Max chased the monkey into the forest with the machete. Chulo jumped into the nearest tree and started lobbing fruit. The monkey's aim was deadly accurate, and a large papaya hit Max squarely in the back, sending him sprawling. Seri, meanwhile, paid no attention to any of it. Such mayhem was evidently beneath her.

Despite Chulo's attempts at disruption, Max finally succeeded in lighting the fire. He was complimenting himself on his newfound survival skills, when Lola's voice interrupted his thoughts: "Who's hungry?"

The two monkeys raced to greet her, dancing about and leaping with joy.

"Gibnut for dinner!" she announced.

"Is that like peanut?" asked Max.

"It's like this," she said, holding up a small animal.

"It looks like a rat."

"It is a rodent," admitted Lola, "but even the queen of England ate it when she came here. I'll skewer it over the fire and it will be the best barbecue you've ever tasted."

"I'm not eating rat on a stick," said Max.

"Suit yourself." Lola shrugged. "Will you help me make the shelter?"

She showed him how to lash saplings together between the trees and cover them with large palm leaves to make a cozy lean-to. While Max laid a floor of wood and moss, Lola prepared the gibnut. Then she pulled a small cooking pot out of her bag and threw in some pointed green leaves.

Max made a face.

"Jackass!" said Lola.

"I just don't like vegetables," said Max, sounding hurt.

"No," explained Lola, laughing, "they're jackass bitters—they're medicinal. I'm going to boil them up to clean your insect bites. They cure everything."

"I'd rather have some antiseptic and a box of Band-Aids."

"Stupid boy! Most of the medicines in your drugstores are made out of rainforest plants! It's just that here you don't pay for the packaging."

"I like the packaging," said Max.

"Spoken like a true city kid," sighed Lola, in mock despair.

"Speaking of packaging," said Max, "what kind of snake

has a black head with a yellow flash underneath and a gray-brown body? It's harmless, right?"

"Where?" Lola looked around in alarm.

"In the forest before. It passed right by my foot."

She put a hand over her mouth in horror. "It sounds like a fer-de-lance. The locals call it the three-step because, if it bites you, that's how far you get. It's one of the deadliest snakes in the world and it's very aggressive. It's not a bit scared of humans. You had a lucky escape!"

Max Murphy, Man of Mystery and Explorer Extraordinaire, went very quiet and pale and huddled closer to the fire. He wondered how he'd ever sleep tonight among all those creeping, crawling, biting things.

"Sure you don't want some gibnut?" asked Lola.

It smelled delicious.

"Just a bite," he said.

Half an hour later, with his belly full of succulent barbecued gibnut, he pulled out his mosquito net to drape across the front of the lean-to and found it ripped and tattered from when he'd fallen out of the tree.

"No problem," said Lola. "I'll throw this old termite nest on the fire and it will keep the bugs at bay all night. Shame it's an old one or we could have eaten the termites for dessert. They're quite tangy; I think you'd like them."

Reflecting that Lola was not like any girl he'd met before, Max Murphy stretched out and went to sleep.

Lola woke him at sunrise for a breakfast of wild papaya,

gathered by the monkeys. Max could tell that Chulo begrudged him every bite.

"Why do we have to get up so early?" he asked blearily.

"If we hike all day, we should get to Utsal by nightfall," said Lola.

Hike all day? Max groaned. He was still tired and aching from yesterday's exertions. "What's at Utsal?" he asked.

"It's on the way to Itzamna. It's where I grew up. I have friends there."

"Sounds good." Max nodded, glad to be heading back to the bright lights of civilization. He reached for the last papaya, but Chulo beat him to it.

"Hey, you've already had three," said Max, chasing the monkey away.

"Boys, stop fighting," called Lola. "We need to get going. It looks like the rains will come early today."

Max looked up. It didn't look like rain at all. There was one wispy little cloud in a clear blue sky. He started to argue, but Lola had already set off.

She walked so quickly that Max had to trot to keep up. He was breathless and panting when, twenty minutes later, the rains came pouring down.

Lola had a knack of springing from one dry spot to another, while Max slogged behind her through solid mud.

"Can't you slow down?" he asked.

"We have to keep up the pace, or we'll never make it in time."

Bossy, bossy, bossy.

He tried to make conversation as they walked, but it felt more like an interrogation.

"What do your parents do?" he asked.

"I have no parents."

"What happened to them?"

"I don't know."

"How can you not know?"

She wheeled around. "Do you know what's happened to your parents?"

He began a new line of questioning.

"How old are you?"

"I don't know."

"Do you go to school?"

"Hermanjilio is teaching me."

"Did he teach you to speak English?"

"Everyone here speaks English."

"What do you speak at home?"

"Yucatec."

"Is that the Mayan language?"

"One of them."

"How many are there?"

"About thirty."

Max gave a low whistle to show he was impressed. "Go on then, say something—"

"*Kanaant awook!*"

"What does that mean?"

" 'Watch out!' "

Too late. Max tripped over a large root and grabbed the nearest tree to steady himself. A searing pain shot through his hand. Several long needles were sticking into the fleshy part of his thumb.

"Let me see," said Lola, inspecting the wound. She slashed

the tree trunk with her machete as if, bizarrely, she was punishing the tree for hurting him.

"It's called a give-and-take palm," she explained. "The thorns give you pain, but"—she peeled off some bark to show him the pink fibrous underside—"the bark takes it away. It's the only thing that works."

Max winced as she pulled out the needles, one by one. "Where did you get that Ramones T-shirt?" he asked, to take his mind off the pain.

"A boy gave it to me."

"What boy?"

"A student from New York."

"Did you go to New York?"

"I will one day."

"So where did you meet him?"

"At Itzamna. Archaeology students come from all over the world."

"Are there students there now?"

"I don't think so."

She pressed the pink fiber onto his injured thumb. The pain stopped almost immediately. "Better?" she asked.

"So is this New Yorker your boyfriend?"

Lola laughed and jumped up. "We need to move," she said.

"How old is he?"

"We'd go a lot faster if you stopped talking."

She set a brisk pace, and Max soon fell behind. This was the opportunity Chulo had been waiting for. When Lola was too far ahead to see, the monkey pelted him with nuts, sticks, and bits of rotten fruit. Whenever a missile bounced off Max's head, Chulo would screech with delight. Once he threw a small iguana, and instead of bouncing off, it dug its claws into Max's scalp.

Lizard wars.

Lola saw none of this. But just as Max was wrenching the iguana off his head to hurl it back at Chulo, she happened to turn around. Her face was a picture of disbelief.

"I'm not even going to ask," she said.

"He started it," said Max, pointing at Chulo.

"You should be flattered," said Lola. "He has the crazy idea that you're a threat to his position as the dominant male."

"Why's it crazy?" asked Max, puffing out his chest and trying to look dominant.

A wild avocado, hard as a rock, hit the back of his neck.

"Did you see that?" he demanded, but Lola had already gone on ahead.

A ball of monkey dung whizzed past his ear.

Max sighed. It was going to be a long and vexing morning.

"Are we stopping for lunch?" he asked, when the sun was overhead.

"I wasn't planning on it," said Lola.

"But I'm starving," protested Max.

"You're always starving," Lola pointed out. "But there's usually something to eat around here if you know where to look."

She inspected a fallen palm tree near the trail. "You're in luck, Hoop," she called, as she hacked into the trunk with her machete. The wood was rotten and splintered easily.

Max wondered what there could be to eat in a dead tree.

And then the answer was there, under his nose.

Three enormously fat white maggots writhed on Lola's outstretched hand.

"They're palm grubs," she said. "Some people think they're delicious."

Strangely, Max wasn't hungry anymore . . .

. . . until, late that afternoon, a waft of smoky fires and cooking smells told him they were close to Utsal.

Hot food and ice-cold soda were within reach.

He picked up his pace. All day long, he'd been imagining a busy town with whitewashed houses, clean bathrooms, and an air-conditioned pizza restaurant. As the hours went by, he'd added an Internet café, a gaming arcade, and an ice-cream parlor.

Now he was really salivating.

"Welcome to Utsal!" cried Lola happily.

All Max could see was a few shacks in a clearing on the riverbank.

"That's it?" he said.

"What were you expecting?"

Max was too disappointed to answer.

There would be no pizza, no soda, no ice cream.

No home comforts of any kind.

At the end of a miserable day was another miserable night.

He hated this place already.

A pack of scrawny dogs trotted out to bark at them, closely followed by a herd of children and a rush of women in embroidered blouses and long skirts.

The women ran joyfully to Lola, arms open, black braids flying behind them. As they hugged her and poured out greetings in Mayan, the children clustered around Max. To his annoyance, the tallest ones yanked his hair to see if it was real. He was just about to ask Lola to have a word with them, when they bounded away like a herd of frightened deer.

Max squinted into the afternoon sun to see what had scared them.

It was a man. An old man. He looked a bit like a Maya version of Gandalf.

His hair flowed down in a thick gray mane. His huge hooked nose protruded out of a face so deeply wrinkled, it reminded Max of a pyramid rising out of the tangled jungle. He wore a long embroidered tunic and a necklace of jaguar teeth. He leaned on a carved wooden cane. His ancient, calloused feet were bare.

Lola pulled Max forward, but his only thought was to get away, to run and keep on running until he had escaped this stranger's penetrating gaze. The closer the old man came, the more his eyes locked on to Max's brain. They read his mind, they burned into his soul, they reflected his past and future in their watery orbs.

These eyes gave new meaning to the term *farsighted*.

Yet, clouded as they were with cataracts, the old man's eyes were almost blind.

Chapter Twelve
THE FEAST

Holding his other hand up as if to stop traffic, the old man pointed at Max with his cane. He cleared his throat. Even the birds in the trees stopped singing as the world waited to hear his words of wisdom.

"Pepperoni Supreme with extra cheese," he said.

Max gaped at him. That was exactly what he'd been thinking about before his mind went numb with terror. He started backing away uneasily.

The old man let out a booming laugh and turned to Lola.

"Your friend likes pizza, Ix Sak Lol," he said.

"You're right"—she smiled—"as always!"

She grabbed Max's arm and pulled him forward. "Max Murphy, meet Chan Kan, village leader and wise man."

"All blessings, Max Murphy, and welcome to Utsal," said Chan Kan.

Max nodded and babbled something, too awestruck to form actual words.

Chan Kan, still chuckling, turned to Lola. "*Biix abeel, chan aabil?*" he said. "How are you, little granddaughter?"

"*Ma'alob, tatich! Kux teech?*" answered Lola. "I'm fine, Grandfather! And you?"

Soon they were jabbering away to each other in Mayan.

Max, still dizzy from Chan Kan's scrutiny, sat down on the grass.

He looked at the village. It was just a few thatched huts on stilts, clustered around a large central square. All the huts had steps up to an open porch, and most of the porches were strung with brightly striped hammocks.

He looked at the river, the famous Monkey River. It was wide, green, and fast-flowing. There were a few dugout canoes on the bank and a rickety bamboo landing stage for bigger boats.

A long-necked white heron settled on a tree stump to eat its catch.

Some women came down for water. Each one carried a large earthenware pot on her back, held by a woven strap over her forehead. As they walked back with their heavy loads, they chatted happily to each other and waved at the men who were building something with poles and palm fronds in the main square.

There was a sense of bustle in the air and a delicious smell of food.

Max's stomach rumbled loudly.

And still Lola talked on.

He was planning how to drag her away without incurring the old man's wrath, when she ran over and sat down next to him. "Sorry," she said. "Chan Kan likes to talk."

"He's your grandfather?"

"No, his family kind of adopted me. But listen, Hoop, he said that Hermanjilio came through here a few days ago."

"With my parents?"

"Alone."

Max threw a stone at a passing iguana. He missed.

"Congratulations," he said. "Your precious Hermanjilio is safe."

"He's waiting for us at Itzamna. He'll be able to tell us what happened." She laid her hand on Max's arm. "I wish your parents had been with him. But I'm sure they're fine."

"How far is it to Itzamna?" said Max in a flat voice.

"Just a few hours upriver. We'll hitch a lift most of the way."

"Whatever."

"Cheer up," said Lola. "I'm sure we'll find your parents soon. People get lost in the jungle all the time."

"I hate the jungle."

"It's been a tough day. But the worst is over, I promise. We'll have an easy boat ride tomorrow. And tonight you'll be guest of honor at the feast."

Max looked up. "A feast?" he said.

A small boy and a tiny boy ran over. The bigger one shyly took Max's hand, trying to pull him to his feet. The little one peeped out from behind Lola.

"This is Och and his brother little Och," she said.

"They have the same name?"

"It means 'possum.' We don't use their real names until they're older," explained Lola. "We call all the children possums to trick the evil spirits of the forest who like to steal human babies. Och and little Och have come to show you around."

Max nodded at the boys. Then he stood up and combed his hair with his fingers. Och did the same.

"You've got an admirer, Hoop," whispered Lola. "Och's copying everything you do."

Max tried to hide his pleasure. He'd often daydreamed about having an adoring younger brother who would hang on his every word.

"Show Mister Max where to wash, and get him some clean clothes," Lola was telling Och. "Then Chan Kan wants to speak with him."

"What if I don't want to speak with Chan Kan?"

"Don't be a baby, Hoop. It's a huge honor to receive a private audience with a Maya wise man. Movie stars would pay a fortune for it!"

"He freaks me out. It's like he can read my mind."

"He can," she said. "See you at the feast."

Dusk was falling as Max washed in the river. Dusk, otherwise known as Mosquito Happy Hour, was not a good time to be naked in the open air. Och and little Och kept guard for crocodiles, while Max swatted bugs and scrubbed away the accumulated grime of the last few days.

Since Och had given him what looked like a handful of potato shavings to use as soap, he'd been skeptical about his chances of getting clean. But as soon as he dunked his hands in the water and rubbed them together, the shavings frothed up into a sudsy lather. Quite luxurious, actually.

"This stuff works pretty good," he called to Och. "What is it?"

"Soap root," answered the boy. "Also good for glue and fish bait."

"Right," said Max dubiously. But he had to admit that his hair felt squeaky clean and, in between the insect bites, his suntanned skin was peachy soft. He seemed to have acquired some muscles in the last week. In fact, by his usual couch-potato standards, he was feeling positively hunky.

Och held out a clean T-shirt and jeans he'd borrowed from somewhere, and Max got dressed as slowly as he could, trying to put off the moment when Och would take him to Chan Kan. When he could delay no longer, he found himself standing on the porch of a large hut at the edge of the village. Och called out in Mayan and pushed open the door.

"*Ko'oten!*" called Chan Kan. "Come! I've been waiting for you, Max Murphy!"

Max went inside. The hut was dark and the air was thick with smoke and incense. At first, he couldn't see anything. Then, at the far end of the hut, he made out a large chair, like a throne, draped in animal skins.

It was empty.

"*Ko'oten waye!*" came Chan Kan's voice again. "Come here!"

Had he made himself invisible?

Max was halfway over to the empty chair when something caught his eye, low down on the other side of the room. It was Chan Kan's hair shimmering in the candlelight.

"*Kulen!*" said Chan Kan, indicating a low stool like the one he himself was perched on. "Sit!"

Max sat.

For a while nothing was said.

Max looked around the room. Behind the old man was a long table covered by a thick striped cloth. Its surface, like every other surface in the hut, was laden with candles, statues, painted pots, and jars of unrecognizable dried-up things. There were no windows, and the walls were draped with animal skins. Masks, carvings, and animal skulls hung from the ceiling.

"It is time for the world to end and start again."

In the dim light, it looked like a witch doctor's lair.

The scent of incense was getting stronger.

The greasy wax candles flared and sizzled.

Max had the strangest sensation that this hut was no longer in Utsal, but spinning in space. If he ran out the door at this moment, he would plunge into empty blackness.

"Have you seen the yellow butterflies, Max Murphy?" asked Chan Kan.

Max nodded.

"Do you know what they are?"

Max shook his head. He hadn't expected a nature quiz.

"I'll tell you, Max Murphy. They are lost souls, trapped between worlds, waiting for the changing of *baktuns*."

Chan Kan looked at Max expectantly.

Max tried to remember everything he knew about butterflies. "Are *baktuns* like cocoons?" he asked.

Chan Kan chuckled. "In the Maya calendar," he explained, "a *baktun* is a period of time, like your century, but nearly four times as long."

Max looked confused. "What's that got to do with butterflies?"

"It has to do with every living thing. For this *baktun* has almost passed. It is time for the world to end and start again."

"I see," said Max, not sure what else to say.

"You see nothing," said Chan Kan. "You are like a burrowing snake, confined in your own little world. It is time to take wing, Max Murphy, to soar far and wide like a hawk in the sky."

Max wished he could take wing on a return flight to Boston.

The minutes ticked by, and the old man said nothing more.

Max began to suspect he'd fallen asleep. His grandfather in Italy did that all the time, often in midsentence. Max was just about to tiptoe out of the room when Chan Kan's eyelids shot open.

"Let us see what is in store for you, Max Murphy."

Chan Kan unwrapped a deerskin bundle and shook its contents in his hand like dice. Nuggets of crystal and dried corn kernels fell onto the rug.

Max had a sudden flashback to Boston: Zia kneeling on the floor with her back to him, bits of something on the carpet in front of her and the Maya figurines arranged around her. She'd said she was cleaning, but now Max wasn't so sure. He was beginning to wonder about Zia. In fact, when he got back to Boston, he had quite a few questions for her. Like where did she get the *Pyramid of Peril* game? Who told her to buy his plane ticket to San Xavier? And how did she know his parents needed him?

A groan from Chan Kan brought Max back to the smoky hut in Utsal. The old man was peering at the crystals and corn kernels and shaking his head violently. He rearranged the pieces in different combinations, all the time frowning and muttering to himself, but no matter what pattern he made, the results never pleased him. "*Bahlamtuuno'ob,*" he muttered crossly.

"The Jaguar Stones?" asked Max. "What about them?"

The old man spat on the ground and began to wail an incantation. His voice was high and unearthly, and it swooped and soared in the room like a trapped bird. Max could almost see it thrashing around and beating the air with exhausted wings.

Suddenly the voice was inside Max's head, and he was the trapped bird. He was a hawk who longed for the wind and the sky and the wide-open spaces. He was looking down on himself from the smoky ceiling. He saw a boy with reddish-brown hair, small like a mouse, too scared to move.

Then the singing stopped and the hawk was gone and he was himself again.

Chan Kan poured out a cup of something, took a swig, and passed it to Max.

"Drink," he said.

"What is it?"

"It is the sacred cup that we must share."

With shaking hands, Max lifted the cup. It smelled innocuous, like coconut.

"Drink," repeated Chan Kan.

Max took a sip. His head exploded. Suddenly, there were twice as many crystals and corn kernels on the rug. They danced a jig for him. He closed his eyes. He heard a voice from far away.

"You face great danger, Max Murphy."

"Is Antonio de Landa coming for me?" he slurred.

"The legions of hell are coming for you."

Max opened his eyes.

"Your path will be perilous and difficult," said Chan Kan, "but it was not by chance you met Ix Sak Lol. Like the Hero Twins before you, you must work together to outwit the Lords of Death. The fate of this world hangs in the balance. For good or for evil, one way or the other, the new *baktun* is upon us, and destruction is all around. The omens are dread indeed."

"But that's your world," protested Max. "It's nothing to do with me."

"There is but one world," said Chan Kan. "And its fate is in your hands."

"But I'm just looking for my parents, I'm not—"

The old man leaned forward and wagged a gnarled finger. "You are like the green macaw, Max Murphy. You flap your wings and complain loudly about nothing. The day is coming when you will be tested."

"Tested?" squawked Max.

"It is time for Lord Macaw to fly away," said Chan Kan. "From this day forward, you must be fearless, brave, and strong like Lord Bahlam, the jaguar."

"Please," begged Max, "stop talking in riddles. If you can see the future, just tell me—yes or no—will I see my parents again?"

"You will see them . . ."

Max sighed with relief. That was all he needed to know.

" . . . in this world or the next!"

The old man's laughter echoed around the hut.

Max's head was swimming.

The candles were blazing; the incense filled his nostrils. Every carved mask, every statue, every skull seemed to mock him. He had to get out.

As he stumbled to the door, Chan Kan called out again. "Max Murphy?"

"Yes?"

"Trust the howlers."

Max sat on the porch steps in the dark and tried to see the funny side of it. Here he was, face-to-face with a Maya wise man in the heart of the rainforest, and the mantra he got to guide him through life was "Trust the howlers." He'd had better advice from a fortune cookie.

But no matter how hard he tried to make light of it, Max felt sick with fear. On the one hand, Chan Kan talked like someone in a bad kung fu movie. On the other hand, he seemed to know what he was talking about.

The legions of hell are coming for you. . . .

Max shuddered and resolved to forget Chan Kan's words as soon as possible.

A mournful booming filled the air.

Had the legions of hell arrived already?

He threw himself to the ground in panic, covering his head with his hands. Och and little Och appeared out of nowhere and lay down next to him, copying his every gesture. They didn't seem at all perturbed by the noise.

"What's going on?" asked Max.

"They are blowing the conch shells, Mister Max," said Och.

"Why?"

"To call the village to the feast."

Some pretty girls walked past and giggled to see Max sprawled in the dirt.

"Why do we lie down, Mister Max?" asked Och happily. "Is it a game?"

"No," snapped Max as he got to his feet. He was too busy brushing off his jeans to notice the hurt look on Och's face.

Och and little Och led him back to the central square, where two thatched canopies had been erected. The feast was to be served under these canopies on low wooden tables, with woven mats to sit on. Many villagers were already seated, the men under one canopy and the women under the other, and they shouted greetings to Max as Och showed him to his place.

Max forgot the indignities of the conch-shell incident when he saw his seat at the head of the men's table. He'd never been a guest of honor before and he was looking forward to it. He sat down cross-legged and beamed graciously at the other diners. Their brown faces smiled back at him, sunburned and wrinkled from working in the fields all day.

Max saw himself through the eyes of these peasants. How rich he must look to them, how well fed and healthy. How envious they must be of his good fortune to be born in a prosperous country. How eager they must be to please this mysterious stranger from the land of plenty.

"Let's get this party started," said Max, helping himself to a gourd of pineapple juice. He drank it down greedily and wiped his mouth with the back of his hand. "Good," he said, looking around and smiling. No one smiled back.

Och looked horrified. "No, Mister Max," he whispered. "We do not start until we have given thanks."

Max rolled his eyes. Why was everyone in the world obsessed with table manners? He surveyed the faces around the table. In the shadows cast by the blazing bamboo torches, their strong Maya profiles echoed the paintings of the warriors on the wall at Chahk. If they were looking for a sacrifice victim tonight, he had a feeling he knew who'd they pick.

The thought made him shiver.

He looked around for Lola and saw her approaching, arm in arm with Chan Kan. Her hair was braided and she was wearing an embroidered square-necked blouse and a long skirt. She looked like all the other women in the village, except that she held her head high instead of demurely cast down. She escorted the old man to his place at the other end of the table, then came to have a word with Max.

"How's it going, Hoop?"

"Did you hear what Chan Kan said—?"

He was interrupted by a blast of conch shell.

"Tell me later," said Lola. "I have to go to the women's table."

"But you can't leave me alone—"

"Och will look after you." Lola assured him. "Just remember, eat whatever you're given or you'll insult the villagers and we won't have anywhere to sleep tonight. Got it?"

"Got it."

"Have fun!"

Chan Kan stood up and said a blessing in Mayan. It was very long and involved much bowing and passing of gourds and drinking of toasts. Everyone applauded, another toast was drunk, and then someone banged loudly on the table. There was an excited silence as two smiling women carried in a big, black earthenware cooking pot. They set it down in front of Max.

A third woman brought a bowl and ladled some soup into it from the cooking pot. This, too, was set down in front of Max.

"*Hach ki' awi'ih!*" chorused the women, giggling.

Max looked at Och questioningly.

"They say they hope you enjoy it," the boy explained, also giggling.

"Isn't anyone else eating?"

"You are guest of honor," said Och. "You must eat first."

He looked in the bowl. Red slop.

"What is it?"

"Specialty of Utsal—spicy soup with peppers," said Och. He licked his lips and rubbed his stomach to show that it was good.

Max took a spoonful. It was spicy, all right.

He took a swig of juice and looked around the table.

"Why's everyone staring at me?" he whispered.

Och giggled again. "They watch your enjoyment."

Max took another spoonful. His gums started to tingle.

It was the hottest thing he'd ever eaten. Sweat broke out on his forehead. When he swallowed, it burned all the way down to his stomach like a trail of molten lava.

He took another swig of juice, but it was like throwing gasoline on a fire, and the flames in his mouth flared up ten times worse. He discovered that the longer he paused between mouthfuls, the worse the burning sensation. The only way to survive this trial by fire was to empty his mind and eat as fast as he could.

Earnest faces willed him on. Even Chan Kan nodded his encouragement. What was it the old man had said? *You must be fearless, brave, and strong. . . .*

Only a few more spoonfuls.

Max's lips had gone numb and his tongue felt twice its normal size. He thought his head might explode. He could no longer taste anything at all.

He put down his spoon in bleary triumph.

Well, one thing was for sure. He hadn't acted like a green macaw tonight.

At the other end of the table, Chan Kan was smiling his approval.

Fearless, brave, and strong. He had passed the test.

Max smiled back—a flinty, heroic kind of smile, like a Maya warrior who'd just wrestled a jaguar and won.

But now Chan Kan's smile was turning to laughter, and his laughter was louder than the thunder of rain in the jungle.

His shoulders were shaking and tears were running down his face. Everyone at both tables—men, women, children, toothless crones—was guffawing and slapping their legs. Och and little Och were lying on the ground holding their sides.

Lola came over from the women's table. She could hardly walk for laughing.

"What's so funny?" rasped Max through his swollen mouth.

"That soup," she gasped, wiping her eyes, "it's a joke they play on tourists. You did great, Hoop!"

Her words were like salt on a slug. In an instant, Max's good mood shriveled up and died. His face, already pink, turned scarlet with rage. How dare these ignorant peasants make fun of him! They could have killed him with their evil concoction. As it was, his stomach would be on fire for days.

A giggling woman took away the soup dish and set down a gourd of thin white liquid.

"Drink it," said Lola. "It will take away the heat."

He sipped it cautiously. It took away the heat.

"Better?" asked Lola.

He looked at her accusingly. "I thought we were a team; I'll never forgive you for this." Another thought occurred to him. "And I suppose it was another of your jokes to get Chan Kan to spook me out?"

"What? No, Hoop—"

"You set me up!"

"But Hoop—"

"My name is Max."

A platter of fried chicken was brought out, and the woman served Max an extra-large helping.

"I'm not hungry," he said, pushing the plate away.

"Oh, come on," said Lola. "Where's your sense of humor?"

"It's back in Boston," said Max, "and I wish I was, too."

Then he jumped up and stomped off into the night.

Och ran after him. "You are to sleep at my house, Mister Max," he said. With his little brother in tow as usual, he led the way to a thatched shack and pointed to a hammock on the porch.

"I'd rather have a bed, if you've got one," said Max.

But he was talking to himself. The boys were gone.

After a few false starts, he worked out how to ease himself into the hammock. It was surprisingly comfortable. The woven fabric shaped itself to his body, and the gentle rocking made him feel weightless. He took off his sneakers and let them drop to the floor. Then he lay there, listening to the sounds of music, speeches, and laughter drifting over from the party. Soon, despite the spicy soup sloshing around in his stomach, he fell asleep.

He was awakened at dawn by the sounds of Och's family going about their day. Still half asleep, he slid out of his hammock and went to put on his sneakers.

A huge, shiny black scorpion looked back at him, waving its claws menacingly. It must have been five inches long and it was standing on the toe of a sneaker. Max guessed it would strike if he moved, so he stood there, frozen to the spot, emitting a low wailing noise to raise the alarm without alarming the scorpion.

Och and little Och and Lola arrived at exactly the same time.

"Why are you making that noise?" asked Lola. "It's time to go."

"Can't move," muttered Max. "Scorpion on shoe."

Lola and the two brothers crept over and looked at the offending creature.

"It's a big one," whispered Lola admiringly.

Och and little Och nodded in agreement.

"Don't just stand there," hissed Max, "do something!"

"Okay," said Lola. In one deft motion, she picked the scorpion up by the tail just below the stinger. "It's one of the biggest I've ever seen," she marveled, showing it to the boys. She carried the scorpion over to where Max was now cowering in the corner and dropped it on his shoulder.

"Oops," she said.

Chapter Thirteen
MONKEY RIVER

The scorpion was climbing slowly up Max's neck.

"Get it off! Get it off!" he cried.

Och ran over and held out his hand to the scorpion, all the time making little kissing noises. The scorpion crawled onto his outstretched palm. He gave Max a big smile. "This is Selma," he said. "My pet."

"Selma?" repeated Max. "Selma is your pet? You have a pet scorpion?"

"Big ones like Selma aren't dangerous," explained Lola. "It's the little ones you have to worry about."

"You could have told me sooner," said Max.

Lola shrugged. "Och wanted to play a joke on you to cheer you up."

"Scorpions aren't funny!" yelled Max. "Red-hot soup isn't funny! And that stuff in Chan Kan's hut wasn't funny, either!"

Little Och started to cry.

"I swear I don't know anything about that," said Lola. "What happened? What did he say to you?"

"As if you didn't know."

"But Hoop—"

"Don't call me Hoop." He turned his back and leaned on the porch rail to sulk.

Before long, a little hand was tugging at his shirt.

"Breakfast." Och was holding up a bowl of glutinous white slop.

Max eyed it suspiciously. "And what village specialty is this?"

"*Saksa*," said Och.

"Is that Mayan for 'stewed maggots,' by any chance?"

Max took the bowl and poured the contents over the side of the porch.

Six dogs appeared out of nowhere and began lapping it up.

Och looked at Max accusingly. Lola stood in the doorway with little Och, her mouth open in horror. Little Och wailed louder than ever.

"What's wrong with him?" said Max.

"That was their breakfast, you idiot," said Lola. "They were going to share their corn porridge with you. I can't believe you poured it away."

"Can't they get some more?"

"More?" repeated Lola contemptuously. "There is no more. They cook what they need and they don't waste anything."

"They wasted that soup last night."

"They were making it anyway. The tourists are coming today."

"Well, that porridge was disgusting. I did the boys a favor, if you ask me."

Max smiled at Och, but the boy's expression was like thunder. With a final black look, he grabbed his little brother's hand and dragged him off, still wailing.

Stupid kid, Max told himself.

But he felt bad.

He sat alone on the porch, waiting for Lola say her good-byes. He couldn't wait to leave this village. But at least he'd learned an important lesson here: from now on, he was going to forget everyone else and look after number one.

When Lola had finally finished kissing all the women and hugging all the children, Max followed her sulkily down to the river. Some girls were scrubbing clothes on the rocks, and they nudged each other and laughed when they saw him. He scowled at them, which made them laugh even more.

Chan Kan was waiting on the bank.

"Eusebio is taking his hot chili peppers to market in Limón," said Chan Kan. "He will give you a ride upriver." The old man chuckled. "Please try not to eat all his chilies, Max Murphy; we saw how much you liked them last night!"

"Ha-ha," said Max unpleasantly.

Lola glared at him. "Thank you for everything," she said to Chan Kan.

"You are most welcome, Ix Sak Lol," he replied, lifting her hand to his lips and kissing it. "Our hearts will travel with you. Please pass on my greetings to Hermanjilio and give him this." He pointed with his cane at a large bamboo cage sitting on the grass.

Max and Lola knelt down to peer in the cage. A mangy little black rooster huddled miserably in one corner.

"His name is Thunderclaw," said Chan Kan. "Hermanjilio will soon have need of him."

"What's the matter with it?" asked Max, sounding disgusted. "Does it have a skin disease?"

"Ah," said Chan Kan, "you refer to his battle scars." He smiled proudly. "The venerable Thunderclaw was once a great fighting cock. His feathers were ripped out over the years, but he was never beaten."

"Poor thing," said Lola. "Well, if anyone can give him a worthy send-off, it's Hermanjilio. He can cook anything."

Chan Kan turned to Max and put a hand on each of his shoulders. Little electric shocks traveled up and down Max's body.

"Trust the howlers, Max Murphy."

Max curled his lip. Surely even Chan Kan realized that the howler joke was wearing thin. He was trying to formulate a smart reply, when Chan Kan took a leather canteen from his belt, drank a little water, and spat it in Max's face.

Well, perhaps not spat exactly. To describe it more objectively, he walked round and round the horrified Max, spraying a gentle mist of water from his mouth until he'd made a ring of tiny rainbows around the boy's head.

"Get away from me!" shrieked Max, trying to shield his face. "That's so gross!"

"You should be honored," said Lola. "Chan Kan has just blessed you with courage."

Max looked quickly from one to the other, but he couldn't catch them smirking. He didn't know if it was another joke or not. "I think you're sick," he said. "You're all sick in the head. I think this village is actually some kind of low-security mental hospital."

"I can't believe you said that!" exploded Lola. "These people have shared everything they have with you. How can you be so ungrateful?"

"Let me think," said Max sarcastically, wiping his face with his shirt. "They poisoned me, they made fun of me, and they spit on me. Yeah, you're right, I've had a lovely time. Remind me to send them a thank-you note."

Lola turned her back on him in disgust.

"I think Eusebio is ready to leave," said Chan Kan. "All blessings."

At the water's edge, a small, round man was loading big, round baskets into a dugout canoe. When he turned to greet them with his twinkling eyes and his leathery face etched with laughter lines, Max recognized him as one of the chief merrymakers of the night before and took an instant loathing to him.

He wasn't impressed by Eusebio's vessel, either. He'd been imagining whizzing down the river on a supersleek speedboat, not a hollowed-out tree trunk with an outboard motor. Surely there wouldn't be room for all of them? The boat was already sitting low in the water from the weight of the chili baskets.

At Lola's call, Chulo and Seri materialized out of nowhere and settled themselves on the bow. Chulo bared his teeth at Max in passing.

There's some extra weight we could lose, thought Max.

Eusebio indicated that Max should sit in the stern with the chicken cage. Then Lola and Eusebio pushed the boat into the water and climbed in next to him. It was a tight squeeze, but soon they were all wedged in and on their way.

A little boy was sitting in a tree at the water's edge.

It was Och.

Little Och sat on another branch, lower down.

Max waved to them, but they didn't wave back.

Lola waved and they waved back enthusiastically.

Max pretended not to care. He dumped the chicken cage on Lola, put on his sunglasses, and stared fixedly upriver.

He was glad to be leaving this crazy village.

His stomach was empty and his heart was, too. He felt like an alien, a hungry alien who didn't speak the language. He longed to be home in Boston, playing video games with characters who followed the rules. In real life people were irrational, unpredictable, annoying, and bossy, bossy, bossy.

An early-morning mist enveloped the boat, and Eusebio concentrated on steering. They zoomed along in silence for an hour or so, until a weak sun broke through and the mist cleared.

"Time for breakfast," said Eusebio, cutting the motor in midstream.

He pulled out a small cooler from under the chili baskets.

Inside were some bottles of water and two tortillas stuffed with beans.

"I am sorry," said Eusebio. "I did not know you were coming, so I did not bring extra food. But you are welcome to share what I have."

"That's very kind of you," said Lola, looking meaningfully at Max, "but we had breakfast at Utsal."

"Speak for yourself," said Max, taking one of the tortillas and gulping it down in three greedy bites.

"For you, Ix Sak Lol?" said Eusebio, offering Lola the remaining tortilla.

She shook her head.

"If you are sure," said Eusebio, about to take the tortilla for himself.

"I'll have it," said Max.

"No!" yelled Lola. "I can't believe you, Max Murphy! A wild pig has better manners!"

"What have I done now?"

"You were going to eat all Eusebio's food."

"He offered."

"He was being polite."

"How was I supposed to know?"

"Well, try thinking about someone besides yourself for a change! You spoiled the party, you threw away Och's breakfast, you insulted everyone at Utsal—"

"What about *your* manners?" demanded Max. "You made me eat the soup, you dropped a scorpion on me—where I come from, we'd never treat a guest that way."

"I'm surprised you have any guests—or any friends at all! The world doesn't revolve around you, you know. The villagers at Utsal work hard every day of their lives. If they like to play their little joke on pampered tourists—and, by the way, the tourists love it—it wouldn't hurt you to laugh along. You could have made a lot of friends last night. But you only know how to make enemies. You're the most selfish person I've ever met!"

"I'm taking care of number one," Max yelled back. "Isn't that the law of the jungle?"

"Stop," said Eusebio. It was the first time Max had seen him without a smile on his face. "You are squabbling like baby parrots."

Lola hung here head. "I'm sorry, Eusebio," she said, but her apology was drowned out by the sound of the boat starting up again.

Max expected to continue upriver but, to his surprise, they made straight for the bank.

Eusebio cut the motor. "Please get out," he said.

"But Eusebio—" began Lola.

"It is the only way," said Eusebio. "Out. Please. Now."

When Max and Lola had reluctantly climbed ashore, Eusebio tied the boat to an overhanging branch and jumped onto land himself.

"Follow me," he said.

As they tramped through the forest, clambering over tree roots and ducking under branches, Max and Lola exchanged angry glances.

Eusebio paid them no attention. He pointed up at some drab flowers garlanding the branches of a tree. "Look, my friend," he said to Max. "This is the rare black orchid. In your country, they fuss over it like a newborn baby. So how does this delicate little flower look after itself in the treacherous jungle?"

The boatman reached up to pick one, but he wasn't tall enough.

"You're not supposed to pick them, Eusebio," said Lola. "They're a protected species."

"So much for looking after itself," muttered Max.

Eusebio waved his hand airily. "My point is," he said, "that the little orchid has trained itself to be the perfect guest. It lives on the tree, but it feeds from the air and the rain. It takes nothing from its host."

"I knew this was about the tortillas," said Max.

But Eusebio had moved on. "Over here," he was saying, "is the trumpet tree—so called because my ancestors made

199

wooden trumpets from its hollow trunk." He handed Max his machete. "Hit it," he instructed. "And stand back."

Max whacked the tree as hard as he could.

An unappetizing smell of blue cheese and coconut filled the air.

"It is the smell of angry ants," said Eusebio.

Even as he said it, hundreds of ants emerged from the trunk and swarmed toward the machete marks. "The tree makes a nectar for the ants to eat, and in return they act as bodyguards for the tree."

"Can we go back to the boat now?" asked Max.

But Eusebio had found another specimen, a sinister-looking tree with black tarlike patches on its trunk. "The mighty poisonwood!" he cried. "Its sap burns worse than pepper soup, and the only thing that soothes it is the bark of the gumbo-limbo." He indicated a nearby tree with a flaky crimson trunk.

"They call gumbo-limbo the tourist tree," added Lola, "because it's always red and peeling."

Max didn't laugh.

"The point is," gabbled Eusebio excitedly, "that gumbo-limbo and poisonwood always grow side by side! It is the same for people. On the surface we are different, but our roots are intertwined. We are connected in ways we cannot see and we must use our talents to help each other. Looking after number one may be the law of the concrete jungle, but it is not the law of the rainforest."

"But I'm *from* a concrete jungle," said Max wearily. "This is not my world."

"Ah," said Eusebio, "so you're a tourist? A guest that takes without giving? Then you are like this strangler fig." He pointed to a huge tree with thick, buttresslike roots. "This started life as a vine in the top of another tree and grew down, stealing its host's food and light, until it reached the forest floor. When it was firmly rooted, it tightened its death grip around its host's trunk and became a living coffin."

"It was only a tortilla!" protested Max.

"And you are welcome to it, my friend," said Eusebio, slapping him on the back. "But have you learned anything from this walk?"

"Yes," said Max ruefully. "I learned that I should've brought sandwiches."

Eusebio roared with laughter. "Come," he said, "let us return to the boat and share that last tortilla."

As they walked along, Max fell into step with Lola.

"I guess I have been acting like a tourist," he said.

"Yeah," said Lola, "you did lose it a bit in Utsal. But hey, maybe I'd act like a tourist if I came to Boston."

"You'd hate it there," said Max. "No snakes, no scorpions, no rat on a stick." He looked at her pointedly. "And the people are normal, too."

She ignored the insult. "You didn't give Utsal a chance."

"They don't have cell phones or laptops or cable TV. That's all I need to know."

"They choose to live without them. Once you join the consumer society, you have to keep making money to buy things you don't need."

"But surely you don't want to live in a shack with no electricity?"

"I think you can have the best of both worlds. I respect the old ways, but I also believe in women's rights and a college education."

"What does Chan Kan think about that?"

"He's hoping I'll get it out of my system and come back and marry some boy he's picked out for me."

"You wouldn't, would you?" said Max, horrified.

She shrugged. "Who knows what the future holds?"

"All aboard!" called Eusebio from the riverbank.

"Race you back to the boat," called Lola, disappearing down the path.

As they thrummed along between high walls of jungle, the boatman pointed out the passing wildlife. It was like traveling through the pages of a children's picture book. There were freshwater crocodiles floating like logs, turtles sunning themselves on rocks, a bright orange iguana on a tree branch, a frigate bird with a chest like a plum tomato, kingfishers, storks, scarlet macaws, and always the clouds of yellow butterflies fluttering along the banks.

It was all so lush and unspoiled and peaceful that Max could easily imagine he was the first explorer ever to navigate these waters.

His fantasy was soon disturbed by a whiny, nasal voice.

"Would ya look at that! See the cute monkeys on the canoe?"

Max looked back in the direction of the voice and saw a white cabin cruiser speeding up the river behind them. Its deck was thronged with overfed passengers in orange life jackets, and every passenger was weighed down with photographic equipment.

As the cruiser passed, it listed to one side with the combined weight of the shrieking mass who rushed to the railing to zoom in on Chulo and Seri.

And then they were gone, leaving Eusebio's boat rocking in their wake.

"What just happened?" asked Max, in shock.

"Tourists!" said Lola. "They're on the Mystery of the Maya cruise. They dock at Puerto Muerto, take a quick trip upriver to Limón, stop at Utsal for lunch, and tick San Xavier off their list. They'll be having margaritas in Mexico tonight."

"It should be called the Mystery of the Tourists cruise," said Max.

"You should know," Lola teased him.

Yeah, thought Max, *I should know.*

In that moment, Max saw the tourists through the eyes of the villagers at Utsal and he understood the pepper-soup trick. He saw himself, last night, sweat pouring down his face, trying to impress the natives.

Yeah, it was funny.

He was glad the rowdy boatload who'd just passed would soon be forcing down the fiery broth. That would quiet them down for a while. And even if their fancy cabin cruiser had a snack bar and a restroom with soft toilet paper, he'd rather be in this hollowed-out log with Lola and Eusebio.

It was time to take sides.

As long as he kept comparing San Xavier to Boston, he was no better than one of those tourists. Like it or not, the jungle was his home right now, and he had to make the best of it. Besides, playing video games alone in his room seemed kind of lame compared to zooming up the Monkey River with the wind in his hair.

He leaned back against the chili baskets to consider this momentous revelation. The sun was getting higher, the day was getting hotter. He closed his eyes. Soon, lulled by the throb of the engine, he fell into a waking dream. It was a parade of disapproving faces, a lineup of everyone he'd upset, offended, or alienated recently—his mom, his dad, Oscar, Raul, Lucky Jim, the entire village of Utsal, especially Och—all set against a hip-hop sound track of Uncle Ted saying, "He's a spoiled brat," over and over again.

Then a new sound joined the beat. A rhythmic *no, no, no*. He opened his eyes.

"No, no, no!" yelled Eusebio, gesturing frantically from the back of the boat. "Get your hand out!"

As Max had dozed, he'd dipped his hand lazily over the side of the boat. He pulled it in quickly. It wasn't the smartest thing he'd ever done, to trail such juicy bait in a river full of crocodiles. But then again, he reflected, perhaps he'd done a few things lately that weren't too smart.

It was late morning when Eusebio pulled the boat into the riverbank. Chulo and Seri leapt off and headed into the trees.

"They know the way," said Lola, laughing. "They'll be there before us."

She hugged Eusebio, thanked him profusely, and showered her blessings on his family. Then she picked up the chicken cage and climbed out of the boat.

Now it was Max's turn to disembark.

He was dithering over whether to shake hands, when the boatman solved his dilemma by catching him in a suffocating bear hug.

"Good-bye, Max Murphy, all blessings," he said.

"Good-bye, Eusebio." Max took off his shades and handed them to the boatman. "Here, you need these more than I do. You're headed into the sun."

Eusebio put on the shades, slapped Max on the back, hugged him again, kissed him on both cheeks, and roared off upriver.

"That was nice of you, Max," said Lola.

"You can call me Hoop, if you like," he said.

Almost as soon as they began to walk, the rain started bucketing down. It was going to be another wet, miserable slog through the mud.

Then Max remembered his new positive attitude. Determined not to be a whiny tourist, he fashioned a rain hat out of a large leaf, gritted his teeth, and followed Lola in stoic silence.

After an hour or so, the vegetation thinned out a little and he could make out a narrow path snaking to and fro up a steep hillside in front of them.

"Nearly there," called Lola. "Are you okay, Hoop?"

"Me? I'm fine," replied Max, as jauntily as he could from under his leaf.

Lola looked at him suspiciously. "Why aren't you complaining about anything?"

"It's the new me," he said. "I've changed."

Lola laughed. "So how does the new you feel about climbing that hill?"

"Lead on!"

When they reached the top, the rain stopped suddenly as it had started, and the sun came out.

The view was incredible. The forest spread out in every direction, from the banks of the Monkey River to the distant purple mountains. But all Max's tired body could focus on was the fact that they were not actually at the top.

There was one more hill to climb. On its summit, the upper terraces closer to sky than earth, were the partially excavated ruins of a huge stepped pyramid.

"That's the Temple of Itzamna," said Lola.

She started to run up the path. Then she stopped and came back. "By the way, there's something you should know before we go up there. . . ."

"What?"

"Hermanjilio is a little"—she searched for just the right word—"eccentric."

"What do you mean eccentric?"

But Lola and Thunderclaw had taken off up the path to the ruined city.

Chapter Fourteen
ITZAMNA

Max followed behind, huffing and puffing up the hill until he reached the Temple of Itzamna. As he got closer, he came face-to-face with a line of monstrous carved faces. One had a pig's snout, another had pop eyes and buckteeth. It wasn't quite the welcoming committee he'd hoped for.

"Lola?" he called.

"Over here, Hoop."

He followed her voice around the side of the pyramid and there, spread out below him, was the glorious ancient city that had once ruled the Monkey River.

Spread out below him was the glorious ancient city.

It wasn't what he'd expected at all. He'd thought Itzamna would be another boring archaeological site like the ones in his parents' photograph albums—a hodgepodge of taped-off trenches and rubble and piles of old stones, meaningless to anyone but the experts. But this place was at once magnificent and welcoming, like coming home to the most beautiful city in the world.

The temple was built into the hillside. They were standing on a platform halfway up, about fifty feet above the central plaza. The top of the pyramid was another fifty feet above them. On this side, steep steps led down to the overgrown plaza. Through the middle of the plaza, a raised stone causeway, flanked by more ruins and grassy mounds, ran to another massive structure at the far end of the site. This, too, was only partially excavated, and trees sprang from its upper terraces. But against the hazy backdrop of the forest, with the afternoon sun bathing its white stones in pinks and purples, it looked like a precious jewel on a bed of dark-green velvet.

"That's the royal palace," said Lola proudly. "It was built over a thousand years ago without metal tools or wheels."

"The Maya didn't have wheels?"

"We had them," said Lola, "but we only used them for children's toys."

"Really? You guys weren't as smart as I thought."

"There's not much point in making wheeled carts if you don't have draft animals to pull them," she sniffed. "Besides, we were busy inventing the Maya calendar, the concept of zero, rubber balls, hot chocolate, chewing gum—"

Max's ears pricked up. "Chewing gum?"

"We call it *chicle*. It's made from the latex of the sapodilla tree. While you're here we could—"

Max gripped her arm. "It's a ghost!" he hissed.

She followed his eyes down to the plaza, where an ancient Maya king had just emerged from behind a pyramid. He wore a richly embroidered tunic, belted at the waist with a woven sash. His straight black hair was pulled into a thick ponytail on top of his head with a gold ornament. Jade spools bobbed from his ears as he walked.

"Hermanjilio!" screamed Lola happily, handing Max the rooster cage and running down to meet this apparition.

"*Biix abeel?*" Hermanjilio shouted up to her. "Are you okay?"

"*Ma'alob, ma'alob,*" called Lola. "I'm fine!"

"I've been expecting you! Chulo and Seri got here ages ago!"

"It's so good to see you," said Lola, hugging him. "And I've got something for you!" She opened her backpack to show him the Red Jaguar.

"But how . . . ?"

"It wasn't easy! I'll tell you everything later. . . ."

As Lola and Hermanjilio chatted on, Max tried to take in every detail of the archaeologist's extraordinary appearance.

He was in his forties, around six feet tall, and as muscular as an Olympic shot-putter. Kindly brown eyes ringed with laughter lines shone out of his leathery face. With his high forehead, prominent cheekbones, and splendidly hooked nose, he was another portrait out of time. Except, Max noted, no ancient Maya king would have worn battered tennis shoes nor carried a wooden spoon.

So this was the last person to have officially seen his parents.

Now, at last, he would find out where they were.

Lola turned to him. "Max Murphy, meet Professor Hermanjilio Bol."

Before Max could say anything, a cloud of yellow butterflies descended on his head and shoulders.

"What an honor to meet you," said Hermanjilio, swatting at the butterflies with his wooden spoon. "These things are everywhere at the moment. They seem to like you, young man."

Max flicked the butterflies away and blurted out the question he'd been waiting to ask. "Have you seen my parents, Professor?"

"Please call me Hermanjilio," he said. "I last saw your parents at Ixchel, Max. I thought they'd be back at your uncle's house by now."

Max looked visibly deflated. He'd been so sure Hermanjilio would have news. "Well, what happened?" he persisted. "Where are they?"

"I don't know. The dig didn't go as planned. We decided to abandon it. The storm came. I'm sure they'll turn up soon. I'm sorry, Max. This business must be awful for you, waiting for them to come back. . . ."

Forgetting he was holding the wooden spoon, he went to put an arm around Max and accidentally poked him in the face. "Forgive me," he said, with a laugh so loud it scared the parrots in a nearby tree. "I've been cooking all day. Tonight we're having a party to celebrate your safe arrival."

Max looked Hermanjilio up and down. "Is it a costume party?"

Hermanjilio chuckled. "Pardon my appearance, but it's an academic experiment. My ancestors lived at Itzamna in the Classic and Postclassic Periods. I've been trying to get closer to my roots by seeing life through their eyes—"

A hideous shrieking sound interrupted his explanation.

"Thunderclaw!" said Lola. "I completely forgot!" She lifted up the cage to show Hermanjilio. "It's a gift from Chan Kan."

"What is it?" asked Hermanjilio.

"His name is Thunderclaw. He's a black rooster."

"Does he have a disease? What are those scales on his skin?"

"Old war wounds. He used to be a champion fighting cock."

"I wonder why Chan Kan would send me a chicken?" mused Hermanjilio.

"To cook?" suggested Max hopefully.

"But Chan Kan knows I'm trying to live like my ancestors, and they didn't have chickens until the Spanish came."

"Beats me," said Lola. "He just said you'd soon have need of him."

"Well, we don't need him tonight, that's for sure," said Hermanjilio. "There's already enough food for twenty people."

At this news, Max's stomach rumbled loudly.

Hermanjilio laughed. "Let's show Max to his room," he said. "Then you can come and talk to me, Lola, while I finish cooking. Follow me."

He strode off, holding the wooden spoon high in the air like a drum major leading a parade. Max and Lola followed behind until they came to a sudden halt in front of a huge tree.

"Look up," said Lola.

Max looked up.

Wow.

Above them, soaring up and up toward the jungle canopy, was an intricately constructed multistoried tree house, with thatched huts at every level linked by rope ladders and slatted walkways.

"This is fantastic!" exclaimed Max. "It's like *The Swiss Family Robinson!*"

Lola looked at him with interest. "People live in tree houses in Switzerland?"

Before Max could explain, Hermanjilio cut in. "Lola, please show Max to my room. I'm not using it at the moment."

"But where will you sleep?" asked Max.

"Don't worry about me," said Hermanjilio. "I've been sleeping in the palace."

"The palace? Isn't that a little spooky?" asked Lola.

"Spooky? You mean haunted?" Hermanjilio considered the question. "Well, there's definitely something in the air, particularly at night—latent vibrations or a sympathetic echo, something of that nature. And I've been having the most extraordinary dreams."

Lola shuddered. "Please be careful, Hermanjilio."

"I like it. It helps me imagine what daily life was like for my ancestors. I'm even grinding my own corn these days—which reminds me! I need to get back to my cooking! Please make yourselves at home."

Hermanjilio padded back down the forest path, silent as a hunting jaguar.

"He's eccentric, all right," said Max. "What a weirdo!"

"Follow me," said Lola coldly.

They ascended the rope ladder in silence. Lola showed Max his room and turned to go, all without saying a word.

"What's the matter? What have I done now?" he asked. He thought quickly. "Is it because I called Hermanjilio a weirdo? I'm sorry, I really am. He took me by surprise, that's all. I was expecting the usual archaeologist type. You know, all beard and khaki shorts."

"Like your father, you mean?" sniffed Lola.

"I guess so."

"Could your father have done a better job of excavating this place?"

"Of course not. It's just Hermanjilio's 'going native' act that threw me."

"Hermanjilio is a native—and so am I."

"Okay, okay! Why are you so touchy?"

"I just want you to understand that, as well as being head of Maya Studies at San Xavier University, Hermanjilio is one of the most brilliant archaeologists in the world. He's actually descended from the lords of Itzamna, so he feels a spiritual connection with this place. One day he's hoping to open it as the first totally Maya-run site. . . ." Lola's eyes were shining. "He may not have a beard and khaki shorts, but Hermanjilio knows more about Maya history than any foreign archaeologist."

"So that's what all this is about? You want me to say that your friend in the dress is a better archaeologist than Mom and Dad? Well, maybe he is. Maybe the Maya are best at everything! But so what? I just want to find my parents and go home. Can't you understand that?"

Lola looked away.

"I'm sorry," he said. "Of course you can understand that. You'd like to find your parents, too, wouldn't you?"

"I don't even know who they are," she sighed. "Chan Kan found me in the forest when I was little. I was holding a white mahogany blossom, so he called me Lady White Flower. I lived in Utsal until a couple of years ago, when I came to study with Hermanjilio. He's taught me so much, and I won't let anyone make fun of him. Especially not someone who's covered in mud and smells like a skunk."

Max put up his hands in surrender. "You're right," he said. "So where's the river and the soap root?"

"I'll show you," said Lola. Her eyes twinkled mischievously. "Unless you'd rather use Hermanjilio's solar-heated shower?"

Max couldn't believe his ears. A hot shower was beyond his wildest dreams. "Hermanjilio really is a genius!" he exclaimed, as a crust of dry brown mud cracked off his clothes and fell to the floor in little pieces.

"Look in Hermanjilio's closet," said Lola. "I think he has some clean clothes in among the jaguar skins."

Later, when Lola appeared for dinner looking amazingly beautiful in a pink-and-orange-striped skirt, a lime-green top, and a brightly woven shawl, with a pink flower behind her ear, Max wished he had tried a little harder to find a shirt that didn't come down to his knees.

"Wow! You look so clean," she said, sounding surprised.

"You, too," he replied, and immediately kicked himself for not paying her a more smooth-tongued compliment. "I mean, you always look clean, that is—"

"*Yum bo'otik teech!*" said Lola.

Max looked at her suspiciously. Was she insulting him, Maya-style?

"It means 'thank you,'" she explained, laughing.

"Enough talking!" announced Hermanjilio. "Let's eat!"

It was a magical scene. The plaza was lit with flaming torches and candles in lanterns strung through the trees. Giant fireflies darted across the path, and above it all, the jungle stars twinkled like diamonds.

But Max had eyes only for the food.

Laid out on a banana-leaf tablecloth was plate after plate of succulent concoctions: a mountain of savory pastries, little fried dumplings, skewers of meat, avocado salad, tortillas, beans, sweet potato fritters, plantains, and a huge platter of tropical fruit.

That night they feasted like kings. It had taken Hermanjilio hours to prepare the banquet, but it took only minutes for Max and Lola to wolf down their first helpings and come back for more. Table manners were forgotten as they ate with their fingers and talked with their mouths full.

As he devoured another whole pastry in one bite, Max imagined what his mother would say if she caught him eating like this. Thinking about her made him sad, and he wiped his mouth (albeit on the back of his hand) in her honor.

He wondered what his parents were eating tonight out there in the jungle. He hoped the smell of this feast would waft to wherever they were and guide them to him. He kept watching the entrance to the plaza, half expecting them to stumble in. But no one came.

Finally, when even Max could eat no more, Hermanjilio stood up and cleared the table. When he came back, he carried a gourd of something that smelled to Max like a mixture of aniseed and gasoline.

"Maya elixir," said Hermanjilio with a wink. "Now tell me again what happened at Chahk. How clever you were to think of using the Red Jaguar and scraping away the jungle like that and rubbing blood on the painting. I would have given anything to be there. . . .Tell me from the beginning."

"I told you everything before dinner," said Lola, "three times."

"Perhaps you could tell your story now, sir," suggested Max, "about what happened the last time you saw my parents?"

Hermanjilio took another draft of liquor and said nothing.

Lola was looking at him strangely.

"Sir?" Max begged him. "My parents are missing, and you're the last person who saw them. You're my only hope."

Hermanjilio groaned and put his head into his hands. When he looked up, he had tears in his eyes.

"I can't lie to you any longer, Max," he said. "I saw it with my own eyes. Your parents vanished into thin air."

Chapter Fifteen
THE OATH OF BLOOD

"Thin air? What's that supposed to mean? How could my parents vanish into thin air? Did a fog come down? Tell me the truth! This isn't one of your Maya legends, this is about my parents! Tell me everything you saw!"

"Calm down, Max," said Hermanjilio. "I don't understand, either. One minute they were there and the next minute they were gone."

"But it doesn't make sense," said Max, getting angry. "There's something you're not telling me!"

Lola was staring hard at Hermanjilio. "There's a lot he's not telling you."

"Lola!" protested Hermanjilio. "You know I'm bound by sacred oaths."

"But you said you didn't believe that stuff. You said you only went through with the rituals to please Chan Kan."

"Since I've been trying to live the old way, my feelings on that subject have changed. Besides, there's something in the air right now, something big, and whatever it is, I don't want you two getting mixed up in it."

"We are mixed up in it, Hermanjilio. You have to tell Max everything. He just wants to find his parents. For my sake? Please?"

Hermanjilio sighed. He knew when he was beaten.

"I will do it on one condition," he said. "The boy must take an oath of silence and seal it with a blood sacrifice."

"He'll do it," said Lola.

Hermanjilio got up for a moment and returned with a long, bony needle and a thin peel of tree bark. He passed the needle to Max.

"It's a stingray spine," he said, "sharper than cut glass. My ancestors would have passed it through their tongues, but you can just prick your thumb."

"I'd rather not," said Max.

Lola grabbed Max's thumb and jabbed it with the stingray spine. Ignoring his cries of pain, she held it over the tree bark and squeezed out a few drops of blood.

"Now say these words," said Hermanjilio. *"If I should betray the secrets of the sacred stones, may the Lords of Death pluck out my living heart."*

As Max repeated the oath, a cold wind blew across the table, making the candles flicker and spit.

Hermanjilio set fire to the bloodstained tree bark and watched in silence as the smoke curled up into the night sky. "The oath is sealed; I would advise you not to break it." He beckoned Max to sit closer. *"Bahlamtuuno'ob,"* he whispered.

"The Jaguar Stones?" said Max, his eyes watering from the toxic cloud of elixir fumes on Hermanjilio's breath.

Hermanjilio nodded. *"Bahlamtuuno'ob* translates as 'Jaguar Stones' but, to me, it means more than just a set of stone carvings. The Jaguar Stones represent everything that is noble about the Maya: our strength, courage, wisdom, creativity, and our enduring spirit. That's why I have sworn to track them down and put them on display, like the crown jewels of the rainforest, to inspire my people and give them hope for the future."

"Couldn't you just tell me what happened to my parents?" interrupted Max impatiently.

"Like everything else in the universe, this story has a natural order," said Hermanjilio. "I am explaining to you how I came to be at Ixchel with Frank and Carla."

The night was getting cool. Lola huddled up to Max and draped her shawl over both of them like a blanket.

Hermanjilio fortified himself with elixir and continued. "With all written record of the Jaguar Stones destroyed by Diego de Landa, they had long ago passed into legend. But like me, Frank Murphy believed they were real and he shared my obsession with finding them. So when he finally got his hands on the White Jaguar, he invited me to Ixchel to witness his experiment."

"What experiment?" asked Max.

"He wanted to try and activate the stone. Of course, I didn't think he'd succeed, because no one today knows how the Jaguar Stones worked. Little did I know he was bringing the instruction manual with him!"

"What?" said Lola, looking puzzled.

"Dad found Friar Diego de Landa's private journal," explained Max.

"No!" she said, her eyes wide in surprise.

"It's true." Hermanjilio nodded. "Before the wily old friar burned our books, he copied down our secrets for his own use. Of course, the journal is very old and many pages are missing. But what remains makes it clear that Landa's plan was to steal the power of the Jaguar Stones for himself."

"And now Count Antonio is reviving that family tradition," added Max.

"But this is incredible!" said Lola. "Why would Frank keep something like that to himself?"

"Think about it," said Hermanjilio. "If the journal was genuine, it was one of the most dangerous documents in human history. Frank feared that some power-crazed madman would seek out the stones and put their power to evil use. He came to Ixchel to end that possibility, once and for all. He wanted to find out if the journal was real or an elaborate fake. If it was real, he intended to burn it—just as Landa burned our books. If it was fake, he would hand it over to the authorities as a fascinating historical document."

"So Dad's a good guy?" said Max in surprise. Since talking to Uncle Ted, he'd got used to the idea that his family were criminal masterminds.

"Of course"—Hermanjilio grinned—"one of the best. So, Lola and I went ahead to Ixchel to get the local workers started on the excavation. Along the way, we discussed the rumors about the Red Jaguar, and Lola decided to go to Puerto Muerto and find out if Ted Murphy was selling."

"But when I got there, he'd already done a deal with Antonio de Landa," said Lola. "So I decided to repossess the Red Jaguar for the Maya people."

"Steal it, you mean," said Max.

"Some people say that all archaeology is theft," said Lola airily.

"Do you two want to hear the story or do you want a moral debate?" asked Hermanjilio.

"Sorry," mumbled Max. "Please go on."

Hermanjilio cleared his throat. "So Frank and Carla arrived at Ixchel and we set to work. Frank told me about the journal and asked for my opinion. Late one afternoon, when the local workers had gone, I was lying in my tent studying the journal when I heard Frank and Carla calling to me. They were out by the cenote, the water hole, mixing up fake blood."

"Why would they do that?" asked Max.

"They needed a bloodlike substance to activate the White Jaguar. Of course, Friar Landa's journal specified blood from a human sacrifice, but even Frank drew the line at that. Still, to find out if the journal was real or fake, they had to follow Landa's instructions as closely as possible. With the fate of the whole world at stake, there was no room for error. So it was quite a scene out at the cenote. The White Jaguar was sitting on a flat rock, surrounded by all these jars of different blood recipes. With a setting sun behind it, it looked like a scene from a horror film." Hermanjilio smiled briefly at the memory. "By the way, it was also the only time I've ever seen your father not wearing that old jacket of his. Carla had made him take it off because he'd spilled fake blood all over it. Anyway, there we were, admiring the color and viscosity of the winning recipe, when we heard a noise from the camp.

"It was getting dark, but we could make out figures swarming around the tents. Later I realized they were working for Antonio de Landa, but at the time we thought they were bandits. We had to hide, and fast. There was a cave at water level in the walls of the cenote, so I whispered to Frank and Carla to grab the White Jaguar and swim with it to the cave. I saw them jump in and I was about to follow, but they never hit the water. There was a flash of white light, and they were gone."

"But there were no bodies in the cenote," said Max. "They must have climbed out when it was over."

"No," said Hermanjilio, "you don't understand. They were gone. *Poof!* They dematerialized, disappeared!"

Max stared at him. "So where are they?"

Hermanjilio's hands were shaking as he reached for his gourd. "I've been thinking about it ever since," he said. "The Jaguar Stone, the blood . . . I believe the cenote became a gateway to Xibalba that night." He pronounced it *she-ball-buh*, and the sound of it set Max's teeth on edge, like fingernails on a chalkboard. "I think that's where you'll find your parents."

"Xibalba?" repeated Max. "Is it far from here?"

Lola looked at him sadly. "Xibalba means 'Well of Fear,'" she said. "I'm sorry, Hoop, but it's the Maya underworld."

"The underworld?" said Max. "Are you saying my parents are dead?"

As he put his head in his hands, a yellow butterfly landed on the table in front of him and started lapping up a spill of sickly sweet guava juice.

Chapter Sixteen

THE COSMIC CROCODILE

It was impossible to sleep. Several times, Max nearly fell out of his hammock as he tossed and turned, imagining the terrifying events at Ixchel and trying to understand what they meant.

As far as he could work out, the good news was that his parents had not technically died. The bad news was that they were trapped in some Maya netherworld.

Two weeks ago, Max would have laughed at such a crazy idea. Now, after his experiences at the Temple of Chahk, he wasn't feeling quite so sure of himself. But even if Hermanjilio's version of events was true, how could two eminent archaeologists like his parents have got sucked into this mess?

It didn't make sense. . . .

He finally drifted off to sleep as the rainforest dawn chorus struck up its overture. He was awakened minutes later by Chulo throwing mangoes at his head.

"If you were going to bring me breakfast in bed, Chulo, you could have chosen ripe ones," he complained.

There was no way he could get back to sleep, so he rolled groggily out of his hammock, pulled on some clothes, and went down to the plaza. Hermanjilio was sitting at the table, deep in thought. There was a plate of tortillas and a bowl of fruit in front of him, but he didn't seem to have touched anything. Max sat down opposite him and sighed heavily.

"Bad night?" asked Hermanjilio.

"Yeah," said Max. "I can't get my head around this Xibalba thing."

Hermanjilio nodded sympathetically. "I'm sure it sounds crazy to you," he said. "But around here, it's the only logical explanation."

Max sighed again. "I was thinking," he said, "if a doorway to Xibalba opened at Ixchel that night, couldn't we just go back there and open it again?"

Hermanjilio shook his head. "For a start, we don't have the White Jaguar. But even if we did, it's not easy to bring people back. According to Maya legend, they would have to be released by special order of the Lords of Death."

Max groaned and laid his head on the table. "This is impossible."

"Nothing's impossible," said Hermanjilio cheerfully. "At least, not around here."

"So tell me about the Death Lords."

"You swore an oath to them last night, remember? There are twelve of them, let me see. . . ." Hermanjilio began counting off names on his fingers. "One Death, Seven Death, Blood Gatherer, Wing, Packstrap, Demon of Pus, Demon of Jaundice, Bone Scepter, Skull Scepter, Demon of Filth, Demon of Woe, and one more . . . ah yes, Scab Stripper."

"Sounds like the lineup for a heavy-metal festival," said Max.

A horrible thought occurred to him.

"If my parents are in Xibalba, they won't meet these guys, will they?"

"I think not. There are nine levels of Xibalba, each more terrible than the last. Your parents would be on the first level, which is said to be more like a waiting room."

Max pictured his dentist's waiting room in Boston. He imagined his parents sitting on those hard chairs, flicking through old magazines, blocking their ears against the sounds of pain from within, waiting for their names to be called. Then, with a pang, he realized it was him they were waiting for. It was up to him to rescue them. "How do I contact the Death Lords?" he asked.

"I don't know," said Hermanjilio. "It's usually the gods who contact mortals. They talk to us through dreams. The Maya dreamworld runs parallel to the waking world, like two sides of a coin; so a message in a dream is as real to us as a letter in the mail."

"You're a university professor. Surely you don't believe that?"

"Since I've been living at Itzamna, I don't know what I believe. In fact, I had a wild dream myself last night. I think it might have been a message from my ancestors."

Max took a banana and peeled it miserably. He was sick of all this Maya mystical garbage.

"I dreamed I was an astronomer here at Itzamna,"

continued Hermanjilio. "I watched myself enter a secret chamber in the observatory and saw how to gain access in every detail." It sounded like an extremely boring dream to Max, but Hermanjilio was bubbling with anticipation and excitement like a child on Christmas Eve. "This morning, Lola and I are going to put my dream to the test."

"Found them!" called Lola, clanking into the plaza, carrying armfuls of hurricane lanterns. "They're a bit old, Hermanjilio. Couldn't we use flashlights?"

"No," he said firmly. "We're going to do this the old way— by the light of beeswax candles, just as my ancestors would have done."

Lola rolled her eyes. "Did he tell you about his dream?" she asked Max. "Are you coming with us to look for the secret chamber?"

Max shook his head. After the Temple of Chahk, he hoped never to enter another Maya pyramid as long as he lived.

"Wish us luck!" called Hermanjilio as they set off across the plaza. Seconds later, he wheeled around and came back. "By the way, Max, would you keep an eye on that boa up there for me? She's due to give birth anytime, and it's really something to see. Most snakes lay eggs, but boas have live young—as many as fifty or sixty babies, each up to two feet long! Can you imagine?"

Max looked up. A huge mottled brown snake was curled around the branch above his head. "Wait," he said, stuffing a tortilla into his mouth. "I'm coming with you."

By the time he'd found a decent lantern and grabbed a few more tortillas, he had to run to catch up. Hermanjilio's voice drifted back across the plaza, chattering with excitement.

"Who would have thought the observatory held such secrets: a hidden chamber beside the ball court. . . . I remember when we were excavating there—the ground radar said it was solid rock. Ha, and we believed it!"

"It was just a dream, Hermanjilio," said Lola. "Don't get your hopes up."

"I'm telling you, I have a good feeling," he insisted, "like everything's been leading up to this moment. Think about it, Lola. I've been looking for years and found nothing. Then—suddenly—two Jaguar Stones surface, and Landa's journal! This dream is the cheese on the tortilla. You can't tell me it's all coincidence."

"That's what worries me," said Lola. "Who—or what—is behind all this? You said yourself there's something in the air."

"You're not getting cold feet, are you?"

"I'm just saying that we need to be careful. It was pretty heavy at Chahk. I'd just like to know what to expect in there."

"Me, too," panted Max, catching up with them.

"Itzamna was Lord of the Heavens, and Lord of Day and Night," said Hermanjilio. "He's depicted as an old man and, unusually for a Maya god, he was a pacifist—so I wouldn't think there's anything to worry about."

They arrived at a flat, grassy space between two steeply sloping walls. One wall was set against the pyramid; the other had wide terraces built into it like bleachers.

"What's this place?" asked Max.

"It's the ball court," said Lola.

"The Maya played basketball?"

"They played a game called *pitz*. See that stone ring sticking out of the wall? You had to knock the ball through it with your hip, knee, or elbow."

"Doesn't sound that difficult," said Max.

"I'd like to see *you* try," replied Lola. "The ball was as heavy as a solid rubber watermelon."

"Although I've heard they sometimes made it lighter," added Lola, "by wrapping a human skull in strips of rubber."

"Now that's what I call taking sports too seriously!" said Max.

"Ah," said Hermanjilio, "but this was literally a game of life and death. The losing team was sacrificed."

Lola pointed to some carved panels on the side of the pyramid. "Look," she said, "it's in the Maya creation story. They're playing it on the wall here."

"Who are the two dudes in loincloths?" asked Max.

"They're the Hero Twins. They've been summoned to Xibalba by the Death Lords to play the ball game for their lives. Their father has already played and lost."

"Do they win?"

"Yes," said Hermanjilio, "they trick the Death Lords and they rescue their father. He becomes Huun Ixim, the maize god. Maize was revered by the Maya. The upper classes even used to squash their babies' heads between two boards to make them look like corn cobs."

"How did they trick them?" asked Max.

"The babies? I don't think they had much choice."

"No, the Hero Twins. How did they trick the Death Lords?"

But Hermanjilio was peering at the carved panels. "Now, in my dream . . . if I press this glyph here . . . like so . . . the door should open. . . ."

"Nothing's happening," said Max. "We should go back."

"Not so fast," said Hermanjilio. "The stone's getting warmer under my hand. I can feel a vibration. . . ."

There was a grinding sound, and the stone in front of them dropped slowly into the ground, revealing a small, dark tunnel.

"It worked! It worked!" Hermanjilio was almost crying with happiness. He stood back and surveyed the tunnel. "It looks a little tight," he said. "My ancestors were a lot smaller than me. Do you think I'll fit?"

"No way," said Max, shaking his head. "Don't risk it. You'll get stuck."

"I'm sure you'll fit," said Lola, with absolute confidence. "If you fit in your dream, you'll fit now."

"I hope you're right," said Hermanjilio. He took a deep breath. "Okay, let's light the lanterns and see what the chamber of Itzamna has in store for us. I'll lead the way."

Hermanjilio had to get on all fours to crawl into the tunnel. His body filled every inch. Lola went next, and Max brought up the rear. As they made their way slowly down that suffocating passage, cobwebs trailing over their faces, Max wondered what might be waiting for them at the end. Tombs? Skeletons? Evil spirits?

Hermanjilio eased himself out.

Then Lola.

Then it was Max's turn.

He could hardly bear to look. . . .

But he needn't have worried. There was nothing. The tiny room at the end of the tunnel was completely empty.

"Well, that was a waste of time," he said with relief.

"Time?" came a voice behind them. "What dost thou know of time?"

The three of them spun around to see a red lightbulb hovering in the shadows. Wait, it wasn't a lightbulb, it was a nose. A bulbous, glowing red nose.

As the rest of the apparition slowly took shape . . .

. . . the nose took its place . . .

. . . on an ancient, wizened face . . .

. . . with sunken cheeks and toothless jaws . . .

. . . on a head topped with a bejeweled turban . . .

. . . from which stringy gray hair fell to bony shoulders . . .

. . . adorned with a heavy bead necklace . . .

. . . above a hunched and scrawny body . . .

. . . his organs visible beneath paper-thin skin . . .

. . . and wearing nothing . . .

. . . but a voluminous and intricately wrapped loincloth.

At first, Max thought it was Chan Kan playing tricks. But the more he stared at the hideous old man, the more he realized that this guy was older than time itself. He turned to Lola to ask who she thought the guy was, but all that came out of his mouth was a strange bubbling sound.

Luckily Lola understood him. "It's not real," she said. "It's like an old hologram or something."

Even so, she followed Max's lead and edged into the farthest corner.

Hermanjilio was on his knees.

"My Lord Itzamna," he said, bowing his head low.

"Who art thou?" croaked the old man.

"My name is Hermanjilio Bol, my lord."

"What dost thou here?"

"I had a dream. I thought my ancestors had summoned me to this place. I am sorry to have disturbed you. We will leave you in peace."

Hermanjilio stood up and tried to take a step backward. But he could not move. He seemed to be rooted to the spot by an invisible force.

The old man laughed an eternity-of-smoking-cheap-cigars kind of laugh. "Thou wilt go when I say and not before. I must know who thou art."

"I spoke the truth, my lord. My name is Hermanjilio Bol."

"Place thy hand against mine," commanded the old man, holding up his ancient palm.

Hermanjilio turned to Max and Lola for moral support. Sweat was pouring down his face. He looked terrified. They tried to give him encouraging smiles.

He put his hand palm to palm against the old man's hand.

And then he screamed.

Hermanjilio was changing. He was becoming different people. Always men, always Maya, always richly attired. As the different faces and bodies appeared in his place, all that was left of him was his scream.

When it was over, he slumped to the floor.

"What have you done to him?" yelled Lola to the old man.

"How darest thou, a mere female, address the great Itzamna?"

"You don't scare me," said Lola, her voice trembling. "You're just a trick they laid into the walls when this pyramid was built."

"A spirited wench, indeed." Itzamna cackled as Lola swept past him to help Hermanjilio.

"Are you okay?" she asked.

"I don't know," said Hermanjilio weakly. "It was the strangest feeling. . . ."

"I did but show thee thy lineage," boomed the old man. "Arise, Hermanjilio Bol, heir to the great city of Itzamna, direct descendant of the keepers of the royal library and all knowledge since thet world began."

As Hermanjilio staggered to his feet, the old man foraged in the billowing folds of his loincloth. Then, with a flourish, he produced a large bundle. It looked like a football, wrapped up in many layers of rags. He held it out, solemnly, to Hermanjilio.

"This day, Hermanjilio Bol, I entrust to thee the future of thy people. When the time is nigh, thou wilt know what to do. May good prevail, may evil be vanquished, may the sun rise again on the glories of Itzamna."

Hermanjilio took the bundle. He looked dazed.

"Open it," commanded the old man.

Cautiously, Hermanjilio peeled away the rags. And there, glowing in the lantern light with all the greens of the forest, was a Jaguar Stone of mottled jade.

He ran a trembling finger over the creature's head, and it seemed to purr with pleasure. Hermanjilio fell to his knees again to thank the old man. "I never dared hope that one day I would hold the Green Jaguar of Itzamna. My grandfather told me it was lost in the days of the conquest."

"Not lost, merely biding its time. And now, Hermanjilio Bol, go forth into the Star Chamber and accept thy destiny."

A doorway appeared in the inner wall. It was black and filled with stars.

Tears were streaming down Hermanjilio's face. "This is the greatest moment of my life . . . I can't believe it. . . ." He was babbling and laughing at the same time, as if he'd just won an Oscar.

"Go forth, Hermanjilio Bol!" commanded the old man. "Go forth, Ix Sak Lol and Massimo Francis Sylvanus Murphy! May you confound your demons!" He straightened up and pointed toward the doorway.

Max and Lola stared at each other in horror.

"How does he know our names?" mused Lola.

"He's pretty realistic for a hologram," observed Max.

When they looked again, he was gone.

Hermanjilio seemed unfazed by these events. He was cradling the Green Jaguar in his arms like a child with a new kitten. "Shall we go in?" he said, stepping inside.

"No!" said Max.

"Let's just take a quick look," said Lola, pulling Max through the door of stars. There was a grinding noise behind them. A stone descended from the lintel and sealed them in.

Max groaned.

"Sorry," said Lola.

"Lord Itzamna means us no harm," said Hermanjilio. "I'm sure there's another door on the other side."

They raised their lanterns to cast some light across the chamber. The room was so high that the ceiling remained pitch-black. But none of them noticed this fact. None of them noticed anything but the enormous cube—maybe thirty feet square—that commanded the center of the room.

Its base was a slab of shiny black stone. On each corner of this slab stood a huge statue of a warrior, his arms raised to support an identical slab. It looked like a massive ice-cream sandwich, with black stone wafers. But instead of a thick slice of French vanilla, these wafers held a complex assembly—all in polished wood—of interlocking gears, wheels, and cogs.

"What is it?" said Lola.

"I've never seen anything like it," replied Hermanjilio. "Just look at this workmanship—every component is inscribed with glyphs."

"But what does it do?" asked Max. "Can you read the glyphs?"

"No, it would take me years to translate them all," said Hermanjilio, walking around the machine. "But I recognize these statues. They're the Bakabs, the four sons of Itzamna and Ixchel. It's their job to hold up the corners of the world. Lola, come here—have you seen this?"

He looked around for Lola, but she was nowhere to be seen.

"Up here!" she called. "Come up! There are steps at the back."

She was standing on the machine.

The steps took Max and Hermanjilio up to a small platform on the same level.

"Jump across!" called Lola. "Wait till you see what I've found!"

She was kneeling over a low stone table in the center of the slab. Its surface was inlaid with a jade mosaic of a headless leaping jaguar, and on the beast's shoulders was an empty niche. Above this were two rows of square windows. In each window was a carved stone glyph. Like the pictures on a slot machine, these carvings were attached to a roller that must have been linked with cogs in the machinery below.

"I recognize these glyphs," said Lola. "They're from the

Maya calendars." She groaned. "When I think of the hours Chan Kan spent drilling me on this stuff."

"Then I'll let you do the honors," said Hermanjilio with a smile. "Let's see how much you remember."

Lola cracked her knuckles like a concert pianist preparing to play.

"Here goes," she said. "I'm fairly sure that the glyphs on the bottom right are from the Calendar Round. They show a day and a month."

"Correct." Hermanjilio nodded. "And the rest of the bottom row?"

"I'm guessing it's the Long Count, which measures time since the world began. You've got the *kin*, or days; the *winal*, or months; the *tun*, or years; the *katun*, which are units of twenty years; and the *baktun*, which are four hundred years."

"Bravo!" cheered Hermanjilio. "Chan Kan would be proud of you! How about the top row?"

She shook her head.

"Then I'll tell you," said Hermanjilio. "Each chunk of time is ruled by a different god, and these are their name glyphs. There must be hundreds of them."

Max groaned. "I can't stand it. It's too complicated."

"I agree," said Lola. "Except for shamans like Chan Kan,

even the Maya don't keep the Maya calendars anymore."

"So, shall we see what happens when we activate it?" asked Hermanjilio, holding the Green Jaguar over the niche. "I vote yes."

"I vote no," said Max.

They both looked at Lola.

"I'm sorry, Hoop," she said, "but I vote yes. Aren't you even a little curious?"

"Curiosity killed the cat," observed Max primly.

The Green Jaguar purred as Hermanjilio went to slot it in. Suddenly he drew back. "Blood!" he said. "We need blood! I mixed up a batch when I got back from Ixchel, but it's sitting on the shelf in my storeroom."

Lola clapped her hand to her mouth. "I thought it was salsa! I put it in my backpack with some tortillas!"

"Perfect!" said Hermanjilio. "I told you this was meant to be."

Lola pulled a small jar out of her backpack and gave it to him.

"Come on, my little beauty," Hermanjilio coaxed the Green Jaguar as he poured the thick red liquid over the niche. Just like the Red Jaguar at Chahk, the stone leapt into place of its own accord.

Hermanjilio blew out the lanterns, and they were plunged into blackness.

A breeze brushed Max's face, and the air in that dank chamber became as fresh as a morning at the seaside. There was a series of loud clicks. The machine was coming to life. The clicks were joined by whirrs and squeaks. As the noise of the machine increased, the whole cube began to rock gently from side to side. The stone table was glowing now, and they grabbed on to it to steady themselves as the cube began to buck like a mechanical bull. Max was wondering how long they'd be able to hold on, when the machine seemed to find its groove and fell into a smooth vibration.

"Look," exclaimed Lola, "the glyphs are changing!"

Hermanjilio was giddy with delight. The carvings were turning over so fast they were just a blur. Gradually they slowed down until each square came to a stop.

"11-Kawak, that's 11-Thunder!" yelled Lola, clapping like a winner on a game show. She looked at Hermanjilio. "Is that today's date?"

"Beats me." He shrugged.

"Never mind that," said Max. "I think this room is getting bigger."

Lola looked around. "It could be a trick of the light."

"It's no trick," said Hermanjilio. "The walls and floor are receding."

"I don't like the look of this," said Max.

"Me neither," agreed Lola.

"What a couple of wimps!" said Hermanjilio. "You're so lucky to share this incredible experience. This might be the greatest moment of your lives."

Or the last moment, thought Max.

The walls and floor fell away. Far below, tiny sparks of colored light rose in spirals and clustered into luminous spheres, spinning out across the blackness to hang in twinkling constellations. Max, Lola, and Hermanjilio looked up in awe as translucent shapes began to form around the star clusters.

It was beautiful, hypnotic, poetic, amazing, indescribable. . . .

"It looks like a crocodile with two heads," observed Max.

"He's right!" cried Lola. "It's the two-headed cosmic monster!"

"It's incredible," said Hermanjilio. "We're standing in the Maya cosmos."

Max was bewildered. "Will someone tell me what's going on?" he wailed.

"Think of this chamber as an ancient Maya planetarium," Lola explained. "Those lights are the stars and planets."

"But what's with the crocodile?"

"The Cosmic Crocodile represents the Maya heavens; its blood is the rain that falls on Middleworld."

"Why is it always blood with you guys?"

Hermanjilio was trying to point something out, but his voice was muffled by what sounded like a truck hurtling past on the freeway. It got nearer and nearer until a great ball of fire suddenly shot up behind them and made a huge arc over their heads.

Whoooooomph!

There was light and heat and a booming, terrifying noise.

Max shielded his eyes from the glare and peered through his fingers.

It was a jaguar.

A fire jaguar.

A massive, flaming, roaring fire jaguar in midleap.

"What's happening?" shouted Lola. She sounded as scared as Max felt.

Hermanjilio didn't look scared at all. He was shining with happiness. "It's the Sun Jaguar!" he exclaimed. "This is more than the night sky; it's showing the passage of time itself!"

"The date's changed! It's on 12-Ahaw—12-Lord! Hermanjilio, did you touch something?" shouted Lola as the fiery beast disappeared behind the edge of the cube.

"I pressed the day glyph," confessed Hermanjilio, "and it moved one day forward. The jaguar was the sun moving across the heavens. At night it crosses into the underworld."

It was dark again. Max leaned over the edge of the cube. There was something down there. Water. He could see the twinkling stars reflected in its glassy surface far below. "Is this some kind of time machine?" he said.

"I doubt it," said Hermanjilio. "I think it just shows the movements of the stars and the planets. It was probably designed to help the king predict eclipses, plan the best days for rituals, that sort of thing."

"So does the machine represent planet Earth?" asked Max.

"There was no such thing," said Hermanjilio. "The ancient Maya believed in twenty-three interconnected worlds, piled up like a stack of tortillas. Our world, which they called Middleworld, was in between the thirteen layers of the heavens and the nine layers of the underworld, Xibalba. So, to answer your question, I'd guess this machine represents Middleworld."

Max looked down at the black waters below them. "Is that Xibalba? Are my parents down there?"

"Forget it, Max," replied Hermanjilio, reading his mind. "None of this exists. It's just a working model, an illusion."

"But what is Xibalba? Is it a spirit world, a parallel universe, another dimension . . . ?"

"It's all of those and none of them," mused Hermanjilio dreamily.

That was it. The final straw. Max had had enough of meaningless Maya double-talk. He began to hatch his plan. . . .

Whoooooomph!

The flaming jaguar leapt through the sky.

"I moved it forward," said Lola. "It's 13-Imix! 13-Crocodile!"

Whoooooomph!

"1-Ik! 1-Wind!"

Whoooooomph!

"2-Ak'bal! 2-Darkness!"

Whoooooomph!

"3-K'an! 3-Maize!"

Whoooooomph!

"4-Chikchan! 4-Snakebite!"

Whoooooomph!

"5-Kimi! 5-Death!" called Lola, like a demented bingo caller.

She surveyed the conjunctions of the planets with the pride of one who can make the sun rise and fall at her command.

"What's that?" she said, pointing to a bright star that was rising in the daytime sky. Instead of twinkling cheerily, it seemed to bristle like a hedgehog.

"Take cover!" yelled Hermanjilio as the star let loose with a barrage of flaming arrows. Max dropped to the floor and covered his head with his hands. Sizzling arrows fell on the slab all around him.

"It's Venus," explained Hermanjilio, "the morning star! To the Maya, it heralded the outbreak of wars and military action. They used to schedule their battles by its cycles."

"Why's it firing at us?" asked Lola.

"Move the day forward and maybe it will stop," suggested Hermanjilio.

Lola pressed the glyph. The Jaguar Sun dove into the sea. Venus shone even more brightly. More flaming arrows hailed down. Max and Hermanjilio took cover with Lola behind the stone control panel.

As they huddled there, a disgusting odor filled the air.

Lola looked accusingly at Max.

"It wasn't me," he said. They both looked accusingly at Hermanjilio.

The smell—an eye-wateringly pungent cocktail of gas, bad breath, and cigar smoke—got worse and worse until it was too strong to be of human origin.

Whoooooomph! Whoooooomph! Whoooooomph!

"Slow down!" Hermanjilio instructed Lola.

"I didn't touch it. The dates are going crazy. . . ."

While the days flashed by and Hermanjilio and Lola huddled over the machine, Max plucked up the courage to put his plan into action.

Dodging arrows, he crawled to the back corner of the platform and quickly slipped over the edge. His searching feet found the shoulders of a Bakab statue, and his hands grabbed its head. He worked his way clumsily down the torso and legs, being careful to avoid the wheels and gears that were spinning at high speed just inches away.

When he landed on the black slab base, he crouched down and looked into the water. It was as flat as a mirror. All he saw was his own reflection, with the erupting universe behind him. He leaned over to touch the surface. It didn't feel like water. It felt like extra-tough Jell-O, a great rubbery mass of seething evil.

This was wrong.

His parents were not here.

He shouldn't have done this.

He had just grasped a Bakab to start climbing back up, when a flaming arrow shot straight into his hand.

He let go.

He was falling.

He was plummeting like a stone into the blackness of Xibalba.

He landed flat on his face.

He managed to turn over so that he could breathe, but he couldn't break free of the gelatinous surface. He was dissolving into it. The evil black Jell-O was sucking out his soul.

He lay there helplessly as the cosmic fireworks went into overdrive all around him. Days and nights flashed by. Fireballs crashed and comets blazed, their fiery tails scorching everything in their paths. Stars collided in showers of burning sparks. A few feet above him, he could make out the machine. It was juddering wildly. Its wheels were roaring and screaming in pain. Gears were spinning out of it, end to end, into infinity. A terrible meltdown was in progress, and it was all his fault. He'd disobeyed the rules. He'd tried to breach the fabric of the universe. And now his life was draining out of him.

Through the smoke and explosions, he saw Hermanjilio's face above him. "Fight it, Max!" he was shouting. He was hanging off the machine, leaning out as far as he could, every muscle straining to reach out.

Slowly, painfully, fighting the Jell-O, Max turned over and inched toward Hermanjilio's outstretched hand.

He was close, so close, when five bony fingers closed around his ankle. He was thrashing and kicking, but he couldn't break free. Something was pulling him down, trying to climb over him, to use him as a bridge between worlds. He felt heavy and drowsy and cold inside, as if mercury had been injected into his veins. His legs were going numb. He was so cold. So cold . . .

He felt Hermanjilio's big warm hand close over his frozen fingers.

Now Max was the rope in a tug-of-war.

"Out! Out! Take the stone out!" someone was shouting, but the voice was distorted and the words made no sense.

If only Hermanjilio would release him and let him sink peacefully down to Xibalba. Maybe he'd see his parents. Maybe he wouldn't. It didn't really matter. Nothing mattered anymore.

With a bang that shook the universe, the wheels and gears of the machine came to a screeching, cracking, shuddering halt.

Everything went black.

The grip on Max's ankle relaxed, and his will to live came flooding back. He could feel the life rushing back into his veins. His legs were tingling as they warmed up.

He squeezed Hermanjilio's hand in the darkness.

Grunting with effort, Hermanjilio hauled him onto the bottom slab. "That was close," he said, half holding him up and half hugging him.

All Max could say was, "Sorry."

A faint light appeared above them. Lola was holding a lantern over the top edge. "Hermanjilio?" she called. She sounded like she was crying.

"I've got him," Hermanjilio called back. "Send down a rope!"

"I thought we'd lost you, Hoop," said Lola when they got to the top.

"Me, too," he replied.

They lit the rest of the lanterns and sat there, shell-shocked, just looking at each other. There were no stars, no planets, no Sun Jaguar. They were suspended in blackness, drifting in eternity, with that awful smell still hanging in the air.

Max was waiting for the other two to start shouting at him.

"I'm sorry," he kept saying, "it was all my fault. The machine went crazy because I fell off—"

"No, it was my fault," Hermanjilio cut in. "I brought you here."

"You saved my life," said Max.

Hermanjilio shook his head modestly. "It was Lola who saved us both. She pulled out the Jaguar Stone."

"But I didn't," said Lola. "It stopped on its own."

"What?" Hermanjilio scrambled to his feet. "Why would it do that?" He lit a match and checked the glyphs. "It says 4-Ahaw, in the month of 3-Kankin."

"4-Lord, 3-Winter Sun," translated Lola. "Do you think it's significant?"

"I don't know." Hermanjilio borrowed a pen and paper from Lola and noted down the dates. "I'll look them up when we get back." He tried to sound calm. "By the way, does anyone have any ideas about how we might do that?"

They began to make suggestions, all of them bad.

Each time one of them drew breath to speak, the other two looked up hopefully, only to have their hopes dashed almost immediately. Most ideas were nixed by their creators before they were even formed.

"What if . . . ? No, that won't work. . . ."

"Perhaps we could . . . Nah, forget it."

"I'm sorry, I'm sorry, I'm sorry," Max said, over and over.

But sorry wasn't going to save them.

He thought about what Eusebio had said in the rainforest. Something about using your special skills to help each other. Problem was, he didn't have any special skills. He was an idiot in an alien world and he didn't understand anything about anything.

"Think, Hoop!" said Lola, sounding desperate. "You got us out of Chahk by thinking like a gamer. If this was a game, what would you do?"

"When a video game crashes, you restart."

"It's worth a try," said Hermanjilio.

He pulled the Green Jaguar out of the slot—it came away easily—and poured on the last of the blood mixture.

"Fingers crossed," he said as he slotted it back in.

Was that a faint breeze?

Slowly, very slowly, the machine shuddered into life. The day glyphs spun back to 11-Kawak, and the Cosmic Crocodile stretched out across the sky.

"Now quit," Max instructed him.

With difficulty Hermanjilio pulled out the Jaguar Stone. It bit him, but he did not let go. The machine stopped, and this time the walls, ceiling, and floor of the chamber came shooting back. The platform and steps reappeared. Then, most beautiful sight, the stone blocking the tunnel rose smoothly up.

"Let's go," said Lola. She sounded exhausted.

As Max followed the other two out of the Star Chamber, he paused and looked back. What had happened in there? Who or what had gripped his foot?

He shuddered and crawled into the tunnel back to the outside world.

He didn't know that the glassy surface of Xibalba had been a two-way mirror, nor that another face had been looking back at him. He'd didn't know he'd been eye to eye with someone he would have recognized, someone who needed a mortal body to return to Middleworld, someone who'd grabbed his ankle and would soon have possessed the whole of him with his evil being.

But if Max had caught a glimpse of his opponent, he would have remembered the two great stone heads in Villa Isabella. He would have recalled the story of Lord 6-Dog's jealous brother who opened a doorway to the underworld and unleashed an army of undead warriors.

He would have recognized the face of Tzelek.

Chapter Seventeen
TRICK OR TREAT

After his ordeal in the Star Chamber, Max wanted to be alone. All afternoon, he lay in his hammock, trying to process what had happened. He couldn't stop the images flooding into his brain. He cowered again from the hologram of the wizened old man, heard the booming of the Sun Jaguar, dodged the burning arrows, and—the image he would most like to erase—fell headlong toward Xibalba.

He shuddered at the memory.

The Temple of Chahk had been physically challenging, like an ancient obstacle course, but the Star Chamber had challenged his very being. His brain told him none of it was possible, but his eyes knew what they had seen. Somehow, the Green Jaguar had opened the door to another dimension where the laws of physics did not apply. It had taken the hunt for his parents to another level. Now there were no rules. Now he understood, for the first time, why people said that anything was possible in the jungle.

But was it real? Or just a theater of tricks and illusions?

His blood ran cold as he remembered the hand pulling

him down as he fought to escape the clutches of Xibalba. He inspected his ankle. It was swollen and bruised. You could clearly see where five sharp fingernails had punctured his skin. That was real, all right.

He climbed down the tree-house ladder and went to look for Lola. She was sitting at the table, chopping a melon.

"Hey, Hoop. Feeling better?"

"Not really," said Max. He looked around. "Have you seen Hermanjilio? I want to thank him again for saving me. He was like Superman in that chamber."

"He's trying to charge up his laptop so he can research all those dates. He's convinced they mean something."

"Hermanjilio has a laptop? He has electricity?"

"I told you he's a genius," said Lola proudly. "He rigged up a generator by the waterfall. It's a bit temperamental, but it does the job. He hasn't used it for ages, so he's trying to get it going again."

A disheveled Hermanjilio came running through the plaza, leaving a trail of dropped tools and wires and bits of pipe. "Can't stop," he shouted as he passed. "I've got to fire up the laptop while the generator's working!"

Later, they took him some food and found him hunched over his laptop, studying a Maya calendar program. Books and papers were strewn around, and he was furiously scribbling notes.

"How's it going?" asked Lola.

When Hermanjilio looked up, he hardly seemed to recognize them. His eyes were big and wild, and his long black hair was sticking out at odd angles. He looked like a mad scientist. "I've been trying to make sense of those dates in the Star Chamber," he said.

"I'm sure they don't mean anything," said Lola. "That machine was so old, I'd be amazed if it still worked properly."

"Then prepare to be amazed." Hermanjilio took a deep breath. "Do you recall the first date it showed when we activated it?"

Lola thought for a moment. "11-Thunder?"

Hermanjilio nodded. "According to my calculations, that's today in the Maya calendar."

Max whistled to show his astonishment.

"There's more," said Hermanjilio. "Remember how we moved through the days until we got to 5-Death and Venus attacked us? Well, 5-Death is in seven days' time—at which point, Venus is set to rise as the morning star!"

"That's incredible," marveled Lola. "This discovery could bring in all the funding you need to finish the excavations."

Hermanjilio coughed in an embarrassed sort of way. "Based on these calendar calculations, I'm not sure there's enough time for that. . . ."

Lola looked baffled for a moment. Then the penny dropped. "Not you as well?" she exclaimed. "You're talking about the so-called end of the Maya calendar, aren't you? You're like those hippies at the Internet café in Limón. They say there's no point in getting jobs because we're in the last months of the thirteenth *baktun* and the world is going to end. But it's garbage. I've heard you say so yourself; it has no basis in fact whatsoever."

"Just hear me out," said Hermanjilio. "Remember when the machine hurtled through the days until it stopped and everything went black?"

"Of course," said Lola.

"And do you remember the date?"

"4-Ahaw 3-Kankin," replied Lola straightaway. "The day of 4-Lord in the month of 3-Winter Sun."

"Just so," said Hermanjilio. "It's the last day of the thirteenth *baktun*."

"I don't care!" Lola was sounding angry now. "This end-of-the-world stuff is just New Age hype, and you know it. When the thirteenth *baktun* ends, the fourteenth *baktun* begins. End of story."

Max opened his mouth to say something, but Lola testily cut him off. "Spare me your spaceship theory, Hoop."

"I was going to say," protested Max, "that Chan Kan mentioned the end of the world to me."

"He did?" Lola narrowed her eyes. "What did he say?"

Max thought back to his encounter in the smoky hut. "He said that for good or for evil, the world must end to begin again. And something about destruction and dread omens."

Lola waved dismissively. "He always talks that way."

"For good or for evil, eh?" murmured Hermanjilio. "That's interesting." He typed something into the computer. "The gods take it in turns to rule the *baktuns*. It says here that Ah Pukuh is next in line."

Awe pooh-coo. It sounded like a cross between spitting and sneezing.

"Ah Pukuh!" said Lola in horror.

"Ah Pukuh?" echoed Max weakly.

"He's the god of violent and unnatural death," explained Hermanjilio. "The Death Lords work for him. He rules the ninth level of Xibalba and he's usually depicted as a bloated corpse, surrounded by dogs and owls. They say he stinks to high heaven. His nickname is Kisin, meaning 'the flatulent one.'"

Lola wrinkled her nose. "Do you remember that foul smell in the Star Chamber?"

"I can't believe you thought it was me," said Max, pretending to be outraged.

"It's not funny," said Hermanjilio, shutting his laptop decisively. "If Ah Pukuh is allowed to take charge, it really could be the end of the world as we know it."

"But it's the ancient Maya world," said Max. "It can't affect us."

"It was the ancient Maya world in the Star Chamber this morning, yet I distinctly saw a bony hand on your twenty-first-century leg," said Hermanjilio.

Max got quiet and rubbed his ankle.

"I need to think," said Lola. "Who wants hot chocolate?"

They drank it under the jungle stars. It was real hot chocolate, too, made from ground cocoa beans mixed with water, cornmeal, and chili pepper. Max sipped it tentatively. The bitter, rich, spicy drink tasted nothing like the chocolate milk they drank in Boston.

"What a day," sighed Hermanjilio, lying back. "How about that Cosmic Crocodile?"

Max tried to trace the outline of the two-headed cosmic monster in the night sky. No matter how weird the Maya concept of the solar system, it was awesome to be gazing at the same stars they'd plotted on their charts a thousand years ago.

Hermanjilio guessed what he was thinking. "Shall I tell

you what the Maya saw on a night like this?" he said. "Right above us are the constellations of Turtle, Rattlesnake, and Owl. Over there, where you see the Big Dipper, we see a bird called Seven Macaw. And your Milky Way is our World Tree, with its roots in the underworld, its trunk on the earth, and its branches in the heavens. In legends, it's sometimes called the Road to Xibalba."

"I think I have to go there," said Max, "to find my parents."

"To Xibalba?" Lola shivered and threw another log on the fire. "Rather you than me," she said.

"I've been thinking," said Hermanjilio. "Mortals are usually summoned to Xibalba by the messenger, Lord Muan. But Frank and Carla weren't summoned, so I'm sure they'll be released soon. It's all a mistake. We just have to be patient."

"Do you know anyone who's come back from Xibalba?" asked Max.

"The Hero Twins?" suggested Lola.

"But that's a legend, right?"

"It's an allegory," explained Hermanjilio. "The Hero Twins represent the sun and moon."

Max sighed. "There's a thin line, isn't there, between real and not real? Since I came to San Xavier, I don't know what to believe anymore."

"Welcome to my world," said Lola.

"But it always comes back to the Jaguar Stones," persisted Max. "Truth and legend, past and present, this world and Xibalba . . . the link is always the Jaguar Stones."

Hermanjilio leaned on one elbow. "If you want to understand the Jaguar Stones, you must understand the Maya worldview. We believe that all things—plants, animals, stones—

have a life force. Our temples are reservoirs for all this natural energy. But it was the great king Lord 6-Dog who worked out how to channel it for the greater good."

Max nodded in recognition at the name. "What did he do?"

"He united the five warring city-states of the Monkey River by giving them each a Jaguar Stone and dividing ceremonial powers between them, almost like government departments." He drew a map in the dirt with a twig. "Ixchel in the north was responsible for culture, Itzamna at the center managed education, Chahk to the east ran agriculture, K'Awiil in the south oversaw lineage, and Ah Pukuh in the west was in charge of military affairs. It was a great success. With the Jaguar Stones to help them, the allied cities built one of the most advanced societies of the ancient world."

"Who made the Jaguar Stones?"

"We think they were Olmec in origin. The Olmecs preceded the Maya and were famous for sculpture. They passed the Jaguar Stones down to the lords of Itzamna, who used them to wage war on their neighbors and subjugate their enemies. Lord 6-Dog's genius was to understand that a lasting peace would bring greater prosperity. He ruled for fifty years and was adored by everyone except his twin brother, Tzelek. When later kings were too lazy or greedy to continue Lord 6-Dog's work, the people lost faith in them. They decided to hide the Jaguar Stones until better times—and worthier rulers—came along. But what actually came along was Friar Diego de Landa." Hermanjilio spat into the dirt. "And the rest is history."

"Until now," said Max. He watched the dancing flames

in the fire and tried not to panic. "Do you still have Dad's old journal?"

"Strange you should ask," said Hermanjilio. "When I went back to my tent after the raid at Ixchel, the journal was the only thing missing."

"Antonio de Landa has it?"

"I assume so. But without a Jaguar Stone, it's not much use to him."

Max winced. "He has the Black Jaguar."

Hermanjilio and Lola sat bolt upright, eyes wide, mouths open in horror.

"How is that possible? Where did he get it?"

"I don't know," said Max. "But I saw him showing it to Uncle Ted."

"Legend has it that the Black Jaguar was destroyed by Lord 6-Dog in his final battle with Tzelek."

"I saw it with my own eyes. I smelled it. It was the real thing."

"I believe you, Max," said Hermanjilio gravely. "It certainly explains why Landa sent raiders to Ixchel. He needed the journal to tell him how to use the Black Jaguar." He gazed into the middle distance, as if he were already watching the terrible events that would soon unfold. "This is what Lord Itzamna was warning us about. From the journal, Landa will know that the Black Jaguar's greatest power is at the rising of Venus in seven days' time. If he uses it to awaken the Undead Army, he will be invincible. Landa will bring Middleworld to its knees, and Ah Pukuh will deal the deathblow."

Lola sighed. "It looks like the hippies were right, after all. The end of the world *is* coming. What can we do?"

Hermanjilio put his head in his hands and repeated her question to himself, over and over. Then he looked up, his eyes shining. "There's only one thing we can do. We must use the Green Jaguar to summon Ahaw Wak Ok, the immortal Lord 6-Dog. There's an old altar on top of the main pyramid that was probably used for just such a ritual. We must bring him back to fight for us. Only he has the power to defeat the Black Jaguar."

"This is madness, Hermanjilio!" cried Lola. "It's too dangerous. You must talk to Chan Kan. There must be another way. . . ."

But Hermanjilio had made up his mind. "This is why my ancestors sent me the dream. This is why Lord Itzamna entrusted the Green Jaguar to me. Don't you understand, Lola? If good men do nothing, evil will win. I must start clearing the altar in readiness for the ritual."

When he stood up, he seemed like a different person. Gone was the eccentric archaeologist. In his place, tall and proud, face ablaze with emotion, muscles gleaming in the firelight, stood a noble Maya warrior. He looked magnificent. "I have found my destiny," he said.

And then he was gone.

Max and Lola looked at each other.

Somewhere in the forest, a jaguar roared.

Max had a feeling that something important, something life-changing, something earthshaking had just happened.

But what?

How had he arrived at this moment?

He tried to remember the city kid who'd stepped off the plane in San Xavier. He'd survived the grueling bus ride over the mountains, only to be plunged into Uncle Ted's shady world of smugglers, shipwrecks, and psychotic Spaniards. What if he'd never followed the Monkey Girl . . . never rafted the underground river . . . never escaped from the Temple of Chahk . . . never entered the Star Chamber . . . never heard Hermanjilio say that his parents were trapped in Xibalba, the Maya underworld? Then again, how sane was Hermanjilio? He seemed to think he could save the world by bringing back some dead Maya king. That couldn't be good news.

It was Lola who spoke first. "I don't like the sound of this," she sighed. "Maybe we can talk him out of it in the morning."

Morning came sooner than they expected. It was well before sunrise when Thunderclaw began to crow—if you could call it crowing. Thunderclaw's idea of a wake-up call was less a *cock-a-doodle-doo* and more a series of hideous shrieks and cackles that belonged in the sound track of a Japanese horror film.

After ignoring the cacophony for as long he could, Max stumbled out of bed. He met a bleary-eyed Lola making her way down the tree-house ladder.

"Thunderclaw seems to have settled in," she said.

"Yeah," said Max, "let's hope it's fried chicken for dinner."

"Surely you couldn't eat Thunderclaw?" said Lola, who'd grown inexplicably fond of the mangy little fowl. "Not now that we've got to know him?"

"Just watch me," said Max in an evil voice, before running into the plaza, calling: "Here I come, chicky-chicken, with my eleven herbs and spices. . . ."

Lola ran after him, laughing wildly, and plowed straight

into him when he stopped dead a few steps later.

"What's happened here?" he said.

"Looks like we've been raided," she whispered.

In the early light, the camp had an eerie, deserted air. Upended boxes, crates, and files were strewn everywhere, their contents scattered on the ground. There was no sign of Hermanjilio.

"Why didn't we hear anything?" said Lola, surveying the mess.

"Blame that demented chicken of yours," said Max.

There was a rustling of branches above them. They looked up to see Chulo and Seri whimpering and clinging to each other. Lola held out her arms to them, but they stayed where they were.

"Something's frightened them," said Lola.

"Where's Hermanjilio?" asked Max, looking nervously around for a corpse.

"Maybe they've kidnapped him."

"But why?"

Their eyes met, and they said in chorus, "The Jaguar Stones!"

"If Landa's taken the red and the green stones as well, we're in big trouble," said Lola anxiously. "In fact, the whole world's in big trouble."

"Do you know where Hermanjilio was hiding the stones?" asked Max.

"No," said Lola, close to tears. "I just hope he's all right."

"Who?" said a booming voice from behind them.

Their first instinct was to scream and run. Apart from his eyes, which were encircled in heavy black, the creature's entire body was painted bright red. He wore a red loincloth, and his hair was twisted in an extravagant topknot, decorated with strips of tree bark and parrot feathers.

"Hermanjilio!" exclaimed Lola. "You scared us!"

Max took in Hermanjilio's costume. "Is it Halloween today?"

"It is like Halloween," said Hermanjilio, "in that the forces of evil are about to run wild among us. But I doubt you'll be getting any candy."

"Very funny," said Lola. "Are you planning to get dressed for breakfast?"

"I am dressed," said Hermanjilio. "This is what my ancestors would have worn for the ritual. I researched ancient Maya spirit transmutation at college, but I never thought I'd have a chance to put it into action. We'll need to create some powerful magic tomorrow night, and it's important to get the details right."

"I don't like it," said Lola. "You're going too far."

"Look at it this way," said Hermanjilio, fixing his topknot. "If I'm wrong, this is just a fascinating experiment in living history. But if I'm right, my paint and feathers might help us bring back Lord 6-Dog. He's the only one who knows how to fight the evil of the Black Jaguar, the only one who can save his people from a living hell ruled by Ah Pukuh and his Undead Army."

Lola pursed her lips. She didn't look convinced. She gestured at the papers scattered on the ground. "Did you make this mess? I thought we'd been raided."

"I'm sorry," said Hermanjilio. "I've been digging out my college notes and looking through my father's old boxes. It's all a bit of a rush. The ancestors would have taken weeks to prepare for something like this. Would you two tidy up for me? I need to fast and meditate to achieve mental purity."

"Sounds like he's going to take a nap," whispered Max.

Hermanjilio winked at him. "I do need to conserve my energy"—he adopted a Shakespearean tone—"for when the Sun Jaguar returns to the underworld, I must arise and gather the creatures of the night: the silent killer who ensnares, the many-footed stalker, and the sacred flying light."

Max and Lola stared at him blankly.

"At sunset, I'm going into the forest to collect bugs," he explained.

"Why?" they asked.

"You'll see. But while I'm away, you need to get yourselves ready."

"Forget it," said Lola. "I'm not wearing body paint."

"That's only for the high priest," retorted Hermanjilio. "You're my acolytes."

"And what do they wear?" asked Lola suspiciously.

"Tunics."

"I'm not wearing a tunic," said Max.

Hermanjilio sighed heavily. "What you fail to understand is that, unless we stop Landa, you may never see your parents again. If evil is allowed to get the upper hand, they will be trapped in Xibalba."

"Tunics it is," said Max.

"Good. Now listen carefully: collect twelve red pods from the achiote bush and six long strips of bark from the *balché* tree. Then crush the achiote seeds and soak them in water to make a red dye. While they're soaking, look in my office for a bolt of raw cotton. Then sew tunics, one for each of you, and dye them red. Dye two bark strips to make red headbands and soak the rest of the bark in elixir overnight. Ideally we'd brew *balché* liquor in a sacramental canoe, but time is not on our side." Hermanjilio wiped his forehead with the back of his hand, like a harassed hostess preparing for a dinner party.

"You're smudging your paint," said Lola.

Hermanjilio pointed to the edge of the forest. "Hurry," he said. "The achiote bush is that way."

Then he turned on his heel, and they watched his tall red frame loping across the clearing toward the main pyramid.

"Do you think he's gone mad?" asked Max.

"I don't know," said Lola. "But in case he's right about the demon army, I think we should do as he says." She cupped her hands to her mouth and roared like a dinosaur to call the monkeys.

"Am I the only one who isn't crazy?" muttered Max.

"I heard that!" she said.

Next morning, having been woken once again by Thunder-claw's maniacal crowing, Max and Lola inspected their handiwork: two reddish tunics, two red headbands, and a bottle of pungent-smelling *balché* liquor.

"That dye's strong stuff," said Max, surveying his crimson-stained forearms and hands.

"I'm glad I didn't get any on me," said Lola, squeaky clean as usual. "I wonder what color Hermanjilio will be today?"

When Hermanjilio arrived, the first thing they noticed was that he was still red, albeit a little streaky. The second thing they noticed was that he held a plastic bag filled to bursting with a crawling mass of bugs.

Of the ones Max recognized, there were centipedes, ants, beetles, slugs, cockroaches, worms, maggots, and spiders of every size and color.

"Come help me thread them onto skewers," Hermanjilio urged him. He made it sound like an honor.

"I'll be right there," lied Max. "Let me wash this dye off my hands. I wouldn't want to contaminate anything."

While Max pretended to scrub, Hermanjilio grilled the bugs over the fire and ground their charred bodies into a black powder. He was in exceptionally high spirits. He even took the daily downpour as a sign that Lord Chahk was purifying the pyramid for the rituals.

"But Hermanjilio," Max pointed out, "it rains every single day."

"There is rain, and there is *rain*," said Hermanjilio. When Max raised an eyebrow, he added, "As we Maya say," and went off with a shake of his ponytail to give thanks to Lord Chahk.

Despite his skepticism, Max felt excited, as if they were getting ready for a party. But what were they getting ready for? He couldn't imagine what the night held in store.

Just before midnight, Hermanjilio appeared in the clearing wearing the pelt of a huge jaguar over his loincloth. The pelt was a little moth-eaten and had obviously been handed down through generations, but it was no less fearsome for that. The creature's snarling head rested on Hermanjilio's head, and the rest of the pelt flowed over his shoulders like a cloak. He had applied more thick red body paint, and he

They began the dizzying climb to the top of the pyramid.

wore a flamboyant creation of feathers and jade beads around his neck.

As Hermanjilio checked over his basket of ritual paraphernalia, Max and Lola put their tunics on over their jeans and fixed each other's headbands.

"Here," said Hermanjilio, passing Lola a small drum to sling over her shoulder.

"I can drum," Max volunteered.

"You take this," said Hermanjilio, ignoring Max's percussive talents and handing him the cage with Thunderclaw.

With a jungle moon shining down and the night birds shrieking and wailing like ghosts, they began the dizzying climb to the top of the pyramid. Chulo and Seri tried to follow, but Lola kept shooing them back. Eventually, Hermanjilio tired of the commotion and signaled her to let the monkeys come.

That was all they needed, thought Max. Now they really looked like a traveling circus. Hermanjilio in his red paint and jaguar pelt, Lola with her drum and her monkeys, himself with a chicken in a cage. What a bunch of clowns.

Eventually the motley procession reached the top platform.

It was completely bare apart from a large stone bowl, which rested on a thick stone column. Around the column was carved a strange creature that was coiled like a snake but feathered like a bird. The creature's wide mouth gaped open, revealing two sharp fangs. Max couldn't help thinking that Chulo would fit beautifully between its huge stone jaws.

"Is that a snake or a bird?" he whispered to Lola.

"It's K'uk'ulkan, the feathered serpent."

Hermanjilio built a small fire in the bowl and stuck candles on the body of the snake to form a ring of light around the pillar.

"Here we go," he said, raising his arms. "Fingers crossed."

"Do you know what you're doing?" asked Max.

"Relax," said Hermanjilio. "I have a good feeling about this."

"I have a bad feeling," said Lola. "Summoning the spirits could be very dangerous. I think we should stop right now."

"It'll be fine," Hermanjilio reassured her. "I studied this ritual in college, remember? Of course, we don't know the actual words the ancestors would have spoken, but we're fairly sure they used ground-up bugs, copal incense, and human sacrifice."

"Human sacrifice?" repeated Max weakly.

"Hermanjilio," said Lola, "you weren't planning on doing any sacrifices tonight, were you?"

"Of course," said Hermanjilio.

Chapter Eighteen

THE CHICKEN OF DEATH

Run for it!" screamed Max, jumping up and pulling Lola with him. Hermanjilio caught them both by the arms and held them in an iron grip.

"Are you mad?" he said.

"Are *we* mad?" said Max. "You're the one who's planning to sacrifice us."

Hermanjilio rolled his eyes in exasperation. "Of course I'm not planning to sacrifice you. That's why we brought the chicken."

"Not Thunderclaw—?" began Lola.

"It is his destiny. This is why Chan Kan sent him. Besides, it is considered a great honor to be chosen for sacrifice," Hermanjilio assured her. A tear rolled down her face. "Thunderclaw is a warrior, Lola. He wouldn't want to end up as chicken stew."

She nodded mutely.

"Will the gods accept a chicken?" asked Max.

"Unless you would like to volunteer . . ."

He shook his head.

"Then a chicken will have to do. Remember, Thunderclaw is no ordinary fowl. Chan Kan said he was a great champion, a fearsome fighting cock."

They regarded the wretched little creature, huddled in a corner and trembling in his sleep. "He doesn't look very fearsome right now," said Max.

"Give me a break," sighed Hermanjilio. "As I understand it, there isn't a precise science to these rituals. They're more about showing swagger and confidence. The Maya gods are like children. They like costumes, special effects, and plenty of action. We just have to put on a good show."

"You're bluffing it?" said Max incredulously.

"In a manner of speaking. And now, if there are no further questions, please sit down. I'd like to get started."

Hermanjilio opened several little packages of incense wrapped in banana leaves and threw them into the fire. The flames flared up and cast an orange glow on his face. Pungent smoke billowed out. He began swaying back and forth, chanting in Mayan. Then he took a handful of the black powder made from ground-up bugs and threw it into the flames. It sent crackling sparks flying in all directions.

More incense.

More smoke.

More black powder.

The smoke was now so thick that Max found it hard to breathe. Through the black clouds, he could see Hermanjilio pouring his blood concoction into the stone snake's mouth before he slotted the Green Jaguar between its gaping jaws.

At Hermanjilio's signal, Lola tapped the drum in the rhythm of a heartbeat.

Tum-tum, tum-tum, tum-tum.

It carried over the jungle and echoed back again. It reverberated through Max's body, and his own heart followed the rhythm.

Tum-tum, tum-tum, tum-tum.

Hermanjilio poured *balché* liquor over the fire. Blue and green flames flickered and hissed like snakes' tongues.

Sitting down between Max and Lola, he pulled out a ceramic flute and played a simple melody, the same four notes over and over. It was a hypnotic sound that seemed to work on the brain like a drug. The heartbeat of the drum and the song of the flute played faster and faster, over and over.

Soon Max felt a crackling energy around him, as if the night air had become electrically charged. The Green Jaguar started to glow. As it grew brighter and brighter, the snake began glowing, too, beginning with the head and spreading down the back, feather by feather, coil by coil, until the whole serpent radiated a green light.

It moved.

A coil uncoiled.

Max rubbed his eyes.

It moved again.

"Stay completely still," muttered Hermanjilio. "Don't move a hair."

As Max watched in terror, the stone snake unwound itself from the column and slithered around the top of the platform, passing inches from where they sat. It formed its massive body into a circle, nose to tail, and shafts of light rose up, until the body of the snake enclosed a thick column of green light.

Within the column, wraithlike images of Maya people emerged, appearing faster and faster, until the whole column writhed with ghostly figures.

Hermanjilio cleared his throat.

"It's now or never," he said, standing up and facing the column of ghosts. From where he sat, Max could see the archaeologist's knees shaking.

"Spirits of my ancestors, we are in desperate need," boomed Hermanjilio in his most commanding voice. "We beseech you to help us. Send us your greatest warlords. Send us the spirits of the mighty Lord 6-Dog and his fearless battle chief, the noble Lord Kukab!"

As Hermanjilio called out these names, the column of light grew brighter still. Waves of green flames flowed out of it, one after another, across the platform and down the sides of the pyramid. The next wave of flame was headed straight for Max and Lola. They looked at Hermanjilio in terror, but he just winked happily as if everything was normal and they were having a lovely time. Chulo and Seri inched closer to Lola and put their hands over their eyes.

Max held his breath as the green flames licked his legs. They were icy cold. When they touched him, he could remember things he had never experienced. Disconnected images of ancient Maya life—a ball game, a ceremony, a market, a harvest, a jaguar at a water hole—strange smells of spices and fire and jungle, the sounds of battles and birds and women weaving flooded into his brain. It was as if each flame contained the soul and the memories of a long-dead Maya.

There was a deep, rolling rumble like distant thunder, and two ghostly figures stepped out of the column. As soon as they did so, the light disappeared and the snake rewound itself around the stone column.

One of the figures strode forward, resplendent in an elaborate plumed headdress. He was covered from head to foot in black body paint, and he held before him an obsidian sword, ready to strike. While the second figure hovered behind, the great warrior peered down at the trembling spectators.

"Who summons Ahaw Wak Ok, the mighty Lord 6-Dog, and his fearless battle chief, Lord Kukab, to walk again in Middleworld?" he boomed.

Mustering all his courage, Hermanjilio stood up and bowed.

"It is I, Hermanjilio Bol, descendant of the lords of Itzamna."

"I will hear thy petition, mortal," said Lord 6-Dog.

The other figure, who'd been hanging back, now stepped forward and pointed a gnarled finger at Hermanjilio. "Where are the human sacrifices? Do you dishonor us with no suitable offering?"

Hermanjilio's jaw dropped open. The second warrior looked and sounded like an old woman, a cross-eyed old woman with four long gray braids.

Lord 6-Dog turned to stare in amazement at his fellow time traveler.

"Mother?" he said.

The old woman nudged him with her wrinkled elbow. "Don't just stand there; introduce me."

With reluctance, the king announced her to the astonished audience. "May I present my mother, Lady Kan Kakaw, First and Most Glorious Wife of the venerable Lord Punak Ha, King of the Monkey River?"

Following Hermanjilio's lead, Max and Lola bowed their heads.

"Welcome back to Middleworld, Your Divine Majesties," said Hermanjilio.

The old woman was still looking around with dissatisfaction. "Where are the bodies, the blood, the severed limbs?"

Hermanjilio took a deep breath.

"Your Divine Majesties," he began, "we would not insult you with a mere human sacrifice. To mark this most illustrious day in the history of Middleworld, we have brought a far greater tribute in the noble body of Thunderclaw, the merciless Fowl of Fear, the notorious Chicken of Death."

Max shot Lola a look of total incredulity. "Fowl of Fear?" he mouthed.

"Chicken of Death?" she mouthed back.

Hermanjilio opened the bamboo cage to reveal the scrawny, balding Thunderclaw, who was still in a dead sleep. "You are familiar with K'uk'ulkan, the serpent with feathers in place of scales?"

Lord 6-Dog and his mother nodded.

"Now meet his nemesis, the bird with scales in place of feathers. The Chicken of Death is a ferocious warrior who tortures humankind with his terrible shrieks. He struts through Xibalba with claws like razors, and the gods themselves tremble with fear."

He shut the cage door, as if to contain a mighty army.

Lord 6-Dog raised an eyebrow. "I believe I have read of this Chee Ken in the Codex of Tikal." He looked into the cage. "Is it true that with one slash of his talons he can rip off thine arm?"

"As you say, Your Majesty," said Hermanjilio solemnly.

"And with one peck of his beak, he can gouge out thine eyes?"

Hermanjilio nodded his assent.

"And with one shriek, he can banish thy soul to the ninth level of Xibalba?"

Hermanjilio nodded again.

Lord 6-Dog looked impressed. He whispered something to his mother, who peered at the bird in disdain.

"Is it not a bit small?" she said. "I would have expected something larger."

Hermanjilio was ready for this one. "With respect, Your Majesty, the chicken is like the scorpion: the smaller the body, the deadlier the bite."

"I see," she said. She seemed to have lost interest in the chicken. "Now tell me, Lord Hermanjilio, why did you summon us?"

"They did not summon thee, Mother," snapped Lord 6-Dog. "They asked for my noble battle chief, Lord Kukab."

She sniffed in disdain. "Kukab? I could beat that milksop any day. His mother said he squealed like a stuck peccary when she had his teeth filed into points for his birthday. Talk about ungrateful."

"In truth, Mother, thou art the Demon of Gossip," sighed Lord 6-Dog.

Hermanjilio coughed to get their attention.

Lord 6-Dog fixed him with a haughty look. "So, mortal, what besets my people in Middleworld?"

"The evil is among us, Your Majesty. The Black Jaguar roams the earth. Soon the Undead Army will be released

"Who summons Ahaw Wak Ok, the mighty Lord 6-Dog?"

and the world will be ruled by Ah Pukuh, god of war and violent death."

The old woman turned to her son. "I told you so," she said. "You should have destroyed that Black Jaguar when you had the chance—and Tzelek with it. Then we could have been sitting under a shady tree in heaven all these years, instead of freezing to death in Xibalba."

"Technically, we're dead already, Mother," said Lord 6-Dog. "But I thank thee for thy counsel. Let us hope thou wilt have less reason to reproach me this time around."

"This time around? You mean, we're staying?" The old woman clapped her hands in delight. "I've been waiting three *baktuns* for something exciting to happen."

Lord 6-Dog bowed to Hermanjilio. "This is a worthy challenge, mortal. It will be my pleasure to lead thine armies and give them victory over the enemies of Middleworld. I stand before thee as a warrior in my prime. Show me now the body I will fight in." He looked around the platform expectantly.

"Where are the human vessels for our spirits?" demanded his mother, eyes glittering with anticipation. "I trust they are of royal birth?"

Lord 6-Dog's eyes came to rest on Max and Lola. "Surely thou dost not propose that my venerable mother and myself should dwell in these runtish bodies?"

Max and Lola shook their heads vigorously.

"Divine Majesties," wheedled Hermanjilio, "forgive my ignorance, but could you not aid us in your present form, as spirits? Times are desperate in Middleworld, and we're a little short on royal personages."

Lord 6-Dog drew himself up to his full height. He

was tall for an ancient Maya, at least five foot six, and his headdress added another three feet of iridescent quetzal feathers. He threw back his magnificently sloped forehead and drew his sword.

"Fool! Dost thou not know that, once summoned, we cannot easily return whence we came? When the Jaguar Stone is disengaged, we will vanish in the wind like smoke from a fire." He slashed his sword through the air. "That will *not* come to pass. Produce a host, or I will take thy body by force."

"One moment, Your Highnesses," stammered Hermanjilio. "I must consult with my acolytes." He crouched down to Lola and Max. "Any ideas?" he asked.

"I can't believe you didn't know about this," whispered Lola.

"Well, it's happened, so what can we do? We need two bodies—quick."

"What about Chulo and Seri?" suggested Max.

"No way!" responded Lola angrily.

"But it's perfect!" said Hermanjilio. "You always say they're more like humans than monkeys, Lola. This will be fun for them."

Lola looked doubtful.

"Frankly," muttered Hermanjilio, "we have no choice. This guy is going to skin me like a gibnut."

"Okay," said Lola reluctantly. "But your new friends want royal bodies."

"Leave that to me." Hermanjilio bowed to the ancient Maya spirits, who were now bickering loudly with each other. They paused in midquarrel to listen to him.

"If I may have your attention, Divine Majesties, I am pleased to present the two noble bodies that are ready for your immediate possession."

"That sounds more like it," said the old woman. "Where are they?"

"Most Beauteous Highness," began Hermanjilio, receiving a flirtatious wink for the compliment, "may I ask you to think once again of the mighty scorpion. For while your new bodies may be small in stature, they are strong in muscle and brave in spirit."

The winking stopped abruptly as the old woman looked around with mounting excitement. "Scorpions?" she asked. "Are we to have the bodies of scorpions? Maybe with the heads of crocodiles? I have seen this fashion on temple walls. . . ."

Hermanjilio seized his chance. "Although Your Divine Majesty would look fabulous in anything, the style these days is for something a little more . . . I believe the word in fashion circles is . . . furry."

He cleared his throat and pointed to Chulo and Seri, who were engrossed in picking lice off each other and eating the proceeds.

Lord 6-Dog held up his hand and a beam of light shot out to illuminate the monkeys. "Howler monkeys? Art thou insane?" He pointed his sword at Hermanjilio's throat. "I am the greatest warrior of the Jaguar Kings, a living god, and thou wouldst have me enter the body of a flea-infested howler monkey? Thou shalt die for this. . . ."

Max could see that Hermanjilio was out of ideas. The archaeologist's eyes bulged in his red-painted face, and his whole body was visibly trembling. Given that he was seconds away from having his throat cut, who could blame him?

Max looked at Lola. She was rooted to the spot, clutching Chulo and Seri to her, all three of them whimpering in terror.

In that split second, Max realized it was up to him to save the day.

In which case, they were sunk.

He didn't want to get involved. He especially didn't want to get hurt. After all, this was a Maya thing, nothing to do with him. But as his brain came up with excuses, his heart told him the truth. He wasn't a tourist anymore. He didn't have the option of watching from the sidelines.

But what could he do?

A trickle of blood ran down Hermanjilio's neck.

"Hey, Featherbrain!" shouted Max, running over to the altar.

Lord 6-Dog's fury made his plumed headdress quiver. "Who dares speak thus to Lord 6-Dog, supreme and sacred ruler of the Monkey River?" he bellowed.

"I do," said Max, putting both hands into the snake's mouth. "Because in exactly two seconds, I'm going to pull this Jaguar Stone out of here, and your little Maya butts are going to be ancient history."

Lord 6-Dog froze, his eyes on the Jaguar Stone.

"So listen up." Max tried to sound braver than he was feeling. "We haven't got two royal bodies. But we do have two healthy howler monkeys. And it's the howlers or oblivion. You choose."

"Thou wouldst not dare," said Lord 6-Dog.

"Watch me."

The old woman stared at Max in terror. "Who is he?" she gasped. "His hair burns like the torches of Xibalba. I think we should listen to him, son. He makes a persuasive argument."

Lord 6-Dog shifted uncomfortably. He had the strangest feeling that this moment was meant to happen. Deep inside him, some half-buried memory stirred like a long-forgotten dream. But a monkey? How could it be?

At that moment, Thunderclaw woke up.

It was nowhere near dawn, but that had never stopped him before. Lord 6-Dog and his mother watched in horror as the Chicken of Death arose and crowed its unearthly shriek.

Before Thunderclaw had finished his first chorus, the spirits of the great warrior-king and his mother exchanged a glance of mutual agreement and flew into the mouths of the monkeys. Like a passing tornado, the force of it knocked the three humans and two monkeys off their feet. All five of them landed flat on their backs with a thud.

For a few moments, Max lay there, winded and terrified. He was aware of nothing but a green glow in the air and the perfume of incense. He closed his eyes. When he opened them a few seconds later, the night was black again. Only the light of the moon and stars remained.

He sat up and looked around.

Slowly the two bodies next to him sat up also.

Hermanjilio massaged his temples as if he had a headache and rubbed his throat where the point of 6-Dog's sword had been.

"So," came his hoarse voice, "I thought that went well."

"What?" said Lola. "You were nearly skewered by a spirit lord, Chulo and Seri have been possessed by who knows what, you brought back a little old lady instead of a battle chief—and you call that going well?"

"I saved the chicken, Thunderclaw," said Hermanjilio defensively.

"You mean Thunderclaw saved you," said Lola.

"It was all part of my plan." He sniffed. "I knew Chan Kan must have sent him for a reason. I'll send him back to Utsal tomorrow."

"I'll miss little Thunderclaw," said Lola. "But I'm glad he's safe."

"How are our guests?" asked Hermanjilio.

Lola shone her flashlight across the monkeys' immobile bodies. Seeing no sign of life, she knelt down and listened to Chulo's chest.

"Is he breathing?" asked Max, trying to sound like he cared.

"Yes," said Lola, "but they're both out cold. We'll have to carry them."

Between them, they hauled the monkeys down the pyramid, across the plaza, and up the ladder to the tree house, where they laid them gently on mats.

"You guys get some sleep," said Lola. "I'll stay with them."

"Everything will seem better in the light of day," said Hermanjilio.

But he didn't sound very sure.

Chapter Nineteen
MONKEY BUSINESS

Lord 6-Dog was awakened by the sound of his own screaming.

For a few moments he lay still on his sleeping mat, trying to shake off the memory of the dream. He told himself to calm down, but still his body trembled and sweat ran down his face.

A howler monkey . . . ?

Groaning, he sat up and ran his hands through his thick black hair. Then a thought occurred to him, and he quickly examined his arms and legs. Upon finding them covered in monkey fur, he let out a muffled scream.

"It was no dream," he moaned.

On the other sleeping mat, Lady Kan Kakaw sat bolt upright and looked around in alarm. Then, seeing her own furry limbs, she instantly relaxed.

"It was no dream," she exclaimed happily.

She held out her monkey hands and tested her opposable thumbs. She clenched her fists and flexed her arms. Then she jumped up, stretched her wiry little body, and scratched herself from head to foot.

"Mother!" protested Lord 6-Dog. "Thou art a royal queen!"

"Yes, son, and I have a royal itch!"

"This vulgarity does not befit thee. Thou mayest look like a flea-bitten howler, but thou dost not have to act like one."

"That's a nice thing to say to your own mother." Lady Kan Kakaw tried to look offended, but her attention was caught by a passing moth. She leapt into the air to swat it, only to fall flat on her face.

"Missed!" She chuckled. "A pox on my old crossed eyes!"

She'd been a cross-eyed queen and now she was a cross-eyed monkey. As an upper-class Maya woman, her crossed eyes had been a sign of beauty. As a monkey, they made it difficult to focus on small objects. She gamely scanned the room for another victim. Soon her skewed gaze came to rest on a large black fly, and this time she did not miss.

Lord 6-Dog watched, appalled, as his mother caught the insect and popped it into her mouth. She noticed his disgusted expression.

"What's wrong?" she asked.

"Thou didst eat the fly. I saw thee."

"I'm sorry, did you want it? Shall I catch another one?"

"Mother, we are royalty. We do not catch flies."

"I do. And I eat them."

"No, Mother! I forbid it. It is unconscionable."

Lady Kan Kakaw considered her son's words. "Our howler monkey hosts are mostly vegetarian, I grant you. But who can resist a fresh, chewy snack?"

"I am ashamed of thee, Mother. Pray have some decorum."

She hid her monkey smile behind a paw. "Cheer up, son. Yesterday, we were spirits floating in a time loop. Today we have living, breathing bodies—what does it matter if they're covered in fur?"

She scampered over to Lord 6-Dog and stroked his bristly little head. "Anyway, I like this stuff, it's very fashionable. I used to have monkey-fur trim around the shoulders of my best robe."

She started making a strange gurgling noise and clutching at her throat.

"What ails thee?" asked Lord 6-Dog. "Did the fly stick in thy gullet?"

All this time, Lola had been lying low in her hammock, watching the monkeys and giving them a chance to settle in. As she told it to Max later, it looked like Seri was deliberately choking herself. In a flash, Lola understood the problem.

"Excuse me, Your Majesties," she began.

The monkeys jumped in surprise, registering her presence for the first time.

"On thy knees, mortal!" thundered Lord 6-Dog. "How darest thou speak to a divine king without permission? How darest thou even look at me? Thou shalt die for this! Mother, call the guards!"

Lady Kan Kakaw staggered to the doorway.

"I see no guards," she rasped, still holding her throat.

"The royal bedchamber left unguarded? This is an outrage," bellowed Lord 6-Dog. "And where are the servants? I am overheated in this fur. Where is the bearer of the royal fan?" His disdainful gaze came to rest once more on Lola. "Where are the other servants? Speak!"

"I'm not a servant, but I will be glad to help your mother.

I think Seri is throttling her from the inside, to punish her for wearing monkey fur on her robe."

"It was just a bit of trim," wheezed Lady Kan Kakaw.

"And who, pray, is Seri?" asked Lord 6-Dog.

"She's your mother's . . . er . . . hostess. Do you mind if I rub her back?"

Lord 6-Dog looked at his mother's furry body, which was now convulsing on the floor. "Proceed," he said.

Lola gently stroked the monkey, crooning all the while in howler language. The monkey responded with a series of protesting squawks. "I know, Seri, it's not easy to wake up and find an ancient Maya queen living in your body," agreed Lola. "But you'll have to learn to live with each other. It's only for a few days."

After a few more whimpers, Seri calmed down and released her grip.

"Thank you, my dear," said Lady Kan Kakaw to Lola.

"I'm sorry about Seri's behavior," said Lola, "it's quite out of character. All this has come as a bit of a shock to her and her brother, Chulo."

"But my dear, I had no idea that monkeys had feelings!"

"Of course they don't," snapped Lord 6-Dog. "They're the lowest form of life, rejects from the Great Sky God's first attempt to make mankind. That's why they're all so ugly. Flat-nosed dwarves—"

Lord 6-Dog fell to the floor, clutching his throat.

Lola and Lady Kan Kakaw watched, fascinated, as the king and the monkey rolled around, slugging it out in the same body. Lola had never seen anyone try to strangle themselves and bite themselves at the same time.

"Who are you, my dear?" Lady Kan Kakaw was asking her.

"What is your bloodline? Who are your family?"

Not wanting to reveal her lack of parents, Lola answered, "I am from the house of Chan Kan in Utsel. My name is Ix Sak Lol, but most people call me Lola."

"Lo-la." Lady Kan Kakaw rolled her tongue around it. "I like it. What does it mean?"

"It doesn't mean anything. It's just a nickname. You know, something your friends and family call you."

Lady Kan Kakaw looked wistful. "Even my mother called me *Ix Kan Kakaw*. I've never had a nickname. . . ."

"Let's think of one, right now!" suggested Lola, glad to change the subject from parentage to nicknames. "*Ix Kan Kakaw* means 'Lady Yellow Cocoa Bean,' doesn't it?"

"Goodness, no! *Kan* can be 'yellow,' but it has an idea of ripeness, something perfect and precious. *Kakaw* is 'cocoa,' but cocoa beans were also money, so there's a sense of treasure and riches. To ancient Maya ears, my name means something like 'Lady Perfect Precious Treasure of Accumulated Wealth Through Judicious Trading of Cocoa Beans.'"

"Lady Precious? Lady Treasure?" suggested Lola. "Lady Coco?"

"I love it!" said the monkey, jumping up and down with excitement. "What do you think, son? Do you want a nickname, too?"

Having managed to pacify Chulo, Lord 6-Dog was standing on a stool, looking out of the window. "6-Dog *is* my nickname, Mother," he said. His voice was still hoarse from the self-inflicted throttling.

"Silly me, how could I forget that? 6-Dog was the date he was born," Lady Coco explained to Lola. "The name his father gave him is unpronounceable even by ancient Maya standards."

Lord 6-Dog put his head against the screen and inhaled. "Aaaah, how I have missed the smell of sweet, wet earth."

Lady Coco sniffed the air. "Yes, these noses are much better than our human ones. I can smell bananas and mangoes and . . . oh, that's disgusting!" She sniffed again. "It's you, 6-Dog! You need a bath."

"By the quetzal!" he exclaimed. "What a torment to have a sensitive nose when one's own body reeks like a dung heap."

Choking noises suggested that Chulo had taken offense again.

"Chulo, stop it!" cried Lola. "It's high time you had a wash. Let me show you to the bathroom, Your Majesties. I think you'll enjoy the technology."

Lola explained how to work the solar shower and, after some hesitation, put out the hand-milled French lavender soap that Hermanjilio had brought back for her from a lecture trip in Europe.

Before she left them to it, she turned to speak again. "Please join us in the plaza for breakfast when . . ." Her voice trailed off as she took in the extraordinary sight in front of her eyes.

Lord 6-Dog, wearing a towel as a cloak, was standing on the sink surveying himself lugubriously in the mirror. Lady Coco was swinging and somersaulting on the shower rail like an Olympic gymnast. Somehow they'd managed to open every single bottle and jar in the cabinet, and the contents were daubed around the bathroom.

"I'll . . . um . . . see you at breakfast, then," said Lola, backing out, but the monkeys didn't notice her.

She was still complaining as she helped Max set the table.

"You should have seen the mess," she fumed. "Well, if they think I'm cleaning up after them . . ."

"I wouldn't get on the wrong side of them if I were you," said Max. "They're not your friendly monkeys anymore. They could have you sacrificed in the blink of an eye."

Hermanjilio emerged from the cooking hut with a plate of tortillas and a bowl of fruit. He was limping slightly and he looked dreadful, as though he hadn't slept a wink.

"I was just saying," said Lola, "that our guests have trashed the bathroom."

"Blame Chulo and Seri," said Hermanjilio. "It probably takes a while for this possession thing to settle down. I'm sure our guests will start acting like nobility soon enough. They just have to learn to control their inner monkeys."

"In that case," said Lola, "I think they're in the wrong bodies. Lord 6-Dog is formal and serious like Seri. But Lady Coco's full of fun like Chulo."

"Lady Coco?" chorused Max and Hermanjilio.

"She wanted a nickname," explained Lola.

"I still have to get my head around talking monkeys," said Max. "You really did it, Hermanjilio! You brought back Lord 6-Dog and his mother!"

"I can hardly believe it myself," said Hermanjilio. "It's taken it out of me, though. I've got the worst headache of my life this morning and I didn't even drink much *balché*." He groaned and sat down at the table, laying his head on his arms. "Wake me up when our guests appear."

In fact, it was the reek of lavender that woke him. You

didn't need a monkey nose to know that the two soft and fluffy specimens descending the ladder had used rather a lot of Lola's precious French soap.

She opened her mouth to protest, but Hermanjilio cut in. "Lord 6-Dog! Lady Coco! It is an honor to make your acquaintance. If there's anything we can do to make your stay more comfortable, you have only to ask."

But the king and his mother didn't hear him. They were standing in the plaza, transfixed.

"What is this place?" asked Lord 6-Dog.

"Itzamna," said Hermanjilio.

"Itzamna?" they repeated in bewilderment.

"Welcome home, Your Majesties," announced Lola with a flourish. To her dismay, the monkeys looked distraught.

"It cannot be," said Lady Coco, looking around. "My Itzamna was surrounded by fields and fertile terraces. Where are the markets, the houses, the workshops? Fifty thousand people lived in this city. Where are they?" Her gaze settled at the far end of the plaza. "My palace," she wailed.

Lord 6-Dog's liquid monkey eyes looked sadder than ever. He pointed mournfully toward the ruins at the other end of the plaza. "Could that be the great Temple of Itzamna," he whispered, "with its red paint all stripped away?"

Hermanjilio nodded.

"My father is entombed beneath those stones," said Lord 6-Dog angrily. "What enemy has dared to desecrate his memory?"

"That enemy was time, Your Majesty," said Hermanjilio. "The golden age of Itzamna was twelve hundred years ago."

"Twelve hundred years," repeated Lord 6-Dog wonderingly. "Three *baktuns*. Like a whirlpool, time encircles me and confounds my memory in its bubbling waters." He stared intently at Hermanjilio. "Who art thou, sir? I feel as if I have known thee all my life."

Hermanjilio looked away from the monkey's intense gaze. "My name is Hermanjilio Bol. My ancestors were the guardians of the royal library. It was I who summoned you here."

"Then I should thank thee, sir, for I am glad to walk in Middleworld again."

While the men were talking, Lady Coco was looking longingly at the bowl of fruit.

"Would you like something to eat?" said Lola.

"Yes, please, my dear. Where is the women's table?"

"We'll all be sitting together."

"Disgraceful!" growled Lord 6-Dog.

"Delightful!" cooed Lady Coco.

"Please make yourselves comfortable, Your Majesties, while I go and fry the eggs," said Hermanjilio.

Lord 6-Dog looked puzzled. "Lord Hermanjilio," he said, "thou hast the look of a noble warrior, yet thou dost act like a kitchen maid. Cooking is woman's work. Let us talk, man to man. Send the girl for the food."

Hermanjilio smiled meaningfully at Lola.

Reluctantly, she went to look for the frying pan. It wasn't that she minded cooking, so much as she was bad at it. She hoped these eggs would turn out better than her last attempts, which had bounced off the plates like rubber balls.

Lord 6-Dog took the stool at the head of the table, where Hermanjilio usually sat. Hermanjilio, who'd been making his way to the same place, was left standing. For a moment, the monkey and the archaeologist locked glances in a battle of wills. Lord 6-Dog glared at his rival autocratically. Hermanjilio's gaze was bleary but unwavering.

"Chill," whispered Lola to him as she brought in the plates.

Hermanjilio blinked rapidly, like someone snapping out of a trance. "Of course," he said, graciously ceding his place.

"What was that about?" Max asked Lola.

"It's the dominant-male thing," she said. "They both think they're king of Itzamna."

"Wilt thou tell me about my people?" Lord 6-Dog asked Hermanjilio. "Tell me everything that has happened in the last three *baktuns*."

As Lord 6-Dog heard about the invasion of the conquistadores, how Diego de Landa had burned all the books, how the Jaguar Stones had been lost, and how all the great Maya cities now lay in ruins, his monkey face grew sadder and sadder.

"Hast thou no tales of heroism?" he asked.

Hermanjilio thought for a moment. "There was Nachankan. He was a great Maya lord from the north. When the Spanish demanded tribute, he said he'd give them 'turkeys in the shape of spears and corn in the shape of arrows.'"

Lord 6-Dog laughed a booming howler-monkey laugh.

"Many Maya lords stood firm," continued Hermanjilio. "In fact, the Maya fought the Spanish for another two hundred years after the Aztecs surrendered."

"The Aztecs? Pah!" Lord 6-Dog sneered. "In my day, they were nothing but a pack of swamp-dwelling scavengers."

"A few hundred years later, they got to be quite big," said Hermanjilio.

"They did?" Lord 6-Dog looked disappointed.

"At their height, they had ten million citizens," continued Hermanjilio. "Of course, they sacrificed them at an alarming rate. Sometimes they ate the corpses."

"That's disgusting," Lady Coco said, grimacing.

"No wonder their empire only lasted three hundred years," said Lola, coming out with a platter of eggs. She sniffed haughtily. "We Maya have been around for three thousand years. And counting."

"Well spoken, Lady Lola," said Lord 6-Dog, cheering up. "I will wager that the Aztecs yielded to the Spanish like a gaggle of old women."

"Excuse me?" Lady Coco turned on him angrily. "That statement is offensive to old women. I'll have you know that an old Maya woman would fight to the death—"

"Eggs, anyone?" said Lola, trying to keep the peace.

"Omelets!" said Hermanjilio. "They look delicious."

Lola glared at him. "They're *fried* eggs actually."

"Thirteen thanks for all our blessings," began Lord 6-Dog. He thanked the wild turkeys that laid the eggs, the earth that grew the corn for the tortillas, the trees that bore the fruit, the rain for water to drink—

Lady Coco's stomach gurgled loudly. "And we thank Lord Hermanjilio for his hospitality," she said. "Let's eat!"

It was the last civilized moment of the meal.

Perhaps the hunger of twelve hundred years superseded the constraints of table manners. Or perhaps Chulo and Seri were venting their inner monkeys.

Whatever the cause, the breakfast was soon in chaos.

Lady Coco started it by sitting on the fruit bowl.

"Mother! Off the table! Hast thou lost thy mind?" shouted Lord 6-Dog.

Lady Coco considered this question for a moment, then lobbed a banana skin at her son, quickly followed by a ripe papaya that exploded on contact and showered him with black seeds. Lord 6-Dog jumped onto the table to retaliate, and the two monkeys started wrestling, tails lashing, pots crashing, food flying until Hermanjilio and Max pried them apart.

"And these guys are going to save the world?" sighed Max.

A small melon bounced off the side of his head. He looked around to see Lord 6-Dog celebrating a direct hit. Remembering that, on the inside, his assailant was a mighty warrior-king, he decided against retaliating. "That hurt, Your Majesty," he said. "We're on the same side, remember?"

Lord 6-Dog looked mortified. "My apologies, young lord, but Chulo made me do it. It seems he bears thee much ill will. I will try to control him."

Balanced giddily on the back of a chair, Lady Coco brushed bits of food off her fur and attempted to muster her dignity, an effort diminished by the raffia fruit bowl she now wore like a rakish straw hat. "I do apologize," she said, trying to sound refined. "I can assure you this is not our usual . . ."

Her concentration lapsed as she watched her son use his tail to grab a mango and bring it to his open mouth. "Let me try that," she screeched.

Soon both monkeys were fully absorbed in experimenting with their newly discovered prehensile tails.

It was the craziest breakfast Max had ever experienced.

At one point, Lady Coco bounced over to perch beside

him. "And who are you, young lord? Are you of royal birth? Who is your father?"

"My father is an archaeologist," said Max. She looked blank, so he added, "He studies history."

"A wise man indeed," said Lord 6-Dog, nodding sagely. He tipped back his head, poured the last of the juice into his mouth, and upended the empty jug. "It is only by studying the past that we can predict the future. What has happened before will happen again." He turned to Hermanjilio. "Speaking of which, art thou sure we have not met before?"

"I am positive," said Hermanjilio quickly. "And now perhaps we could discuss more pressing matters. How do you propose we stop Count Antonio de Landa from using the Black Jaguar to raise the Undead Army?"

"Landa, didst thou say? Was that not the name of the varlet who burned our books?"

"That was Friar Diego de Landa. Antonio is his descendant."

"Then it will be my pleasure to take him captive and flay him alive."

"He has bodyguards," interjected Max. "And guns."

Lord 6-Dog stroked his chin. "How many armies dost thou command, Lord Hermanjilio? How many warriors will join us in this battle?"

"Four."

"Four armies?"

"Four warriors."

"This is no time for jest."

"It is the truth. There are four of us: you, me, Lola, and Max."

"Make that five, Lord Hermanjilio; you can count me in," said Lady Coco. "But in all that you have told us, there is one name you have not mentioned."

"And who would that be?" asked Hermanjilio.

"Tzelek!" She spat out the word like a curse.

"My twin brother?" said Lord 6-Dog. "What has this to do with him?"

"His old crony, Ah Pukuh, is about to take the reins of power. Do you really think Tzelek would miss such an opportunity to make mischief? It was common knowledge in Xibalba that he was hanging around the surface, trying to find a way through."

Max remembered the grip on his ankle in the Temple of Itzamna.

"Does Tzelek have long, bony fingers?" he asked.

Lady Coco nodded. "He kept his nails specially sharpened for ripping out hearts with his bare hands. You mark my words, if there's evil afoot in Middleworld, Tzelek is involved in it up to his villainous neck. I'll wager ten baskets of cocoa beans that he's already here. I expect he glimpsed a hole in the gateway and squeezed through it like the cockroach he is."

"Then the question we should be asking," said Hermanjilio, "is whose body is Tzelek living in? And I'm sorry to tell you, I think I know the answer."

"Is it me?" said Max in a small voice. "I think he grabbed my ankle in the Star Chamber and tried to suck out my soul."

"Surely you'd know if you'd been possessed by Tzelek," said Lola. "Do you get black moods? Do you think evil thoughts? Are you bad-tempered and irrationally angry?"

"Yes." Max felt nauseous. "It's me, isn't it?"

"Of course it's not you!" snapped Hermanjilio in exasperation. "Let us not confuse the emotional turmoil of adolescence with the inner workings of one of history's most evil villains! Guess again."

Blank faces stared back at him.

"Isn't it obvious?" said Hermanjilio. "Who's been playing around with Jaguar Stones? Who has an interest in the black arts? Who would welcome an ally like Tzelek?"

"Count Antonio de Landa!" burst out Max in horror.

Hermanjilio nodded gravely.

"Well, that explains why he's been too busy to look for us," said Lola.

"This just gets worse and worse," groaned Max. "Now the evil descendant of one of the most evil men in history has been possessed by the evil spirit of an evil Maya priest. And my parents are caught in the middle of it."

Chapter Twenty
COUNTING THE DAYS

It was too awful to contemplate: the fiendish Tzelek in league with the ruthless Count Antonio de Landa. Between them, they represented twelve hundred years of absolute evil. Who knew what warped scheme they were hatching?

"But why would Tzelek come back? What does he want?" asked Lola.

"He wants what he has always wanted," said Lord 6-Dog, "to be the supreme and sacred ruler of Middleworld."

"It's such a cliché," said Max. "Why do bad guys always want to rule the world?"

"Deep-seated emotional insecurity masquerading as a superiority complex?" suggested Lola.

They all looked at her in amazement.

"I'm thinking about majoring in psychology," she explained.

"Whatever," said Max. "It's stupid. An ancient Maya madman can't just suddenly appear and declare himself king of the world."

"With his friend Ah Pukuh in charge of the new *baktun*,"

said Lord 6-Dog, "he can do whatever he wants."

"And this time," said Hermanjilio, "his power will not stop at the limits of the Maya realm. This time, all humanity will be under his dominion."

Lady Coco pulled a branch off a nearby tree and stripped the leaves with her teeth. "At least we know where and when he'll make his first move," she said, in between bites.

"We do?" said Max.

"We do," confirmed Lord 6-Dog. "The place will be the Black Pyramid of Ah Pukuh. And the time will be at the rising of Venus on 5-Kimi—or 5-Death, in thy parlance. It is an auspicious day, a day of sacrifice and mourning. . . ."

"Most importantly," interrupted Lady Coco, "it is in four days' time."

Max swallowed. "And how far is it from here to the Black Pyramid?"

Lord 6-Dog and Hermanjilio spoke at the same time.

"One day," said the ancient Maya king. "It is an easy march."

"Two days," said the archaeologist, "and it won't be easy."

They looked at each other in surprise.

"The straight stone roads your warriors marched on are long since overgrown," said Hermanjilio. "We'll have to hack our way through. We must leave tomorrow. And now, if you'll excuse me, I have much to do."

"Thou art dismissed," said Lord 6-Dog imperiously. As Hermanjilio strode away, the king furrowed his monkey brow. "He is so familiar to me, and yet I cannot place him. Does he remind thee of someone, Mother?"

"He has shifty eyes," said Lady Coco.

"Oh no, not Hermanjilio," Lola insisted, getting up to clear the table. "He's the kindest man you could ever meet."

"When is his birthday?" Lady Coco asked Max.

Max shrugged. "I have no idea."

"And you, young lord?" persisted Lady Coco. "On what day were you born?"

"In the Maya calendar?" he said. "Who knows."

Lord 6-Dog and his mother looked at each other in alarm.

"No wonder Middleworld teeters on the brink of destruction," said Lord 6-Dog. "For if mortals have forgotten how to read the days, they are doomed to stumble through time like children wandering across a battlefield."

"What's the big deal?" asked Max.

Lola threw him a cloth to wipe the table. "Our royal guests believe that a person's entire character and destiny are decided by the day of their birth," she explained. "Like a horoscope—except a bad one could ruin your life."

"And a good one could ensure success," pointed out Lady Coco.

"But how could anyone look at a newborn baby and pronounce it a liar or a thief?" said Lola.

"When your future's been decided by the gods, you don't question it," replied Lady Coco.

"Well, maybe you *should* question it," said Lola. "Did you know that the Spanish used your beliefs against you? They convinced your priests that your defeat was written in the stars, and it became a self-fulfilling prophecy."

"All history is a self-fulfilling prophecy," said Lord 6-Dog. "What has happened before will happen again."

Lady Coco looked thoughtful. She lowered her voice. "But you do believe you can beat Tzelek this time, don't you, son?"

Max and Lola pretended to be engrossed in washing up, while straining to hear the great king's reply.

"Why dost thou doubt me, Mother?"

"Because Tzelek has always wrapped you around his little finger. You must face the truth, 6-Dog. He is evil from his balding head to his stinking feet. You must not give him another chance. He must be stopped."

"I understand the situation, Mother."

"Then why didn't you finish him off last time?"

"He is my twin, my flesh and blood."

Lady Coco spat a nutshell onto the ground. "No," she said. "No, he isn't."

"What art thou saying?"

"Tzelek was born a few minutes after you, but he was not my child. His mother was a witch. She died in childbirth that very day—but not before she'd made me promise to adopt her evil spawn."

"Why wouldst thou, a royal queen, adopt a witch's son?"

"His mother vowed that, from that day forward, your lives would be intertwined as you grew up. If I abandoned Tzelek or he failed to thrive, you, too, would wither and die. Your father knew nothing of this curse, and for three *baktuns* I have kept my silence."

"Tzelek is not my brother? But I always thought he was thy favorite."

"He was always so very jealous of you. When your father died and you became king, he plotted against you constantly. I thought you might be safer if I pretended not to care for you.

But all the while, I was trying to help you in unseen ways. I used to pray to the spirit of your father to show me what to do. He was so proud of you, 6-Dog. He still is."

"If I had not gone hunting that day, he might have lived," said Lord 6-Dog, looking across to the pyramid of Itzamna, his father's final resting place.

It had been a day of merrymaking, a *katun* celebration to mark Punak Ha's first twenty years on the throne. As the elder twin, 6-Dog was expected to stand by his father's side at the ceremony. But he'd slipped away to go hunting instead. How could he have known that Punak Ha would come looking for him? Or that he'd be ambushed while calling his son's name?

When 6-Dog had returned with his catch (an armadillo too small to bother cooking), the conch-shell horns and the wooden trumpets were sounding their laments. The next day, preparations began for 6-Dog's coronation.

His father's murderer was never caught.

Lord 6-Dog swore to honor his father's memory by becoming the greatest king that Middleworld had ever seen. Gorgeous and terrible in his black body paint, jaguar pelts, and quetzal-plumed helmet, he had won every battle and subdued every enemy.

But he had never vanquished his own conscience.

"Dost thou believe our lives are written in the stars, Mother?"

"I believe in second chances, son. What has happened before will happen again. But this time, you can change the outcome."

"I cannot bring my father back."

"But you can sit next to him under the great ceiba tree for

all eternity if you win this victory. He is waiting for you, son, in the heroes' heaven. You must deal with Tzelek once and for all."

"Even the mighty 6-Dog may not be strong enough to defeat the combined forces of Tzelek and Ah Pukuh."

"This time," declared Lady Coco, "I will fight by your side. This is my second chance, too, 6-Dog. I promise to be your most loyal and devoted warrior."

"May good prevail," he said.

She nudged him playfully. "Here's what I think of Tzelek and his cronies."

Lord 6-Dog watched in amazement as his mother, First and Most Glorious Wife of the Great King Punak Ha, pointed her bony monkey posterior in the air and noisily broke wind.

And then, for the first time in more than a thousand years, he laughed until his sides ached.

Chapter Twenty-one
PREPARING FOR BATTLE

A s I see it," said Max, "all that stands between humankind and the end of the world is two talking monkeys, a crazy archaeologist covered in red paint, and a couple of kids with blowguns? Am I right?"

"Wrong," said Hermanjilio. "I'll be wearing my black paint this time. Now keep practicing."

Max and Lola had been honing their blowgun skills for hours. It was late afternoon, and Max's cheeks were aching, but at least he was starting to hit the target. Lola had graduated to trick shots, and several surprised parrots could vouch for the accuracy of her aim.

"But it's going to rain," said Max. "Couldn't we take a break?"

"What, and miss the chance to practice in wet conditions?" said Hermanjilio. While Max and Lola shot their blowguns in the pouring rain, Lord 6-Dog brewed up a potion to coat the tips of their darts.

"Could we not make it a little stronger, Lord Hermanjilio?" he asked as he stirred his mixture. "If we added just one small poison dart frog, we would have enough toxin to slay Landa and all his men. . . ."

"A sleeping draft will be fine, Lord 6-Dog," Hermanjilio assured him hastily. "These days, we tend to shy away from human sacrifice."

"Have it thine own way," muttered Lord 6-Dog. "But let us hope that Tzelek is equally well versed in the etiquette of modern warfare."

When all was ready for their journey, they gathered around the campfire for one last meal.

"This meat is delicious," said Max. "What is it?"

"Iguana," said Lola. "Would you like another skewer?"

As Max chowed down on the juicy lizard, he marveled that his mother had ever called him a picky eater. He reckoned that, these days, he could even eat Zia's tamales without complaint.

Everyone was quiet around the campfire, thinking about the next day's journey to Ah Pukuh. Hermanjilio tried to boost their confidence with tales of daring deeds from Maya legends, but his stories fell as flat as stale tortillas. "Well, good night, then," he said in resignation. "Get some sleep, all of you. We leave for the Black Pyramid at dawn."

The rest of them murmured their good-nights and began to gather their things. But somehow, with Hermanjilio gone, the atmosphere lightened and they lingered under the stars.

"Look, son," whispered Lady Coco, "look up at the moon rabbit."

Max overheard. "The moon rabbit? You guys know about that? My mom used to make me wave to the moon rabbit when I was little."

Lady Coco smiled. "Mothers have been pointing out the

moon rabbit since the world began. It is a good omen that we see it so clearly tonight. It tells us that its owner, Ixchel, is watching over us."

"Ixchel?" said Max suspiciously. "The moon goddess? Do we *want* her watching over us? The waiter at the hotel in Puerto Muerto said she's bad news."

"Like any woman, she has her moods," agreed Lady Coco. "As the old moon, with a serpent headdress and human bones on her skirt, she can be quick to anger. But as the young moon, with her pet rabbit, she's a beautiful woman, creative and caring, a patron of motherhood, weaving, and medicine. It is the young goddess that has smiled on us tonight. She is the mother to us all, and she will protect us like a doe protects her fawn."

Lola was staring glumly up at the moon rabbit. Max guessed she was thinking of her own mother, whom she had never known.

He reached out to touch her arm.

"I'm going to bed," she said curtly.

He got up to walk with her, but Lord 6-Dog pulled him aside. "Thou hast won favor with Chulo tonight, young lord. It seems that baby howlers also know the moon rabbit. I think he likes thee better now."

"Well, that's one less enemy to worry about," Max said with a grin. "Good night, Chulo; good night, Your Majesties."

"Good night," replied Lord 6-Dog, with a courtly bow.

"Don't let the vampire bats bite!" added Lady Coco.

Max felt like he'd only just gone to sleep when Lola was calling him to wake up and get going. As he dragged himself down the tree-house ladder, his fear felt like a lead weight in his stomach. For the first time in fourteen years, he wasn't hungry for breakfast.

It was a somber party that made their way through the jungle, following the overgrown course of the old Maya causeway. Even the monkeys, who usually kept up a constant chatter and crashing of branches, crept silently through the trees as they scouted ahead. Everyone was tense. Every creature that rustled in the undergrowth made them jump, and every new turning seemed fraught with danger.

As they walked, Lola tried to take Max's mind off things by teaching him about the jungle birds. But the screams of the macaws, the croaks of the toucans, and the screeches of the parakeets made him feel like he was in a haunted house.

"Why are the birds so noisy in the jungle?" he asked her.

She shrugged. "What do the birds in Boston sound like?"

Max thought about it. "I don't have a clue. I guess I'm always wearing headphones."

They made camp before sunset by a rock pool.

As Max gathered wood, he saw a small green lizard running across the surface of the water on its hind feet, like a miniature Godzilla.

"Look! Look!" he called to Lola.

"It's a basilisk," she said. "Something must be chasing it."

They watched as the little creature reached dry land and ran up a tree.

"What are you two doing sitting around?" asked Lady Coco crossly. "Come and help me get this fire going."

"Sorry, Your Majesty," said Lola. "Max had never seen a basilisk before."

"A basilisk? Where is it?" Lady Coco sounded horrified.

"You don't like them?" asked Lola in surprise.

"It's nothing personal, but it makes me think of Tzelek. His name means 'Basilisk Lord,' you know. And that's what he is. A slimy, cold-blooded lizard. He even leaves a trail like a lizard, with that crippled foot that drags behind him."

There was a rustling of leaves, and they turned to watch a bright yellow iguana, maybe seven feet long, skin like chain mail, emerge from the bushes. It stopped in its tracks to check them out.

Lady Coco regarded it with disgust. "You could learn a lot about Tzelek by studying his fellow lizards. They are cunning escape artists and masters of disguise. Most of them will shed their own tails to avoid capture. The horned lizard squirts blood out of its own eyes to defend itself." She waved her arms wildly at the iguana. "Scoot! Scram! Shoo!"

The iguana, unimpressed by its first encounter with a talking monkey, flicked its tongue at her a couple of times before lumbering down to the rock pool.

Lady Coco shivered. "I sometimes think that all the reptiles in Middleworld are in league with that monster Tzelek."

Max surveyed the huge scaly body of the iguana as it drank at the water's edge. As if sensing his scrutiny, it stopped drinking and slowly looked up, its hooded eyes appraising him without a trace of fear.

"Let's build a big fire tonight," said Max.

Next day, through rain and sun, they tramped steadfastly on. By late afternoon, the monkeys' noses detected the first tang of sea air. As they rounded one last hill, a fierce storm blew up out of nowhere. And there in front of them, set against a backdrop of black clouds and angry waves, was the city of Ah Pukuh.

It was every bit as forbidding as Max had imagined it.

As the thunder raged and the lightning flashed, he looked across at this ancient city that had taken the ways of darkness to its heart. Through the driving rain, he saw how it was built on a finger of rock pointing into the ocean. At the tip of the finger were the ruins of several overgrown buildings, dominated by a tall, thin-stepped pyramid.

The Pyramid of Death.

As Max watched, a bolt of lightning struck the pyramid and threw the stones into sharp relief. For a few seconds, the temple on the top platform was illuminated, and he saw to his horror that a huge skull, maybe twenty feet high, had been carved over the doorway.

Max knew that very soon, maybe tomorrow, he'd have to go through that doorway. It seemed unlikely that anyone who entered would live to tell the tale, and his heart beat wildly at the prospect.

Then all was calm again.

The storm stopped as suddenly as it had started. The sky turned dusky blue and the birds began to sing. As the setting sun cast its glow over the pale green sea, it looked like a scene out of a travel brochure.

"It all looks so pretty now," said Lola, amazed at the transformation.

"Don't be fooled, my dear," said Lady Coco. "Malevolence hovers over this place like gas off a swamp."

Lord 6-Dog nodded sadly. "It was here that the priests of Ah Pukuh developed their dark powers and Tzelek raised the Undead Army from their slumbers."

"Look!" whispered Lola.

Squinting into the sunset, Max could see several armed guards moving about on the top platform of the pyramid. Perched high up on the decorative roof comb, on a level with the wheeling vultures, another armed guard scanned the surrounding area.

"They look like Landa's men, all right," said Max.

Lola craned her neck, trying to count the guards. "Hermanjilio, you're the tallest. How many do you see?"

Hermanjilio didn't hear the question. He was staring at the Black Pyramid in a daze. "This is my destiny," he whispered. Max guessed he was giving himself a pep talk for the coming battle and resolved to do the same before he went to sleep that night. Having seen the Black Pyramid, he wished he'd never got involved in this mission.

Lord 6-Dog ran up a palm tree. "I count ten guards. But I cannot see the whole plaza."

"How many do you think there are altogether?" asked Lola.

"There is only one way to find out," replied Lord 6-Dog. "The first rule of war is to know thine enemy. I therefore propose that Mother and I infiltrate the guards' camp. We will try to ascertain the whereabouts of the Black Jaguar."

"No!" cried Lola. "It's too dangerous."

"It's all right, Lady Lola," said Lady Coco. "I know you're worried about Chulo and Seri, but Landa's men have no reason to shoot two friendly howlers."

"They don't need a reason," said Lola.

Lord 6-Dog stood straight and proud like the warrior he used to be. "Allow us to do the task we were summoned here to do," he said, and started off toward the city.

"Don't worry," said Lady Coco, "we'll be careful." She gave

Lola a quick hug before following her son into the valley.

Lola stared after her.

"She'll be fine," said Max. "Come and help me find some firewood."

They busied themselves making camp at the edge of the jungle.

Night fell.

Occasionally, a shout or a curse or a burst of raucous laughter would drift over from the guards' camp. But no monkeys returned.

"What's taking them so long? Why aren't they back yet?" fretted Lola.

"They can take care of themselves," Max reassured her.

Hermanjilio was less sympathetic. "Lola, you must get a grip on your emotions," he said. "This is a war. There will be casualties."

A shot rang out in the distance.

Lola froze.

"We're doomed, we're doomed," wailed Lady Coco, leaping into the middle of the campsite.

Lola held out her arms to the monkey, who was shaking with fear. "Are you all right? What's happened? Where's Chulo?"

"He's here," said the voice of Lord 6-Dog, climbing down a tree.

"Are you hurt?" asked Lola. "What was that shot?"

"I know not. It was behind me . . . probably a guard discharging his weapon at a tree squirrel. Landa's men are as jumpy as a barrel of bullfrogs."

"Tell them the bad news," said Lady Coco. "Tell them what we heard!"

Lord 6-Dog took a deep breath. "I am sorry to tell thee that the Chee Ken of Death is in Landa's pay. We heard its infernal crowing from behind the cooking hut. I doubt my sleeping draft will work on that scaly devil."

"A chicken? You were scared by a chicken?" said Max. He and Lola looked at Hermanjilio expectantly. Surely it was time to come clean about Thunderclaw?

Apparently not.

"Don't worry, Lord 6-Dog," said Hermanjilio. "I believe I am more than a match for this Chee Ken."

"Thou art truly a brave man, Lord Hermanjilio."

"To think you would attack a chicken single-handed," said Lola in mock admiration.

"Will you use a knife—or a fork?" asked Max.

Hermanjilio had the grace to look embarrassed. "Forget the chicken," he said. "Were you able to find out where they're keeping the Black Jaguar, Lord 6-Dog?"

"That we were. The lily-livered coward Landa is still hiding out at sea. It is my assumption that the Black Jaguar is with him."

"That sounds likely," mused Hermanjilio. "He probably won't show himself until the last minute. We must be ready to move quickly. How many guards does he have?"

"No more than a score."

Max looked blank.

"That's twenty," Lola explained. "Four to one."

"Let's make this easy on ourselves," said Hermanjilio. "I propose that we drug the guards' food and knock out any stragglers with blowgun darts. When Landa comes ashore, we'll ambush him, steal the Black Jaguar, and be long gone before his guards wake up."

"And then?" objected Lola. "Surely he'll track us down and kill us? Landa-slash-Tzelek won't give in just like that. There's too much at stake."

"And let's not forget my parents in all this," said Max.

"First we find the Black Jaguar," said Hermanjilio. "Everything else will follow."

Max felt intensely irritated. These archaeologists were all the same. Worrying about their precious artifacts when they should be thinking about human beings. Still, at least the Black Jaguar would give them a bargaining chip with Landa. And if this stuff about Tzelek and Ah Pukuh were true, they might even avert the end of the world. Not a bad day's work.

"So how do we make a clean getaway?" he asked.

"I can answer that," said Lord 6-Dog. "I know this place like the back of my, um, paw."

"Why would you know the Black Pyramid?" asked Max suspiciously. "I thought only bad guys hung out here."

"While Ah Pukuh himself has always been the most cruel and feared of the Maya gods, the city that bore his name was not always rotten to the core. Before it was corrupted by Tzelek, in the days when good and evil were in balance, Ah Pukuh was one of the five sacred pyramids of the Monkey River. We used to come here to celebrate victories in war. The royal party would stand on the top platform and wave to the cheering crowds below. Then—*poof!*—when the smoke cleared, we were gone!"

"How?" asked the rest of them in unison.

"We would make our way down inside the temple to a secret passage known only to the Jaguar Kings. It led to a labyrinth of caves and tunnels that crisscrossed the whole region. There were exit points all over the jungle."

"Like a Maya subway system?" suggested Max.

"I know not about this subway, but I can tell thee it was a merry trick. The people loved it. It was almost as popular as sawing the slave in half."

"Except that sawing the slave in half wasn't a trick," pointed out Lady Coco. "You really did saw him in half."

"If I may bring you back to our escape plan," said Hermanjilio, "why doesn't Tzelek know about this passageway?"

"Despite their best efforts, high priests did not know everything," replied Lord 6-Dog. "Passageways like this one were a closely guarded secret, passed down from king to king. It was not just a matter of knowing the way. Tests and traps were built into the walls—a trespasser would not survive."

"How do we know the passage is still there after all these centuries?" asked Lola.

"Good question," said Hermanjilio. "Lord 6-Dog, perhaps you could check it out for us? As a monkey, you'll be able to sneak around without arousing suspicion."

"I would do so gladly, Lord Hermanjilio, but this stunted body cannot operate the secret door. One of thy number must accompany me."

"I'll go," said Lola without hesitation.

"Thou hast the heart of a true Maya warrior," said Lord 6-Dog.

"Thank you." Lola smiled proudly. "So where's the nearest entrance?"

"There are many places to exit the secret passageway, but there is only one point of entry."

Lola's smile was fading. "Don't tell me . . ."

Lord 6-Dog nodded. "We must enter through the Pyramid of Death."

"Rather you than me," said Max. Then he felt guilty because he could see that Lola was having second thoughts. "No, I'm sure it'll be fine," he said. "I mean, it can't be worse than Chahk or Itzamna, can it?"

Lola turned to Lord 6-Dog. "Please tell me what to expect."

"Tell her the truth, son," instructed Lady Coco. "Forewarned is forearmed."

"It is not possible to arm thyself against the Undead Army, but I will protect thee, Lady Lola, I promise thee."

Lola and Max exchanged anxious glances.

"I don't like the sound of this," said Max. "It's too dangerous. Who are the Undead Army? What are they?"

"Before Tzelek cast his spell on them, they were the lords of Ah Pukuh, all thirteen generations of them, entombed in their final resting place. Now they are the earthly bodies for the Demon Warriors of Xibalba. They lie sleeping in the Black Pyramid, dressed in battle gear, awaiting the call to arms. They feel no pain; they have no fear; they cannot die, for they are dead already."

"But you said they're sleeping, right?" asked Lola in a small voice.

"Tzelek cannot awaken them until the rising of Venus—"

"We better be quick, then," she said, with a note of hysteria.

Lord 6-Dog took a deep breath. "Just one more thing . . . ," he said.

She looked at him, her face a mask of fear.

"As thou knowest, the god Ah Pukuh will rule Middleworld in the new *baktun*. It is possible that he has come to the Black Pyramid to prepare for his coronation. He may be in there at this moment, feasting with his cohorts and planning his reign of terror. I think it unlikely that our paths would cross. As to what would happen if they did, thy guess is as good as mine. But I have sworn to protect thee, Lady Lola, and I will keep my word."

It was Hermanjilio who broke the stunned silence.

"That's settled, then," he said.

"You mean they shouldn't go?" said Max, relieved.

"No, I mean Lord 6-Dog will take good care of our precious Lola. Meanwhile, I'll take a closer look at Landa's defenses. Lady Coco, please come with me and provide the necessary distractions."

"My pleasure," said Lady Coco.

"I order thee to be careful, Mother," commanded Lord 6-Dog. He dropped his voice. "Remember, thou art my most loyal and devoted warrior. I need thee by my side in the final battle."

Lady Coco smiled at him tenderly. "Don't worry about me, son. After a lifetime of waving off the menfolk, I'm ready for some action. And now, if you'll excuse me, I must go and practice my most entertaining monkey mannerisms."

They all got up to start preparing for their various missions.

"What about me?" asked Max. "What should I do?"

Hermanjilio put a hand on his shoulder.

"To you, Max, falls the most important job."

"What's that?" said Max warily.

"You will stay here and guard the camp."

Max could have cried with relief. He could have thrown himself at Hermanjilio's feet and kissed his battered old tennis shoes. *Yes! Yes! Yes!* He didn't have to go inside the Black Pyramid. He didn't have to go anywhere near Landa's camp. All he had to do was keep the campfire going and toast the odd tortilla.

Then he realized that Lola and Lord 6-Dog were listening.

"That's not fair," he said. "Why can't I go on a mission like everyone else? I've trained as hard as anyone. I'm ready to go into battle."

"Then take your orders, soldier," barked Hermanjilio. "You don't have the skills to move through the jungle without endangering us all. We all have our own tasks in this unit. You're staying here, and that's final."

Max was so happy he could have danced a jig. He pretended to clench his fists in anger. "Yes, sir," he replied, in the surliest voice he could muster.

Lola and Lord 6-Dog shot him sympathetic glances.

He shrugged as if to say, *You go ahead and enjoy yourselves; don't worry about me.* He attempted a brave smile, then turned away quickly so they wouldn't see it broaden into a grin. No zombie armies for him.

"Get some rest, everyone," said Hermanjilio. "You're going to need it."

Chapter Twenty-two
THE BLACK PYRAMID

Sometime in the early hours, Max was awakened by someone grabbing his shoulder and shaking him.

"Rise and shine," said Hermanjilio. "It's time to get ready."

"Ready for what?" slurred Max groggily.

"You can't guard the camp if you're sleeping."

Max rubbed his eyes and peered at Hermanjilio. At first he thought he was still dreaming. In the moonlight, all he could see of the archaeologist were the whites of his eyes and the pink of his mouth. The rest of him was covered in black body paint.

"Great camouflage," he said. "They won't see you coming."

Hermanjilio put his hands on his hips and turned his head sideways like a warrior on an ancient Maya fresco. "They won't see me coming," he said, "because I am the Invisible Jaguar of the Night."

Max laughed, then realized that Hermanjilio wasn't joking.

"Go get 'em, tiger," he said under his breath, as Hermanjilio melted into the jungle with Lady Coco scampering at his heels.

Lola and Lord 6-Dog were getting ready to head off in the other direction. "Art thou ready?" said Lord 6-Dog.

She nodded.

Max tried not to show his glee at being left behind. "Good luck in the Pyramid of Death," he said, trying to sound envious.

Lola looked at Lord 6-Dog.

Lord 6-Dog looked at Max.

"Art thou ready?" he asked.

Max's stomach sank into the ground. "But Hermanjilio said . . ."

"I do not see him here, young lord, dost thou?"

Lord 6-Dog tossed Max a blowgun. He dropped it. "But I can't come with you," he said. "Who's going to guard the camp?"

"It can guard itself, Hoop," said Lola. "Don't let Hermanjilio bully you."

"Thou wast trained as a warrior, not a night watchman. It is only fitting that thou shouldst join us on this skirmish. It will limber thee up for the main battle tomorrow."

"You looked so disappointed when Hermanjilio ordered you to stay behind," said Lola. Her voice was filled with admiration, and Max savored it for a moment before pulling himself together.

"The thing is," he said, "much as I would like to come with you, Hermanjilio is my commanding officer, and I have to obey him. For all I know, this is a test he's set for me. I can't put my own selfish desires before military discipline. I have to stay here."

Lola stared at him openmouthed. "You're scared," she said.

"Am not," said Max.

"Prove it," she said.

Max hesitated. What should he do? Save his skin and let a girl think he was scared? Or bluff it out and face the horrors of the Black Pyramid?

"Ready when you are," he said, picking up the blowgun.

Lola slapped him on the back. "Way to go, Hoop!"

Almost as soon as they set off, he stumbled over a fallen branch and sent assorted jungle birds flapping out of the trees in fright.

"Maybe Hermanjilio was right about you," whispered Lola crossly. "Watch where you put your feet!"

"Sorry," said Max. "Should I go back?"

"Keep marching, soldier."

Nearly an hour later, they approached the base of the Black Pyramid.

The closer they got, the more forbidding it looked.

The main pyramid had been excavated, but dense jungle covered the rest of the site and gave them cover as they crept closer.

"Wait here," whispered Lord 6-Dog.

Max and Lola waited. The jungle around them was shrouded in the sinister monochrome of night. Black flowers, gray leaves, vines like industrial steel cables, thorns like barbed wire. There was no buzz of life, and the air was as thick and heavy as molten tar.

As they stood in tense silence, Max's heart was in his mouth. It nearly stopped beating altogether when Lord 6-Dog dropped silently out of a tree in front of them.

"There are two guards on the pyramid. One keeps

watch from the topmost platform, one patrols the base," he whispered.

"Wait here, Hoop," said Lola. "Let us deal with them."

Max nodded gratefully. He watched them go, then sat down on a log and waited. And waited. Each minute seemed like an hour.

At last, Lord 6-Dog returned.

"Follow me," he said.

With a heavy heart, Max followed him up the side of the pyramid. It was an easy climb for a monkey, but steep and difficult for a boy. By the time they reached the top, Max was sure someone would hear his breathless panting.

But they were safe. The guard was crumpled on the floor, a blowgun dart sticking out of his shoulder.

Lola appeared out of the shadows, and Max helped her drag the sleeping guard beneath the carved skull and into the temple. Max shivered. Evil hung in the air like the smell of fried onions around a hot-dog stand.

"Light thy torches," commanded Lord 6-Dog.

They switched on their flashlights and gasped. The walls were made entirely of human skulls. While Max and Lola gazed around the chamber in horror, Lord 6-Dog pointed up to a particularly gruesome skull.

"Reach into the eye sockets, young lord," he instructed.

"How about we lift you up and you do it?" suggested Max.

"Art thou afraid of a carving?" said Lord 6-Dog. "These skulls are cut out of the limestone."

"They look real to me," said Max.

Lola pushed him out of the way and wiggled her thumb and forefinger into the eye sockets of the skull. "I feel something," she said. "It's a lever."

The walls were made entirely of human skulls.

"Good," said Lord 6-Dog. "Now push it down with all thy might."

There was a grinding sound, and the wall began to rotate. As one panel of stone covered the doorway, another panel slid away to reveal a small opening in the back wall.

"Make haste," ordered Lord 6-Dog, stepping through the gap, with Lola behind him. The gap was getting smaller all the time, and Max slid through just before it closed up completely.

He looked back. All along the wall, holes were drilled into the rock to let observers peer through a row of eye sockets into the first room. Max wondered what horrors had been witnessed from this vantage point.

"From this moment, be on thy guard," said Lord 6-Dog. "The pyramids were always gateways between worlds. But remember that, as the new *baktun* draws near, they are more alive than ever. Watch thy step and do not deviate from the path. Trust nothing, not even thine own perceptions. Have no fear, or they will use thy fears against thee." He patted each of them with a gentle paw. "Stay close," he said.

The passageway spiraled steeply downward. The atmosphere was damp and musty. With each step, Max felt the air close in.

He wished he had blinders like a horse so he couldn't see the walls on either side of him. They were covered from top to bottom in gory frescoes that looked horribly realistic in the dim light. Muscular warriors in jaguar-skin tunics plunged their lances into bulgy-eyed enemies. Cowering captives begged for mercy. A Maya priest held a human heart above the blood-spattered body of his victim. Shuffling past these terrifying scenes, Max found it all too easy to imagine himself as a captive being led to the sacrificial altar.

They made their way down the passageway for another twenty feet or so, until they came to a dead end.

"We'll have to go back," whispered Max, trying to sound disappointed.

"Wait," said Lola, "maybe this is one of those tricks Lord 6-Dog told us about."

They were both wrong.

Lord 6-Dog stared infently at the floor and poked in the dust with his foot until he located some finger holes in one of the flagstones. "Help me, young lord," he said.

Together the boy and the monkey heaved up the ancient trapdoor to reveal a staircase disappearing down into darkness.

"After you," said Max. Then, almost trembling with fear, he followed Lord 6-Dog and Lola into the unknown.

The staircase led them into an enormous chamber.

"There's another pyramid inside this one!" said Max.

"They used to build new temples on top of old ones," explained Lola.

"Silence!" commanded Lord 6-Dog. "We are entering the burial chamber of the lords of Ah Pukuh. Woe betide the fool who dares disturb their slumber. Touch nothing. Tread only in my footsteps."

Max wanted to turn tail and run, but Lola pushed him forward.

"Don't look," she said. "Just follow Lord 6-Dog."

They began to work their way down the steep stairs cut into the terraced walls of the inner pyramid.

Max knew he shouldn't look.

He tried not to look.

He looked.

On both sides of the steps, reclining on every surface, lay the richly attired bodies of hundreds of dead Maya warriors. Some were nothing but crumbling bones. Others moldered in various stages of decay. But many of them looked fresh, as if they had only just died, their skin still glistening with body paint. All of them wore battle gear, and clutched an arsenal of swords, axes, and spears.

It was too much. Max made a noise. A sort of muffled scream.

The eyes of the corpses who still had eyes opened in unison. With a creaking of bones, they sat bolt upright, even the skeletons. Their heads swiveled toward Max.

This time, Lola screamed as well.

"They will not hurt thee," said Lord 6-Dog. "I am sure of it." He didn't sound sure. "Only the Black Jaguar can bring them to their feet. But let us hurry."

Max and Lola did not need telling twice. They went flying down the rest of the steps until they reached the base of the inner pyramid. From there, more steps led down through a hole in the floor.

Max plunged through the hole after the other two and into another long, narrow passage. Lola and Lord 6-Dog were already out of sight ahead of him.

"Wait for me," he called. In his panic to catch up, he missed his step and fell flat on his face. The impact knocked his flashlight from his hand. He watched in horror as it skidded along the floor, bounced off a wall, flickered, and went out.

"Lola! Lord 6-Dog! Help me!"

Only the echoes of his own voice replied.

He got down on his hands and knees, gingerly feeling around on the dusty floor for the flashlight. Eventually, he found it.

Please work, he prayed.

It didn't.

"Lola! Lord 6-Dog! Where are you?"

This time he thought he heard a faint response.

"Lola! Lord 6-Dog! Come back!"

"Max? Is that you?" The voice was far away but getting closer.

"I'm over here! My flashlight's gone out."

Now he could definitely hear footsteps getting closer. He breathed a long and heartfelt sigh of relief. For a moment there, he'd thought he was a goner.

Far down the corridor, a light was flickering toward him.

"Max, where are you?"

"Straight ahead," he called.

Who was that? Was it Lola? It didn't sound like her. And yet he knew that voice.

"Stay there, Max! I'm coming!"

"Mom?"

The nightmare was over! Here he was, alone in the dark in the Pyramid of Death, convinced he was about to be captured by demons, and who should come along to rescue him but the person he loved most in the world! He was weak with amazement and happiness.

"*Bambino!* It is you!" Carla Murphy hugged her only son and kissed his head. "How can this be? I thought you were still in Boston! I am so happy to see you, but what are you doing here?"

"What are *you* doing here?"

"We have so many questions for each other! But all that matters is that we're together again. Come, let's go and tell your father the good news." She took Max's hand and began to lead him down the passageway. "He's just down here with his friends. . . ."

"What friends?"

"Oh, they're such nice people. I can't wait for you to meet them."

What was going on? It crossed Max's mind that a group of nerdy archaeologists must have got together to watch the rising of Venus from the Black Pyramid. In which case, he had to warn them to get out.

"Mom," he said, "it's not safe in here."

"Sì, sì, bambino," she said absentmindedly as she looked around to get her bearings. "Ah, here we are. . . ."

Her candle illuminated a set of ornately carved double doors. She reached out to knock, but before her hand touched the wood, the doors were flung open. Max blinked with surprise as bright light spilled out into the corridor, bringing with it a pungent aroma and a wave of chattering voices.

A figure stepped out to greet them.

It was Lola.

"Hoop!" she cried. "Isn't this fantastic? I was going to come back for you, but Carla insisted on getting you herself. She wanted to surprise you."

"And she succeeded," said Max.

Now that he could see his mother properly, he registered that she was wearing a long, embroidered dress with a huge jade necklace and a feathered headdress.

"That's quite an outfit, Mom!"

"Isn't it fun? Now come and join the party, *bambino*."

Max opened his mouth, but nothing came out. He didn't know where to begin. Taking an arm each, Carla and Lola escorted him into a large room lit by flaming torches. Someone had gone to a lot of trouble to clean it out and decorate it to look like a lavish Maya palace. Woven rugs hung on the walls, and a roaring fire blazed in the hearth. All around the room, alcoves had been carved into the walls. If it had been a church in Italy, figures of the saints would have looked down from these niches. But in this room, each space was filled by a large owl. At first Max thought they were stuffed, but as he moved, he noticed their unblinking yellow eyes were following him. At ground level, men dressed as Maya lords reclined on cushioned ledges or stood around in merry groups, filling the air with their cigar smoke and raucous laughter. The festivities were evidently in full swing.

On a raised platform in the center of the room was a stone table, laden with food and drink. Seated at this table, deep in conversation, were Lord 6-Dog and two other Maya lords. Lord 6-Dog appeared to be demonstrating to them the advantages of his monkey body. It was only when Max drew closer that he realized he knew one of the men.

"Dad?"

Like his wife, Frank Murphy was dressed in traditional Maya costume. He stood up when he heard Max's voice and beckoned his son over to join them.

"Max! What a wonderful coincidence! 6-Dog here has been telling me all about it! But you must come and meet our host! I know you're going to get on famously!"

Max had never seen his father so animated. He was usually

a shrinking violet at parties, just looking for an opportunity to escape. But tonight he was smiling and talking ten to the dozen, like some cheesy TV presenter.

Max guessed he'd been drinking elixir.

Party on, dude, he thought. *Tomorrow, we go home.*

The nightmare was over.

It was over.

He hugged his father and shook Lord 6-Dog's hand, then waited politely to be introduced to the third Maya lord at the table.

He was obviously supposed to be someone very important because his chair was bigger than the others' and was draped with jaguar skins. He was enormously, disgustingly fat, and his chalky white skin was covered in hideous black bruises. He looked like a bloated body washed up on a beach, the corpse of a plague victim perhaps. To make the effect even more ghastly, he wore rouged cheeks and bright red lipstick.

As if this character's appearance was not striking enough, his tentlike tunic was covered in little bells that looked like they were carved out of real bone and jingled dully at their wearer's every move. As a finishing touch, his thick black hair was tied in an elaborate headdress, decorated with dried human tongues and shriveled eyeballs that bounced on their nerve cords as he spoke.

Max had never seen someone go to so much trouble for a masquerade costume. The fat suit alone must have cost a fortune, and the makeup was incredible. No expense had been spared. He'd even brought along five massive, vicious-looking dogs that sat behind him in a semicircle, growling and slavering.

"Eat! Drink! Let us celebrate this joyous reunion!"

"Max, I'd like to introduce you to our host, Lord Ah Pukuh."

"Pleased to meet you," said Max, reluctantly going along with the joke.

Ah Pukuh held up a finger, as if asking Max to wait a moment. Then he leaned to one side, lifted up one of his huge buttocks, and noisily passed gas—the most noxious gas that Max had ever smelled. He thought he might faint from the fumes. Meanwhile everyone else in the room was laughing, cheering, and clapping. Max's mother was leading the applause. Was this the same woman who had a fit if Max drank from the milk carton? She'd evidently relaxed her standards since she'd been in San Xavier.

Carla indicated that Max should sit next to their corpulent host, while she and Lola took chairs opposite.

"Welcome!" boomed Ah Pukuh as Max sat down.

Whoa! The blast of foul breath from the guy's black hole of a mouth nearly knocked Max right off the chair. He tried, surreptitiously, to cover his nose with his hand as the fat guy continued to speak. "Eat! Drink! Let us celebrate this joyous reunion! What will you have, young lord?"

"Nothing, thanks," said Max, who was feeling queasy.

"But I insist!" said Ah Pukuh. He clapped his hands. "Bring roast gibnut and hot chocolate for our guest!" he bellowed.

Immediately, a servant appeared with a loaded plate and a pottery goblet. The gibnut still had its head and tail attached. It lay on the plate like a burned rat. Max surveyed it miserably as the servant filled his goblet with a viscous brown liquid the color of old blood.

"Dig in," urged Ah Pukuh.

Carla screamed with laughter. "Dig in! It's an archaeologist joke," she explained to Max. "Do eat something, *bambino*; you don't want to offend dear old Pookie."

Max gave the gibnut a desultory poke with his fork. He pushed back from the table in horror as the rodent opened an eye and turned its head toward him. "Aaaaagggghhhh," he shrieked, jumping to his feet.

The rodent sat up, looked nervously from side to side, leapt onto Max's shoulder, and sprang from there onto the floor. With a nod from Ah Pukuh, the waiting dogs ran after it and gobbled it down.

"Mom," whispered Max, "can we get out of here?"

"But why, *bambino*? The party has only just started."

"I just want to go home."

"Home? But, *caro mio*, this is our home now."

"You mean we're going to live in San Xavier?"

"I mean that Pookie has invited us to live here, in the Black Pyramid."

"Can we just drop the joke, Mom? I'm tired. I've had enough. You have no idea what I've been through. I thought you might be dead."

"Dead?" Carla threw her head back and laughed. "We will never die!"

"I'll drink to that!" Lola cackled as they clinked their goblets in a toast.

"Mom, have you been drinking elixir?"

"Yes, and it's even more delicious than Chianti. Be a good boy and find me some more, would you?"

Max went over to his father. "I think Mom's had too much to drink," he said. "I can't get any sense out of her. Will you tell me what's going on?"

"Of course I will, Max. We have such good news for you."

"Good news?"

"Yes, jumping into that cenote was the best thing we ever did."

"It was?"

"If we hadn't done that, we'd never have met Ah Pukuh and the gang. We made friends with them in Xibalba. They're a great crew. And they'll be running the world soon, so we're in a good position. It's all ours for the asking, Max . . . we'll be rich beyond our wildest dreams."

"Thy father speaks the truth," said Lord 6-Dog. "It pains me now to think of all the time I have wasted in pointless combat with my brother Tzelek. Far better that he and I should work together. The entire world will be ours to command."

"You've both gone mad," said Max. "Why are you obsessed with money and power all of a sudden?"

"Isn't that what everyone wants, Max? It's why we all go to work."

"No, it's not. You love archaeology, Dad! You've always said you'd do it even if they didn't pay you."

"I've had it with old pots! Be honest, Max, haven't you ever wished that we led a more glamorous life? Or that we lived in a bigger house? What about a hot tub? An indoor pool? One of those plasma TVs you like so much?"

"Dad, you sound like the shopping channel. I thought you disapproved of the consumer society."

"That's what I'm trying to tell you, Max. I've changed. Everything's changed. From now on, we're going to live like Hollywood stars. We'll take our vacations in the south of France or anywhere you want to go. We'll reserve a permanent suite at Disney World, if you like. We'll employ a chef to make

330

you fresh pizza every day and all the homemade ice cream you can eat. How does that sound?"

"I don't want any of it, Dad. I just want our old life back."

"Oh, come on, Max, there must be something you want. What was that game you kept asking me to buy back in Boston?"

"The new limited edition *Hellhounds 3-D?*"

"That's the one. Limited edition, my foot! We'll commission the designers to create an edition just for you—*starring* you, if you like. Now that's what I call a limited edition! And you'll have all the time in the world to play it, because you need never go to school. You'll have enough money to buy everything your heart desires, so you can just laze around for all eternity."

"Professor Murphy!" scolded Lola. "Life isn't just about buying things."

"At last," said Max, "the voice of reason."

"Life is also about the things that money can't buy," Lola continued, "like revenge. Think about it, Max. Chan Kan really made a fool of you with that pepper soup. Wouldn't you like to give him a taste of his own medicine?"

"And dost thou not hate the way Lord Hermanjilio orders thee around?" asked Lord 6-Dog. "Wouldst thou not like to turn the tables?"

"What about that teacher who failed you in woodworking just because you sawed his desk in half?" put in his father.

"And that girl who stood you up in seventh grade?" added his mother. "She'll be sorry when she sees you driving around Boston in a red Ferrari. . . ."

Max put his hands over his ears. "What are you all saying?"

he cried. "I know I used to be greedy and materialistic—"

"And selfish," interrupted Lola.

"And selfish," added Max, "but I'm not like that anymore."

"Of course you're like that," boomed Ah Pukuh from his throne. "All boys your age are like that. And I'm happy to say that most of them never grow out of it. Why, I can remember . . ." His reminiscences were drowned out by a barrage of flatulence.

"The question is, *bambino*," said Carla, "are you with us?"

"I'm your son, aren't I?"

"The continuation of that filial arrangement," said Frank Murphy, "depends on whether or not you decide to turn over a new leaf."

"Is there something in particular you want me to do?"

"Since you ask, there is. We would like you to sign in blood right now, committing yourself to the protection of Lord Ah Pukuh. He'll be like a godfather to you and spoil you rotten."

"Just sign," wheedled his mother, "and we'll be together for all eternity."

"Obey thy parents," commanded Lord 6-Dog.

"It's a good deal, Hoop," added Lola.

"I'm not sure," said Max. "It sounds creepy. I need to think."

The mood in the room changed instantly. The light hardened from a rosy glow of flames to a cold blue ashy glare. The laughter died down. The dogs growled and licked their chops.

"He needs to think," said his mother, mimicking him.

"He's never needed to think before," said his father. "Why start now?"

"What a loser," agreed Lola in disgust.

"Make him breathe smoke from burning chili peppers until he obeys," suggested Lord 6-Dog.

"Why are you all picking on me?" asked Max. "What happened to the happy reunion?"

"It might have been a happy reunion for you," said his father pointedly.

"What do you mean?"

"To be honest, son, we were happier without you."

"The truth is, *bambino*, we've never liked you, not from the moment you were born." Carla leaned over to Lola. "You know the type," she said in a stage whisper, "always crying and puking. The mess he made on my silk shirts! I used to pay strangers on the street to hold him so I wouldn't have to. Then there was all the bed-wetting and the nose-picking and the whining. He made my life a living hell."

"Mom . . . ?"

His father put an arm around him. "The truth hurts, eh, son? But having you ruined our lives. We never risked having another child in case it turned out to be as boring as you. I know you thought I worked long hours because I was so interested in the ancient Maya. But, in truth, I just didn't want to come home to you. Half the time, I wasn't even in the office—I was at the movies or a ball game. Other fathers would be there with their sons, but not me. I couldn't bear to be near you. . . ."

Max's jaw dropped. He couldn't believe his ears. Occasionally, when his parents had refused to let him stay out late or said no to the most expensive sneakers, he'd suspected he was adopted. But he'd never dreamed they hated him this much.

"You need to start pulling your weight in this family, Max. Just sign the paper and we'll make a fresh start," said his father.

"Yes," said his mother, smiling. "We'll forgive you for everything and be a happy family. It's up to you, *bambino*."

It was tempting to sign and have it done with.

He was afraid that, if he didn't, he'd never see his parents again.

Afraid that he'd be alone in the world . . .

Afraid that . . .

Afraid?

They will use thy fears against thee.

Max took a deep breath.

What was he afraid of?

That these sadistic bullies could possibly be his parents?

That any parents were better than no parents?

That his parents had never loved him?

He considered the evidence.

He remembered when he was little, sitting on his mother's knee and waving to the moon Dog. He remembered all those Saturday-morning soccer games when his father had cheered him on in the rain. He remembered the night the laser printer broke down, and his parents had stayed up till dawn trying to get his fifty-page project on state capitals printed out. He'd gone to bed in tears. But when he came down for breakfast, there was his project, all fifty pages, tied up in a big red ribbon.

Would they have done these things if they thought he was just a nuisance?

Then he remembered his mother's expression on the evening they left for San Xavier, and he knew beyond a shadow of a doubt that his parents loved him.

He looked at the faces around the table and saw their hate-filled eyes for what they were. He'd let himself be tricked by the demons of hell.

Mustering all his courage, he leaned over to Ah Pukuh. "Is that all you've got, fatso?" he said.

Ah Pukuh laughed loud and long, like the sound of a saw cutting down trees. His multiple chins rippled and shook with merriment.

Max felt very small and very crushable.

"I've only just begun," said Ah Pukuh. "I have the next four hundred years to torture you, Max Murphy. I know everything about you and I will make you suffer in ways you cannot yet imagine. Surrender now, or you will regret it."

"No," said Max. He wanted to sound brave and manly and defiant, but his voice came out as a squeak.

"Don't do this to us, son," cried his parents, as chunks of flesh fell off their faces and Max could see patches of white skull peeking through their peeling, shriveled scalps.

Lola touched his arm with a skeletal finger. "Save me," she said. "There's still time to sign."

"No," said Max.

And when he looked again, she was a decomposing corpse.

The stench was overpowering.

"I told you it wouldn't work," said the corpse of Lola. "We should have just ripped out his heart, like I said. Come on, Pus, you lost the bet. Pay up."

"Not so quick, Scab Stripper. How about double or nothing?" said the demon of pus, who had so recently been posing as Max's mother.

"Let's suck his brains out," suggested the remains of Lord 6-Dog, who was now just random bits of fur and gristle.

"Not for me, Blood Gatherer. I'm on a diet," said the skull of Frank Murphy. One of his eyeballs fell out, bounced on the table, and rolled onto the floor. An owl swooped down and carried it back to his perch.

"Set the hounds on him," ordered Ah Pukuh.

"Perfect!" said the demon of pus. "Apparently, the boy likes to play a game called *Hellhounds 3-D*. Let us see how he likes the real thing."

The five massive dogs were snarling and foaming at the mouth, waiting for the signal to attack. Max was shaking. He was out of tricks. He was going to be torn limb from limb by a pack of devil dogs in the halls of Ah Pukuh, god of violent and unnatural death. It was certainly a fitting end for a gamer.

And then he realized how to win. These guys were no more real than the characters in his games. They didn't understand love or courage or truth. They were casebook cartoon bad guys, motivated by hate and greed. If he refused to play by their rules, he might be able to blow the cosmic circuitry.

Ah Pukuh clicked his fat greasy fingers.

The dogs leapt.

"I know my parents love me."

Max saw the dogs' yellow eyes and their sharp yellow teeth.

"I am not afraid of you."

He smelled their foul breath and felt their burning saliva that dripped like acid from their foaming jaws.

"Lord 6-Dog will protect me."

Their bodies barreled against him, and their claws knocked him down. He closed his eyes, bracing himself for the first bite.

All was quiet.

He didn't move.

"Hoop?" said a voice.

He opened his eyes slowly. He was back in the corridor, lying flat where he'd fallen in the dark. Lola was crouching over him, holding his flashlight.

"Hoop!" she cried. "What happened to you?"

"You won't believe it," said Max as she helped him to his feet. "I've just met Ah Pukuh. But I stood my ground. You would have been proud of me."

"You weren't scared, then?"

"A bit. But old Pookie is basically all talk."

Lola raised a sardonic eyebrow. "He's not the only one," she said.

"What do you mean?" asked Max, baffled.

She pointed at his jeans.

He looked down. There was a large wet patch at the top of his legs. Had he really been so scared of the dogs that he'd wet himself?

Probably.

He was mortified.

"There were these five huge dogs—"

"Oh, did the doggies scare ooo? Poor lickle baby!" She sneered. "We should've bwought some diapers for the lickle baby!"

"Stop it! I'm not a baby!" yelled Max. "You don't know what it was like."

"You're a bit old to go around wetting yourself, Hoop. I'd see a doctor, if I were you. Just wait till the others hear about this—"

"No, please," begged Max, "don't tell them."

"Why not?"

"Because it's embarrassing."

"Are you worried about what they'll think of you?"

"Yes."

"Well, I can tell you what they think of you. They think the same as I do—that you're a jerk. A useless little jerk with stupid red hair and a face like a rat with acne."

"Stop it, Lola! I thought we were friends!"

She snorted with derision. "Why would a hot girl like me ever be friends with a jerk like you? I've been leading you on for a laugh, but now I'm going to tell you the truth. You're sad, you're ugly, you're boring, and you're disgusting. Even when you're not soaked in pee, you smell. You've got bad breath, and those zits on your chin make me feel sick. Nobody likes you, Massimo Francis Sylvanus Murphy. Even your name is stupid. Everybody's laughing at you behind your back, and they'll laugh even harder when I tell them about this. If I were you, I'd just run away now while there's time."

Max sank back to the floor in misery. He felt as gutted as a fish on a slab. It was so unfair. He could see that the old Max Murphy, the couch potato who'd landed at San Xavier airport, hadn't been much of a catch. But he thought he'd improved since then. His face was tan and his body was fitter. He'd tried to be a better person on the inside, too, since that day on the Monkey River.

But, apparently, it all counted for nothing.

All Max's bravado melted away.

There was no point in going on.

Maybe his parents didn't love him after all. How could anyone love him? He was a failure. A creep. He'd always suspected that girls found him repulsive. Now his worst fear had come true.

Wait a minute . . .

His worst fear!

They will use thy fears against thee.

He looked up. Lola was grinning triumphantly.

"Give me a kiss," he said.

Her smile disappeared.

"Come on," he coaxed, "why not? You're not such a catch yourself, you know. You've got a big nose and a bad haircut, and you're so bossy you give me a headache. I think you'd be lucky to kiss a hunk like me."

"What?" she said incredulously.

"Face it, Monkey Girl, you can't get to me because you're not real. You're a product of my imagination. I don't have to listen to anything you say."

He just had time to grab the flashlight before she melted back into the wall.

Phew. That was a close one.

Max got to his feet and started to make his way quickly down the corridor. Running around a corner, he ran smack into Lola.

"Hoop!" she cried. "What happened to you?"

"My flashlight broke. . . ." He flicked the switch to demonstrate, and it came on instantly.

"It seems to be working now," she said.

Was she real or was she a ghost?

He shone the flashlight on his crotch.

"What are you doing?" she asked, appalled.

It was dry. She was real.

"Hoop, what are you doing?" she repeated.

"Nothing." He pointed the flashlight away from him. "It's just that things got a bit weird for a while."

He told her all about the phantom party, except for the bit at the end where her evil twin had appeared to him in the passageway. No need for her to know that his worst fear in the world concerned girls and what they thought of him.

"Poor Hoop, that sounds awful. Let's get out of here."

"So, while we were separated, did Ah Pukuh get at you, too?" he asked.

She nodded.

"What with?"

She shuddered. "I'll tell you another time. Now, which way? This place has as many tunnels as a termite nest. . . ."

"Wait!" said Max. "There's something I have to ask you."

"What is it, Hoop? We have to hurry—"

"Do I have bad breath?"

"What? This isn't the moment to discuss personal hygiene," she snapped. "We have to find Lord 6-Dog."

"Thou hast found him," said the monkey, stepping out of the shadows.

Max peered into the monkey's eyes. "It is you, isn't it?"

Lord 6-Dog held his gaze. "Indeed it is," he said. "But am I to assume that the spirits have been testing thee with phantasms?"

Max nodded. "Did they test you, too, Your Majesty?"

"My test will be Tzelek," said Lord 6-Dog gravely. "Remember, this is but a rehearsal. No matter what thou hast endured this night, young lord, worse is to come. So far thou hast been menaced with magic and illusion; on the morrow, thou wilt face the reality of pure evil. Until Tzelek is vanquished, each one of us is in immeasurable danger."

"Do you still think we can vanquish him?" asked Max doubtfully, but Lord 6-Dog had bounded ahead down the passageway and didn't hear. Max and Lola hurried after him, wrapped in their own thoughts.

"Was that a yes or a no on the bad-breath question?" he asked.

She stopped dead and made a noise like a cat when someone steps on its tail.

"That bad?" he said, horrified, cupping his hand on his chin and trying to direct his breath upward so he could smell it himself.

But Lola was pointing straight ahead. "Oh no!" she said. "I can't bear it."

Once again, the passageway ended in a solid wall. But this time there was no trapdoor, no way forward.

"What now?" wailed Lola, reprising her tortured cat noise. "I just want to get out of here."

"Please don't say we have to go back," said Max. "Anything but that."

"Tsk, tsk," Lord 6-Dog chided them. "Have faith."

Using faint indentations in the wall, he began to climb up the stones. When he reached the ceiling, Max and Lola were astonished to see his head and then his body and finally his tail disappear through the solid rock. A few moments later his head reappeared upside down.

"The passage is free to the caves," he announced. "We have our escape route. Now follow me and do not hesitate."

Max prepared himself for pain as he forced his head up

against the ceiling. To his surprise, he met with no resistance, and was able to climb straight through, up into another passageway. The air was less oppressive here and, giddy with relief, he sensed that their escape plan was going to work. The rest was easy, and Lord 6-Dog led them through a network of caves and tunnels, out into the sweet, wet, humming, buzzing, living forest.

It was daylight by the time they got back to the camp, but Lady Coco and Hermanjilio had not returned.

"Take a rest," said Lord 6-Dog. "I will keep a lookout."

He took off through the trees.

Max and Lola were dead tired and threw themselves down on the grass.

"What a night!" said Max.

"*Sí, ¡qué noche!* A most interesting night," said a voice behind them.

They jumped to their feet and spun around.

A dark-haired man dressed all in black clicked his fingers loudly. Men in black sidled out from among the trees and surrounded Max and Lola.

"Who are you?" asked Max, but he knew the answer.

"I am Count Antonio de Landa," said the Spaniard, pointing his goateed chin in the air and making that melodramatic cape-flicking movement that Max had first seen at the hotel in Puerto Muerto.

"But the big question"—the count sneered, striding over to Lola and grabbing her roughly by the jaw—"is who are you?" As she fought to free herself, he held her face steady in his black leather gloves. "The gods always like the pretty ones," he said. "They will be pleased with you. Are you ready to sacrifice yourself, my dear? You have an appointment at the altar."

"Spanish scum!" she yelled, and spat in his face.

He slapped her hard across the cheek. "Take them to the ship."

Chapter Twenty-three
CAPTURED

Whump. Whump. Whump. The high-powered speed-boat met each wave head-on as they raced across the ocean. Max and Lola were lying on the floor of the boat, drenched by rain and saltwater spray, their hands and feet bound with rope, their mouths tightly gagged.

It had all been going so well. Max had been so relieved to get out of the Black Pyramid and get back to the safety of the camp. He was proud of himself for standing up to Ah Pukuh and his demons. And even though their impersonations had been grotesque, their attempts had reassured him that his real parents weren't far away.

Against all odds, victory had been within their grasp. Now Hermanjilio, Lord 6-Dog, and Lady Coco would have to fight the forces of evil alone. When Venus rose in the morning, Lola would be tied to the sacrificial altar and . . . what? What fate did Landa have in store for Max? Would he be sacrificed, too?

He strained to turn his head until he could see Lola. Her hair was plastered to her face. She looked as seasick as he felt.

He thought he might puke at any moment. How would that work with the gag? It was too disgusting to contemplate.

Just when he thought he could hold it in no longer, the boat stopped.

A white yacht towered over them.

La Espada, Cadiz.

Someone yanked him up roughly and hustled him and Lola into a cargo net. Before he knew what was happening, they were scooped off their feet and winched into the air. Next minute they were hanging a few feet above the surface of the ocean. Max thought he could see a shark fin cutting through the water toward them.

Would he rather be eaten first or watch Lola being eaten?

There was no time to decide, for the cargo net suddenly lurched, swung around, and dumped them heavily onto the deck, like two fat codfish.

Lola was carried away in one direction, while Max was dragged off in the other. Two guards manhandled him roughly along gangways and up stairways until they reached a carpeted corridor on an upper deck. Here the guards untied him and removed his gag.

"Where are you taking me?" asked Max.

One of the guards answered in a torrent of Spanish. Max was none the wiser.

"Is it to Landa?" guessed Max. "I have nothing to say to that pig."

The guards seemed to find this hilarious. They nodded and leered as they pushed him toward a set of varnished wooden doors at the end of the corridor.

So this was it. The long-awaited confrontation with Count Antonio de Landa.

Max wondered if the count had an onboard torture chamber. Well, at least if he was busy torturing Max, it meant he wasn't engaged in sacrificing Lola. Wow! Max got a lump in his throat as he realized that was probably the most selfless thought he'd ever had in his life. But what was the point of being a reformed character if a sadistic Spaniard was about to pull out your fingernails one by one?

Max's thoughts were spiraling into hysteria when the guards pushed him headlong through the doors.

He went sprawling onto the carpet. When he staggered to his feet, he found himself in a plush, wood-paneled stateroom. There was a long table in the center of the room and red velvet banquettes around the edge. At the far end, a man was standing with his back to the room, gazing out to sea. He was wearing a white linen suit.

"Uncle Ted!"

Uncle Ted turned around. His face looked even more furrowed. He had dark shadows under his eyes. He looked like he hadn't slept for at least a week.

"Uncle Ted, what are you doing here?"

"I could ask you the same question, young man."

"This is Landa's yacht! Are you in league with him? I might have known it!"

"I think we should start this discussion with an apology."

"It better be good," said Max.

He waited.

"An apology from you," clarified Uncle Ted.

"Me? For what?"

"Let me think," said Uncle Ted. "For betraying my trust, perhaps? For stealing the Red Jaguar? For doing your utmost to destroy my business?"

"Your business?" Max stared at him in disbelief. "Don't you understand that the world is about to end and you won't even have a business if we don't stop your friend Landa from waking the Undead Army?"

Uncle Ted looked alarmed. "What have they done to you? I heard you've been keeping bad company, Max. Have they brainwashed you?"

"Me, brainwashed? That's a good one. So how long have you been involved in this plot, Uncle Ted?"

"Plot?" Uncle Ted sounded genuinely puzzled.

"The plot for Landa-slash-Tzelek to take over the world."

"That's enough, Max!" said Uncle Ted. "Can you imagine how worried I've been? First your parents disappear. Then you run off into the jungle with a band of thieves. If this is what it's like to have children, then—" He stopped himself abruptly and continued in a colder, more businesslike tone. "All I'm trying to do is recover a valuable artifact for my client. If you'd just tell me what you've done with the Red Jaguar, perhaps we can sort it out without recourse to the law."

Max narrowed his eyes and looked hard at Uncle Ted. Either he was an Oscar-worthy actor or he really didn't know Landa's plans.

"Your client has been possessed by the spirit of an evil Maya priest. He's using the Black Jaguar to release the demon warriors of the underworld."

"Oh, grow up, Max! I don't think you understand how serious this is. Larceny, assault, sabotage, property damage . . . you and your girlfriend are in a lot of trouble."

"She's not my girlfriend," muttered Max. "If you could just get us off this boat, I'll tell you everything. . . ."

Uncle Ted ran his hands through his hair.

"I'm afraid that's not possible. The matter is out of my hands. Thanks to your delinquent behavior, Count de Landa is calling the shots." Uncle Ted lowered his voice. "You know I'm no fan of his, Max, but you've forced me to take his side. He's my client and I made a deal with him. Now he wants his merchandise and he won't give up until he gets it. He's ruthless, Max. So stop all this nonsense right now."

"It's not nonsense. It was you who told me that if Landa's journal was not a fake, it could destroy the world."

"I should have kept my mouth shut."

"But Uncle Ted—"

Max saw a movement out of the corner of his eye. He turned, once again expecting to see Landa. But it was Lucky Jim. He was sitting there, arms folded, staring straight ahead.

"Lucky, you're a Maya—you know I'm telling the truth. Or is it you who's in league with Landa? I don't know who to trust anymore."

Lucky Jim ignored him.

Uncle Ted stepped forward and stared into Max's eyes. "Paranoia, stealing, delusions . . . Have you been taking drugs?"

"Of course not! I'm telling you the truth, Uncle Ted! You said yourself that anything can happen, that things are never what they seem around here. If you don't help me stop him, Landa is going to sacrifice Lola to Ah Pukuh."

Uncle Ted sat down heavily on a banquette. He looked like he was trying hard to keep his temper. "Let me spell it out. All the count wants is the return of the Red Jaguar."

"No, Uncle Ted, you're wrong! Landa wants to rule the world! Why do you think he's collecting Jaguar Stones?"

"It's not my business, Max."

"It is your business! It's all our business! Someone has to

stop him! I know you deal with some shady characters, Uncle Ted, but surely even you can recognize pure evil when you see it?"

"That's enough, Max!" Uncle Ted put his head in his hands.

Max turned back to Lucky Jim.

"Lucky, you know what I'm talking about!" he said. "You understand the power of the Jaguar Stones!"

Lucky Jim shrugged. He looked uncomfortable.

"You were right," Max continued, "the ancient Maya are still trying to run things in this jungle. Last night, in the Black Pyramid, I met Ah Pukuh—"

"You tourists should stay out of our temples," said Lucky Jim.

"No!" yelled Max. "We've gone way past that. It's not about who's a tourist and who's a Maya. We're all in this together. You can't ignore history anymore, Lucky Jim, because it's playing out right in front of us. Your children will ask you why you didn't try to save them from the living hell that will be their lives when Ah Pukuh takes over. Are you going to blame that on the tourists? Or are you going to do something about it, while there's still time?" Max's face, red with fury, was right in Lucky's face. Their noses almost touched. "At least you could tell Uncle Ted that I'm not crazy."

Silence.

Max took a softer tone. "We need you, Lucky! There's going to be a huge battle tonight between good and evil. The immortal Lord 6-Dog is out there right now. We used the Green Jaguar of Itzamna to bring him back. He's inside the body of a howler monkey, and Tzelek is inside Landa. . . ."

Max's voice trailed off as even he realized how ridiculous it all sounded.

Lucky Jim got up and left the room.

"Now you've gone too far," said Uncle Ted, "making fun of Lucky's heritage. I'm disgusted with you, Max. Here I am, trying to protect you. . . ."

"Don't give me that," said Max. He was past caring what he said. "You hate me just like you hate my father."

Uncle Ted looked genuinely appalled. "That's not true," he said quietly. "It took me a day or two, but I grew fond of you, Max. You reminded me of myself at your age. Sure, you were a little spoiled, but I thought a few weeks in San Xavier would change that."

"I have changed, Uncle Ted."

"But, sadly, not for the better. Listen to yourself. Evil spirits, human sacrifices, demon warriors . . . I'm too frustrated to talk to you anymore. You should have stayed in your room that night, Max. You gave me your word and you broke it."

"But my word wasn't good enough for you, was it? I was going to stay in my room until I realized you'd locked the door. Why couldn't you have trusted me? You locked me away like a prisoner."

Uncle Ted sounded close to tears. "No, I locked you away like something precious. I just wanted to keep you safe, Max." The pain in Uncle Ted's eyes hardened into resolve. "But now I can see the error of my ways. I'll give you a little time to think about things, and then I'm handing you over to Landa."

With that, Uncle Ted swept out of the stateroom.

The two guards, who'd evidently been waiting outside the door, barged in and grabbed Max again. They looked disappointed to find him in one piece and did their best to injure him themselves as they pushed and pulled him through hatches and down ladders to the bottom of the ship.

At the end of a long metal gangway, a door was unlocked

and Max was pushed in. He found himself in a small cabin with no porthole and no furniture except for a sink and a metal bunk bolted to the wall.

Now what? Max checked every inch of the cabin for a way out. He pressed his ear against the door, but he could hear nothing. He tried kicking the door for a while, but no one came. He paced up and down. He lay on the bunk. As the hours went by, he grew more and more wretched. This waiting and not knowing was as bad as any torture the creepy count could have devised.

What was happening? Where was Lola? How would Hermanjilio and two talking monkeys be able to outwit Landa and all his men? The more he thought about it, the more his heart sank. Whichever way you looked at it, they were in big trouble. And there was nothing he could do to help.

As he lay on the bunk in that airless cabin, he gradually dozed off. He awoke with a start to the blaring of an alarm. There were men shouting and the sounds of running feet all over the boat. Someone ran past his door and up the stairs. He heard motorboats starting up, revving their engines, and roaring off.

Then all was quiet again.

What was going on? Had something happened onshore?

Had Hermanjilio made his move?

Max banged on the door. He kicked the walls. He shouted. After a while, he thought he heard a noise in the corridor. He held his breath and listened as closely as he could.

Yes, there it was again. There was something or someone out there.

"Let me out! Let me out!" he shouted.

He heard the lock slowly turning.

Suddenly, the door flew open and a familiar figure half stepped and half fell into the cabin.

"Uncle Ted! What's happening?"

"Some kind of emergency . . . all gone ashore . . . good time to escape . . ."

Max took in his uncle's slurred speech, his unsteady gait, and the whiskey fumes that wafted from his pores. "Are you all right, Uncle Ted?"

"Had a drink or two with the captain . . . to get him out of the way. . . . He's sleeping it off . . . on the bridge. . . . You must go now."

Before Max could ask any more questions, Uncle Ted lurched back down the gangway toward the stairs. When Max caught up with him on the deck, he was leaning perilously over the guardrail and pointing at something off to stern.

"That'll get you to shore. . . . Think you can handle it?"

Max peered over the side. A little boat with an outboard motor bobbed below, straining at its rope.

"I don't understand," said Max.

"Zodiac inflatable . . . jus' pull the cord and slam it into gear. . . ."

"No, I mean, why are you helping me escape?"

Uncle Ted looked like he might cry. "Turns out I do owe you an apology, Max. . . . The way they dragged that poor girl off . . . I think you were right about Landa. . . . I should have listened—"

"Lola?" interrupted Max. "Where did they take her?"

"To shore . . ."

"I have to go; I have to save her."

"Save your own skin, Max. . . . Get as far away from here as possible."

"I'm going to find Lola. Are you coming?" said Max coldly.

His uncle shook his head. "What we should do"—he staggered slightly—"what we should do is call the police."

"There's no time! Don't you understand? Landa's going to sacrifice Lola. We need to stop him!"

Max was pulling his uncle toward the ladder down to the Zodiac, but Uncle Ted clumsily disengaged himself.

"Uncle Ted, come on. Lola needs us!"

"Sorry, Max . . . I'm not the hero type. . . ."

"Are you scared of Landa?" sneered Max.

"Yes," said Uncle Ted.

"So you'd let Lola die rather than face up to him?"

"We Murphys look after number one."

"Well, this Murphy has learned that you can't live your life that way."

"I tried to be a hero once. . . . It went wrong. . . . She died. . . . I should have just called the police—"

Max impatiently interrupted, gripping his uncle's arms to call him back from his drunken ramblings. "Where's Lucky Jim? He could help me."

"Lucky? I think you've upset him, Max. He's locked himself in his cabin and he won't come out. I can hear him chanting, and it smells like he's burning incense. If I didn't know him better, I'd think he was doing some sort of Maya ritual. I don't know what's come over him." Uncle Ted hiccuped loudly.

"With Lucky on our side, we might have stood a chance."

"Do you want me to try and talk to him?"

"There's no time," said Max, climbing over the side of the yacht. "Wish me luck."

"Max . . . wait!"

"Are you coming with me?"

"No, I just want to give you this."

Uncle Ted passed down a diver's knife on a belt.

"Good luck, Max."

When Max was safely aboard, Uncle Ted untied the rope and shouted down instructions. Max pulled the cord with all his might, and the engine roared to life. After a few false starts when he butted the yacht like an angry ram, he got the hang of steering and the Zodiac sped away.

Soon Max could make out the shore and the sinister outline of the Black Pyramid. He headed straight for it, with the motor flat-out. His heart surged, happy to be free again. His stomach, which apparently knew something his heart did not, shrank into a tight ball of fear.

What grisly sight would be waiting for him at the temple?

After a while, he heard the motor of the yacht behind him. The captain must have woken up and discovered him missing.

He willed his little boat on across the waves. But, as fast as his inflatable was, the yacht quickly gained on him. The bow got closer and closer until he could feel it looming over him. The captain was clearly trying to run him down.

Max turned sharply. The yacht turned as sharply as it could, but it was no match for the agility of a Zodiac. He was confident that he could outmaneuver it. His only worry was that the captain might radio ahead and tell Landa's men to meet him in their high-speed motor launches.

In fact, Max should have been worrying about something else entirely.

Like the fact that, at that very moment, the captain was out on the flying bridge, aiming a rifle at him.

As the yacht closed the gap and loomed over him again, Max started to make his next turn when—*crack*! A bullet tore into the outboard motor. The engine sputtered. Max turned sharply and started zigzagging to make himself a more difficult target. He was losing speed.

Crack! Crack! Crack!

Spouts of water shot up around his boat where the bullets had missed. Max silently thanked Uncle Ted for plying the captain with whiskey. He was horribly aware that it would take only one good shot to deflate the Zodiac and scupper his escape.

But the damage was done. The outboard motor coughed and shuddered to a halt. He was dead in the water. As he pulled on the cord, praying for the engine to start, he saw the captain taking aim. Even drunk, he couldn't miss now. Max steeled himself.

Suddenly, the captain pitched over the railing and into the ocean. In his place was Uncle Ted, with a big grin on his face. He threw a life ring to the flailing captain and took the wheel of the ship.

"Pull out the choke," Uncle Ted called down through cupped hands.

With the choke fully out and a few more tugs on the cord, the outboard motor roared shakily back to life.

As the yacht veered sharply away, it gave a loud blast of its horn.

Max turned and waved, then once again headed for the shore.

Chapter Twenty-four
THE SHOWDOWN

It wasn't quite the James Bond moment that Max could have hoped for.

When he'd first sped away in the Zodiac, he'd planned to make straight for land and take cover in the jungle before anyone noticed him.

Unfortunately, it hadn't worked out that way.

Now he was puttering along in his bullet-ridden craft, stalling continually and leaving a trail of greasy black engine fluid. He suspected he had a slow leak, as the boat seemed to be getting lower and lower in the water. Eventually the engine gave up altogether, and he had to reach for the oars.

If one of Landa's guards spotted him now, he was a goner. But why hadn't they spotted him already? Or maybe they had? Maybe they were planning a reception at this very moment?

Max felt distinctly uneasy as he paddled the last few hundred yards to shore.

It was getting dark. He could make out the shapes of Landa's motorboats pulled up on the sand, about half a mile down the beach. But there was no sign of any crew. There was also, he realized, no sign of any way up to the Temple of Ah Pukuh. A line of cliffs, hidden from the water by a grove of palm trees, formed an impenetrable barrier between the beach and the jungle.

How had Landa's men got up there? There had to be a trail near their boat landing. He crept along through the palm trees, as fast as he dared. His only thought was to get to the pyramid and find Lola before it was too late. In a few hours, Venus would rise and Landa would initiate the rituals.

By the motorboats, a thug in black lay facedown in the sand, with a blowgun dart sticking out of his neck.

Yay, Hermanjilio! One down, nineteen to go.

Then he saw the way up. A zigzag stairway had been carved into the cliff face. It was steep and narrow and completely exposed. Max knew that once he started climbing, he would be at the mercy of anyone above or below.

Trying not to look down, not to think about snipers, not to think about anything but getting to Lola, he slowly made his way up. The steps were weatherworn and cracked. As he got higher and his head started to spin, he turned his back to the water and climbed up sideways, his fingers clinging painfully to the crumbling rock.

When he got to the top, he sat down for a moment to recover. The moon was rising over the sea. No sign of Uncle Ted and the yacht. A bright star hung low in the sky. Could that be Venus?

He jumped up and headed inland. A path plunged into the forest. Mindful of Hermanjilio's disparaging remarks about his clumsiness, he moved as quickly and as silently as he could.

He didn't notice the body until he nearly fell over it.

The guard was sprawled across the path, with a blowgun dart in his neck. The Invisible Jaguar of the Night had struck again! A hundred yards farther on, Max found two more bodies, then another, and another. All felled by blowgun darts.

Maybe they could beat these guys after all. Max was just starting to feel hopeful when he heard the crack of gunfire ahead. The fight was still going on.

When he got close to Landa's camp, he left the path and crept on his belly, inching forward until he could spy on the camp from under a bush. Everywhere looked deserted. The rising moon cast a ghostly light over the scene.

Where was everyone?

Max lay still, his every nerve on high alert. He tried to filter out the cacophony of the rainforest and listen for voices or gunfire.

He had the unnerving sensation that someone was behind him.

He thought of the bodies on the path. Had those guards had the same sensation just before they'd been hit?

Slowly, very slowly, he turned his head and looked over his shoulder. There was someone in the bushes, he was sure of it.

Crouching now, Max pulled out his diver's knife. He scanned the undergrowth, but all he could see was the trembling of a fern frond that had recently been disturbed. His heart was beating fast. He listened hard, his ears straining for a clue.

Out of the bushes came a loud fart, followed by peals of laughter.

"Lady Coco?" whispered Max.

"I am in top form tonight," she said with a giggle, emerging from her hiding place.

There was a rustling in the trees and Max looked up to see a small figure in a Red Sox cap climbing to the ground.

"Lord 6-Dog! I am so pleased to see you!"

"I can only apologize, young lord, for the unseemly behavior of my mother," said Lord 6-Dog. "She has been making an exhibition of herself all day."

Lady Coco emitted another barrage.

"Ignore her, I beseech thee," said Lord 6-Dog.

"But what's happening? Where are Landa's men?" asked Max.

"They sleep like newborn babes."

"All of them? But how?"

"Last night, as we had planned, Lord Hermanjilio slipped into the camp. To our most glorious luck, the cook is a local man named Eligio, whom Lord Hermanjilio knows well. When he heard about Landa's evil plans, Eligio agreed to pour a bottle of my sleeping draft into the lunchtime stew. An hour later, all who had partaken of the stew were out cold."

"It worked!" cheered Max. "Then what?"

"Eligio hid in the jungle to wait for Landa, while we pursued the stray guards who did not eat the stew."

"Who's 'we'?"

"Lord Hermanjilio and myself."

There was a squawk of protest from Lady Coco.

"Mother helped, too," sighed Lord 6-Dog. "Her duty was to create a loud and malodorous diversion of the kind you just witnessed. While the guards were transfixed in horror, Lord Hermanjilio and I took aim with our blowpipes."

"Way to go, Lord 6-Dog!" said Max admiringly.

"Excuse me," interrupted Lady Coco, poking a hairy finger into Max's chest. "Perhaps the young lord would like to compliment me on my diversionary skills. It's not easy maintaining such a high quality of flatulence, you know."

Max nodded politely. "Way to go, Lady Coco!"

"Thank you," she said with a regal air. Then she gave a few little toots of acknowledgment and jumped back into the trees to groom herself.

Max turned back to Lord 6-Dog.

"Did you get all the guards?" he asked.

"Unfortunately not. One of them was able to escape and make contact with the Spanish vessel."

"So that's why they all left the yacht in a hurry," reflected Max.

"We were ready for them," said Lord 6-Dog. "When Landa arrived with reinforcements, we ambushed them on the path."

"I fell over some of your victims! Did you get Landa?"

Lord 6-Dog shook his head. "Instead of leading from the front like a Maya warlord, he hid at the rear like a coward. While we battled his men, he scuttled into the forest with Lady Lola and two of his bodyguards."

"Poor Lola! Where are they now?" asked Max.

"They're heading toward the Black Pyramid," said Lady Coco. "Eligio the cook has been taking potshots at them to slow them down. We're hoping Lord Hermanjilio will get there first."

"I thought I heard gunfire. I hope the cook doesn't hit Lola by mistake."

"As I understand it, Eligio is not trying to hit anyone," said Lord 6-Dog. "He is merely taunting them, like a buzzing mosquito. Meanwhile, Mother and I are taking up position to attack Landa's flank, if thou wouldst care to join us."

He made it sound like an invitation to tea and scones.

A shot rang out somewhere in the distance.

"Come," said Lord 6-Dog, "we must hurry."

They worked their way around the edge of the camp to the side of the pyramid. When they had taken cover behind a fallen tree trunk, Lord 6-Dog handed Max his blowgun and his last pouch of darts.

"Here, young lord," he said regretfully. "Thy lungs are bigger than mine. There are but three darts left. Use them wisely."

"What will you do?" asked Max.

"Mother and I will collect some tactical ammunition."

Before Max could ask what that meant, the two monkeys had vanished into the trees.

He surveyed the scene in the moonlight. Looking up at the Black Pyramid, he thought he could make out Hermanjilio on the top step, blowgun at the ready. Max gave a little wave. Hermanjilio nodded, held his finger to his lips, and pointed across the clearing. Evidently, that was where Landa was expected to emerge.

Max waited nervously. He loaded one of the darts into the blowgun and carefully placed the other two in front of him.

All was quiet.

Suddenly, a flock of parrots exploded from the trees, shrieking and squawking, and three men burst out of the rainforest. One of them pushed Lola in front of him. The other two shot at anything and everything as they ran across the clearing toward the steps of the pyramid.

The noise was terrifying—guns shooting, men shouting,

birds screeching—but Max tried to stay calm, waiting for the right moment. He knew he would only get one chance. And, armed with only a blowgun, he also knew the odds were against him.

In the end, it happened so quickly that he hardly had time to think.

Just as Landa reached the bottom step, the two monkeys let loose with a volley of nuts and fruits from high above Max's head. The bodyguards paused to blitz the treetops with bullets. Max crouched behind the log, not daring to breathe, as leaves and twigs exploded and rained down onto the forest floor. An animal shrieked and fell through the branches, landing with a thud somewhere behind him.

It was now or never.

Adrenaline pumped through his veins as he fired his three darts in quick succession. At the same moment, Hermanjilio fired from the top of the pyramid.

Yes! Yes!

The two bodyguards staggered and then collapsed.

No!

Landa pulled Lola in front of him like a shield. One arm was around her throat; the other pointed a gun into her back. She looked half asleep, as if she was drugged, but she was swaying and making little moaning noises as her entire body tried to fight whatever he had given her.

"Hold your fire!" Landa shouted. "Or I will kill the girl."

Max kept completely still.

"And now, I will to count to three. *Uno, dos, tres.* If you do not step out with your hands up, your little friend is dead."

Max looked up at Hermanjilio but couldn't see him. What should he do?

He could make out Hermanjilio on the top step, blowgun at the ready.

"*Uno!*"

His mind raced. Each second seemed like eternity. If he didn't come out, Landa was probably ruthless enough to shoot Lola in cold blood.

"*Dos!*"

But if he did come out, Landa might shoot *him* in cold blood.

"*Tres!*"

"Stop!" yelled Max. "Don't shoot, I'm coming out."

"No . . . urgh," groaned Lola as Landa choked her words by pulling his arm tighter around her windpipe.

Max slowly stood up and put his hands in the air. As he emerged from the underbrush, he took in the whole scene for the first time.

The brooding menace of the Black Pyramid.

The two guards sprawled on the lower steps.

Landa swiveling around to shoot him.

Then he saw something out of the corner of his eye, something soaring into the sky behind Landa. So unexpected was the sight that it took his brain a moment to register what it was.

A pineapple. It was a pineapple.

It sailed through the air in a graceful arc. When it reached its high point, it seemed to hang there for several seconds like a little UFO, hovering in the moonlight. And then the pineapple started its downward trajectory, plummeting to earth with increasing speed.

Landa became aware that Max was focused not on him but on something above him. He turned to look up, only to catch the pineapple squarely in the face. It exploded, sending pineapple chunks and juice in every direction.

Landa staggered, and Lola groggily pushed him away.

Now Hermanjilio had a clear target and, as Max watched, a silent dart embedded itself in Landa's forehead. The Spaniard didn't even have time to flick his cape before he crumpled to the ground.

A loud whoop came from the jungle in the same direction as the pineapple.

Max vaulted the log and ran toward Lola, who was slumped on the bottom step of the pyramid.

Lady Coco leapt out of the trees and got to her first. "Lady Lola! Are you all right?"

Lola groaned. She put her hands to her head. "I feel like I've been drinking Hermanjilio's elixir," she said.

"Landa drugged you," explained Max, "but it seems to be wearing off. Luckily for us, his sleeping potion isn't as strong as ours." A loud snore erupted from the Spaniard. "Anyway, he's getting a taste of his own medicine now."

Lady Coco jumped up and down in excitement. "Did you see that?" she asked. "What a perfect shot! And I've had no military training, you know."

"It was incredible, Lady Coco," said Max. "You saved my life."

Lady Coco smiled modestly, but her crossed eyes were shining with pride. "Did you hear that, son?" she asked, looking around for Lord 6-Dog. "I promised I'd make a good warrior—"

"Enough talking!" came a booming voice from the pyramid.

They looked up to see Hermanjilio making his way down. He seemed to be limping.

"Are you hurt?" Max shouted up to him.

"We will all be hurt," Hermanjilio called down through cupped hands, "if we don't get the Black Jaguar and get out of here."

"The Black Jaguar? Landa must have it," said Max, running over to the count's prone body. When he moved the Spaniard's cape aside, he saw a large pouch hanging from his belt.

Quickly, Max cut it free with his diver's knife and opened it.

A smell of rotting flesh filled his nostrils, just as it had when Landa had opened his case and showed the Black Jaguar to Uncle Ted in the hotel garden.

"Found it!" called Max.

He turned back to the group in triumph, but Lola and Lady Coco had no interest in Jaguar Stones. They were looking around and calling into the jungle.

"What is it?" asked Max.

Lady Coco looked distraught. "My son—where is he?"

Max had a sinking feeling.

"I heard something fall through the trees in all the shooting. . . ."

Hermanjilio was getting impatient. "What are you doing?" he shouted down. "Bring me the Black Jaguar and let's go."

"We have to look for Lord 6-Dog," Max called to him. "We think he might be"—he saw Lady Coco's anguished face—"hurt."

"Just hurry!" commanded Hermanjilio.

"I'm too dizzy," groaned Lola. "I'll sit on the steps and wait for you."

So they left the Black Jaguar with her and went back into the trees to look for Lord 6-Dog. It was not an easy task. Very little moonlight filtered down to the forest floor, and the thick foliage made it difficult to search. They found a Red Sox cap hanging on a branch, but no sign of Lord 6-Dog.

In the end, it was Lady Coco's finely tuned nose that located the spot where her son had landed when Landa shot him out of the trees.

They found his limp, blood-soaked body under a thorn-bush.

Max put an ear to the brave monkey's chest. Tears welled in his eyes.

"Is he . . . dead?" whispered Lady Coco.

Max held the monkey close and burrowed his ear into its fur. He could just make out a faint heartbeat.

"No. He's badly hurt, but he's alive."

Max tenderly put the Red Sox cap back on Lord 6-Dog's head. Then he carried the monkey's limp body to the base of the pyramid.

"Lola!" he called. "Lola! We found him! We're going to need some of your rainforest remedies."

No answer. She wasn't there. She must have felt better and gone up with Hermanjilio to show him the escape route.

Max laid Lord 6-Dog out in the moonlight where he could take a proper look at his wounds. He'd been shot through the arm, and a second bullet had grazed his hip. It was bad, but not as bad as it had looked at first. Max took off his T-shirt and tore it into bandages while Lady Coco mopped her son's brow with a banyan leaf.

"Mama's here, little dog," she whispered in his ear.

When they'd done all they could to tend Lord 6-Dog's wounds, Max gathered up the injured monkey and began to stagger up the temple steps with him. It was surprising how much one howler monkey could weigh. Lady Coco tried to help, but it was slow going.

"Lady Coco," gasped Max, exhausted and only halfway up, "I think you need to get Hermanjilio. Ask him to come down and help me."

She hesitated. She didn't want to leave Lord 6-Dog's side.

"He'll be okay," said Max.

Lady Coco licked her son's face tenderly, then bounded off up the temple steps. When she reached the top, she leaned over and waved before disappearing from view through the skull doorway.

Max kept looking up hopefully, but no one appeared to help him.

Eventually he hauled Lord 6-Dog up to the top by himself.

He was breathing hard from the weight of the monkey and the steepness of the climb. He carried the monkey through the doorway and into the chamber of skulls. He was ready to give Hermanjilio a piece of his mind. How could he let his comrade-in-arms struggle all the way up on his own?

Then Max's resentment was replaced by a new feeling.

It was called fear.

Make that terror.

The hairs on the back of his neck rose up.

Something felt very wrong.

As his eyes adjusted to the darkness, he looked around the chamber. What was that dark shape on the floor? He gasped as he made out the inert body of Lady Coco, a blowgun dart sticking out of her back.

Max had only one thought. He had to get out of there fast.

Still carrying Lord 6-Dog, he lurched around to go back.

As he did so, he caught sight of Hermanjilio's arm swinging down with the glowing Black Jaguar in his hand.

The stone hit Max hard on the side of his skull.

His head exploded into stars, and he dropped to the ground unconscious.

Chapter Twenty-five
HUMAN SACRIFICE

Max struggled, but he couldn't move. He was pinned down to something. A hideous face leaned over and leered at him. She was the ugliest girl he'd ever seen. And as she smiled, he saw that she had fangs like a vampire bat.

There was a sickly smell of incense. He could hear the abrasive scraping of a knife being sharpened.

"Prepare to die, my little fool," crowed the Maya vampire girl.

She licked his face.

Her breath was foul. Her tongue was rough and slimy. He pushed her away, but she kept coming back and licking him. He tried to scream, but she held her hairy black hand over his mouth.

He was still struggling when he woke up.

His head hurt. A monkey was licking his face.

He tried to protest, but a paw was clamped over his mouth.

"Make no noise," said the monkey.

A talking monkey!

"If he hears thee, he will kill thee," it whispered.

Max had heard that voice before. He looked hard at the monkey. Its fur was matted with blood. It was wearing a baseball cap. It curled back its lips and attempted a reassuring smile, which made it look even more freakish.

"I am Lord 6-Dog," said the creature, "summoned from Xibalba to help thee. . . . Dost thou remember?"

It sounded familiar. Crazy, but familiar.

"I beg thy pardon if the ministrations of my tongue were offensive. It was the only way to rouse thee. Dost thou promise not to scream?"

Max nodded.

Lord 6-Dog removed his hand. Max considered screaming.

"No, young lord," said the monkey, wagging a hairy finger. "We have no time for games. We have to stop him."

"Stop who?" said Max thickly. He was having trouble getting his thoughts together. His fingers explored the huge lump on his head. It felt wet and sticky. The slightest touch sent pain shooting through his brain.

Where was he?

He looked around. The walls seemed to be made entirely of human skulls.

That couldn't be good.

An eerie gray light flooded in through an open doorway. On the floor, he could make out the body of another monkey.

Its name was Lady Coco.

How did he know that?

Trust the howlers, said a voice in his head.

And then, in a flash, it all came back to him.

"Lord 6-Dog," he whispered, "are you all right? I was carrying you when . . . when . . ." His voice trailed off. He was about to say, *when Hermanjilio hit me*—but that couldn't be right. Could it?

"I am well enough, young lord," said Lord 6-Dog. "The force of the blow knocked me to the floor and brought me to my senses. I feigned death, but I saw everything. Mother is sleeping; we can leave her for the moment. Come now, we must stop him. . . ."

Lord 6-Dog helped Max to his feet.

"Stop who?" said Max.

"Tzelek!"

"Tzelek? You mean Landa-slash-Tzelek?"

"No, young lord, I mean Lord Hermanjilio-slash-Tzelek."

"What? I don't get it," said Max. "How did Tzelek get out of Landa and into Hermanjilio?"

"It appears he was never in Landa. It is my belief that when Lord Hermanjilio opened the gateway at Itzamna for Mother and me, Tzelek sneaked through at the same time. He has been hiding inside Lord Hermanjilio ever since."

"But why didn't we notice?"

"It suited Tzelek's purpose to lie low. Like a strangler fig, he lived in harmony with his host until he had taken what he wanted. He has used Lord Hermanjilio to bring him to the Pyramid of Ah Pukuh this night and give him the Black Jaguar. Unwittingly, we have all done his bidding." Lord 6-Dog indicated the gray light beyond the doorway. "And now the rituals have begun."

The horror of the situation sank into Max's throbbing brain.

He crawled over to the doorway and peered out.

He was not prepared for the shock of what he saw and he had to clap his own hand over his mouth to keep from crying out.

Hermanjilio/Tzelek was dancing rhythmically around the sacrificial altar. The altar was a huge stone slab, supported at each corner by a column of human skulls. Set into the end facing Max was the body of a jaguar inlaid in black obsidian. On the headless shoulders of this beast, the Black Jaguar radiated its murky light. At its feet, the Red and Green Jaguars added their own glow. The air stank of rotting flesh mingled with pungent incense.

In the center of this nightmare, lashed to the altar stone by her hands and feet, was Lola.

She was dressed in a blue tunic, and her skin was daubed in blue paint. She seemed to be awake, but she was limp and lethargic. Her half-open eyes tried to follow Tzelek as he pranced around the altar, chanting. His dance was made all the more macabre by the strange half-limping, half-lurching gait caused by the twisted foot he dragged behind him. In one hand, he carried a small stone bowl. In the other hand, he brandished a long knife.

Each time he circled the altar, Tzelek slashed his own ears and collected the dripping blood in the bowl. When it was full, he stopped in front of the Black Jaguar and let out a piercing howl. Then he lifted the bowl with both hands and dribbled his blood onto the Black Jaguar. The pyramid started to vibrate, as if the whole structure was awakening. Tzelek cackled in delight.

As Max watched in horror, the Black Jaguar opened its glittering mouth and roared. When the other Jaguar Stones roared in reply, Tzelek smiled like a proud mother.

Glowing eyes flicked on in the black recesses of the skulls supporting the altar stone, and their jaws began to chant a dirge. Rings of light pulsed in waves out of the altar, getting bigger and bigger like ripples in a pond. They rolled across the top of the pyramid and over the edges. They flowed down the steps, vaporizing stray vegetation. When they reached the bottom, they consumed the sleeping bodies of Landa's guards without leaving a trace of them.

When the pyramid was as clear as the day it was built, a gray light shone out of the cracks between the stones. Behind the altar, a jagged black hole, a void of nothingness, shimmered like a supernatural heat haze, as if the fabric of the world had ripped apart.

Tzelek dipped the tip of his knife into the bowl of blood and traced an incision line on Lola's tunic above her heart. Still crouching at the doorway, Max was transfixed with horror. He nearly jumped out of his skin when Lord 6-Dog tapped him on the shoulder.

"The time has come, young lord," he whispered. "I will fell Tzelek with a dart. Thou shouldst be ready to pluck out the Black Jaguar from the altar." Lord 6-Dog picked up Hermanjilio's blowpipe from the floor of the chamber. It was

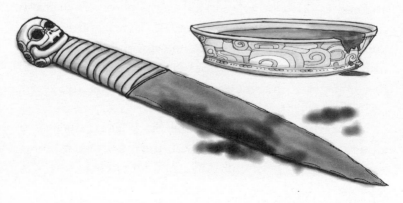

twice as tall as he was. He loaded it with a dart, lifted it, and took aim. His injured arm buckled instantly from the weight and length of the blowpipe.

"Blast this feeble body," he muttered.

Tzelek raised the knife high above his head. The obsidian blade glinted in the moonlight. Seconds before the knife was about to plunge into Lola's chest, Lord 6-Dog gathered every ounce of his strength, lifted the blowpipe, and fired.

The dart sped straight toward Tzelek's neck.

Max thought he would faint with relief. He crouched like a runner on the starting blocks, ready to sprint to the altar the second the dart hit its target.

Tzelek looked up and smirked.

The dart stopped in midair, inches from his face, and burst into flames. It dropped harmlessly to the floor.

Tzelek turned to Lord 6-Dog, hands on hips, and laughed.

"Oh, puh-lease! You've had three *baktuns* to prepare for this moment, 6-Dog. Is that really the best you can do? But then, I see you have shrunk in stature since last we met. And you've given up shaving, too. I'm sure the ladies don't find you quite as handsome this time around. You pathetic buffoon! You can't stop me from killing this girl any more than you could stop me from killing your father."

Lord 6-Dog froze, his monkey eyes fixed on Tzelek.

"Yes, you heard me!" crowed Tzelek. "I killed Punak Ha, your father! I would gladly have stood by his side at the ceremony, but it was you he wanted. It was always you. So I killed him. And I vowed that one day I would have more power than either of you." Tzelek raised the knife again. "This is my day."

There was a bloodcurdling scream—like a dinosaur in pain, like a soul in torment—a roar that awakened every howler in the jungle, and Lord 6-Dog sprang across the platform as if he'd been shot from a cannon. He propelled himself high into the air and landed on Tzelek's face. His tail wrapped around the neck while his paws gripped the head in a vise. A savage expression contorted his features as he sank his teeth deep into Tzelek's nose.

Tzelek screamed.

This was Max's chance. He raced across to the altar and grabbed the Black Jaguar. It writhed and jerked and snapped at his fingers. Pain shot through him, but he did not let go.

He saw something flying at him.

He was knocked to the ground by the body of Lord 6-Dog, which Tzelek had pulled off his face and flung at him.

Before Max knew it, Tzelek had him by the throat. It was Hermanjilio's nose and mouth that breathed their fury on him, but the rest of the face he did not recognize. The eyelids were hooded like an iguana's, and Hermanjilio's laughing brown eyes were black coals glowing red with evil. Max could feel his life being squeezed out as Tzelek's icy-cold hands tightened their grip and once again his sharp nails pierced Max's skin as they had done in the Star Chamber.

With one last almighty effort, Max tried to fight off the evil priest.

Tzelek's lip curled in scorn.

"You little worm"—he sneered—"do you think you can spar with the mighty Tzelek? You disgust me. You are not even fit for sacrifice. Go and join your idiot parents in Xibalba!"

He raised Max above his head and prepared to pitch him

into the blackness behind the altar. Max tensed and closed his eyes. So this was how his story ended.

"Drop the boy."

Max opened his eyes and looked down in time to see Lucky Jim land a mighty punch on the side of Tzelek's head.

There was a sound of bone crunching. The evil priest staggered in surprise and dropped Max onto the platform. Lucky Jim dragged him clear and took a flying leap at Tzelek. "You're going back to Xibalba where you belong!" he shouted. His huge body hit Tzelek high in the chest, and the two men hurtled together into the void.

There was no flash, no scream, no smell of burning.

All that remained was silence.

In a daze, Max lurched to his feet and tried once again to pull out the Black Jaguar. It scratched and clawed him, but he didn't care anymore. In one supreme effort, he wrenched it out and threw it down.

It was done.

Like a speeding car suddenly thrown into reverse, the whole pyramid shook from top to bottom.

There was a crashing sound like thunder. The stones of the pyramid jumped up and down; some even shot out of place. The edges of the black void were sucked back together. In an instant, the hole was gone.

For a moment, Max lay there, gasping for breath, replaying it all in his mind. Then he sat up and moved his head stiffly, like someone in a neck brace, to look around the platform for Lord 6-Dog.

The monkey-king was slumped against the temple wall. He was covered with blood, and chunks of his fur were missing.

Max crawled over to him and they sat there, exhausted, leaning against each other.

It was over. They had won.

"Tell me, young lord, who was that brave Maya warrior who sent Tzelek back to Xibalba?" asked Lord 6-Dog.

"His name is Lucky Jim," said Max. "He works with my uncle. We owe him everything. We have to get him out."

"All in good time, young lord. We have won this battle, but we have not won the war. First I must do what I should have done before and destroy the Black Jaguar. I will grind it into powder and scatter it to the winds, that it may never again menace the mortal world."

Max pointed to the altar stone. "It's rising! What's happening?" he cried hysterically. "Is Tzelek coming back?"

The stone was hovering in midair, supported by a shimmering curtain of red light.

"Calm thyself," whispered Lord 6-Dog. "I know not what sorcery this is, but as long as the stones are dormant, Tzelek cannot return."

"So who's that?"

A figure was stepping through the curtain. He had the head of an owl and the body of a man with four gnarled talons on each foot. He wore a feathered cape. The owl-man opened his beak to speak, and the voice that came out was raspy and screechy like a barn door swinging on a stormy night.

"I am Lord Muan," he announced, pronouncing it *moooo-an* like the hooting of an owl. "On behalf of their lordships One Death, Seven Death, Scab Stripper, Blood Gatherer, Demon of Pus, Demon of Jaundice, Bone Scepter, Skull Scepter, Demon of Filth, Demon of Woe, Wing, and

Packstrap, I bring a message for Massimo Francis Sylvanus Murphy."

He looked at Max for a response, but seeing that the boy was paralyzed by terror, he unrolled a scroll and began to read from it. "My masters bid me thank thee for the sport thou hast provided since they summoned thee."

"It was the D-D-Death Lords who summoned me?" stammered Max.

"It was indeed," said Lord Muan. "They have greatly enjoyed watching thy tribulations and laying wagers on thy survival. They have now commanded me to reveal that thy parents await thee in Xibalba."

"I know that," said Max, finding his voice. "But how do I get them out?"

"That," said Lord Muan, "is why I have come to speak with thee."

He made a series of retching noises, stretched his neck forward, and slowly ejected an owl pellet. Max watched in disgust as the hard gray slug of compacted fur and bones rolled along the floor.

"As I was saying," said the messenger, "their benevolent lordships wish for nothing more than to reunite thee with thy parents."

"They do?" said Max. "That's fantastic!"

"Do not trust him, young lord," gasped Lord 6-Dog through his pain. "That accursed beak vomits pellets, tricks, and lies."

"I am but the messenger, 6-Dog. And I would rather talk through the beak of an owl than through the hindquarters of a howler monkey."

"How darest thou speak thus to me? I will have thee plucked for thy insolence, thou hooting fool." The monkey-king's voice was growing weaker.

"I think not, 6-Dog. If thou wert worthy of my respect, thou wouldst now be sitting in the heroes' heaven, not in a stinking bag of monkey fur."

"Leave him alone," shouted Max. "Can't you see he's injured?"

The owl-man's ear tufts lay flat, his feathers bristled, and he opened his yellow eyes wide. "I must warn thee, young lord, this discourteous attitude may not be helpful in our negotiations."

"I'm sorry," said Max. "Just tell me what to do. I'll do anything to get my parents back."

"No, young lord!" cried Lord 6-Dog. "Do not bargain with the Lords of Death. Thou canst not win."

"One moment, please . . . ," said the messenger. His ear tufts perked up and he seemed to be listening to voices in his head. Max assumed the Death Lords were giving him instructions, like ghoulish TV producers speaking from some cosmic control room. At one point Lord Muan broke off to check a technicality. "Thou didst say thou wouldst do anything?"

Max nodded.

Lord 6-Dog groaned.

The messenger stepped forward. "Good news: thou hast won favor with their lordships. They are prepared to release thy parents."

Max's face lit up. "Did you hear that, Lord 6-Dog?"

Lord 6-Dog was unimpressed. "It is a trick," he said, "and it stinks like a rotting fish."

The owl blinked rapidly. "Thy cynicism is unwarranted. In return for the release of Frank and Carla Murphy, my magnanimous masters ask only for one small favor, if and when they should ever need it."

"That sounds fair enough," said Max.

"No," said Lord 6-Dog, sounding weaker than ever, "the Lords of Death cannot be trusted. Who knows what this small favor might entail? Thou canst not make a pact with evil."

"I have no choice," whispered Max to Lord 6-Dog. "At least it will buy us time to rescue Hermanjilio and Lucky Jim."

"I warn thee, young lord, do not underestimate the Lords of Death."

Max took a deep breath. "I will be honored to owe their lordships a small favor in return for the release of my parents."

"Thou hast spoken wisely, Massimo Francis Sylvanus Murphy. My masters will contact thee at the appointed hour." Like a used-car salesman clinching the deal, the messenger took a moment to attempt a cheesy smile and then launched into the small print. "I am required by cosmic law to inform thee that the size of the favor can go up as well as down. If thou shouldst break this pact, thy parents will be dragged back to Xibalba and sacrificed forthwith."

"No good will come of this," muttered Lord 6-Dog.

"Can't you say something positive?" Max begged him.

Lord 6-Dog winced with pain. "I like the name Sylvanus."

Meanwhile, Lord Muan was hunting.

His owl head rotated to scan the platform until his bulbous eyes settled on the Jaguar Stones. To Max's horror, he picked them up, one by one, and balancing all three in his feathered arms, melted back into the curtain of red light.

"Did you see that?" asked Max indignantly. "He took them all!"

"I can talk no more, young lord," sighed Lord 6-Dog. "This body needs to heal and I must rest. For the moment, it is over." He stretched out his hairy little limbs and instantly fell asleep.

Seconds later, Frank and Carla Murphy stepped cautiously through the curtain.

Chapter Twenty-six

MORNING

His mother's hair was greasy and matted. She wore a grubby white shift, and her face looked tired and old. His father, who always looked a mess, was even more disheveled than usual. But, for once, Max didn't care what they looked like. He was just happy to see them.

But was it really them?

Or had Ah Pukuh sent two more demons to fool him?

He watched them closely.

Please let it be them.

They were squinting in the early light. They must have come from somewhere dark. They were shielding their eyes with their hands and looking nervously around. Max's heart felt like it would burst.

Please let it be them.

His mother saw him first.

"*Bambino!* It is you!" Carla Murphy hugged her only son and kissed his head. "How can this be? I thought you were still in Boston! I am so happy to see you, but what are you doing here?"

He stood there awkwardly, staring at her matted hair.

Please let it be them.

After his experience with the demonic doppelgängers, he needed proof that these two hobos really were his parents. He needed to test them in some way. But he was so tired, he could hardly think. He ran his fingers through his hair and wiped his nose on the back of his hand.

"Massimo Murphy! Use a Kleenex!"

No one else in the universe would fuss about manners at a time like this.

"Mom! It's really you!" Now he hugged her properly.

She stepped back and looked at him. "What's happened to you, *bambino*? Your head is hurt . . . and what's that on your skin?"

Max looked down at himself. He was bare to the waist, having ripped up his T-shirt to make bandages for Lord 6-Dog. His arms were still red from dye, and his chest was smeared with black body paint from his tussle with Hermanjilio-slash-Tzelek. Blood from his head wound trickled down his face.

"It's been a long night," he said.

"It's wonderful to see you, Max," said his father, "but what are you doing here?"

Max smiled. "I've been testing my inner resources, Dad, just like you wanted."

Behind him, the altar stone sank slowly back into place.

"Excuse me," said a drowsy voice. "Could somebody please untie me?"

"Lola!" cried Max, jumping up and running to cut her free. To his relief, she looked fine—sluggish and hollow-eyed and covered with blue paint, but basically fine.

She sat up slowly and looked around her. "Where am I?"

"You're safe," Max whispered, "and so are my parents."

"*Ciao*, Lola!" called Max's mother, rushing over. "Are you all right?"

Lola regarded her blankly.

"It's me, Carla Murphy—we met at Ixchel, remember?"

Lola looked from Max to his mother and father, then her eyes lit up with happiness. "Hoop, it's your parents! That's wonderful!"

"Yes," said Max. "Yes, it is."

A new day was dawning in the rainforest. The air was fresh, the sea was blue, and the forest below them buzzed with the sounds of early morning.

But there was another sound that was getting louder and louder.

It was the sound of someone puffing up the pyramid.

A look of terror crossed Lola's face. "It's not that snake Landa, is it?"

Frank Murphy looked over the edge. "No, but it *is* a snake."

First Ted Murphy's hands, then his hat, and then his sweaty face appeared as he hauled himself over the top step.

"Good morning, Frank," he said. "It's good to see you, even if you did just call me a snake. What do you say we bury the hatchet, right here and now? You're the closest family I have, and I thought for a moment I might never see you again!"

He stood there on the pyramid, arms open wide, a big grin on his face, until Frank started laughing, too.

"I never thought I'd say this, Ted, but it's good to see you—it really is."

With that, Frank walked over and hugged his older brother, tentatively at first, but soon with a real rib-crusher of a bear hug.

"At last!" cheered Carla, who was laughing and crying at the same time.

Uncle Ted turned to Max. "I'm glad to see you in one piece."

"We won," said Max, "but we lost Lucky Jim."

Uncle Ted nodded sadly and patted him on the shoulder. "Lucky knew exactly what he was doing, Max. He said it was time to accept his destiny." He looked along the line of bedraggled people and saw Lola. "And you must be the young lady that Max has told me so much about."

Lola smiled drowsily.

"She's still recovering from the drugs," Max explained. "And, of course, she's not usually painted blue." It wasn't the greatest introduction to make for a potential girlfriend.

"It seems to me," said Uncle Ted, "that you could all use a hot shower and a square meal. I hitched a ride over here with the police. I'm sure they'll give us all a lift back. Is everyone fit to travel?"

Frank Murphy assessed the scene. "It looks like no one was hurt," he said, "except for that howler over there."

"He's actually Lord 6-Dog, the greatest king of the Monkey River," said Max, "and his mother is inside the temple. We need to get them to a vet."

Frank, Carla, and Ted stared at him in bafflement.

"I think he has a concussion," said Carla, feeling Max's forehead.

"Back me up, Lola! It's true, isn't it?" Max demanded. "Lord 6-Dog came back as a monkey."

386

"Yes, I remember that bit," said Lola, still sounding dazed, "but who was that maniac pretending to be Hermanjilio?"

"Hermanjilio Bol?" said Carla. "Is he here? Is he all right?"

"It's a long story, Mom. Can we talk on the way down the pyramid? I'm starving."

"Follow me," said Uncle Ted, "for the best brunch in Central America."

Which was how, on the morning of 5-Death, Max came to be speeding along the coast in a police launch, headed back to Villa Isabella. The monkeys were laid out on banquettes. Frank and Ted were deep in conversation on deck. Carla was in the bathroom trying to fix her appearance. And Lola was sitting in the cabin with Max.

"How are you feeling?" he asked her.

"Much better, thank you," she said, "but it creeps me out to think about it. Can you believe that Tzelek was inside Hermanjilio all that time?"

"Remember when he clashed with Lord 6-Dog and we put it down to the dominant-male thing?" Max reminded her. "And how Lord 6-Dog kept saying Hermanjilio seemed familiar? No wonder Hermanjilio wanted us all to think that Tzelek was inside Landa."

"I should have known something was wrong," fretted Lola. "I kept wondering why Hermanjilio didn't take advantage of having a real, live Maya king at Itzamna, ask him more about the history of the site and so on. It all makes sense now. Poor Hermanjilio. I feel like I let him down."

"You couldn't have known. Even Hermanjilio didn't know."

"We have to rescue him, Hoop."

"Yeah, and Lucky Jim. Any ideas?"

"Well, how did your parents get out?"

Max lowered his voice to a whisper. "Don't tell Mom and Dad, but I promised to do a favor for the Lords of Death."

"What favor?"

"I don't know yet."

"It's been nice knowing you," said Lola.

"Thanks for the vote of confidence."

"It's just that the Lords of Death are ruthless; you can't trust them an inch. They lie and they cheat and they're compulsive gamblers, all of them. And they're completely barbaric. I've heard they like to flay humans and wear their skins as capes."

"I'm dead meat," groaned Max.

He laid his head on his arms. Lola ruffled his hair. He didn't stop her. He turned his head to look at her.

"You'll help me, won't you, Monkey Girl?"

"I don't know about that."

"What? You can't just go back to your old life and forget about me. We're a team."

"What about your old life, Hoop? You'll want to forget that any of this happened when you get back to Boston."

"No chance," said Max. He was already imagining how cool it would be to tell the guys at school that he had a Maya girlfriend.

He tried to take her hand.

"What are you doing?" she said, pulling it away.

He decided to tell the guys she was his girlfriend anyway. It wasn't like they were ever going to fly to San Xavier to check it out.

388

And so, eleven days after he'd followed the monkeys into the rainforest, Max returned to Villa Isabella. As he tramped across the beach with Lola, his parents, and his uncle, he could see Raul waiting at the door.

Max waved enthusiastically, but Raul's smile of welcome wavered as he took in their appearance. For a second, Max thought he might shoo them away like beggars.

You could see his point.

Max was black with red arms.

Lola was blue.

His mother, with her grubby shift and crazy hair, looked like she'd escaped from a lunatic asylum.

His father and his uncle were carrying what looked like dead monkeys.

Raul surveyed them, one by one, and quickly regained his composure. "Brunch will be served in twenty minutes. Please make yourselves at home."

Lady Coco stirred.

"I smell food," she said, springing out of Frank Murphy's arms, her nose twitching furiously to identify the various cooking smells.

"It's a talking howler monkey!" exclaimed Raul.

"Raul," said Max, "may I introduce you to Lady Kan Kakaw, First and Most Glorious Wife of the great King Punak Ha and mother of the immortal Lord 6-Dog. That's him lying over Uncle Ted's shoulder."

Raul looked at Uncle Ted, who gave a little nod to confirm Max's story.

If there was one thing Raul had learned in a lifetime's butlering, it was to keep cool under all circumstances. He drew upon that training now, bowing low to the monkey as if it were the most normal thing in the world.

"I am honored to meet you, Your Majesty," he said.

"Likewise," she said, "but please call me Lady Coco. Now tell me, Raul, is that banana bread I smell? With just a little hint of nutmeg, if I'm not mistaken?"

"My secret recipe," said Raul, with a wink.

"Perhaps I can persuade you to share it." She giggled flirtatiously. "Would you be so kind as to give me a tour of the kitchens?"

"But, of course, Lady Coco," said the butler. "Follow me."

"Raul—such a manly name . . . ," came Lady Coco's voice as they disappeared down the corridor together, deep in conversation.

"Apparently, monkeys have extraordinary powers of recovery," Uncle Ted commented with a smile. "Looks like Lady Coco's fine." He patted Lord 6-Dog gently on the back. "There's a vet on his way to look at His Majesty here. Meanwhile, we should just let him sleep."

He laid the unconscious monkey down on a sofa in the great hall.

"Now, ladies and gentlemen," he said, "there's just time to freshen up before brunch. Let's meet on the terrace in twenty minutes."

Max and Uncle Ted made it in fifteen.

"I just wanted to say to you, Uncle Ted, that, well, you said you weren't the hero type, but you saved my life yesterday. Pushing the captain off the boat like that . . ."

"No, Max, you were the hero. You and Lucky Jim."

"What made Lucky come and help me? I thought he didn't want anything to do with the ancient Maya."

"Lucky has always thought the old ways were nothing but

trouble. He wanted his people to join the modern world and leave all that superstition behind. But when he heard you say that Tzelek and Lord 6-Dog had returned, he realized that the past and the future are all one. He said it was time to stand up and be counted."

"And now he's trapped in Xibalba—"

"Those ancient Maya won't know what's hit them when they meet Lucky Jim!" interrupted Uncle Ted with a chuckle. "I have a feeling he can look after himself."

"This is a lovely house, Mr. Murphy," said Lola as she sat down opposite Max. She was wearing one of Uncle Ted's linen shirts as a very fetching dress. The skin on her arms was red from scrubbing, but it still had a distinct blue tinge.

"So what was it like," asked Max, "being a human sacrifice?"

"Max!" protested Uncle Ted. "I'm sure Lola doesn't want to talk about it."

"I honestly don't remember," she said.

"What? Nothing at all?"

"Well, I remember when you left me sitting on the steps with the Black Jaguar. And I remember Hermanjilio coming down to get it. He was standing over me with those red eyes...." Her voice was little more than a whisper.

Uncle Ted put an arm around her.

"It's okay," he said, "you're safe now."

Safe. *Such a cozy, comforting word*, thought Max. A word that couldn't apply to him until he'd sorted out this deal with the Death Lords.

His reverie was interrupted by the arrival of his parents.

"*Buongiorno*," trilled his mother, looking like her old, well-groomed, shiny-haired self. She'd wrapped one of Uncle Ted's white tablecloths around her as a long dress, with a hibiscus flower for a corsage. She was as elegant as any New York socialite arriving at a dinner party.

With perfect timing, Raul appeared with a huge serving dish of crispy bacon and juicy sausages and a platter piled high with barbecued ribs and steaks. These were soon joined by plates of scrambled eggs, fried eggs, and golden hash browns; racks of thickly sliced buttered toast and all kinds of jams; baskets of banana bread, bagels, doughnuts, and pastries; a massive bowl of tropical fruit salad; homemade yogurt; and jugs of cream. Finally, when there was not an inch of space left on the table, he came out empty-handed and whispered something to Uncle Ted.

"Excuse me, everyone," said Uncle Ted. "Please start without me, and I'll be back in a moment."

For the next few minutes, Max forgot everything that had happened and concentrated on eating. He felt like a warrior returning home to a victory feast. It was only when he thought his stomach was so full it might explode that he applied his mind to the situation again.

"So what was it like in Xibalba?" he asked his parents.

"Wet and misty and cold," said his mother, "like Venice in winter. Everything was in black and white, except for the flaming torches on the street corners and the blood-red water in the canals."

"Hermanjilio thought you'd be in some sort of waiting room," said Lola.

"Exactly right." Max's father nodded. "Mostly, we passed the time talking about you, Max."

"What were you saying about me?" he asked.

"For one thing," said his mother, "we agreed that we

would never again go away without you. We want to enjoy every second with you while we can."

Max laughed nervously. "You make it sound like I'm going to die or something."

His father put down his knife and fork and looked at him with misty eyes. "I've learned my lesson, I promise you. I've had a lot of time to think about things, Max. From now on, we're going to do a lot more together, you and me."

"We are? Like what?"

"Well . . . let me see. . . ." His father cast around for suitable activities. "You could teach me to play some of those exciting video games of yours."

"Actually, Dad, I think I've had all the excitement I can take for a while. But you could teach me more about the ancient Maya. I hate to admit it, but they're not as boring as I thought."

His father beamed at him.

"What's that on your tooth, Dad?"

Carla rolled her eyes. "I told him he'd regret it, but he wouldn't listen."

Max's father pulled down his lower lip to reveal a small piece of jade studded into one of his bottom teeth. "I took the opportunity to research ancient Maya cosmetic dentistry. It was all the rage in their day."

"Cool!" said Max. "Can I get one of those?"

"No!" said his mother firmly. "It looks like a piece of creamed spinach."

"How about a nose ring? Or some body piercing? Or a tattoo?" wheedled Max. "It's all very Maya. . . ."

"No! No! No!" His mother laughed and threw her hands up in mock despair.

Uncle Ted slipped back into his chair at the head of the table. As soon she saw his face, Carla stopped laughing.

"That was the chief of police," he said. "I called him from Landa's yacht last night, once I was sure Max had made land safely. The whole force came speeding out and searched the yacht from top to bottom. Turns out they've been after Count de Landa for quite a while."

"So what's the news?" asked Max.

Uncle Ted looked nervously at Lola. "Not good, I'm afraid. Antonio de Landa has vanished without trace, and his yacht has disappeared from police custody."

"So he's still out there, flicking his cape somewhere," muttered Lola.

Max sniggered.

"It's no laughing matter," said Uncle Ted. "He's a dangerous man and he won't stop until he gets what he wants."

"But what does he want?" asked Max. "The Jaguar Stones?"

"Something even more precious by the look of things," said Uncle Ted. "The police found these when they searched his yacht." He handed Lola an envelope, and she looked inside.

"They're photographs," she whispered. "Of me."

"Apparently, he had hundreds of them. Your face, your eyes, your nose, your ears . . . all taken long-range. He seems to be obsessed with you."

She put her face in her hands. "Why me?"

"Whatever Landa's up to," said Uncle Ted, "you can't go back to Itzamna on your own. It's just not safe."

Lola looked down at the table. "I'll be fine," she said. "I'm used to looking after myself."

"A loner, eh?" said Uncle Ted. "What will you do?"

Lola shrugged. "Maybe I'll go back to Utsal. I could carry on with my studies, sort through Hermanjilio's notes, get all his research ready for when he comes back. . . ."

"You can't go back to Utsal," protested Max. "Chan Kan will try to marry you off to someone."

"Then I'll go to Limón," said Lola. "I told you, I'll be fine."

"You know, Lola," said Uncle Ted, "I used to think of myself as a loner, until young Max here changed my mind. This big house felt very empty without him. I was wondering if you'd like to stay here until Hermanjilio gets back. I could be your temporary guardian. You could go to school in Puerto Muerto, and I'm sure we could persuade Max to come and visit now and again."

"It's a great idea!" agreed Max.

"What do you think, Lola?" asked Uncle Ted.

"It's very kind of you, Mr. Murphy," she began politely, "but I couldn't. I don't think . . . it's just that . . . well, Hermanjilio said . . . I mean, I don't . . ." She was tying herself up in knots, trying not to offend him.

"What are you trying to say?" cut in Uncle Ted gently.

"You're a smuggler!" she blurted.

Silence fell around the table. Max thought he detected the hint of a smirk on his father's face, but no one said anything. They were all waiting to see Uncle Ted's reaction.

"Oh, that," he said. "Truth to tell, after my brush with Landa, I've lost the taste for it. If you'd do me the honor of living under my roof, Lola, I promise to give up my little sideline. I might even take up painting again."

"Say yes! Say yes!" urged Max.

Lola looked around the table. Everyone, including Raul and Lady Coco, was nodding furiously.

"I'll think about it," she said. But she was smiling.

"Splendid!" said Uncle Ted. "That's settled, then." He looked happier than Max had ever seen him.

"More coffee, sir?" asked Raul. "And perhaps you'd like to sample one of Her Majesty's muffins?"

"I beg your pardon?" said Uncle Ted.

His eyes fell on Lady Coco, who was standing behind Raul, wearing a child-size white apron and carrying a tray of little cakes.

"Cashew and mango," she said proudly. "I made them myself."

"I didn't know you could cook, Lady Coco," said Max.

"Ah yes, young lord. Even queens had to make tortillas for their families. And my tortillas were famous throughout the Monkey River."

"Excuse me, Lady Coco," ventured Max's mother, "but I'd love to know what you think of the kitchen here at the villa. It must be very different from what you were used to in the palace at Itzamna."

Lady Coco's little monkey face lit up like Times Square. "It's amazing!" she gibbered. "Raul showed me everything! That mixing machine and the refrigerating unit and the cooking fire that turns on and off. . . . Even the greatest brains of the mighty Maya did not invent such things!"

Max's father shook his head in amazement. "I don't know what's harder to take in," he said. "An ancient Maya queen singing the praises of modern kitchen appliances—or a talking howler monkey!"

"They'll never believe this back at Harvard, that's for sure," agreed Max's mother.

"Speaking of which," said his father, "are you looking forward to going back to Beantown, Max?"

Max considered the question. Not so long ago, back in Boston was the only place he wanted to be. But now he wasn't so sure.

"I guess so," he said. He looked at Lola. "But I'm going to miss this place."

His mother smiled. "I hope normal life won't be too boring for you, after all these adventures."

Normal life? Max thought about the words. What was normal?

His mother was wearing a tablecloth. His father had a jade-inlaid tooth. They certainly weren't normal parents. But now he knew that was a good thing. He wasn't sure what he'd promised to get them back, but it was worth it.

Wasn't it?

"Mom," he said, "I've been wanting to ask you about Zia. . . ."

But his mother was deep in conversation with Lola about Maya weaving techniques. As Max waited for an opportunity to interrupt, a yellow butterfly landed on his hand. He tried to flick it away, but it clung on.

"What do you want?" he muttered. "Leave me alone."

The butterfly waved its antennae at him.

"You're making a big mistake," he whispered. "I can't help you. I'm not the one. I'd pick another champion if I were you."

The butterfly hovered in front of his face for a moment and then did a little dance, fluttering backward and forward between his chair and the glass doors that led from the terrace into the house. Even Max could not ignore the butterfly's meaning. It wanted him to follow it.

Curious to find out what the insect was trying to tell him, he got up and wandered into the house. He was going to go up to his room, but a movement in the great hall caught his eye. He went in to check on Lord 6-Dog.

An extraordinary scene awaited him.

The monkey king was sitting on top of his own great stone head, staring across at the head of Tzelek. The vet had obviously come and gone, as 6-Dog was patched and bandaged.

"Thy devilish scheme has failed," he was saying to the statue of his rival. "But like a rat who can squeeze through the smallest of holes, thou wilt find a way out of Xibalba. So hurry back to Middleworld, Tzelek, for we have unfinished business. There is still a great battle in the stars for thee and me. But I warn thee, the world has changed and so have I. We are no longer brothers. So go ahead and lay thine evil plans. I will be waiting for thee."

After a few moments, Lord 6-Dog noticed Max standing below and climbed down to him. "We have no time to lose, young lord," he said. "I will teach thee everything I know and then, shoulder to shoulder, we will face the legions of hell."

The legions of hell were coming for him.

"I can't do it," whispered Max. "I'm afraid."

"What talk is this, young lord?" said Lord 6-Dog kindly. "And thou a noble warrior? Did we not fight alongside each other on the Black Pyramid? And hast thou not learnt that anything is possible? Why, if the great Lord 6-Dog can hang from a tree by his tail, who knows what else can happen? Perhaps a boy with hair as red as fire can defeat the powers of evil like the blazing Sun Jaguar defeats the night."

"My hair is brown, actually," said Max. "Do you really think I stand a chance against the Death Lords?"

Lord 6-Dog bared his monkey teeth in what he hoped was a reassuring grin and hid his crossed fingers behind his hairy back.

"Of course I do. Now let us get to work."

To be continued . . .

What favor will the
Death Lords ask of Max?

Why is the crazy count,
Antonio de Landa,
collecting photographs of Lola?

What will happen to
Hermanjilio and Lucky Jim?

Will Tzelek escape Xibalba to wreak
more terror on the mortal world?

What is Zia's secret?

Where is the long-lost Yellow Jaguar?

These questions and
many more will be answered in
The Jaguar Stones: Book Two.

GLOSSARY

AH PUKUH (*awe pooh coo*): God of violent and
unnatural death, depicted in Maya art as a bloated,
decomposing corpse or a cigar-smoking skeleton.
His constant companions are dogs and owls, both
considered omens of death. Ah Pukuh wears bells to
warn people of his approach (possibly an unnecessary
precaution, since one of his nicknames is Kisin, or
"the flatulent one," so you'd probably smell him
coming, anyway).

BAKABS (*baw cobs*): Four brothers, the sons of ITZAMNA and
IXCHEL, who stand at the corners of the world and support the
heavens.

BALCHÉ (*ball chay*): A ritual drink brewed from fermented honey,
water, and the bark of the purple-flowered balché tree.

CENOTE (*say note eh*): A deep, water-filled sinkhole, like a natural
reservoir. There are at least three thousand cenotes in the Yucatán.
The name is a Spanish corruption of the Yucatec Maya word
tz'onot.

 CHAHK (*chalk*): God of storms and warfare, Chahk
was one of the oldest and most revered of the ancient
Maya deities. He has two tusklike breath scrolls
emitting from his mouth to convey his humid nature;
bulging eyes; and a long, turned-up nose. Frogs were
thought to be his heralds, because they croak before
it rains. Just as the Norse god Thor carries Mjolnir,
his enchanted hammer, so Chahk wields the god
K'AWIIL as his fiery lightning ax.

CHICLE (*cheek lay*): A natural gum made from boiling the milky
latex of the sapodilla tree. Chicle had been chewed by the Maya for

centuries but didn't reach North America until 1870 when Thomas Adams, a New York inventor, opened the world's first chewing gum factory. These days, manufacturers mostly use synthetic rubber.

CODEX (plural CODICES): Strictly speaking, any book with pages (as opposed to a scroll) is a codex, but the term is most closely associated with the books of the ancient Maya. Written and illustrated on long strips of bark paper or leather, folded accordion-style, these books painstakingly recorded Maya history, religion, mythology, astronomy, and agricultural cycles. All but three were destroyed during the Spanish conquest. (See DIEGO DE LANDA.)

GLYPHS: The name given to more than eight hundred different signs used by the Maya to write their books and stone inscriptions. The Maya writing system incorporates signs for sounds and signs for whole words. It is considered to be the most sophisticated system ever developed in MESOAMERICA and did not begin to be decoded until the 1950s. About 80 percent of the most common glyphs have now been deciphered.

HERO TWINS: The twin brothers Xbalanke (*sh-ball-on-kay*) and Hunahpu (*who gnaw poo*) are the main characters in the Maya creation story. Like their father and uncle before them, the twins are challenged to a ball game in XIBALBA by the LORDS OF DEATH. But where their father and uncle died in the attempt, the twins outwit the Death Lords and take their places in the heavens as the sun and the moon. Their father is resurrected as HUUN IXIM, the Maize God. The story of the Hero Twins is part of the Maya creation story, as told in the POPOL VUH.

HOWLER MONKEYS: With an extra-large voice box that makes them the loudest land animals on the planet, howlers can hear each other up to three miles away. Only the blue whale, whose whistle carries for hundreds of miles underwater, is louder.

HUUN IXIM (who *knee shim*): The reborn father of the HERO TWINS and the Maya god of maize. Huun Ixim has an elongated forehead that resembles an ear of corn. Maya nobility often molded babies' skulls into this shape by binding the infants' heads between wooden boards.

ITZAMNA (*eats um gnaw*): Ruler of the heavens, lord of knowledge, lord of day and night, and all-round good guy. Itzamna gave his people the gifts of culture, writing, art, books, chronology, and the use of calendars. As a patron of healing and science, he can bring the dead back to life. With IXCHEL, he fathered the BAKABS. Itzamna is usually depicted as a toothless but sprightly old man.

IXCHEL (*each shell*): Like most Maya deities, Lady Rainbow had multiple personalities. As the goddess of the old moon, she is depicted as an angry old woman with a coiled snake on her head, fingernails like claws, and a skirt decorated with human bones. In this guise, she vents her anger on mortals with floods and rainstorms. But as the goddess of the new moon, she is a beautiful young woman who reclines inside the crescent moon, holding her rabbit in her arms. IXCHEL was the patroness of childbirth, medicine, and weaving.

JAGUAR: Called *bahlam* by the ancient Maya who revered it for its hunting skills, the jaguar is the largest and most ferocious big cat in the Americas. Today, due to the fur trade and the destruction of its natural habitat, the jaguar is in danger of extinction.

JAGUAR STONES (*bahlamtuuno'ob*): A literary invention of the Jaguar Stones trilogy, along with the five sacred pyramids, these five fictional stone carvings embody the five pillars of ancient Maya society: agriculture, astronomy, creativity, military prowess, and kingship. As far as we know, no such stones ever existed—nor did the Maya ever relax their warlike ways enough to forge an equal alliance of five great cities.

JUNGLE/RAINFOREST: All tropical rainforests are jungles, but not all jungle is rainforest. A tropical rainforest receives at least eighty inches of rain per year. It is home to more kinds of trees than any other area of the world, most of them growing closely together. The tops of the tallest trees form a canopy of leaves about 100 to 150 feet above the ground, while the smaller trees form one or two lower canopies. Between them, these canopies block most of the light from reaching the ground. As a result, little grows on the forest floor, making it relatively easy to walk through a tropical rainforest. If the canopy is destroyed, by nature or by humans, a tangle of dense fast-growing greenery springs up in the sunlight. This is jungle. Its growth provides shade for the rainforest species to reseed and grow tall enough to block out the light once more. This cycle can take one hundred years to complete.

K'AWIIL (*caw wheel*): A god of lightning and patron of lineage, kingship, and aristocracy. He has a reptilian face, with a smoking mirror emerging from his forehead and a long snout bursting into flame.

K'INICH AHAW (*keen each uh how*): The great sun god. By day, he traces the path of the sun across the sky and by night he prowls through the underworld in the form of a jaguar, before emerging in the east each morning.

K'UK'ULKAN *(coo cool con)*: The feathered serpent, a divine combination of serpent and bird, one of the great deities of MESOAMERICA.

DIEGO DE LANDA (1524–1579): The over-zealous Franciscan friar who tried to wipe out Maya culture by burning their CODICES and thousands of religious artworks in the square at Mani on July 12, 1549. Even the conquistadores thought he'd gone too far and sent him back to Spain to stand trial. Ironically, the treatise he wrote in his defense, *Relación de las Cosas de Yucatán (1565)*, is now our best reference source on the ancient Maya. Landa was absolved by the Council of the Indies and returned to the New World as the bishop of Yucatán.

LORDS OF DEATH: In Maya mythology, the underworld (XIBALBA) is ruled by twelve Lords of Death: One Death, Seven Death, Scab Stripper, Blood Gatherer, Wing, Demon of Pus, Demon of Jaundice, Bone Scepter, Skull Scepter, Demon of Filth, Demon of Woe, and Packstrap. The Lords of Death delight in human suffering. It's their job to inflict sickness, pain, starvation, fear, and death on the citizens of MIDDLEWORLD. Fortunately, they're usually far too busy gambling and playing childish pranks on each other to get much work done.

MAYA: Most historians agree that Maya civilization began on the Yucatán peninsula sometime before 1500 BCE. It entered its Classic Period around 250 CE, when the Maya adopted a hierarchical system of government and established a series of kingdoms across what is now Mexico, Guatemala, Belize, Honduras, and El Salvador. Each of these kingdoms was an independent city-state, with its own ceremonial center, urban areas, and farming community. Building on the accomplishments of earlier civilizations such as the Olmec, the Maya developed astronomy, calendrical systems, and hieroglyphic writing. Although most famous for their soaring pyramids and palaces (built without metal tools, wheels, or beasts of burden) they were also skilled farmers, weavers, and potters, and they established extensive trade networks. The Maya saw no boundaries between heaven and earth, life and death, sleep and wakefulness. They believed that human blood was the oil that kept the wheels of the cosmos turning. Many of their rituals involved bloodletting or human sacrifice, but never on the scale practiced by the Aztecs. Wracked by overpopulation, drought, and soil erosion, Maya power began to decline around 800 CE, when the southern cities were abandoned. By the time the Spanish arrived, only a few kingdoms still thrived, and most Maya had gone back to farming their family plots. Today, there are still six million Maya living in Mexico, Guatemala, Belize, Honduras, and El Salvador.

1500 BCE		250 CE	900	1500	1800
Maya	Preclassic	Classic	Postclassic	Colonial	Modern
			Aztecs		
			Incas		

MAYAN: The family of thirty-one different languages spoken by Maya groups in Central America.

MESOAMERICA: Literally meaning "between the Americas," Mesoamerica is the name archaeologists and anthropologists use to describe a region that extends south and east from central Mexico to include parts of Guatemala, Belize, Honduras, and Nicaragua. It was home to various pre-Columbian civilizations, including the Maya (from 1500 BCE), the Olmec (1200–400 BCE), and the Aztecs (1250–1521). (The Incas of Peru in South America date from 1200 to 1533.)

MIDDLEWORLD: Like the Vikings, the Egyptians, and other ancient cultures, the Maya believed that humankind inhabited a middle world between heaven and hell. The Maya middleworld (yok'ol kab) was sandwiched between the nine dark and watery layers of XIBALBA and the thirteen leafy layers of the heavens (ka'anal naah).

MOON RABBIT: The shadows that look like a man in the moon to people in northern climes are viewed sideways in Central America, where they look like a leaping rabbit. The moon rabbit was the companion of the young moon goddess, IXCHEL. Due to the different vantage point, the moon appears to wax and wane vertically in the tropics, which is why Ixchel is often depicted holding her pet as she reclines on the crescent moon.

OBSIDIAN: This black volcanic glass was the closest thing the ancient Maya had to metal. An obsidian blade can be one hundred times sharper than a stainless steel scalpel, but it is extremely brittle.

PITZ: The Maya ball game was the first team sport in recorded history. It had elements of soccer, basketball, and volleyball, but was more difficult than any of them. Using only their hips, knees, or elbows, the players tried to knock the heavy rubber ball through a stone hoop high on the side wall of the ball court. The game had great religious significance, and the losers were frequently sacrificed.

POPOL VUH (*poe pole voo*): The Maya Book of the Dawn of Life, the sacred book of the K'iché (*kee chay*) Maya who lived (and still live) in the highlands of Guatemala. The title literally means "Book of the Mat" but is usually translated as "Council Book." The Popol Vuh tells the Maya creation story and explains how the HERO TWINS rescued their father from XIBALBA.

QUETZAL (*ket sahl*): The Maya prized the iridescent blue-green tail feathers of the Replendent quetzal bird for decorating royal headdresses. After the feathers were plucked, the birds would be set free to grow new ones. In Maya times, the penalty for killing a quetzal was death. Today, without such protection, the quetzal is almost extinct.

RAINFOREST: See JUNGLE.

SAN XAVIER: The setting of the Jaguar Stones books, this is a fictional country based on modern-day Belize.

VISION SERPENT: When Maya kings wished to communicate with their ancestors or with the gods, they would hold a bloodletting ceremony to summon the Vision Serpent. The ritual required members of the royal family to pierce themselves and drip their blood onto strips of bark paper. The paper would then be burned and the Vision Serpent was supposed to appear out of the smoke, with the desired ancestor or god emerging from its mouth.

XIBALBA (*she ball buh*): The K'iché Maya name for the underworld, meaning "well of fear." Only kings and those who died a violent

death (battle, sacrifice, or suicide) or women who died in childbirth could look forward to the leafy shade of heaven. All other souls, good or bad, were headed across rivers of scorpions, blood, and pus to Xibalba. Unlike the Christian hell with its fire and brimstone, the Maya underworld was cold and damp, and its inhabitants were condemned to an eternity of bone-chilling misery and hunger.

MAYA COSMOS

What did Max, Lola, and Hermanjilio see in the Temple of Itzamna?

This illustration (based on a painted plate from the Late Classic Period) depicts the three realms of the Maya cosmos: the heavens above, Middleworld (the world of humans), and the waters of Xibalba, the underworld. In the heavens, the two-headed Cosmic Monster (or Cosmic Crocodile, as Lola called it) contains the sun, Venus, and the Milky Way. In the middle of it all is the World Tree, which was brought into being by the king during bloodletting rituals. With its upper branches in the heavens and its roots in Xibalba, the World Tree was the doorway to the otherworlds of gods and ancestors. Communication with these spirits took place through the mysterious Vision Serpent. At the top of the World Tree sits Lord Itzamna as the bird of heaven.

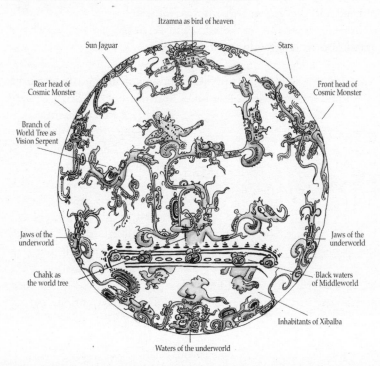

Itzamna as bird of heaven

Sun Jaguar

Stars

Rear head of
Cosmic Monster

Front head of
Cosmic Monster

Branch of
World Tree as
Vision Serpent

Jaws of the
underworld

Jaws of the
underworld

Chahk as
the world tree

Black waters
of Middleworld

Inhabitants of Xibalba

Waters of the underworld

THE MAYA CALENDAR

The Maya were fascinated by the passage of time and they developed a variety of astonishingly accurate calendars to track the movements of the sun and the stars. The Maya kings and priests used their advanced knowledge of astronomy to plan their rituals, wage their wars, and manage their agricultural cycles.

The Long Count

The Long Count counts the days (kin) since the beginning of this creation. (The Maya believed there were three creations. The first two, when humans were made out of mud and wood respectively, were failures. The third creation, this one, when men were made out of corn, was deemed a success.) According to the Long Count, this third creation began, in our terms, on August 11, 3114 BCE. In the Long Count, the Maya year (tun) was 360 days long. Just as our 10-based counting system marks the decade (10 years) and the century (10 x 10 = 100 years), the Maya's 20-based counting system marks the katun (20 tuns) and the baktun, (20 x 20 = 400 tuns). Some say that the third creation lasts 13 baktuns, giving us an end date of December 21, 2012. There is no archaeological evidence for this claim and Mayan inscriptions indicate that the world will continue far beyond 2012.

The Haab

The Haab is the Maya calendar closest to our own. It tracks the solar year and is made up of 18 months, each consisting of 20 days, plus a 5-day period called the Wayeb to make a total of 365 days. The Wayeb was thought to be a time of uncertainty and bad luck, when the doors between the mortal realm and the underworld were opened and demons roamed the earth.

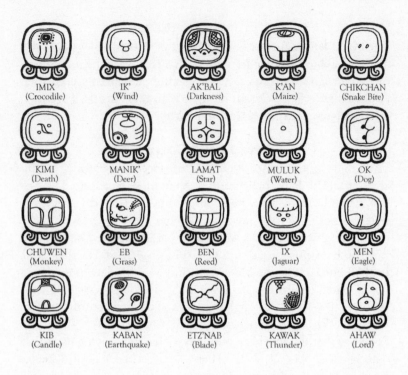

IMIX
(Crocodile)

IK'
(Wind)

AK'BAL
(Darkness)

K'AN
(Maize)

CHIKCHAN
(Snake Bite)

KIMI
(Death)

MANIK'
(Deer)

LAMAT
(Star)

MULUK
(Water)

OK
(Dog)

CHUWEN
(Monkey)

EB
(Grass)

BEN
(Reed)

IX
(Jaguar)

MEN
(Eagle)

KIB
(Candle)

KABAN
(Earthquake)

ETZ'NAB
(Blade)

KAWAK
(Thunder)

AHAW
(Lord)

The Tzolk'in

The Tzolk'in was the sacred calendar, used to predict the characteristics of each day and determine the days for rituals, like a daily horoscope. It is made up of 20 day names and 13 numbers, and takes 260 days to go through the full cycle of name-and-number combinations. Each day name has a quality, some good, some bad. For example, Imix ("Crocodile") is full of complications and problems, and thus bad for journeys or business deals. The number (1–13) determines how strong the characteristic would be. So on 13-Imix, you might want to stay home.

The Calendar Round

The Calendar Round brings together the Haab and Tzolk'in calendars. It takes 18,980 days (about 52 years) to work through the 260 Tzolk'in days and the 365 Haab days. The Calendar Round is usually depicted as a series of interlocking cogs and wheels—which, in *Jaguar Stones: Middleworld*, was the inspiration for the "time machine" in the Temple of Itzamna.

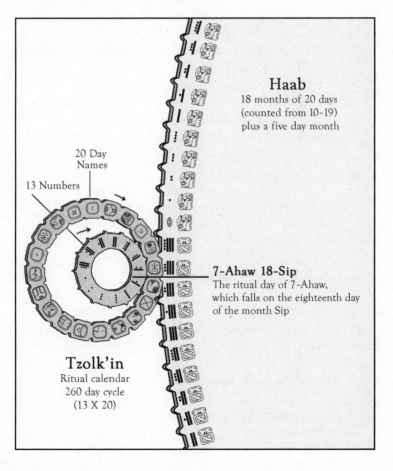

20 Day Names

13 Numbers

Haab
18 months of 20 days
(counted from 10-19)
plus a five day month

7-Ahaw 18-Sip
The ritual day of 7-Ahaw, which falls on the eighteenth day of the month Sip

Tzolk'in
Ritual calendar
260 day cycle
(13 X 20)

EASY CHICKEN TAMALES

Everyone in Central America has their own recipe for tamales. Even Max Murphy would like this one.

Ingredients

1 bag of corn husks
1 roast chicken, off the bone and shredded
1 jar of salsa verde or tomatillo sauce
6 cups of Maseca corn masa mix for tamales
1 cup of corn oil
6 cups of chicken stock or broth
2 tsp salt
1 tsp baking powder
1 tsp cumin
1 green chili, seeds removed, finely chopped
1 clove garlic, crushed and finely chopped

Method

1. Soften the corn husks by soaking in warm water for at least 3 hours. You'll need to put something heavy on them to keep them under the water.

2. Marinate the shredded chicken in the salsa verde.

3. In a mixer combine the masa mix, oil, chicken stock, salt, baking powder, cumin, chili, and garlic. Mix until you have a soft dough. Add more chicken stock if needed.

4. Spread a heaped tablespoon of the masa mixture into the center of a corn husk (smooth side up, with the wide end of the husk toward you) to make a 3-inch square. Put 2 teaspoons of the marinated chicken and salsa verde on top of the masa. Fold first the left side of the corn husk over the filling, and then overlap with the right. Fold the pointed end toward you. Fold up the wide end over the tip of the pointed end. Tie with a strip of corn husk or kitchen string to make a little package. Continue until all the masa and chicken are used up.

5. Place tamales in a large steamer and steam for about 40 minutes. You'll know the tamales are cooked when they easily separate from the corn husks.

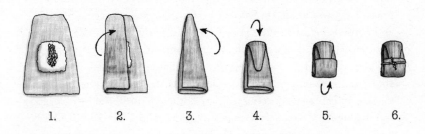

1. 2. 3. 4. 5. 6.

ACKNOWLEDGMENTS

In the course of researching this book, we met a Maya shaman who explained the importance of being bound to others in a tangle of obligations and favors that can never be unraveled or repaid. Certainly words don't seem enough to thank Daniel Lazar, our agent, and Stephen Barr. Thank you also to our wise and witty editor Elizabeth Law and to Mary Albi, Saint Nico Medina, Doug Pocock, Alison Weiss, Rob Guzman, and everyone at Egmont USA for their brilliant ideas, their enthusiasm, their patience, and their commitment to protecting the world's remaining rainforests by using only sustainable paper stocks. Huge, humble, heartfelt thanks to our own personal superhero, Dr. Marc Zender of the Peabody Museum at Harvard, for sharing his immense knowledge so generously and with such good humor. Thanks to Patsy Holden at the University of Central Florida for her thoughts on the Maya worldview, Mark Van Stone at Southwestern College for his insights on 2012, Kathryn Hinds for her eagle-eyed copyediting, and Jordan Brown for letting us use his line. Thank you to Dustin Schaber for fortitude and showmanship above and beyond the call of duty. Also to Alan, Christy, Andrea, Max, Nicole, Heather, Jack, and Mary Anne for their extraordinary help and support in so many ways for so many reasons at so many times and always at such short notice. Thank you to Geraldo Garcia, Karina Martinez, Franklin Choco, and Hugh Daly in Belize; Jesus Antonio Madrid and Jose Cordoba in Guatemala; Oscar Vera Gallegos, Vicente, and Chan Kin in Mexico; Cee Greene, Paul Verbinnen, and Big Guy in New York. Thank you to all the booksellers who've been rooting for us, especially Penny McConnel and Liza Bernard at the Norwich Bookstore, Jill Moore at Square Books Junior in Oxford, Mississippi, Lisa Sharp at Nightbird Books in Lafayette, Arkansas, and Jennifer Stark at Barnes & Noble, Lincoln Center. Thank you to Lucinda Walker and Beth Reynolds at the Norwich Public Library. Thank you to all the teachers and schools who've supported and encouraged us, especially Wakefield Middle School in Tucson, Canarelli Middle School in Las Vegas, Edmonds Middle School in Burlington, and the Marion Cross School in Norwich. Thank you also to Donald Kreis, Jessica Carvalho, Trina Boyd, Peter and Hetty, Graham Sharp, James Bowen, the SBJ Book Club, Erik Roush, Andy the chef, Peter Kraus, and Emilio Ortiz. And did we mention Dan Lazar?

YUM BO'OTIK TE'EX!